A KILLER'S OBSESSION

"He's back."

Jax reached out to grasp his shoulder. "We can't jump to conclusions, Ash."

Ash understood his brother's warning. There was nothing more dangerous for an investigator than leaping to a conclusion, then becoming blind to other possibilities.

But he was no longer a detective, and his gut instinct was screaming that this was the work of the killer who'd destroyed the lives of so many. Including his own.

"There's more." Feldman cleared his throat, lowering the pad. "She's had plastic surgery."

"Not that unusual," Jax said, echoing Ash's own thoughts. "Lots of women, and men for that matter, think they need some nip and tuck."

Feldman grimaced. "This nip and tuck was for a particular purpose."

A chill crawled over Ash's skin. Not the frigid air of the morgue, but something else. Perhaps a premonition. "What purpose?" he forced himself to ask.

"If I had to make a guess, I would say it was to make Angel Conway look like Remi Walsh . . ."

Books by Alexandra Ivy

Guardians of Eternity
WHEN DARKNESS COMES
EMBRACE THE DARKNESS
DARKNESS EVERLASTING
DARKNESS REVEALED
DARKNESS UNLEASHED
BEYOND THE DARKNESS
DEVOURED BY DARKNESS
BOUND BY DARKNESS
FEAR THE DARKNESS
DARKNESS AVENGED
HUNT THE DARKNESS
WHEN DARKNESS ENDS
DARKNESS RETURNS
BEWARE THE DARKNESS
CONQUER THE DARKNESS

The Immortal Rogues
MY LORD VAMPIRE
MY LORD ETERNITY
MY LORD IMMORTALITY

The Sentinels
BORN IN BLOOD
BLOOD ASSASSIN
BLOOD LUST

Ares Security
KILL WITHOUT MERCY
KILL WITHOUT SHAME

Romantic Suspense
PRETEND YOU'RE SAFE
WHAT ARE YOU AFRAID OF?
YOU WILL SUFFER
THE INTENDED VICTIM

Historical Romance
SOME LIKE IT WICKED
SOME LIKE IT SINFUL
SOME LIKE IT BRAZEN

And don't miss these
Guardians of Eternity novellas
TAKEN BY DARKNESS in
  YOURS FOR ETERNITY
DARKNESS ETERNAL in
  SUPERNATURAL
WHERE DARKNESS LIVES in
  THE REAL WEREWIVES OF
  VAMPIRE COUNTY
LEVET (eBook only)
A VERY LEVET CHRISTMAS
  (eBook only)

And don't miss these
Sentinel novellas
OUT OF CONTROL
ON THE HUNT

Published by Kensington Publishing Corporation

THE
INTENDED
VICTIM

ALEXANDRA IVY

ZEBRA BOOKS
KENSINGTON PUBLISHING CORP.

www.kensingtonbooks.com

ZEBRA BOOKS are published by

Kensington Publishing Corp.
119 West 40th Street
New York, NY 10018

All Kensington titles, imprints, and distributed lines are available at special quantity discounts for bulk purchases for sales promotion, premiums, fund-raising, educational, or institutional use.

Special book excerpts or customized printings can also be created to fit specific needs. For details, write or phone the office of the Kensington Sales Manager: Attn.: Sales Department. Kensington Publishing Corp., 119 West 40th Street, New York, NY 10018. Phone: 1-800-221-2647.

Zebra and the Z logo Reg. U.S. Pat. & TM Off.

First Printing: January 2020
ISBN-13: 978-1-4201-4383-6
ISBN-10: 1-4201-4383-2

ISBN-13: 978-1-4201-4384-3 (eBook)
ISBN-10: 1-4201-4384-0 (eBook)

10 9 8 7 6 5 4 3 2 1

Printed in the United States of America

Prologue

The sun was still struggling to crest the horizon when Angel Conway entered the small park next to Lake Michigan. Shivering, she hunched herself deeper in her heavy coat. Shit. Was there anywhere in the world colder than Chicago in the winter? She doubted even the North Pole felt as frigid. Especially this morning, with the wind whipping the icy droplets from the nearby lake. They stung her face like tiny darts.

Unfortunately, she had no choice but to drag herself out of her bed at such a god-awful hour to brave the cold. It was the same reason she snuck out every Friday morning.

When she came to Chicago, she'd intended to have a clean start. No drugs. No men. Nothing that would screw up her one opportunity to climb out of the sewer she'd made of her life. But after the operation, she'd been given painkillers, and the hunger had been stroked back to life. Within three weeks of her arrival in the city, she was back to the same old habits.

Stomping her feet in an attempt to keep blood flowing to her toes, she scanned the shadowed lot. Where was her john? Usually she was the one running late. She did it deliberately to avoid being turned into a human Popsicle. She wanted to arrive at the park, climb into the man's expensive Jag, do her business, and get her pills. No fuss, no muss.

And no frostbite.

"Come on, come on," she muttered, rubbing her hands together.

Maybe she should bail. She could sneak out this weekend and find a street dealer. Of course, what little money she had . . .

Her thoughts were shattered by the sharp snap of a branch. She frowned, glancing over her shoulder at the trees directly behind her. She'd chosen this spot because it offered her an open view of the lot, but at the same time gave her cover in case a cop decided to drive through the park. Now she felt a weird sense of dread crawl over her skin.

She was from the country. She knew the difference between a critter scrambling through the underbrush and a human footstep.

There was someone moving in the darkness. The only question was whether it was an early morning jogger. Or a pervert who was spying on her.

She never considered there might have been a third possibility.

Not until she felt the cold blade press against her throat . . .

Chapter One

Dr. Ashland Marcel entered his office on the campus of Illinois State University. It was a small, dark space that had one window overlooking the parking lot. An office reserved for a professor who hadn't yet received his tenure. Not that the cramped space bothered Ash. As much as he enjoyed teaching criminal justice classes, he hadn't fully committed to spending the rest of his life in an academic setting. Especially after his hectic morning.

With a grimace, he dropped into his seat behind the cluttered desk. A sigh escaped his lips. It was only noon, but he was grateful he was done teaching his classes for the day.

The students weren't the only ones looking forward to the end of the semester, he wryly acknowledged. Early December in the Midwest meant short, brutally cold days. A bunch of twentysomethings trapped inside for weeks at a time was never a good thing. His classroom was choking with their pent-up energy.

But it was Friday. And Monday the students started finals. Which meant that in less than seven days, he could look forward to a month of peace and quiet.

Pretending he didn't notice the tiny ache in the center of his heart at the thought of spending the holidays alone in his small house, Ash opened his laptop. He needed to get through his email before he could call it a day.

He'd barely fired up the computer when the door to his office was shoved open. He glanced up with a forbidding glare. His students were told on the first day of class that they could come to him during his posted office hours. He'd discovered his first year of teaching that they would follow him into the toilet with questions if he didn't set firm guidelines.

His annoyance, however, swiftly changed to surprise at the sight of the man dressed in a worn blue suit who stepped through the opening.

Detective Jackson "Jax" Marcel.

At a glance, it was easy to tell the two were brothers. They both had light brown hair that curled around the edges. Ash's was allowed to grow longer now that he was no longer on the police force, and had fewer strands of gray. And they both had blue eyes. Ash's were several shades darker, and framed by long, black lashes that had been the bane of his childhood. And they were both tall and slender, with muscles that came from long morning jogs instead of time in the gym.

Ash rose to his feet, his brows arching in surprise. It wasn't uncommon for his family to visit. The university was only a couple of hours from Chicago. But they never just appeared in his office without calling.

"Jax."

Jax stretched his lips into a smile, but it was clearly an effort. "Hey, bro."

Ash studied his companion. Jax was the oldest of the four Marcel brothers, but they had all been born within a six-year span, so they were all close in age. That was perhaps why they'd always been so tight. You messed with one Marcel, you messed with them all.

"What are you doing here?" Ash demanded.

"I need to talk to you."

"You couldn't call?"

Jax grimaced. "I preferred to do it face-to-face."

Fear curled through the pit of Ash's stomach. Something had happened. Something bad. He leaned forward, laying his palms flat on the desk.

"Mom? Dad?"

Jax gave a sharp shake of his head. "The family is fine."

"Then what's going on?"

"Sit down."

Ash clenched his teeth. His brother's attempt to delay the bad news was twisting his nerves into a painful knot. "Shit. Just tell me."

Perhaps realizing that he was doing more harm than good, Jax heaved a harsh sigh.

"It's Remi Walsh."

Ash froze. He hadn't heard the name Remi in five years. Not since he'd packed his bags and walked away from Chicago and the woman who'd promised to be his wife.

"Remi." His voice sounded oddly hollow. "Is she hurt?"

This time Jax didn't torture him. He spoke without hesitation.

"Her body arrived in the morgue this morning."

Morgue.

"No." The word was wrenched from Ash's lips as his knees buckled and he collapsed into his chair.

Jax stepped toward the desk, his expression one of pity. "I'm sorry, Ash."

Ash shook his head. "This has to be a mistake," he said, meaning every word.

It *was* a mistake. There was no way in hell that Remi could be dead.

"I wish it was a mistake, bro," Jax said in sad tones. "But I saw her with my own eyes."

Ash grimly refused to accept what his brother was telling him. He'd tumbled head over heels in love with Remi from the second she'd strolled into the police station to take her father for lunch. Ash had just made detective and Gage Walsh was his partner. Thankfully, that hadn't stopped him from asking Remi out. She'd been hesitant at first, clearly unsure she wanted to date someone who worked so closely with her father. But from their first date, they'd both known the sensations that sizzled between them were something special.

That's why he couldn't accept that she was gone.

If something had happened to Remi, he would know. In his heart. In his very soul.

"How long has it been since you last spent time with her?" he challenged his brother.

Jax shrugged. "Five years ago."

"Exactly. How could you possibly recognize her after so long?"

"Ash." Jax shoved his fingers through his hair, his shoulders stooped. He looked like he was weary to the bone. "Denying the truth doesn't change it."

Anger blasted through Ash. He wanted to vault across the desk and slam his fist into his brother's face for insisting on the lie. It wouldn't be the first time he'd given Jax a black eye. Of course, his brother had pounded him back, chipping a tooth and covering him in bruises, but it'd been totally worth it.

Instead, he forced himself to leash his raw emotions.

"It's official?" he demanded.

Jax gave a slow shake of his head. "Not yet. The medical examiner is overwhelmed, as usual. It will be hours before they can run fingerprints, even with me putting pressure on them."

The anger remained, but it was suddenly threaded with hope. Nothing was official.

The words beat through him, echoing his heavy pulse.

At the same time, he continued to glare at his brother. "Why come here before you're sure it's Remi?"

Jax coughed, as if clearing his throat. "I wanted you to be prepared."

Ash narrowed his gaze. The shock of Jax's announcement had sent his brain reeling. Which was the only explanation for why he hadn't noticed his brother's hands clenching and unclenching. It wasn't just sympathy that was causing his brother's unease.

"No. There's something you're not telling me," he said.

Jax glanced toward the window, then down at the scuff marks on his leather shoes. Was he playing for time? Or searching for the right words? "Let's go for a drink," he finally suggested.

"Dammit, Jax. This isn't the time for games," Ash snapped. "Just tell me."

Jax's lips twisted before he forced himself to speak the words he'd clearly hoped to avoid. "She was found with her throat slit."

Ash surged to his feet, knocking over the chair. It smashed against the wooden floor with a loud bang, but Ash barely noticed.

"Was there a mark?" he rasped.

It'd been only a few weeks after he'd started dating Remi that Gage had put together the connection that a rash of dead women was the work of a serial killer. They'd tagged him the Chicago Butcher because it was suspected he used a butcher's knife to slice the throats of his victims. Only the cops knew that there had been a hidden calling card left behind by the killer: a small crescent carved onto the women's right breast. No one knew if it was supposed to be a "c" or a moon, or perhaps some unknown symbol. But it was always there.

"Yes."

"Like the others?" he pressed.

Jax nodded. Ash reached into his pocket to pull out his keys. He'd gone from white-hot emotion erupting through him like lava to an ice-cold determination.

The Chicago Butcher had destroyed his life five years ago. If the bastard was back, Ash was going to track him and kill him. He didn't care if he had a badge or not.

He tossed his keys to his brother. "Go to my house and pack a bag."

Jax caught the keys, his brows tugging together. "Ash, there's nothing you can do."

"I have to see her," Ash muttered, not adding his secondary reason for returning to Chicago. His brother was smart. He knew Ash would be hungry for revenge. "She was my fiancée."

Jax grimaced. "It was all a long time ago."

Ash snorted. It had been five years, not an eternity. And most of the time it felt like it had all happened yesterday. "We both know it doesn't matter how long ago it was or you would never have come down here to tell me."

The older man hunched his shoulders. "I didn't want you to hear it on the news."

Ash didn't believe the excuse for a second. "Pack a bag," he commanded, reaching down to right his chair. "I'll be ready by the time you get back."

"What about your classes?" Jax tried a last-ditch effort to keep Ash away from Chicago.

"Finals are next week." Ash sat down and reached for the cell phone he'd left on his desk. He might be under thirty, but he held the old-fashioned belief that there was no need for phones in his classroom. Including his own. "I'll call the dean and warn him there's been a family emergency. If I'm not back by Monday, my teaching assistant can proctor the exams."

"Ash—"

"I can go back with you or I'll drive myself," Ash interrupted.

"Hell, I don't want you behind the wheel." Jax pointed a finger toward Ash. "Don't move until I get back."

Ash ignored his brother as he turned and left his office. He not only needed to contact the dean, he wanted to make sure that his assistant knew he would be expected to take over his classes if necessary, as well as making his excuses to the dozens of holiday invitations that were waiting in his in-box.

He was just finishing his tasks when his phone pinged with a text, telling him that Jax was waiting for him in the parking lot.

Grabbing his laptop and the coat that hung in the corner, he left the office and closed the door behind him. Then, using the back stairs, he managed to avoid any acquaintances. Right now, he would be incapable of casual chitchat.

Pushing open the door, he stepped out of the building and headed for the nearby parking lot. The sun was shining, but there was a sharp breeze that made him shiver. Like all his brothers, he enjoyed being out in the fresh air, either jogging or spending the weekend camping near the river. But with each passing year, he found he was less willing to brave icy temperatures.

Soon he'd be spending the long winters sitting in front of a warm fire with a comfy sweater and his favorite slippers.

Shaking away his idiotic thoughts, he stopped next to his

brother's car. Opening the door, he slid into the passenger seat and wrapped the seat belt across his body.

"Have you heard anything from the medical examiner?" he demanded as his brother put the car in gear and pulled out of the lot.

"Not yet." There was silence as Jax concentrated on negotiating the traffic out of town. It wasn't until they reached the interstate that Jax glanced toward Ash. "Mom will be happy to have you home for a few days. She complains you never bother to come to see her anymore."

Ash pressed his lips together. It was that or snapping at his brother that this wasn't a damned social visit. Eventually, however, he forced his tense muscles to relax. He wasn't so far gone that he didn't realize that Jax was trying to distract him. And that there was no point in brooding on what he was going to discover once they reached Chicago.

"Mom's too busy planning Nate's wedding to notice whether I'm around or not," he managed to say.

Nate was the youngest Marcel brother, who'd moved to Oklahoma after leaving the FBI. He had proposed to his neighbor, Ellie Guthrie, a few months ago, and she didn't have a relationship with her own parents, so June Marcel had eagerly stepped in to act as her surrogate mother.

Jax released a short laugh. "She's been in heaven running around the city to find the perfect flower arrangements and sewing the bridesmaids' dresses," he agreed. "The poor woman assumed with four sons she would never have the opportunity to be so involved in all the froufrou nonsense that comes with a wedding." Jax set the cruise control and settled back in his seat. "Still, you must have been gone too long if you've forgotten Mom's ability to concentrate on more than one thing at a time. I remember her baking cupcakes for Ty's Boy Scout club while helping

Nate with his math homework and at the same time making sure I raked every damned leaf in the backyard because I missed curfew."

Ash's lips curved into a rueful smile. His mother was a ruthless force of nature who'd occasionally resorted to fear and intimidation to control her four unruly sons. Mostly she'd smothered them in such love that none of them could bear the thought of disappointing her.

"True. She has a gift." He felt a tiny pang in the center of his heart. It'd been too long since he'd been home. "I could use her in my classroom."

"Lord, don't say that. She'll be waiting next to your desk with a ruler in her hand," Jax teased.

Another silence filled the car, then Jax cleared his throat and abruptly asked the question that had no doubt been on his mind for the past five years.

"I never knew what happened between you and Remi." Jax kept his gaze focused on the road, as if knowing that Ash wouldn't want him to witness the pain that twisted his features. "One day you were planning your wedding and the next the engagement was off and you were moving away."

Ash's breath hissed between his clenched teeth. "The Chicago Butcher happened."

He expected his brother to drop the issue. His breakup with Remi was something he refused to discuss. His family had always respected his barriers.

But whether he was still trying to keep Ash distracted, or if it was the shock of seeing a woman he believed to be Remi at the morgue, Jax refused to let it go. "You both suffered when she was captured by the Butcher and her father was killed trying to save her," he pointed out. "I thought it would draw the two of you closer together."

Ash turned his head to gaze at the frozen fields that lined the road. The memories of that horrifying night were firmly locked in the back of his mind. The frantic phone call from Remi telling her father that she was being followed. Gage Walsh's stark command that Ash drive Remi's route in case the killer forced her car off the road on the way home, while he went to his elegant mansion on the North Shore. And then Ash's arrival at the mansion to discover that he was too late. Gage's blood had been found at his home, but his body had never been discovered. No one knew why the Butcher would have taken it, unless he feared that he'd left evidence on the corpse that he didn't have time to remove. The killing, after all, wouldn't have been planned like the ones of the females he stalked and murdered. Thank God Remi had been alive, although she'd been lying unconscious in the kitchen.

But while he wasn't about to go into the agonizing details, Jax deserved an answer. The older man had been an unwavering source of strength over the past few years. Whether it was to shut down his father's angry protests when Ash announced that he was leaving the police department, or driving down to the university and getting him cross-eyed drunk when he was feeling isolated and alone.

"After I brought Remi home from the hospital she started to shut me out," he said in slow, painful tones. "At first I assumed she would get her memory back, and that she would be able to heal from the trauma she'd gone through."

"But the memories never came back," Jax murmured.

"No, they never came back." Ash grimaced. He'd wasted a lot of emotional energy trying to convince Remi to get professional help to retrieve her memories. As if the return of them could somehow heal the growing breach between them. It was only with time and distance he could see that they were struggling with more than the trauma of her being attacked by the Butcher. "But it was the guilt that destroyed our hopes for the future."

His brother sent him a sharp glance. "Guilt for what?"

Ash gave a sad shake of his head. "Remi felt guilty for her father's death. She had a crazy idea that if she hadn't called to say she was being followed, her father would still be alive. And to be honest, it only made it worse that his body was never found. I think a part of her had desperately hoped he would miraculously return. With each passing day, she blamed herself more and more."

"And your guilt?" Jax pressed.

"I should never have let Gage go there alone. I was his partner."

Jax muttered a curse. "His *younger* partner. Gage was your superior, and it was his call to split up so you could cover more ground. Just as it was your duty to obey his order."

Ash shrugged. Easy to say the words; it was much harder to dismiss the gnawing remorse. If only . . .

Heaving a sigh, he leaned back his head against the seat and closed his eyes. He'd given Jax the explanation he demanded. He didn't have the strength to argue whether it made any sense or not.

Ash kept his eyes closed even as the traffic thickened and they slowed to a mere crawl. He'd driven to the morgue enough times to know exactly when they were pulling into the side parking lot.

Lifting his head, he studied the long, cement-block building with two rows of narrow windows. Nothing had changed in the past few years. Maybe the trees lining the street had grown a little taller, and they'd replaced the flags out front. Otherwise, it was the same stark structure he remembered.

Jax switched off the engine, turning his head toward Ash. "I wish you wouldn't do this."

"I have to." Ash unbuckled the seat belt and pushed open the door before stepping out.

Behind him was the sound of hurried footsteps as Jax rushed to keep up. Not that Ash was going to get far without him. He was no longer a cop, which meant he would have to hang on to the hope that Remi still had him listed as an emergency contact to get past security.

Much easier to let Jax do his thing.

Quickly at his side, Jax took charge as they entered the building. They were halted twice, but Jax flashed his badge and quickly they were stepping into a harshly lit room that felt ice-cold.

Ash shivered. He hated coming here. Even when it was a part of his job. Now his stomach was twisted so tight, it felt like it'd been yanked into knots.

They were led by a technician down a long row of steel racks where bodies wrapped in heavy plastic waited for an official ID. Or perhaps for an autopsy. He'd tried not to really notice what was going on behind the scenes. Now he felt as if he was in a dream as the technician waved for them to stop and Jax wrapped an arm around his shoulders. No, it was more like a nightmare. One that wasn't going to end if it truly was Remi who was being slid out on a steel slab.

Taking care not to disturb the body any more than necessary, the technician slowly pulled back the plastic cover. Ash made a choked sound as he caught sight of the long, black hair that was glossy enough to reflect the overhead light. It was pulled away from a pale, beautiful face, just like Remi liked to wear it.

He swayed to the side, leaning heavily against his brother as pain blasted through him. "Christ."

"Steady," Jax murmured.

Ash's gaze absorbed the delicate features. They were so heart-wrenchingly familiar. The slender nose. The high, prominent cheekbones. The dark, perfectly arched brows. The lush lips.

"I didn't want to believe," he rasped, his voice coming from a long way away. As if he was falling off a cliff and was waiting to hit the bottom.

Would he die when that happened?

He hoped so.

What would be the point of living in a world without Remi Walsh?

"I'm sorry," Jax said, his own voice harsh with pain.

Ash's gaze remained locked on Remi's lips. It'd been five years, but he still remembered their last kiss. He'd just told her that he intended to take a job at the university. Deep inside, he'd hoped she would be furious at his decision. He wanted her to fight for their future together. Instead, she'd offered a sad smile and leaned forward to brush her mouth over his in a silent goodbye.

He'd nearly cried even as he'd savored the taste of her strawberry lip balm . . .

Ash stilled. Lip balm. Why was there a warning voice whispering at the back of his fuzzy brain? Maybe he was going crazy. What the hell did her lips have to do with anything? He frowned, telling himself to turn away.

He'd done what he came there to do. What was the point of gawking at Remi as if he hoped she would suddenly open her eyes? It was time to go.

But his feet refused to budge. He knew Jax was staring

at him in confusion, and that the technician was starting to shift from one foot to another, but still he continued to run his gaze over Remi's pale face.

Something was nagging at him. But what?

Then his gaze returned to her mouth, and he realized what his unconscious mind was trying to tell him.

She was wearing lipstick. A bright-red shade. And more than that, there was makeup plastered on her skin and what looked like false lashes stuck to her lids. The harsh lighting had washed everything to a dull shade of ash, which was why he hadn't noticed it the minute the cover had been pulled back.

"That's not her," he breathed.

"Ash." Jax's arm tightened around his shoulder. "I know this is tough, but—"

"It's not her," Ash interrupted, his heart returning to sluggish life.

How had he been so blind? Remi never wore makeup. Not even when her mother insisted on dragging her to some fancy-ass party. She claimed that it made her skin itch, plus she didn't feel the need to slap paint on herself to try to impress other people. If they didn't like her face, they didn't have to look at it.

Her down-to-earth attitude was one of the things he'd loved about her.

Of course, as far as he was concerned, she was gorgeous. She didn't need anything artificial to make his palms sweat and his pulse race.

"How can you be sure?" Jax demanded, his voice revealing his fear that Ash had gone over the edge. "Like you said, it's been five years. She could have changed in that time. Unless there's something you haven't told me?"

Ash jutted his chin. He wasn't going to explain about the makeup. Jax would tell him a woman might very well alter her opinion about cosmetics as she started to age. Or perhaps she had a boyfriend who wanted her to plaster her face with the gunk. Besides, now that he was looking at the dead woman with his brain and not his heart, he could start to detect physical differences. The nose was just a tad too long. Her brow not quite wide enough. And her jaw too blunt.

"I'm sure." His voice was strong. Confident. "It's not her."

"He's right." A new voice cut through the air, echoing eerily through the racks of dead bodies. "I just got back the results from the fingerprints."

They all turned to watch as Dr. Jack Feldman, one of the city's top medical examiners, stepped out of the shadows. A short man with salt-and-pepper hair and a neatly trimmed beard, he was wearing a white lab coat that didn't hide the start of an impressive potbelly. He'd been a good friend of Gage Walsh, and had extended that friendship to Ash when he'd become Gage's partner.

He'd also adored Remi, treating her like she was his own child. It must have been a hideous shock to have a woman who looked so much like her show up in his morgue.

"Feldman," Ash murmured, stepping away from his brother so he could pull the older man into a rough hug.

They shared a silent moment of tangled emotions, then the doctor slapped him on the back and pulled away to study him with a sympathetic gaze.

"Good to see you, Ash, although not under these circumstances."

Ash cleared his throat, his attention moving toward the electronic pad clutched in Feldman's hand. "Did you get an ID?"

Feldman held up a hand before he glanced toward the silent technician.

"I'll take it from here, Jimmy," he told the young man.

They waited until Jimmy turned and left the room before Feldman led them to a distant corner. His dark gaze rested on Ash's face. "I shouldn't be talking to you, but I'm pretty sure you'll get the information one way or another. Plus, you're one of us, even if you did jump ship for a while. Eventually you'll come back where you belong."

They were words he'd heard from a dozen different lawmen when he'd announced his decision to leave the Chicago Police Department and take a job teaching. And in truth, a part of him had secretly agreed.

Being a detective was in his blood.

He shook away the thought, nodding toward the electronic pad. "Who is she?"

Feldman lifted the pad and touched the screen to call up a file. "Her name is Angel Conway. She's a twenty-five-year-old white female. Five feet, six inches tall. One hundred thirty pounds."

Ash frowned. "Is she local?"

"No." Feldman brushed his finger over the screen. "Her address is Bailey, Illinois. A small town fifty miles south of the city."

Ash glanced toward Jax, who gave a shake of his head. He'd never heard of the town.

"Do you have any other info?"

Feldman was silent as he read through the short report. Ash knew Feldman must have shouted and bullied and called in every favor owed him to get any information so quickly. The Chicago coroner's department was notoriously understaffed and overworked. It was only because of their dedicated staff that they weren't completely overwhelmed.

"It looks like she worked at a convenience store and has a rap sheet for petty crimes," Feldman murmured. "Mostly stealing and one count of prostitution."

Ash tried to process what he was being told. Not easy when his brain was still foggy from the extreme emotions that had battered him. Fear. Shock. Grief. Soul-shaking relief.

He did, however, tuck away the information so he could pull it out later and truly consider what it all meant. "Where did they find her?"

"Jameson Park," Feldman said.

Ash lifted his brows in surprise. Jameson Park was built along the shores of Lake Michigan, and popular enough to be crowded this time of year despite the frigid weather. Plus, it would have a regular patrol officer who would do sweeps through the area.

A dangerous place to do a dump.

"That doesn't fit the pattern," he said.

"No. But everything else does," Feldman told him, turning around the pad so Ash could see the photos taken of Angel Conway's naked body.

For a second his stomach rolled in protest. It'd been a while since he'd seen death up close and personal. And the violence one person could inflict on another. Then he sucked in a slow, deep breath.

Shutting down his emotions, he studied the picture with a professional attention to detail. He'd learned as a detective it was too easy to be overwhelmed by death. He had to break it down to small, individual pieces to keep himself focused on what was important.

Leaning forward, he studied the cut that marred the slender throat. It was thin and smooth and just deep enough to slice through the carotid artery. There were no hesitation marks, no ragged edges to indicate nerves or anger. It was a precision kill that seemed to be oddly lacking in emotion.

Next, his gaze moved to the small wound on the woman's

upper breast. It was carved into a neat crescent shape. This was the one detail they'd never revealed to the public.

"Christ," he breathed as he straightened. "He's back."

Jax reached out to grasp his shoulder. "We can't jump to conclusions, Ash."

Ash understood his brother's warning. There was nothing more dangerous for an investigator than leaping to a conclusion, then becoming blind to other possibilities.

But he was no longer a detective, and his gut instinct was screaming that this was the work of the killer who'd destroyed the lives of so many. Including his own.

"There's more." Feldman cleared his throat, lowering the pad. "She's had plastic surgery."

"Not that unusual," Jax said, echoing Ash's own thoughts. "Lots of women, and men for that matter, think they need some nip and tuck."

Feldman grimaced. "This nip and tuck was for a particular purpose."

A chill crawled over Ash's skin. Not the frigid air of the morgue, but something else. Perhaps a premonition. "What purpose?" he forced himself to ask.

"If I had to make a guess, I would say it was to make Angel Conway look like Remi Walsh."

Chapter Two

Remi Walsh was seated at a small table at the back of the youth center. She was a tall, slender woman with long, black hair she kept pulled into a braid and green eyes she'd inherited from her mother. Her skin was winter pale and smooth even though she was closer to thirty than twenty. Today she was wearing a pair of jeans and a heavy cable-knit sweater to combat the icy December day.

Across the table sat a fifteen-year-old girl. Julie Stewart had reddish-blond curls and a round face sprinkled with freckles. She looked like any typical teenager. Young and innocent. But Julie had endured more than most people in her short life. Remi had only gotten an abbreviated version, but she knew that Julie had been bounced from one foster home to another after being taken away from her abusive mother.

Now she was in a stable home that was ensuring she attended school every day. They also insisted that Julie stop by the youth center after classes twice a week for tutoring.

Remi sat back and tapped her red pen on the table. "Okay. We've identified the mistakes. You need to correct them and retype the paper before Monday."

Julie grimaced as she glanced at the term paper criss-crossed with red marks. It was late on Friday afternoon and the teen was no doubt envisioning a weekend filled with lazy mornings spent in bed and her nights at the mall with her friends. "I'll try."

"No," Remi said in firm tones. "You'll do it or you won't pass your English Comp class and you'll be taking it again next year. Got it?"

Julie heaved a sigh that indicated she considered herself the most mistreated teen in the world. Still, she gave a nod as she grabbed for her backpack and coat. "Yeah, yeah," she muttered, rising to her feet and shoving the paper into the backpack. "I got it."

"Good girl." Remi watched in silence as Julie pulled on her jacket and headed toward the door. Before she could leave the room, however, Remi called out, "Julie."

The teen reluctantly halted, clearly eager to be on her way. "What now?"

Remi hesitated. She hated to discuss one of her students with another, but she was genuinely worried.

"Have you seen Drew?"

Drew Tyson was a sixteen-year-old boy who'd started coming to the center with Julie a few months before. Remi suspected the only reason he'd agreed to be tutored was for an opportunity to spend time with the pretty girl.

Remi didn't care why he came. She just wanted the opportunity to help him finish his education. He was too smart to be lost to the usual traps that came along with grinding poverty. Drugs. Crime. Violence. And, more often than not, an early death.

Julie paused, obviously trying to think back to the last time she'd seen Drew.

"Not since last Wednesday," she finally said.

Remi's heart sank. She'd hoped that Drew had simply decided he was tired of coming to the youth center, but that he was still going to school. "I tried to call his father, but I didn't get an answer," she said.

Julie shrugged. "It's possible his old man is back in jail. Drew told me that he found an empty baggie in his car. He's probably using again."

The words were said in the jaded tones of a teen who'd seen too much in her short years. Her own mother was currently serving time for drugs.

"Where does Drew go when his dad's in jail?" she asked.

"I think he has an aunt in Minnesota, but he usually stays on the streets." Julie glanced toward the one window in the room that offered a view of the bus stop in front of the building, making sure she wasn't about to miss her ride home. "Do you want me to go look for him?"

"No." Remi gave a sharp shake of her head. The last thing she wanted was Julie putting herself in danger. "I'll do that."

Julie ran a disbelieving glance over Remi. "You?"

Remi rolled her eyes. Although she dressed in casual clothes and never wore makeup or jewelry, the kids easily sensed that she wasn't from their neighborhood. It was like a second sense they possessed.

"I'll see you Monday," she told the younger girl.

Julie gave a wave and hurried out of the room. She no doubt had big plans for the night. Remi on the other hand . . .

She sighed as she cleaned off her desk. She didn't want to think about the empty weekend that stretched ahead of her. It was her own fault, of course. She had friends who'd invited her out to dinner or to the movies. And her mother had mentioned she was hosting yet another gala to raise money for . . . hell, she couldn't even remember. Or, more likely, she hadn't been listening.

If she didn't want to be alone, she shouldn't have said no to everyone.

With her desk clean, Remi was reaching for her purse when a large man appeared in the doorway.

"Knock, knock," he said with a smile.

Lamar Hill was a retired NFL player who'd returned to Chicago after he'd been injured. He could easily have retired on his earnings, but instead, he'd devoted his time and money to starting this youth center that provided hot meals, clothing, medical care, computer access, and tutoring for any kid who walked through the door. In the very back were a few beds that he made available to the homeless adults in the neighborhood. It was a safe place, a beacon of light for people who had very little. Plus, it had the bonus of being a cool spot for the older teens to come and spend some time.

Who didn't want to hang with an NFL player?

Remi tilted back her head. Lamar was over six five, with a broad body that moved with surprising grace.

"Hi, Lamar, what's up?" she asked. The man was usually too busy to stop by to chat.

"You have a couple of visitors," he said.

"Now?" Remi wrinkled her nose. On rare occasions she had parents stop by to ask about their child's progress, or even teachers who brought by missing homework assignments they hoped she could help students complete. Usually she welcomed their arrival, but it was five o'clock on a Friday and she still had an hour of traffic to battle through. "I was just about to leave."

"Sorry, but it's the cops," he said, his tone more curious than alarmed.

When one of the kids got in trouble, they often offered the names of staff members at the youth center to vouch for them.

"Oh." Remi had a sudden surge of hope that they were here about Drew. She didn't want the boy to be in trouble, but at least she would know he was safe. "Okay."

"Can I send them back?"

"Of course."

Lamar flashed his charming smile before he turned to disappear across the large central room where a dozen volunteers were setting up chairs and heating up the popcorn machine for movie night.

Remi swallowed a yawn and reached into her purse to switch on her cell phone. It was doubtful she'd missed any urgent messages, or even a friend with a last-minute invitation.

The screen glowed to life. Nothing. No missed calls. No messages.

Look at her. Miss Popularity.

Her lips twisted as she shook off her bout of self-pity. It was just the short days and cold weather that were making her feel blue. What she needed was a few days on a beach with a drink that had lots of alcohol and a little umbrella. That would perk her right up.

Maybe after the new year . . .

"Hey, Remi."

Lost in her daydreams of a tropical island drenched in golden sunlight, Remi abruptly jerked her head around at the sound of a familiar voice. "Jax?" she breathed, her gaze sweeping over him as he stepped into the office.

He hadn't changed much. There might be a little more silver in his hair, a few fine lines fanning from his eyes, but he was still as handsome as ever. And she'd bet good money he was wearing the same blue suit.

"It's been a while," he said with a rueful smile.

Dazed by his appearance, it took Remi a second to even consider why he might be at the youth center. Then an icy fear spread through her. Jax was a homicide detective. This couldn't be good news. She placed her palms flat on the desk and pushed herself to her feet. "Are you here about Drew?"

He looked puzzled by her question. "No." He stepped away from the doorway. "Actually, I brought an old friend."

She released a shaky breath. He wasn't here about one of her kids. The relief was so overwhelming, she didn't even wonder who the old friend might be. Or even how Jax had known that she worked at the youth center.

Her distraction meant she was utterly unprepared when the second man stepped into the room. A painful mistake, as the ground shifted beneath her feet and her brain froze. Ashland Marcel. Lord have mercy. It'd been five long years since he'd walked away from her, but the time melted away at the sight of his lean face.

How many hours had she spent tracing each chiseled feature? The wide brow. The bold nose and astonishing blue eyes. He was more striking than handsome, but just the sight of him had been enough to make her heart thunder in her chest. And that hard, male body . . .

She knew every inch.

Intimately.

Remi's knees went weak and she dropped into her chair. Ash grimaced and hurried around the desk to crouch in front of her.

"Sorry, I didn't mean to shock you," he said in a soft voice, grasping her limp hands in a firm grip.

Remi cleared the lump from her throat. "I'm fine," she lied.

She wasn't fine. She felt like she'd just been sideswiped by a speeding freight train.

"I'll wait for you in the car," Jax murmured.

Coward, Remi inanely thought, watching as Jax backed out of the room.

"Your hands are freezing," Ash said, rubbing her fingers between his big palms.

She shivered. But not because she was chilled. The shock was beginning to wear off enough for her to react to his familiar touch.

Christ, it'd been so long. And no one had ever been able to cause those potent sparks of awareness. Just Ash.

"This building is always cold," she said, forcing herself to pull her hands free.

Her poor brain was already struggling to process Ash's sudden appearance. She didn't need his touch adding to her befuddlement.

Thankfully, he seemed to sense her need to regain command of her composure. Straightening, he turned to study the wooden shelves that were loaded with books and the five computers set on tables at the back. Everything was basic, but it served its purpose. The kids who came here needed the support of people who cared, not fancy equipment.

Remi allowed her gaze to roam over his broad back that was covered by a silver cashmere sweater that he'd matched with charcoal slacks. She could detect the muscles beneath the soft material, but he looked thinner. As if he'd honed his body to pure bone and sinew.

"Is this your classroom?" he asked, at last breaking the silence.

Remi willed her heart to slow its frantic pace before she answered. "Not really a classroom," she admitted. "I tutor the kids who come to the center."

He pivoted back to meet her wary gaze. "That's what you always wanted to do."

Her lips twisted. They both knew it wasn't exactly what

she wanted to do. She'd gotten her master's in education with the intention of becoming a full-time teacher who concentrated on at-risk students. She was going to change the world. Instead, she was a volunteer at a small center that made a minimal impact on the kids who walked through the door.

Still, she at least was working her way back toward her dreams. She took great pride in her grim determination. "I'm enjoying it, at least for now," she said with a shrug. "Of course, it's not like being a college professor."

He rolled his eyes, shoving his hands in the front pockets of his slacks. "True. You actually make a difference."

Her breath caught at his soft words. Lord, she'd missed this man over the past five years. She missed sleeping in his arms. And sending him a thousand texts a day just because she saw something that captured her imagination. But what she'd truly missed was his unique ability to make her feel good about herself.

When she was with Ash, she could pretend that she was the smartest, most capable woman ever born. As if she could take on the world and win.

Was it any wonder she'd tumbled head over heels in love with him?

"Thanks," she breathed.

He cocked his head to the side, studying her with a puzzled gaze. "For what?"

"Not many of my old friends understand why I would waste my degrees volunteering in this place."

His features softened. They both knew the reason she was there. And the effort it'd taken to get to this point.

"You don't have to explain yourself to anyone," he assured her. "Your true friends will support you no matter where you decide to work."

They shared a long, mutual glance of understanding. The sort of glance that only two people intimately connected could share.

Time ticked past. A second—then ten—passed before the sound of someone walking nearby jerked Remi out of her strange sense of enchantment.

Awkwardly, she cleared her throat. The days of lingering gazes were over. She'd made certain of that. Or at least she thought she had.

"I assume you're in town to spend the holidays with your family?" she asked, belatedly wondering why Ash would be at the youth center.

Pity? Nostalgia? The ghost of Christmas past?

His features hardened, as if her question had reminded him of something unpleasant. "I'm sure we'll get together while I'm home."

Remi frowned. She knew that tone. There was something bothering Ash. "What's going on?"

She half-expected him to shrug aside her question. Whatever was troubling him couldn't have any connection to her. Not after five years apart.

Instead, he studied her upturned face with a brooding gaze. "I'm back because I thought you'd been hurt."

"Me?" She frowned in confusion. "Why would you think that?"

His jaw tightened, his hands curling into fists. As if he was battling the urge to reach out and touch her. "Because there's a woman who looks just like you in the morgue."

Remi blinked. "Why were you in the morgue?"

"Jax came to the college and told me that you were there."

"Oh." She was surprised by the thought of Jax upsetting Ash before he'd double-checked to see if he'd made a mistake. Even if they were no longer together, she'd once been Ash's fiancée. Jax had to know that his brother would be devastated by the news. "It wasn't me."

"Thank God. For a few hours . . ." With a fluid movement, Ash was once again bent down by her chair, reaching out to brush his fingers over her hair. "I don't want to go through that again."

Her heart picked up speed as the warm scent of his skin teased at her nose. A renegade pang of yearning clutched at her heart.

"I'm sorry you were worried, but as you see, I'm alive and well," she said, forcing herself to speak in a bright voice. Having Ash so close was bringing back memories she'd put a lot of effort into burying in the back of her mind. "Just a case of mistaken identity."

His fingers smoothed over her temple and down her cheek. "Maybe not so mistaken."

Pleasure sizzled through her at his light caress, but Remi grimly concentrated on his strange words. Later she would lie in bed with a glass of wine and recall the feel of his gentle touch. "Excuse me?"

He paused, no doubt considering his words with care. Unlike the rest of the Marcel men, Ash preferred a slow, methodical approach rather than charging rashly into a situation.

"The medical examiner found indications that the woman had recently undergone cosmetic surgery," he finally said.

"And?"

"It was done to make her more closely resemble you."

Remi jerked, her heart slamming painfully against her ribs. A woman had surgery to look like her? And now she was in the morgue?

No. That was insane.

She gave a sharp shake of her head. "You can't know that."

"No, not for sure," he grudgingly conceded. "But there's no doubt she had surgery."

She shrugged. "It was probably just a coincidence. I look like a hundred other women."

Ash made a strangled sound, his fingers cupping her chin. "Trust me, Remi. You don't look like any other woman. You are unique. Something I've tried to forget."

She studied his pale face. There was a brittle tension in his expression that warned her he hadn't told her everything. Not yet.

She hesitated. Did she want to know? Right now, her life might be boring, but at least it was peaceful. Something she'd worked hard to achieve. Why risk having that taken away?

The questions whispered through her mind, even as she stiffened her spine. What the hell was wrong with her? She wasn't a coward. "What's going on, Ash?"

His thumb rubbed up and down the line of her jaw, a muscle twitching next to his eye.

"Sorry," he said in a rough voice. "I'm still trying to recover. My nerves are a little raw."

She held his guarded gaze. "There's something bothering you besides the fact that this woman looked like me."

He slowly straightened, his expression bleak. "Yeah, there's something else."

Anxiety feathered through her. A depressingly familiar sensation. "Tell me."

"Her throat was slit," he admitted, his voice so low she could barely catch the words. "And there was a crescent-shaped wound on her breast."

Remi's lips parted, but no air entered her lungs. Had someone wrapped steel bands around her chest? That's what it felt like. At the same time, her brain was churning with a thousand thoughts, all of them so tangled they didn't make any sense.

Vivid images formed and then shattered, then formed again. A memory of her standing in the police station, laughing with her father. His gruff warning to be careful and a kiss on the cheek before she was turning to walk away. The paralyzing fear when she woke in the kitchen of her parents' house to realize she'd been heavily drugged. The groggy night spent in the hospital, Ash pacing the floor with short, angry steps.

"The Butcher," she managed to croak.

His hands clenched and unclenched at his sides. "Or a copycat," he suggested.

She shuddered, not believing for a second that this was some copycat. Her father had told her that they specifically withheld the information that the killer left a mark on his victims. Besides, she'd always known it was just a matter of time.

She had no idea why the Butcher had disappeared from Chicago. Or exactly when he'd be back. But his return had been as inevitable as the rising sun.

Pressing a hand to her stomach, Remi battled back the urge to throw up. "Oh God."

Ash made a choked sound. Remi didn't know if it was pity or frustration. Probably a combination of the two.

"I didn't want to scare you, but you need to be careful," he said.

"I'm always careful," she assured him. And she was. She had moved into her grandparents' house in a nice, quiet suburb. Plus, she never left home without a can of pepper spray tucked in her purse.

"Do you have a gun?"

She gave a sharp shake of her head. "No."

He didn't try to press her. Remi had never hidden her dislike for guns, despite the fact that her father was a cop.

His glance lowered to his feet, as if he didn't want to look at her when he asked his next question. "I know it's none of my business, but do you live alone?"

Remi felt heat creep over her face at his unexpected question. Was she embarrassed to admit that she was still single? Quite likely.

"I have Buddy," she muttered.

Ash seemed to flinch. "Buddy?"

"My dog."

His gaze slowly lifted. "Is he big?"

Her lips curved into a wry smile. Buddy was a rescue dog she'd chosen nearly two years ago. He was a mangy mix of breeds, with a goofy smile and mismatched eyes. He was also large and powerful and fiercely protective of her.

"Big enough."

Ash frowned, seemingly not satisfied with her answer. "It would still be safer if you moved back home for a while."

Remi sucked in a sharp breath. She loved her mother. She truly did. But the two of them had never managed to forge a comfortable relationship. Just a few hours together and Liza Harding-Walsh would be driving her nuts.

"I'd rather get a gun," she told him.

Regret darkened his glorious blue eyes. A regret that was etched on her own soul. "How is your mother?"

Remi released a harsh sigh. "She acts like everything is the same. She stays busy with her charities and society events." She gave a shake of her head. Her mother's brittle smile couldn't disguise the shadows that lurked just below the surface. "But I suspect she is still grieving for my father."

"We all miss him," he breathed.

"Yes." With an abrupt movement, she rose to her feet and crossed the room to grab her coat. Ash's unexpected arrival had stirred up a hornet's nest of memories. Not to mention smashing her fragile sense of peace. She needed time to regroup and repair her shredded nerves. Something that would be impossible when Ash was in the same room. "I should get home." She forced herself to send Ash a meaningless smile. "It was good to see you."

He grimaced, smart enough to realize she was done discussing the Chicago Butcher and whether or not she was capable of protecting herself.

"Remi, it wasn't a fluke that the killer chose a woman who looked just like you," he said in harsh tones. "Be careful."

Her mouth went dry as she gave a jerky nod. "I will."

With a last, lingering glance, Ash slowly walked out of the room. Remi watched him go, her courage leaking out of her like a deflating balloon.

She desperately wanted to call him back. The only time she ever felt safe was when Ash was holding her in his arms. But she kept her lips grimly pressed together.

Her father had died trying to protect her from the Chicago Butcher. She wasn't going to let Ash be the next man she loved to be sacrificed.

Chapter Three

Darkness pulses inside me. A heavy, malignant tumor that continues to grow. I've cut. And cut and cut and cut. I prune the cancer, but it returns. Why?

I know, although I don't want to see the truth.

The evil is a part of me.

It has lurked in the shadows, waiting for the opportunity to grow and fester, destroying me from the inside out. I should have ended it the moment it sparked in my soul. But I was weak . . .

My attention is captured by the bloody knife lying on the counter. It needs to be cleaned. Or perhaps tossed in a fire so it can be purged of the contamination. But I hesitate. The tiny red droplets that stain the silver blade remind me of the sensation of sliding the knife through the soft flesh.

It'd happened sooner than I wanted. I had intended to savor my creation for months and months, not just a few paltry weeks. It was meant to leach the pus from a festering wound. But it had been more difficult than I'd anticipated to create the perfect antidote for my illness. I had allowed it too much freedom. The cure was tainted and I had no choice but to destroy it. Even worse, I'd been sloppy. Something I'd been so very, very careful to avoid.

Still, the deed was done. And in the end it had been . . . cathartic.

I shiver as the memory sears through my mind. For those brief seconds, I felt in utter harmony with the world. As if a light had combusted inside me to drive away the darkness. Even now I can feel the lingering warmth. I want to cling to the peace for as long as possible.

Reaching out, I run my hand along the edge of the blade. Crimson stains my skin and I open my lips to press my finger against the tip of my tongue. The taste of blood is sharp and oddly heavy.

Another shiver races through me.

The battle against the darkness continues.

Ash climbed into the passenger seat of his brother's car and slammed shut the door.

"How is she?" Jax demanded, putting the car in gear and pulling away from the curb.

Gorgeous. Sexy. Heart-wrenchingly vulnerable . . .

The words whispered through his mind, but he didn't allow them to pass his lips. Later he would deal with his intense reaction to being near the woman who'd once held his heart in her hands.

"Rattled," he told his brother.

"Yeah." Jax gripped the steering wheel, zipping through the backstreets to avoid the worst of the Friday traffic. "So am I."

"Get in line," Ash said dryly.

They traveled in silence. Jax concentrating on his driving, while Ash tried to banish the panic that was a heartbeat away. Remi was safe. At least for now. And he'd soon be taking steps to ensure that she was properly protected.

First, however, he needed to get started on his hunt for

the Butcher. The sooner the bastard was dead, the sooner Remi could have a normal life.

Almost as if capable of reading his mind, Jax sent him a quick glance. "Do you want me to take you to Mom's house?"

It was always "Mom's house." Never their parents' house. Or Dad's. No doubt because it was June Marcel's domain. She was the heart of the family, and wherever she was, that was home.

Not that his dad had been a bad father. But he'd been consumed by his duties as a cop, happy to leave the primary caregiving to his wife.

"No." Ash motioned for his brother to take the next turn. "I need to get my old files."

Jax followed his directions. "What files?"

"The ones on the Chicago Butcher."

"You still have them?"

Ash frowned. Did Jax think he would have thrown them away?

"Of course."

"Where?"

Ash parted his lips, only to hesitate. His skills as an investigator were no doubt rusty, but he had faith they would quickly return. And without the rules and regulations that came with his job as a detective, he was free to use whatever means necessary to get information.

Still, he needed to know what leads the police were following and if they found any forensic evidence that might offer a clue to the killer.

"Are you going to include me on this case?" he abruptly demanded.

Jax's fingers tightened on the steering wheel. "You realize you no longer carry a badge?"

Ash shrugged. "You can keep me in the loop or I'll find someone else who will," he said.

Jax's jaw tightened, but he didn't bother to claim that Ash couldn't find the information he wanted. Even after five years, he still had friends on the force. Most of them would be happy to share whatever was necessary to help him catch the bastard who'd killed one of their own.

Jax released a low hiss. "You compromise this case and—"

"I have no intention of doing anything that will compromise the case," Ash interrupted.

"But you're going to investigate it," Jax said, his words a statement, not a question.

"Don't bother to try to stop me," Ash warned.

Jax sent him a frustrated glare. "Then you have to give me the same promise you demanded of me. You'll tell me what you discover." His eyes narrowed. "*Everything* you discover."

"Agreed," Ash said without hesitation.

"Shit," Jax muttered. "This is a bad idea."

Ash ignored his brother's grumbling. It wasn't the first time and it most certainly wasn't going to be the last that Jax was annoyed with him.

"We need to go to the storage unit that's down the street from my old apartment."

"That's where you have the files?"

"Yep."

Jax turned onto a main road that would lead to the neighborhood where he'd lived during his time as a detective. It wasn't fancy, but it had been close to the precinct and it had been cheap enough that he didn't have to live on ramen noodles.

It was nearly dark by the time they were pulling into a fenced parking lot, and Ash hurried into the office. He hadn't brought his key, which meant he needed the manager. Ten minutes later, they were pushing up the roller door and stepping into the long, narrow space.

Ash flipped the switch, blinking as the harsh fluorescent glow seared away the darkness. Beside him, Jax drew in a sharp breath.

"Christ, Ash. I wondered why your new place seemed so empty when I went to pack you a bag. You haven't moved in," he said.

Ash allowed his gaze to skim over the piles of boxes that lined the walls and the heavy furniture that he had stacked at the back. "I've been busy."

"Or maybe it's not home," Jax suggested, moving forward to pull open one of the boxes.

Ash refused to consider his brother's words. "I've been there five years."

"And all you have is a few clothes, three plates, two glasses, and a roll of toilet paper. That should tell you something."

"That you're a nosy bastard," Ash groused even as he silently admitted his brother had a point. He clearly needed to rent a moving van and haul his belongings to his house. It was no wonder he'd never felt comfortable there.

"True," Jax agreed without shame, pulling out the bottle of champagne and engraved glass that Ash had bought as a graduation present for Remi. He'd moved away before he could give it to her. "If you want me to get rid of some of this stuff—"

"No," he growled, moving toward the back of the unit with jerky steps.

"Sorry." Jax replaced the items and closed the box before he hurried to join Ash.

"I'll deal with my personal stuff later," Ash promised, a hint of apology in his voice. He hadn't meant to snap at his brother. Then he bent down to grab a plastic bin from the floor. "These are my private notes on the Butcher, as well as Gage's."

Jax arched his brows. "You didn't give them to the department after he died?"

Ash shook his head. "They have our official reports. These are mostly filled with our investigations that turned out to be dead ends and interviews with witnesses who we didn't really trust to tell us the truth."

There were also the more sensitive inquiries they'd kept on the down low. They didn't want anyone to know that they'd interviewed a lawyer who worked in the district attorney's office, as well as the son of a prominent businessman. Not when the evidence had been sketchy at best. No need to ruin any reputations.

"Why keep them?" Jax demanded.

"At the time I just wanted to hide them away and forget. Now . . ." Ash allowed his words to trail away.

"Now what?"

Ash grimaced, a shiver of disgust spreading through his body. Just holding the container with the files made him feel tainted. As if a portion of the killer's evil had managed to seep into the files inside.

"I think I knew this day would come," he said, lifting his head to meet his brother's somber gaze. "None of us truly thought the Butcher would just stop killing. It was only a matter of time before he returned to Chicago."

"I never worked the case. Did you believe that the Butcher left the area after Gage died?"

That period in his life was a blur in Ash's mind. He'd been consumed with grief and guilt, and at the same time he was terrified by the thought the killer was still out there, just waiting for his opportunity to strike again.

"Either that or he was incarcerated for some other crime. Serial killers rarely start and stop on a whim," he said.

Jax furrowed his brow, as if Ash's words had struck a sudden inspiration. "You know, it's possible that the Butcher changed his MO." He slowly spoke his thoughts out loud. "He had to know that killing a cop would have put him on the radar of every law enforcement agent in the country. I might pull a few of our unsolved cases and give them a second glance."

Ash blinked. He'd never considered the idea that the Butcher had remained but changed his method of killing. Sadly, there were enough unsolved murders in Chicago that his victims might have been labeled as random deaths. "A good idea."

Jax smiled with wry amusement at the surprise in Ash's tone. "I might not have a fancy degree, but I'm a kick-ass cop," he boasted.

Ash snorted. "I'll agree to the ass part."

Jax rolled his eyes. "It's colder than crap in here. Let's go."

Remi pulled into the garage of her bi-level home with its green siding and a large bay window. It'd belonged to her grandparents for forty years. When they'd decided to move to Florida, Remi had purchased the house and moved in. The neighborhood had once been an upscale area for solid, middle-class workers like her grandfather, but over the past few years it'd started to edge toward shabby. Remi didn't mind. It was a nice, peaceful area where she felt isolated from the hectic bustle of the city.

Entering through the side door that led into the kitchen, Remi was braced when her dog came pounding forward. Buddy possessed an unshakable belief that she wanted to be mauled by a seventy-pound dog as soon as she entered the house.

With a laugh, she bent down to give the mutt a good back scratch, allowing the beast to slobber over her face before she grabbed the leash off a nearby hook.

"Come on, boy," she said.

Buddy responded with an excited bark, barely allowing her to clip the leash to his collar before he was dragging her through the house to the front door. Remi jogged to keep up, her dark thoughts shattered by the enthusiastic dog.

Not that she could completely turn off her fear that the Butcher had returned to Chicago. Or the lingering shock at seeing Ash. But no matter what happened during her day, Buddy could always lift her mood.

Opening the door, she was careful to ensure she had her pepper spray in her pocket before heading out for their evening walk. The icy night air added a speed to their trip through their neighborhood as they were both anxious to return to the warmth of the house. Once back home, Remi closed and locked the door before leading Buddy into the kitchen. Expecting the dog to rush to his food bowl, Remi's heart slammed against her chest as he instead barked toward the glass sliding door that led to the back porch.

Trying to tell herself it was a squirrel, or maybe a stray dog, Remi flipped on the outside light. Still, she paused to grab a large knife from a drawer before she slid open the door. Better safe than sorry, right?

She also waited for Buddy to join her before stepping onto the porch and glancing around. Buddy growled and Remi froze. She strained to see through the darkness. Had there been a shadow moving at the edge of her property?

"Hello?" she called out. "Who's there?"

There was a loud rustle from the side of her house

before a man strolled into the light that pooled around her back porch.

"Trouble, Remi?"

She managed to swallow her primitive scream, feeling like a fool. Doug Gates was a short man with thinning blond hair and a round face. Six months ago, he'd moved into the ranch-style house next door. Since then, he'd made a habit of appearing whenever she was outside. Like the Jack-in-the-box she had when she was young. She hated how it would suddenly pop up and make her scream.

She pasted a smile on her face, feeling guilty for her less-than-neighborly thoughts. Doug was a perfectly respectable banker with a couple of kids who lived with his ex-wife. He'd been nothing but nice to her.

"No. I thought I saw someone in the yard, but it must have been my imagination playing tricks on me," she told him, hiding the knife behind her back.

Doug strolled toward her, putting his foot on the first step before he froze at the sound of Buddy's low growl. He cleared his throat, trying to pretend he wasn't embarrassed by the dog's overt dislike. "I wouldn't be too sure it was your imagination. I thought I saw someone peeking through your front window earlier in the day," he said. "Do you want me to do a circle of the block to see if there are any strangers hanging around?"

She shivered, giving a shake of her head. It would be crazy to leap to the conclusion that it was the Butcher. The killer was too skilled to be creeping around her house and peeking through her window. He would have to realize it would attract the attention of her neighbors, who were mostly elderly and nosy enough to keep an eye on what was going on around them.

Still, she didn't want Doug getting himself killed.

"No. I might give the cops a call later," she assured him.

Doug paused, as if trying to think of some excuse to keep the conversation going. "You could come to my house and give them a call if you feel uneasy being alone."

"Thanks, but I'll be fine." She reached down to pat Buddy's head. "I have plenty of protection."

Another awkward pause before Doug forced a smile. "Well, if you need anything, just holler out the window and I'll come running."

"That's very generous of you."

"I like to be neighborly."

"Thanks," Remi muttered, turning to herd her dog into the kitchen and sliding the door behind her. "Yikes."

She shuddered, turning the lock before she busied herself with feeding Buddy and then heading into the bathroom to take a hot bath. It'd been a long day. And the night promised to be even longer.

Pulling on a pair of fuzzy PJ bottoms and a faded T-shirt, Remi braided her damp hair. She was at the point of deciding whether she intended to eat dinner or crawl into bed with a good book when there was a knock on her door.

Warily, Remi made her way to the living room. Buddy was already at the door barking, and Remi wished she had circled through the kitchen to get her knife. Instead, she held her phone in her hand. She punched in the numbers 9-1-1, her thumb hovering over the Call button.

Inching closer to the door, she flipped on the porch light. Then, leaning forward, she peered through the peephole she'd had installed shortly after she'd moved in.

"Ash," she breathed, her knees going weak at the sight of his finely sculpted face and the dark curls that had been tousled by the breeze.

A part of her wanted to be annoyed by his uninvited arrival. He'd already disrupted her day. Now he was no doubt intending to disrupt her night. A larger part of her, however, was fiercely glad not to be alone.

Clearly the fear that someone had been creeping around the house had freaked her out more than she wanted to acknowledge.

Chapter Four

Remi slid back the dead bolt and pulled open the door. Her brows lifted as she took in the boxes he held in his hands.

"What's going on?"

His gaze skimmed over her casual clothing before moving to Buddy, who'd strangely halted his barking. Almost as if he sensed that Ash was a friend. Then he returned his attention to her wary expression. "Can I come in?"

"Come in or move in?" she demanded.

His lips twitched. "I think you'll be interested in what I brought with me."

"Fine." She stepped back, allowing him to walk through the doorway. It was too cold to argue on the front porch. Plus, that sense of relief was still helping to banish the fear that was lodged in the pit of her stomach. She pointed toward the open living room that was filled with furniture chosen for comfort rather than style. "You can use the coffee table for your boxes."

"Thanks." With fluid strides, he was moving to lower the boxes on the low table, along with a large backpack. Then he straightened and turned in a slow circle. "This is your grandparents' house, isn't it?"

"Yeah, they moved to Florida three years ago."

"We came here for Thanksgiving when we were dating," he said. "It looks different."

She tried hard not to remember how she'd snuggled close to Ash on the couch while her grandparents insisted they sit through hours of home movies. Ash hadn't complained once, and her grandmother had pulled her aside to assure her that Ash Marcel was a "keeper."

He had been, but that hadn't prevented her from pushing him away.

She swallowed a sigh. "Not really. I pulled up the carpet to expose the hardwood and painted the walls," she said.

He released a sharp laugh. "It's a lot more than I've done."

She didn't want to think about him in his own house. Perhaps he was sharing it with some beautiful professor who hadn't retreated into a brittle shell.

Remi's heart twisted and she reached down to lay her hand on Buddy's head. He was studying Ash with more curiosity than distrust, but she needed his solid comfort.

"Are you going to tell me why you're here?"

Holding her gaze, Ash slid off his jacket and tossed it onto a nearby chair before he settled on the couch. "To bargain with you."

"Bargain?"

He patted the cushion next to him. "Have a seat."

Her heart jerked and skidded before it lurched back to a steady rhythm. She wanted to sit next to him. She wanted to feel the heat of his body seeping through her. And catch the warm scent of his skin.

That was why she deliberately took a chair near the bookshelves that also served as a TV stand.

"Should I be scared?" she asked, keeping her tone deliberately light.

He studied her for a long moment, as if considering his words. "Do you trust me?"

She didn't hesitate. "Yes."

It was true. There was no one in the world she trusted more than Ash.

Something that might have been satisfaction smoldered in his eyes, but as he leaned forward, his expression was grim.

"I think the Butcher is back in Chicago."

She wasn't shocked by his words. She'd had a few hours to absorb the fact that a young woman had turned up in the morgue with her throat slit and the Butcher's mark on her breast.

"So do I."

He continued to hold her gaze. "And I think he's obsessed with you."

She frowned. She was willing to accept that the Butcher was back, but she wasn't convinced that he was obsessed with her personally. Most serial killers chose their prey for a specific purpose. The Butcher had a thing for dark-haired women with green eyes.

"Because he killed a woman who happened to look like me?"

"Because she looked *exactly* like you."

She made a sound of impatience. "So what are you saying? Do you think he saw her and mistook her for me?"

His jaw tightened. "I'm not entirely sure. I just know I'm worried."

A tiny spark of warmth flared to life in the center of her heart. It'd been a long time since she'd felt as if someone cared about her. Really and truly cared.

Her mother loved her, of course, but Liza Harding-Walsh found it difficult to display her emotions.

"I don't know why he'd be obsessed with me," she muttered.

"You're the one who got away," he said with a blunt simplicity. "His failure has no doubt been festering for the past five years."

She pressed a hand to her stomach, mentally willing herself not to return to that dark, horrifying night.

"What about your bargain?" she demanded.

"I want to stay here until the Butcher is caught," he told her, his expression hardening. "Or dead."

"Here?" It took her a second to process what he was saying. Then her heart started doing that crazy jerking and skidding again. She forced herself to take a deep breath. "Can't you stay with your mother?"

He gave a dramatic shudder. "Various family members have already started to descend for the holidays, and unfortunately, they'll no doubt stay until after Nate's wedding at the end of next month. They tend to be like roaches who refuse to leave once they've invaded the place. Trust me, the house is filled to the rafters."

"What about one of your brothers? I'm sure they have their own places with spare bedrooms."

"They snore."

"Then what about a hotel?"

"Too expensive. I'm just a poor teacher."

She flattened her lips to keep them from curving into a smile. No one could be more charming than Ash Marcel when he put his mind to it. And no matter how hard she might pretend to be indifferent, she inwardly accepted that she was just as susceptible as she'd always been.

With an effort, she squashed the unnerving realization.

"I'm not an idiot. I know you think you need to protect me," she said.

He shrugged without apology. "I want to make sure you're safe."

She glanced toward the large window that overlooked the front yard. "It's no longer your job."

She thought she heard his breath hiss between clenched teeth. Was he angered by her words?

"It will always be my job," he told her in soft tones.

She flinched. "Because of Dad."

"Because of us," he insisted.

The soul-deep yearning she kept firmly locked deep inside her threatened to crack open. She gave a sharp shake of her head. *No. Not now.*

With an effort, she forced herself to turn to meet his gaze. "I appreciate your concern, Ash, but—"

He interrupted her assurance that she was just fine on her own. "I'm not done."

She heaved a sigh. He could be as stubborn as a mule. "Okay. What do I get out of letting you stay here?"

He arched a brow, as if puzzled by her question. "I don't think you understand, Remi. Your reward is having me as a guest."

She made a choked sound. "Really? And what do you get out of the deal?"

"Your help in tracking down the Butcher."

She stared at him in genuine surprise. He was asking for her assistance in looking for the killer?

"Are you being serious?" she rasped.

"Never more so." His voice was somber, assuring her that he truly intended to ask for her help.

"But the last time you wouldn't even discuss the case with me," she reminded him.

He lifted his hands. "It was my job. I wasn't allowed to discuss it with anyone."

She studied him. He wasn't giving her the full truth. Ash had never gossiped about private police matters, no matter what the case. But she suspected her father had been insistent that he keep his mouth shut about the Butcher. Her father had always tried to protect Remi from the ugliness of his job.

"And now?" she pressed.

"Now I'm a private citizen. I can do whatever the hell I want."

She stiffened, struck by a sudden fear. "If you're hoping I remember something about that night, you're going to be disappointed."

His eyes darkened to a deep indigo at the mention of her kidnapping. They'd both been scarred by that night.

"I know you can't force the memories. Either they'll return or they won't," he said.

She'd braced herself for the predictable sympathy. For months after the kidnapping—and her father's death— she'd been smothered in pity. Thankfully, Ash seemed to remember just how much she hated it. His voice was brisk, almost indifferent.

She studied him in confusion. "Then how can I help?"

He reached out to touch the boxes he'd stacked on the coffee table. "I brought the notes your father and I made during the investigation. I hope we can go through them together. You might see something we missed."

She released her breath on a shaky sigh. Until this moment, she hadn't realized how desperate she was for an opportunity to actively search for the Butcher.

For the past five years, she'd been treading water, as if she was caught in a quagmire she couldn't escape. How could she move forward when the past continued to hold her hostage?

Ash was offering her the chance to break free of her prison.

"Yes," she breathed.

He gave a slow nod, clearly sensing the emotions churning through her. "I also thought we might take a drive tomorrow."

She took a second to gather her scattered thoughts. She didn't want Ash regretting his offer to include her in the investigation.

"Drive where?" There. That was a perfectly intelligent question.

"To Bailey."

"Bailey?" The name didn't mean anything to her. "Is it a store?"

"No, it's a little farm town south of here."

"Why would we go there?"

"Angel Conway."

She sent him an impatient glance. Was he being deliberately vague? "Who's that?"

"The woman who was killed," he clarified. "She lived in Bailey."

Oh. Now she understood. "Is that where she was murdered?"

He shook his head. "No. Her body was found in Jameson Park. The cops believe that's where she died."

Remi considered his words. "How did Angel Conway end up in a park in Chicago?"

"I think he took her there."

Remi's stomach threatened to revolt as a jagged image of walking through darkness, a sense of evil looming behind her, flickered through her mind before disappearing as swiftly as it formed. She didn't bother to try to hold on to it. Her memories from the night she was kidnapped were like a shattered window. She might be able to grasp a fragment for a few seconds, but it was impossible to put them together.

Belatedly realizing that Ash was regarding her with a frown, Remi rose to her feet.

"I'll get the spare room ready," she said, her tone brisk.

The last thing she wanted was Ash worried that she couldn't handle the investigation.

His gaze lingered on her face before he rose to his feet. "Have you had dinner?"

"No."

"I'll order something." He pulled his phone from the front pocket of his slacks. "Pizza okay?"

"I can cook," she offered.

Ash flashed a quick smile, no doubt well aware that her cupboards were bare. Her lack of culinary skills had been a running joke between them.

"Pizza it is."

Jax grimaced as he tossed away the last of his salad and headed out of the kitchenette just down the hall from his office. Getting old sucked. There was a time when he could eat two bacon cheeseburgers, a plate of fries, and polish it off with a slab of cake without putting on a pound. Now he couldn't walk past a pastry display without his belt tightening.

What he really needed was to return to his morning jogs, he wryly acknowledged. How long had it been since he'd last exercised on a regular basis? A year ago? Two?

He swallowed a sigh. His mother was right. He was too old to be a bachelor. Living alone meant that he didn't have any reason to stop working at a reasonable hour. No one cared if he was home for dinner, or if he made plans for his weekend. It also meant that he didn't take care of himself like he should.

Too many takeout meals eaten at work and not enough time on the treadmill.

He shook his head, dismissing his bout of self-pity. It wouldn't matter if he had a wife and ten kids waiting for him at home; he wasn't going anywhere for a while.

The Butcher was back, and if Ash was right and the bastard was hunting Remi Walsh, Jax's every waking minute was going to be spent chasing down leads. Eventually, one of them would lead him to the killer.

Refusing to contemplate the thought of failure, he rounded the partition wall and came to a sharp halt. His eyes narrowed as he took in the sight of the man who was leaning over his desk, flipping through the tall stack of files.

What the hell?

He moved forward, watching as the man abruptly straightened and whirled to face him.

Bruce O'Reilly.

The detective was a year younger than Jax, although he looked like he was a decade older. He had a big, square head with dark hair he kept buzzed next to his skull. His skin was ruddy and sagged near his jaws, giving him the appearance of a bulldog. His body was equally square, with a growing paunch that threatened to bust through his white shirt.

"Jax." The man pushed his hands in his pockets, trying to act as if he hadn't been nosing through Jax's desk.

"O'Reilly." Jax glanced toward his desk. "Are you looking for something?"

O'Reilly folded his arms over his chest. "Just curious."

"About what?"

"I heard you caught the Jane Doe from the park."

Jax shrugged. "She's not a Jane Doe. We have an ID."

O'Reilly barely listened. Clearly, he wasn't interested in the identity of the murder victim. "The rumor is that you're claiming it was the work of the Butcher."

Jax tensed as he felt prickles of unease dance over his skin. O'Reilly wasn't just being nosy. He was here with a purpose.

"I'm not claiming anything," Jax said with complete honesty. He wanted to keep a lid on his Butcher theory. The longer he could go without the press breathing down his neck, the better. Unfortunately, he needed to coordinate between several units, which meant it was inevitable that gossip would spread. "I'm just working the case."

"Was her throat slit?" O'Reilly demanded.

"I don't have the coroner's report yet."

O'Reilly glared at him. Something that would have been a lot more intimidating if he wasn't four inches shorter than Jax.

"Don't be an ass."

"The only one being an ass is you, O'Reilly."

"Just like your brother."

Jax chuckled at the muttered words. "I take that as a compliment."

"You shouldn't," O'Reilly snapped. "If he'd listened to me, he would still be a detective."

Jax bristled. He'd never liked the younger detective. He was crude, brash, and overbearing. As far as he knew, O'Reilly didn't have any friends in the department. "What are you talking about?"

O'Reilly glanced around, as if making sure there was no one close enough to overhear their conversation. "Look, it might be politically incorrect to talk bad about the dead, but Gage Walsh was blinded by his ambition."

Jax snorted in disbelief. "That's bullshit."

"Is it?" The man shrugged. "You know I was his partner?"

Jax had a vague memory of O'Reilly being teamed with Gage for a short time. It'd been several years ago. "So?"

"Walsh wasn't a bad detective." O'Reilly turned so he could settle his fat ass on the corner of the desk. "But he was always looking to score a high-profile case."

"I never heard that about him."

"It's not something he spread around, but I think he had political aspirations." He spoke stiffly. Almost as if he'd practiced the words.

"Gage?" Jax made no effort to disguise his skepticism. "You're out of your mind. He hated bullshit politics."

O'Reilly jutted his chin to a stubborn angle. "Maybe it was his wife pushing him. But he drove me nuts with his complaints that we were stuck investigating gangbangers and drug dealers."

Jax rolled his eyes. "We all get frustrated. Don't tell me you don't ever complain."

"Yeah, but he started exaggerating our reports."

Jax might not have known Gage Walsh as well as his brother, but he did know that he'd been a damned good detective. And an honest one. "You're going to have to be more specific."

"Sometimes he implied our perp was a drug lord or that the case was connected to government corruption," O'Reilly said, keeping his accusations vague enough it would be difficult to call him a liar. "When I refused to back up his claims, he dumped me for your brother. He assumed a hotshot Marcel would play his game. And he was right."

Jax took a quick step forward, barely resisting the urge

to punch the jerk in the face. "Be very, very careful of what you say next, O'Reilly," he warned, his voice lethally soft.

O'Reilly tried to look casual, but Jax didn't miss the nerve twitching next to his eye. The man knew he was asking for trouble, but still he pressed on.

"I'm not saying Ash was corrupt, but he was eager enough to jump on the bandwagon that there was a serial killer in Chicago."

"Probably because there *was* a serial killer in Chicago."

"We had a spate of women getting their throats slit," O'Reilly said, his tone indicating he thought it was the women's fault. "Maybe they were connected and maybe they weren't. Either way, Walsh and your brother made sure they were the center of attention."

Jax grimly leashed his flare of fury. There was no one in the Chicago Police Department who had doubted there was a serial killer. Or ever implied they thought Gage or Ash were camera hogs in search of personal fame.

So why was O'Reilly making his wild accusations? Sour grapes? Or something more nefarious?

Suddenly, Jax thought back to standing next to his brother in his storage unit. Ash had kept his and Gage's notes hidden. Did he suspect someone in the department might be overly interested in the case?

Tucking the suspicion in the back of his mind, Jax studied the detective's ruddy face. "So, if your theory is that there was no Butcher, who do you think killed Gage?"

O'Reilly gave a lift of one shoulder. "That daughter of his was obviously unhinged. Who knows what happened that night?"

Abruptly, Jax had endured enough. Remi Walsh had been kidnapped, terrorized, and then was plagued with guilt at the death of her father. Now this jackass was implying she was somehow responsible.

"Get away from my desk," he rasped.

O'Reilly paled, but he took his time backing out of the cubicle. "Stay out of the past, Marcel," he warned Jax. "You won't like what you stir up."

Jax scowled as the detective disappeared from view.

He didn't know what O'Reilly had hoped to achieve. But he intended to keep a close eye on the man.

A very close eye.

Chapter Five

After a late night of organizing his old files, Ash was up and out of bed before dawn the next morning. He'd slept remarkably well considering he'd been in a strange place. It could have been because he was exhausted, both physically and emotionally. But he suspected it had more to do with the knowledge that Remi was sleeping on the other side of the wall.

For the first time in years, he hadn't felt that empty ache in the center of his being. As if just having Remi near was enough to ease his need.

The sensation should have worried him, but he shrugged off the strange thought and hopped in the shower, then pulled on the heavy sweatpants and shirt his brother had packed for him. Next, he headed into the kitchen, starting the coffee maker and searching through the cabinets until he found a packet of dog treats.

He was seated at the kitchen table sipping his coffee with Buddy on a chair next to him when Remi strolled out of her bedroom.

She was already dressed for her morning run with her hair pulled into a high ponytail as she stepped into the kitchen. She came to a halt, her brows lifting at the sight of Buddy wagging his tail and offering her a goofy grin. Quickly, her gaze moved to the empty packet on the table.

"Are you bribing my dog?" she demanded.

Ash scratched the mutt under his chin. "He's a beauty."

"He is," she readily agreed. "Why are you up so early?"

He rose to his feet. "Getting ready to go for a jog."

She hesitated, clearly searching for an excuse to avoid his company.

"You don't have to go with me," she said. "I always take Buddy."

He strolled toward the door to the garage where he'd left his coat. He turned back to meet her wary gaze as he pulled it on. "I've been running alone for years. It'll be nice to have some company."

His soft words seemed to catch her off guard. Slowly, her tension eased. Grabbing her own coat, she bundled it around her and took the leash.

"Okay, but you have to keep up or we'll leave you in our dust." Buddy scrambled to her side, eager to be out. She snapped the leash to his collar before dropping a kiss on top of his broad head. "Won't we, boy?"

"Don't worry about me, I'll keep up," Ash assured her, feeling a tiny tug on his heart. Remi was so warm and affectionate. She needed someone in her life to smother with love.

Of course, if she chose another man . . .

He slammed the door on the painful thought as his hand instinctively reached for the gun he no longer carried. This morning he just wanted to enjoy spending time with Remi.

In silence, they headed out of the house, walking a block to warm their muscles. Then, without needing to speak, they fell into a comfortable pace as they jogged through the early morning darkness. This was one of many rituals they'd enjoyed during their time together.

The sun was just beginning to crest the horizon when they turned back. The faint light allowed Ash ample opportunity to catch sight of the shadow that moved across her front porch.

Reaching out, he grasped her arm and brought her to a sharp halt. "Wait," he commanded.

She sent him a puzzled glance. "What's wrong?"

"There's a man on your porch."

She stiffened, the dog growling as she turned her head to peer through the darkness. After a minute, she released her breath with a harsh sigh.

"That's just Doug," she said in dismissive tones.

"Doug?"

"Doug Gates."

He glanced down at her unconcerned expression. "A friend?"

She shrugged. "My next-door neighbor."

Ash frowned. If she thought he would be comforted by her explanation, she was wrong. He didn't like the thought there was a man living so close who thought he had the right to wander around her property.

"Does he spend a lot of time on your porch?" he demanded.

She sent him a puzzled glance, easily catching the edge in his voice. "He's a nice guy," she assured him.

Ash ignored her words, his gaze remaining locked on the man who'd moved to glance through Remi's front window. He was going to have a word with Doug about creeping around a woman's house. Either he was a pervert or something worse.

"Married?" he asked.

"Divorced."

"How long has he lived next door?"

"Around six months."

Ash's suspicion went up a notch. Certainly, it could be a coincidence. But then again, if the Butcher had returned to Chicago with the specific purpose of playing some sick game with Remi, moving next to her would fit the pattern.

"Hmm."

He heard Remi heave a deep sigh. "You're going to run a background check on him, aren't you?"

Ash shrugged. "Not me personally."

With a shake of her head, Remi cut through the yard and climbed on the porch. "Hi, Doug."

The man whirled around, an eager smile curving his lips. "Morning, Remi."

Ash strolled up behind her, pleased to hear Buddy growling low in his throat. The dog clearly thought Doug was sketchy. Yet another reason to discover everything he could about the neighbor. He halted beside Remi, barely resisting the urge to wrap his arm around her shoulder.

Doug glanced toward him, his smile fading as his eyes narrowed.

Remi broke the thick silence. "This is Ash Marcel. He's staying with me for the holidays."

Doug allowed his gaze to run over Ash, his jaw tightening. "A relative?"

Remi answered before Ash could speak. "An old friend."

"I see," Doug said, his tone indicating he didn't understand at all.

"Did you need something?" Remi demanded.

Doug gave Ash one last, lingering glance, almost as if he thought he could intimidate him. Idiot.

"Just making sure your lurker hadn't returned."

Ash was immediately distracted. "What lurker?"

"It's nothing." Remi sent a stiff smile toward Doug. "Everything's fine."

It was an unmistakable dismissal and Doug grudgingly

headed off the porch. "Okay, then. If you need anything, just give a yell."

Waiting until the man had disappeared into the house next door, Ash glanced toward Remi. "Tell me about the lurker."

"After we get out of the cold."

Remi reached into the pocket of her coat to pull out her keys. Unlocking the front door, she entered the house and unhooked Buddy's leash. The dog moved to flop on a pillow next to the couch while Ash closed the door.

He pulled off his coat and tossed it on a nearby chair. "Talk," he commanded.

She sent him a wry glance, tugging off her own jacket. "Last night I took Buddy for a walk. When we came back to the house, he ran into the kitchen and started barking. I went out and looked around, but there was no one around. There might have been a shadow at the back of the yard, but it was too dark to say for sure."

Ash made a mental note to go out later to check for any indication there'd been someone sneaking around her backyard. For now, however, he concentrated on his suspicions swirling around Doug Gates. "How did your neighbor know?"

She absently pulled her hair from the ponytail, allowing it to spill over her shoulders. Ash's hands twitched. He'd loved running his finger through the satin strands. Or, better yet, feeling her hair brushing over his bare skin when they were in bed.

"He came out when I was looking around," she said.

Ash crushed the fantasies that threatened to distract him. Right now he was trying to keep Remi safe. Later, he would discover if her hair was as soft as he remembered.

"Came out or was already out?" he demanded.

She paused, considering his question. "I didn't notice. He just appeared."

"Definitely a person of interest," Ash murmured. He'd get Jax to run the background check ASAP.

She rolled her eyes. "You sound like a detective, Dr. Marcel."

He gave a lift of his hands. He did sound like a detective. Probably because deep in his heart, he still felt like one.

"I'll try to sound more scholarly in the future," he promised.

Their gazes met and held, a strange understanding passing between them. It was like the first time they'd crossed paths in the squad room. She'd come to take her father to lunch and he'd been sitting at the older man's desk. They'd stared at each other in silence, both caught off guard by the intensity of their first glance.

Ash had known in that moment his life was never going to be the same.

And he'd been right.

Remi's face flushed, her eyes darkening with need before she was abruptly turning away. "I need a shower," she muttered.

He forced himself not to reach out and pull her back to him.

"I'll make some breakfast," he said, his tone deliberately light. "And we can head to Bailey."

She nodded, scurrying toward the hallway without looking back. Ash smiled wryly as he headed toward the kitchen. He didn't know whether to laugh or cry at the awkward awareness that smoldered between them.

He hated the realization that the easy relationship he'd taken for granted between them was gone. But then again, he would have been devastated if she'd felt nothing.

Entering the kitchen, Ash distracted himself with cooking a decent breakfast. It wasn't easy, considering that Remi's cabinets were nearly bare. She'd never enjoyed spending time in the kitchen and it appeared that hadn't changed.

He had the plates on the table when she entered the dining room smelling like soap and delicious strawberry lip balm. She'd pulled her damp hair into a braid and wrapped herself in a pair of jeans and a warm, fuzzy sweater. She looked like she should still be in college, not teaching troubled teens.

They ate in silence, then Remi poured out food and water for Buddy and they headed back out of the house. Ash led her toward the sleek, silver Mercedes coupe, his lips twitching as Remi arched her brows. Clearly, she hadn't paid any attention to the vehicle before now.

"Is this your car?" she demanded in surprise.

"I rented it," he explained, lifting his hand as her eyes widened. "And no, I'm not going through some midlife crisis. The rental agency had this car, a van that could fit twelve people, and a sedan with a broken defroster."

"'Tis the season," she murmured.

"No crap."

She glanced up at the sky. The sun was shining, but this was the Midwest. Any second the clouds could roll in and the snow could start flying.

"Maybe we should take my car," she offered.

It made more sense to take the sensible sedan. But while Remi had been in the shower, Ash had considered a dozen different ways to approach the people of Bailey and ask questions. He'd been in enough small towns to know they were friendly enough with one another, but they didn't like strangers. They were going to need a tempting excuse to get them to share information about Angel Conway.

"I was thinking we might pass ourselves off as reporters," he told her. "Maybe even imply we're making a documentary. The flashier our transportation, the better."

She sent him a startled glance. "That's actually a good idea."

Ash snorted, pressing the button on the key fob that would unlock the doors. "I do have them now and again."

With a chuckle, Remi pulled open the passenger door. Ash hurried around the car to settle behind the steering wheel. Once they were both buckled in, he loaded the address into the GPS and fired up the massive engine. In less than ten minutes they were on the interstate headed south.

Settling into the butter-soft leather seat, Remi remained silent as she watched the tightly packed neighborhoods spread out to sprawling suburbs and finally to farmland.

"Has the family been notified?" she finally demanded.

"Yeah. Jax called while you were in the shower," he said. Jax had already been at his office when he'd phoned Ash. "Angel's mother is expected to ID the body today."

She sent him a startled glance. "Shouldn't we wait until she's back home?"

"No. Jax will interview Ms. Conway after she's done at the morgue," he said. "I'm more interested in Angel's friends. She would be more likely to tell them her true reason for going to Chicago. Especially if it was something she wanted to keep hidden from her family."

"That makes sense," she agreed. "But how are we going to find her friends?"

That was one part of the plan to which Ash hadn't given much thought. He shrugged. "It's a small town. We'll be able to figure out where Angel would hang out."

She didn't bother to argue as Ash exited the interstate onto a narrow county road. Probably because he was using the long, empty stretch of highway to see precisely how the expensive car would perform. He grinned at the throaty sound of the engine and the way the vehicle hugged the pavement as they rounded a curve.

"Maybe I am going through a midlife crisis," he admitted.

She blinked in confusion. "Why do you say that?"

"I'm liking this car."

She released a startled laugh. "I'm sure your students would be impressed. A hot professor in a sports car."

He pounced on her teasing words. "You think I'm hot?"

She blushed, quickly looking away. "Do you like teaching?"

"For now."

Ash turned his attention back to the road, slowing to a reasonable speed. The turnoff into Bailey was only a few miles away. He didn't want to miss it.

He sensed her curiosity. "But?"

He didn't have an easy answer. There was a part of him that enjoyed being a teacher. Most of his students were eager to learn and it was fulfilling to know he was helping to train the lawmen of the future. Still, another part of him had started to chafe at being in the classroom. Especially when that classroom was so far away from Chicago.

"I'm starting to reconsider my future," he told her in soft tones.

"You miss being a detective?"

"I miss a lot of things."

She shifted in her seat, no doubt sensing he was talking about more than his job. Before she could respond, however, the GPS was telling him to turn right and they were driving into Bailey.

There was a cluster of fading houses that marked the beginning of town. A few were decorated for Christmas, but many looked like they'd been abandoned over the past few years. Rural America was struggling to recover from the recession.

Slowing his pace to a leisurely crawl, Ash turned on to First Street. It looked to be the main thoroughfare through town. He drove past a bank, an old movie theater with a sagging marquee, an auto shop, a hair salon, and an insurance office.

"There," Remi said, pointing toward the corner building.

Not hesitating, Ash angled the car along the curb, ignoring the small parking lot across the street that was almost full. Turning off the engine, he read the gold lettering in the window of the brick building.

Blue Moon Restaurant and Pool Hall.

Hmm. It seemed a little late in the morning for the breakfast crowd, but it was clearly the hot spot in town.

Crawling out of the car, he was joined by Remi, who never waited for him to open her door. She was a woman who enjoyed her independence, and if she needed help, she would ask for it. Together, they walked the short distance to enter the restaurant.

Ash grimaced. The heat hit him first. After being in the chilled breeze, it felt like it was a hundred degrees inside the dining room. Next, he was hit by the smell. There was a strange combination of coffee, deep-fried potatoes, and the sawdust that was spread over the floor.

Not particularly appetizing.

He allowed his gaze to roam over the dining room that was nothing more than a few booths along one wall. Down the center of the floor was a row of wooden columns that separated the space from the five pool tables on the other side.

There was one middle-aged man seated in a booth

with an empty plate in front of him, but the majority of the customers were sitting or standing next to one of the pool tables where a game was in progress.

At a glance, he guessed them to be in their midtwenties, although they were roughhousing and telling the sort of crude jokes that were more appropriate for teenagers than young adults.

A middle-aged woman in a white shirt and tight slacks appeared from the back. She had a mound of suspiciously blond hair that was pulled into a knot on top of her head and bright red lipstick. She waved a hand toward empty tables.

"Take your pick," she told them.

"Thanks," Remi murmured, crossing the worn plank floor to take a seat at the nearest booth.

Ash followed closely behind her, sliding onto the bench seat across the table from her.

The waitress, who had the name "Joy" pinned on her ample breast, pulled out an order pad.

"Just two black coffees, please," he said with a smile.

The older woman swallowed a sigh, no doubt assuming any hope of a tip was lost. Still, she turned to head toward the counter, where she grabbed a silver coffeepot and returned to fill the cups already on the wooden table. Then, with a shake of her head at a shrill laugh from the crowd on the other side of the room, she headed back to the kitchen.

Ash barely noticed. His attention had been captured by a young man who had moved to gaze out the window. He looked younger than the others—maybe eighteen—and was dressed in jeans and a flannel shirt with a Cubs baseball cap covering his head.

After a few minutes, he turned to glance toward Ash. "Hey, man, is that your ride?"

"Yep."

A hint of envy darkened the younger man's eyes. "It's sweet."

Ash slid out of his seat and leaned casually against the edge of the table. "What's your name?"

As Ash had hoped, the boy took a couple of steps in his direction. "Mason Curry."

"Do you want to take a look at the car, Mason?"

Mason remained wary even as he shuffled closer to the table. His gaze flicked toward Remi before returning to Ash.

"Depends."

"On what?" Ash demanded.

"What you expect in return."

"Information."

The younger man released a sharp laugh. "Then you're shit out of luck. I ain't got none. I live in the middle of nowhere and work at the local window factory. Do you need any information about those things?"

"You'd be surprised." Ash deliberately paused, as if trying to decide whether to share a secret or not. At last he spoke. "I'm here to learn more about Angel Conway."

"You're a cop," Mason said in disgust, revealing that the gossip of Angel's death had already made the rounds through town.

"Not guilty," Ash instantly denied.

"Then why are you interested in Angel?"

Ash waved a hand toward Remi, who sipped her coffee in silence. "We think her story might make a good documentary."

"Documentary?" Mason tested the word, his brow furrowed. "That's one of those short movies?"

"Exactly."

He looked skeptical. "You know she was murdered in Chicago, not here in Bailey?"

"I do," Ash assured him. "That's what first intrigued me. The death of a small-town beauty in the big city."

He watched as Mason's suspicion was forgotten as the younger man suddenly realized he might benefit from Angel's death. "Are you going to interview me on camera?" he demanded. "Do you pay people for stuff like that?"

Ash heard Remi make a low sound of disgust, but his attention remained on the younger man.

"Right now we're just trying to get a feel for her story. I need to find out if she might interest the public."

"Gotcha." Mason nodded in what he no doubt hoped was a sage manner. "Angel was older than me, but Dana was friends with her."

Ash arched a brow. "Dana?"

"My sister." Mason turned his head to bellow across the room. "Hey, Dana."

A woman in her midtwenties turned to glare at Mason. She had the prettiness that came with youth, but her features were too sharp, her eyes set too close together for true beauty. Her hair was a light brown shade that hung limply down her back and her skinny body was covered by a pair of faded jeans and a furry sweater.

"What the hell do you want?" she yelled back.

"Come here."

She stepped closer to a man who was older than the others and drinking a beer despite the early hour.

"No . . ." Her words trailed away as her gaze moved from her brother to Ash. Her eyes widened, her annoyance fading as she forgot the local bad boy. With a sway in her hips, she sauntered across the floor, halting next to her brother while she kept her attention locked on Ash. "What's going on?"

"They're here to make a movie about Angel," Mason explained.

"Angel?" Dana frowned. "She's dead."

"They know that, stupid." Mason rolled his eyes. "That's why they want to make the movie."

Dana elbowed her brother in the side even as she pasted a smile to her lips.

"Really?" she asked Ash.

Ash shrugged. "We're just gathering information right now."

"She was my best friend."

Mason snorted, but no one paid him any attention.

"Can you tell me about Angel?" Ash asked in soft tones.

"Sure." Dana stepped toward him, any grief at the loss of her best friend hidden beneath the excitement that simmered in her blue eyes. "What'd you want to know?"

Ash took a second to consider his words. He didn't want to sound like a cop interrogating a witness. Still, there was information he needed.

"Did she have a happy childhood?" he finally asked.

"She wasn't abused, but I don't know if it was happy," Dana said with a shrug. "Her dad took off when she was in grade school. Angel never talked about him, but someone told me that he ran off with another woman."

Ash made a mental note to do a check on the missing Mr. Conway. If he had moved to Chicago, that might have been a reason for Angel to travel there.

"What about her mother?"

"During the day she works at the convenience store near the interstate and at night she cleans the bank. I don't think she was home very much when Angel was growing up."

Ash felt a pang of pity for Ms. Conway. It sounded like she'd done her best as a single mother to keep a roof over their heads and food on the table. Now her daughter was dead. It didn't seem fair.

"Did Angel have any brothers or sisters?"

"No." Dana lifted a hand to her lips to smother a sudden

giggle. "Well, everyone said her father got half the women in town pregnant before he took off, but none of them admits to having his kid."

Ash grimaced. He definitely needed to check out Mr. Conway.

"Was Angel a good student?" he asked.

Dana released a sharp crack of laughter. "She didn't give a shit about school. She was planning to haul ass to Hollywood as soon as she turned eighteen."

"Did she?"

"Yep. She went to California for a year. She thought that she was going to be a big star just because everyone was telling her how pretty she was." There was a hint of bitterness in Dana's voice. Ash suspected she'd been unfavorably compared to her supposed best friend since they were in kindergarten.

"I assume it didn't work out?"

"Naw." Dana tried to hide her hint of satisfaction. "She came back and started working at the store with her mom."

Ash was beginning to get a sense of Angel Conway. A girl who'd been raised by a distracted mother and an absent father who had been desperate to escape her small-town life. "Did she have a boyfriend?"

"Lots of them, but none were serious." It was Mason who answered, a hint of bitterness in his voice. Had he nurtured a crush on his sister's friend? Probably. "She thought she was too good for the local guys."

Ash nodded, turning the conversation in the direction that most interested him. "Did she ever have any trouble with the law?"

Dana's brows snapped together with genuine outrage. "Angel was poor, but she wasn't trash."

He offered an apologetic smile. "I never thought she was. Believe me, the last thing I would ever want to do is tarnish Angel's memory, but a multidimensional person is more interesting than a saint, don't you think?"

There was a long silence as Dana battled between her loyalty to her dead friend and the opportunity to grab her fifteen minutes of fame.

Fame won out.

"I suppose," she agreed, leaning forward. "Angel liked pills."

He guessed the most likely drug of choice. "Painkillers?"

Dana nodded. "She started them when she was out west. She said they helped her nerves when she was auditioning."

"And continued the habit when she came home?" Ash asked.

Dana hesitated, sending a quick glance over her shoulder. Ash suspected the local dealer was standing in the crowd across the room.

"When she could get the money," she finally muttered.

Ash didn't press. He could sense that Dana would clam up if she thought she might get one of her friends in trouble. Especially if it happened to be the beer-drinking man who was sending suspicious frowns in their direction.

He turned the questions to a less-sensitive topic. "Did she spend a lot of time in Chicago?"

Dana released a small breath of relief. "No. The bank repossessed her car last year. Even if she had the money to go to the city, she didn't have any wheels to get there."

"How did she get to the city?"

The young woman shrugged. "I'm not sure. I just know that a couple of months ago she told me that she had a fabulous opportunity in Chicago and she'd be gone for a while. That's why I didn't worry when she just disappeared."

He shared a quick glance with Remi before returning his attention to Dana. They both had the same thought.

This was how the killer lured Angel to Chicago. Or maybe he came and picked her up in his own car.

He needed to find out. Even in this small town there were plenty of security cameras. It was possible one of them had caught an image of the Butcher's vehicle.

"What was the fabulous opportunity?" he asked Dana.

"She couldn't say. She had to sign some piece of paper that said she wouldn't tell anyone about it."

"A nondisclosure agreement?" he suggested.

"I guess that's what it's called." Dana grimaced, clearly uninterested in legal documents. "I thought at first that Angel was making up shit. She did that when she was feeling depressed about being a nobody stuck in this god-awful town. But one day she came by the hair salon—" She paused to send Ash a flirtatious smile. "I'm a fully trained manicurist if you happen to be in the mood for a pedicure. I give the best foot rubs in town."

She waited for Ash to respond. When he refused to be lured by the promise of—actually, he wasn't sure what he was being offered—she continued with a shrug. "Angel was there to show off a stack of money she got in the mail. She said it was a down payment."

"Someone sent her cash?" he demanded in confusion.

A few serial killers created elaborate games to toy with their prey, but during the investigation five years ago they'd never had any indication that the Butcher did more than select his victim and slit their throat.

Was the killer evolving? Or were they completely off base in trying to pin this latest murder on him?

"That's what Angel told me," Dana said, her tone puzzled.

Ash gave a small shake of his head. He was losing focus. He'd sort through the variations in the murders once he returned to Chicago. Right now, he needed to finish his questioning and get out of town. Eventually, someone was going to walk into the restaurant who wasn't so easily convinced that he was there about a documentary.

"You didn't hear from Angel after she left town?" he asked.

"No. I sent her a couple of texts, but she ignored them. I assumed she thought she was too big a deal to waste her time with me."

Ash glanced toward the crowd that was starting to file out a side door. It was obviously time to move on to the next hot spot. "Is there anyone else in town she might have contacted?"

Dana considered before giving a slow shake of her head. "She didn't have a lot of friends. She might have called her mom, I guess."

Sensing he'd pressed his luck far enough, Ash nodded toward Remi, who promptly slid out of the booth to head for the door. Ash dropped a five-dollar bill on the table and sent Dana and Mason a professional smile.

"Thanks for taking time to talk to me. You've both been a lot of help."

"Hey, when will we know about the movie?" Mason called out as Ash headed toward the exit.

He pushed open the door before looking over his shoulder. "We're still in research mode. But I'll let you know if I have any more questions."

Chapter Six

Remi climbed into the expensive car, barely pulling on her seat belt before Ash was settled behind the steering wheel and starting the engine.

She hadn't minded remaining in the background as he'd questioned Angel's friends. Ash was a trained detective. He knew exactly what questions to ask and how to ask them. Plus, it'd been obvious that the young Dana had been eager to impress Ash.

She cast a covert glance at Ash's perfectly chiseled profile, suppressing a sigh. He wasn't exactly handsome. None of the Marcel boys were. But there was a compelling strength in their features and an irresistible charm in their smiles. Women had been tripping over their feet to capture their attention as long as she'd known them.

It had been inevitable that she would be attracted to Ash. But it wasn't until she'd actually gotten to know him that she tumbled head over heels in love. It was his heart and soul that made him special.

Aching regret clenched her heart as they pulled away from the curb and headed out of town. If only things had been different . . .

Remi clenched her teeth, forcing away her futile thoughts. There was no way to change the past. All she could do was make certain that she didn't allow Ash's return to Chicago to create even more pain.

"So what's our next step?" he said as they pulled onto the interstate. His voice was low, and she suspected he was speaking more to himself than her.

"You sound just like my dad," she told him, her lips curving into a wistful smile. "He'd sit next to me while I was doing my homework and say 'Well, Remi girl, what's the next step?'"

"Everything I know as a cop I learned from Gage Walsh," he admitted. "I couldn't have had a better teacher."

Remi forced herself to concentrate on the happy times with her father. It was too easy to fall into the vast grief that lurked in every memory.

"He said you were the most stubborn, relentless, brilliant detective he'd ever met," she told Ash. "He was certain you were going to end up as a Chief of Detectives one day."

"I wanted him to be proud of me."

"Me too."

Ash's fingers tightened on the steering wheel, his gaze locked on the road. "We need to do better," he breathed.

Remi winced. She knew exactly what Ash meant. Her father had expected great things from both of them. He would be deeply disappointed to know that his death had caused Ash to walk away from the force, and that she had lost the glorious confidence that she was going to change the world.

"Yeah, we do." They shared a sad smile, then Remi gave a shake of her head. Enough of the past. They needed to concentrate on tracking down the killer. "Okay. What's the next step?"

"We need to know who offered Angel her fabulous opportunity in Chicago, and how they found her," Ash said. "It doesn't sound like she'd recently traveled to the city."

"Maybe she met him when she was living in Los Angeles."

"I suppose it's possible."

Remi sensed he wasn't willing to jump to any conclusions. Her father had told her that a detective had to keep his mind open to several possibilities, even when the solution to a case seemed obvious. She gave a mental shrug. They had to start somewhere.

Laying her head against the buttery leather of the seat, she closed her eyes and tried to imagine how a killer might have crossed paths with a convenience store worker in Bailey. She couldn't think like a detective. Or even a killer. But she did know young girls who were willing to do anything to attract attention. "If our theory is right and the killer is using some mysterious offer to lure women, he might be using social media to find them," she suggested.

Ash sucked in an audible breath. "Shit. I never thought about that."

"I deal with teens who can barely look away from their phone long enough to do their homework," she said, reaching into her purse to pull out her own phone. With a couple of swipes across the screen, she was logged into Facebook and searching for Angel's page. "I found her," she finally announced.

Turning the steering wheel, Ash had the car smoothly zooming off the nearest exit. He took another turn, pulling into the lot of a large truck stop before he put the engine in Park and swiveled in his seat.

"Let me see."

Remi handed over her phone, prepared as Ash's eyes widened as he scrolled down her page. Angel Conway had made a habit of posting provocative pictures of herself. Plus, she had listed "actress" as her occupation. Any lunatic could have seen her profile and known exactly how to bait the perfect trap.

"Christ," Ash muttered, handing back the phone. "It would have been easy to target her."

Remi nodded, scrolling down the updates. "Here." She stopped to read the post out loud. "The first of October she says she has exciting news that she's going to announce in a few weeks."

Ash leaned toward her, the crisp smell of his warm male skin teasing at her nose.

"What's the last date she posted on her page?" he asked.

"Six weeks ago. She put up a picture of the Chicago skyline with a heart emoji."

Ash was silent as he considered the various possibilities.

"So either someone else posted for her, or she didn't feel in any danger after she arrived in the city," he finally said.

Remi read through the various reactions to Angel's post. They were mostly "yay" and "you go, girl." Then over the past couple of days were questions about when the announcement was coming, but no demands to know if she was okay. "It doesn't look like any of her friends were worried about her."

"Jax will be able to get a warrant to look into her social media accounts," Ash said. "If someone contacted her with the fabulous offer, he should be able to track the IP address. I also need to tell him about the cash. If it was delivered by mail, Angel might have kept the envelope it came in."

"Along with the nondisclosure contract," Remi added, a shiver racing through her as she considered just how simple it would be for a killer to lure an eager woman into his grasp, and even ensure that she didn't tell a soul about him.

"True," Ash said, his expression distracted.

Remi lowered her phone and studied him with a curious gaze. "What is it?"

"Let's go over what we think might have happened."

"Okay. You start."

"Angel Conway is a frustrated actress and drug user who feels trapped in her small town," Ash said. "She regularly posts half-naked pictures of herself in a desperate hope of finding fame."

"She catches the attention of the Butcher, who contacts her through her Facebook page and offers her an opportunity to travel to Chicago."

He nodded. "We still need to figure out how she got to the city, but once she was there, she has surgery to make her look more like you."

Remi stiffened. "We don't know that for certain. She might have—"

"Damn."

She frowned. Not because he'd interrupted her protest, but because he'd put the car in gear and whipped it out of the parking lot. A minute later, they were humming down the interstate at a speed that made her blood race. "What's going on, Ash?"

"Someone had to perform the surgery," he told her. "I want to know if Jax has managed to track down a doctor. And I need to let him know what we discovered in Bailey."

"It's Saturday," she reminded him. "Is Jax working today?"

He nodded. "Yep."

Remi swallowed a sudden curse, lifting her arm to glance at the watch strapped around her wrist. Until she'd mentioned the day of the week, she'd completely forgotten her weekly lunch date.

"If you want to drop me off at home, you can go see him," she said.

He sent her a surprised glance. "You don't want to go?"

She wrinkled her nose. Of course she wanted to go. Jax

had no doubt discovered all sorts of valuable information. Plus, she wanted to hear his response to what they'd learned about Angel. But she had a duty she couldn't avoid. "I always meet my mother for lunch on Saturday," she said, her flat tone revealing that her decision wasn't up for debate.

Ash slowed the car as they reached the sprawling suburbs. "I suppose I should visit my mother as well," he said, keeping his tone light. "She'll hunt me down and whack me with a wooden spoon if she finds out I'm in town and I haven't come by."

Remi smiled. She loved her mother, but Liza Harding-Walsh was a complicated woman who was difficult to please. June Marcel, on the other hand, was exactly what a mother should be: warm, loving, and fiercely loyal. The older woman did, however, expect her boys to obey a few simple rules.

"Yes. She will," Remi readily agreed.

A few minutes later, Ash had pulled into her driveway, and before she could protest, he was out of the car and doing a quick circle around her house, clearly searching for any intruders. Inside, Buddy was barking with excitement. It didn't matter if she'd been gone for a day or an hour, he always welcomed her home.

Ash smiled at the sound, meeting her at the front door. "I'll be back before dinner," he assured her, his fingers tracing the length of her jaw as his gaze lingered on her lips. "What do you want me to pick up?"

Remi flushed as she tried to squash the wicked urge to tell him that all she wanted for dinner was a bottle of wine. And him. It didn't help that the image of a naked Ash spread across her bed formed with perfect clarity.

He narrowed his gaze almost as if he was able to read her mind and Remi quickly tried to distract him.

"I'm not that bad of a cook."

A mysterious smile curved his lips. "I'll swing by our favorite Chinese restaurant on the way back."

His smile remained as he stepped off the porch and walked toward the car.

"Jerk," she called out, but the word didn't have any sting. Not when they both knew that his lack of confidence in her culinary skills wasn't the reason for her blush.

Chapter Seven

With a shake of her head, Remi unlocked the front door and braced herself as Buddy launched himself toward her. With a laugh, she forgot her list of worries, which was growing longer by the hour, and bent down to give her dog a full-body rub. It was only when Buddy rolled onto his back for her to scratch his belly that she noticed the torn piece of paper that was lying on the linoleum floor of the entryway.

Fear curled through the pit of her stomach even as Remi told herself that Ash had probably dropped it earlier. They'd been shuffling through the boxes of files. There were dozens of notes that had been written on cocktail napkins, tissues, and other scraps of paper. It would have been easy enough for one to have gone astray.

Reaching out with a shaking hand, she grabbed the paper and turned it over.

I need to see you

That was it. It wasn't signed. No indication of who might have written it. Just a few words scribbled on a piece of lined notebook paper.

Remi straightened. Had it come from the files or had someone shoved it under the door? Impossible to know for certain. With a grimace, she tossed the paper on a table next to the front door. She'd show it to Ash when he returned. For now, she had to get Buddy some exercise before jumping in her car and heading across town.

Unnerved enough to keep her pepper spray in one hand, she braved the cold to walk Buddy to the nearby dog park. He was well-behaved, but if he didn't have an opportunity to run and play, he would find some other way to release his energy. Usually by eating something she didn't want eaten. A shoe. A pillow. The corner of her couch.

Once his tongue was hanging out and he flopped at her feet, Remi took him back to the house and climbed into her car. The drive to the north side of town took nearly half an hour, and Remi's nerves were stretched tight by the time she drove through the wrought-iron gates and up the long, tree-lined driveway.

She parked in front of the white, colonial home that had tall windows framed by black shutters and a portico. It was large enough to easily house a dozen people and was surrounded by manicured grounds that included a pool and a pool house, a tennis court, and a six-car garage.

The estate had been built by her mother's grandfather, or maybe it was her great-grandfather, and she'd inherited it after their deaths when Remi was just a child. Her father had hated the place, but he'd been willing to live there to please his wife.

Remi swallowed a sigh. They all did things to please Liza.

Crawling out of her car, she hurried up the stairs to the porch and pressed the bell. The minutes ticked past as she shivered in the frigid air. At last the door was pulled open to reveal her mother.

Liza Harding-Walsh was a short, curvaceous woman dressed in an expensive, ivory pantsuit and shoes that had four-inch heels. Her black hair was as sleek as satin and pulled from her round face. She had pretty features, but her eyes were her most stunning asset. They were a deep emerald green and thickly lashed. Remi's father claimed he'd been a goner the first time he'd seen those eyes.

Liza allowed that stunning gaze to run over her daughter's disheveled appearance, her lips curving into a meaningless smile. As if she was looking at Remi, but not really seeing her.

Just once, Remi wished her mother would be mad, or disappointed, or . . . anything.

"Hello, Mother," Remi said, swallowing a resigned sigh.

"Hello, Remi," the older woman politely murmured, stepping back so Remi could enter the house. "I thought you might have forgotten the time."

Remi entered the foyer. It was almost as large as her house, with a marble floor and a vaulted ceiling. On one side, a curved staircase led to the upper floor with a bannister that had once graced an English manor house. Straight ahead was an arched opening that led to the living room. Remi hadn't been in there since the night her father had been murdered. She didn't know if it would be worse to see it and realize that everything had been changed or to have it be exactly the same.

Maybe if Remi could remember what happened that dreadful night it would give her and her mother a sense of closure. Instead, they both tried to pretend they were moving on with their lives.

With an effort, she thrust away her dark thoughts.

"Sorry," Remi automatically apologized. It was something she did a lot when she was in her childhood home. "I had an appointment this morning."

Liza nodded, watching Remi as she shrugged out of her coat and hooked it on a coatrack in the corner. In silence, they entered the second arched opening that led to the dining room. In the center of the room was a long, glossy table with a dozen matching chairs. The walls were paneled and decorated with a collection of charcoal etchings that depicted Chicago from the mid-eighteen-hundreds to the nineteen-fifties. They'd been commissioned by her great-grandfather. Remi had heard a friend of her mother's say that they were worth a fortune, but Remi didn't care about their value. She just liked them. Overhead was a large chandelier that had been brought over from Italy by some distant ancestor, and beneath her feet was a Persian rug that had been a gift from a diplomat from one of the Middle Eastern countries.

Her mother moved directly to a heavy sideboard that had a full bar setup. She poured herself a glass of her favorite wine. "I hope your appointment wasn't at that center," Liza said. "That neighborhood isn't safe."

It was a familiar argument. Her mother wanted Remi to get a job at a nice private school. Understandable. The youth center *was* in a dangerous neighborhood.

"No, I wasn't at the center," Remi assured her.

Liza sipped her wine, waving a hand toward the bottles on the sideboard. "Do you want a drink?"

Remi shook her head. "No, thank you."

"Then I suppose we might as well get started." Liza moved to take her seat at the head of the table.

Remi followed to take her place on her mother's right, unfolding the linen napkin and laying it across her lap as her mother rang a small bell. Instantly, a middle-aged woman appeared with lunch on a silver tray.

Remi felt a pang of guilt as she caught sight of the beef stroganoff and homemade bread on the delicate china plate. Her mother knew it was her favorite. Sometimes,

Remi was so busy looking for her mother's disappointment in her that she forgot to see the tiny acts of love.

"How was your gala?" Remi asked between bites of savory noodles and the melt-in-the-mouth bread.

"Successful." Liza polished off her wine while barely tasting her lunch. "We raised over twenty-thousand dollars for the Chicago Police Memorial Fund."

"Oh." Another stab of guilt sliced through Remi. "I didn't realize that was the charity you were promoting. I'm sorry I wasn't here."

Liza shrugged. "I didn't really expect you to attend."

Remi ignored the unmistakable lack of interest whether she was there or not. The stress of Ash's sudden arrival, not to mention the fear the Butcher had returned to Chicago, was making her more irritable than usual. Plus, it'd nearly made her forget that she had a delicate subject she wanted to discuss with her mother.

Taking another bite of bread, Remi wiped her mouth and considered her words. "Have you made plans for the holidays?" she asked at last.

Her mother arched a brow. "I assume you'll be here for Christmas dinner?"

"Yes," Remi quickly assured the older woman. "But I thought you might enjoy spending a few days with Uncle Lawrence in Palm Beach. I know he invited you."

"How do you know?"

Remi blinked. "Excuse me?"

"How do you know Lawrence invited me to Florida."

"He called me."

With a smooth motion, Liza was on her feet. "So you and my brother have been talking behind my back."

Remi watched her mother move to the sideboard to pour herself another glass of wine. Remi wasn't entirely certain what had happened between Liza and her younger brother, Lawrence Harding, although she suspected it had something to do with their inheritance. Liza had ended up with the lion's share of the estate, plus a trust fund that ensured she never had to worry about money. But neither of them ever discussed the frosty relationship.

In fact, Remi couldn't remember the two of them speaking until her father had been murdered. Lawrence and his wife had traveled from Florida to Chicago to stay with Liza, clearly concerned when Liza had retreated to her bedroom, refusing to attend Gage's funeral.

It'd taken months before Liza had shaken off her deep depression and returned to her normal routine. At the time, Remi had been grateful to her uncle for being there to offer her support, but once Liza had decided to crawl out of her bed, the older woman had insisted Lawrence and his wife leave her home.

"He's worried," Remi told her mother. Lawrence had called Remi last week, urging her to convince Liza to spend a few days at their beach house.

Liza frowned. "Why would he be worried?"

"He believes you're lonely."

Liza narrowed her gaze, clearly offended. "I'm not lonely. I have a very full life."

"That's what I told him," Remi said in soothing tones. "Still, it might be nice to get away from the cold for a week or so."

"I have too much to do." Liza curled her lips as she took a sip of her wine. "Besides, your aunt has that obnoxious dog she treats like a child. I can't abide being covered in fur and listening to its constant yaps."

Remi had to agree with her mother. She loved Buddy, but her aunt's dog was obnoxious. He'd peed on the carpet, tried to bite Remi when she'd taken him out for a walk, and barked from dusk to dawn. No one had been sad when they'd taken the tiny beast back to Florida.

"Okay." Remi sucked in a breath and prepared herself to make the ultimate sacrifice. "If you don't want to go to visit Uncle Lawrence, I'll come and stay with you for the holidays."

Liza was clearly caught off guard by Remi's offer. But instead of being pleased, she looked . . . flustered.

"Don't be silly." She abruptly drained the wine before setting aside the empty glass. "You don't have to drop everything to babysit me. I'm fine."

Remi studied her mother. Usually, the older woman was far better at disguising the fact that she had no desire for her daughter to be underfoot.

What had her rattled? Maybe a new man in her life?

Remi didn't know if the thought pleased or horrified her. "Okay." Feeling strangely off-balance, Remi rose to her feet and grabbed her empty dishes. "If you change your mind—"

"What are you doing?" her mother interrupted with a frown.

Remi glanced down at the plates in her hands. "Taking these into the kitchen."

Liza clicked her tongue. "How many times must I tell you that there's no need? I pay my housekeeper an outrageous sum to take care of me and my guests."

Remi resisted the urge to continue into the kitchen. Annoying her mother was all too easy and something she was trying to avoid. Wasn't she? "Okay. Thanks for lunch," she said, placing the plates back on the table. "I'll call you later in the week."

She walked out of the dining room and into the foyer. Grabbing her coat, she was just pulling it on when her mother appeared in the entrance.

"Remi, be careful," the older woman said without warning.

Remi sent a startled glance toward her mother. Had the older woman heard about the murder? It was possible that one of her father's old friends had contacted her. "Careful about what?" she demanded.

Liza looked uncomfortable, as if she was regretting her impulsive words. "Just be careful," she muttered.

"I will."

Stepping forward, Remi brushed her lips over her mother's cheek and turned to leave the house.

She would never understand Liza Harding-Walsh, she decided.

As expected, Ash found his brother in his small cubicle. Jax was like all Marcel men: an incurable workaholic.

He quickly shared what he'd learned in Bailey, watching his brother take notes as he spoke. Once he was done, he expected a few questions about his impressions of Angel's friends.

Instead, Jax leaned back in his chair and folded his arms over his chest. "Do you remember O'Reilly?" Jax asked.

"O'Reilly?" Ash leaned against the edge of his brother's desk and dredged through his memories. At last, he recalled the weasel of an officer who was always lurking around trying to cause trouble. "Yeah, I remember him. He was an asshole. And a terrible detective. Gage had to turn him in to the Internal Affairs unit."

"For what?"

"Gage claimed he took drugs off a perp and they never showed up in the evidence room."

A disgusted expression settled on Jax's face. There was nothing worse than a dirty cop. "Did he get in trouble?"

"No. Gage didn't know if the crime was too petty to

warrant an investigation or if someone up the food chain squelched his complaint. I know he was pissed as hell when nothing happened."

Jax studied him with a steady gaze. "Do you think he was trying to interfere in your investigation of the Butcher?"

Ash jerked in surprise at the unexpected question. "Why do you ask?"

Jax revealed his encounter with the detective, as well as his vague warning not to stir up the past.

Ash scowled, mentally reviewing his handful of encounters with O'Reilly. The man was a year or two older than Ash and had clearly been bitter about Gage dumping him for another partner. And once Ash had suspected that O'Reilly had been snooping through the evidence they'd collected on the Butcher. That was when Gage had suggested they start keeping their own notes that weren't included in the official files.

After Gage's death, he'd forgotten about his partner's suspicions. Now he realized he needed to do more than skim through the files he'd just taken out of storage.

"Do you think he's just jealous, or is he somehow involved in the murders?" he bluntly demanded.

Jax grimaced. "Hard to say. It's possible he's just being a dick, but I'm going to keep my eye on him," he said, his voice hard.

Ash nodded. He knew without a doubt that O'Reilly wouldn't be able to so much as fart without Jax knowing about it. "Have you started searching for the plastic surgeon?"

Jax shook his head. "I'll do that on Monday. Most of the clinics are closed on the weekends."

Ash squashed his flare of frustration. He better than anyone knew that detective work wasn't like on the TV shows. It was slow, and methodical, and, a lot of the time, boring as hell.

Still, he couldn't resist hoping for some break in the case.

"Anything new?" he demanded.

"Not really." Jax reached up to rub his nape. "I have the patrols scouring the park for anyone who might have been there on the morning Angel was killed. They're also pulling any surveillance footage in the area. We might get lucky."

"Did she have a phone with her?"

"Still looking for it," Jax admitted.

Ash tried to imagine a young woman without her phone in her hand. It was impossible. Still, if it was missing, it didn't necessarily mean the killer had it. People could be stone cold and it wasn't unusual for a passerby to steal the phone or wallet off a corpse.

"Have you checked out her social media?" he asked, holding up his hands in apology when he caught sight of the irritation flaring through his brother's eyes. "Okay, I'm not trying to tell you how to do your job."

Jax released a short laugh. "That would be a first."

Ash grimaced. In hindsight, it was easy to see that he'd come into the department with an arrogance that must have pissed off a lot of people. Including his brother.

He'd been a young hotshot who assumed he knew it all. Age had, thankfully, tempered his ego. "Only because I'm always right, bro."

Jax flipped him off and they both laughed. There'd been occasions when it'd been a pain to work in the same unit, but most of the time they'd cherished the opportunity to share what they both loved.

Ash's smile slowly faded. "While you're in such a good mood, I need a favor."

Jax unfolded his arms and leaned forward in his chair. "What now?"

"I want you to run a background check on a Doug Gates."

Jax grabbed a pen and jotted down the name. "Is he connected to my vic?"

"No, he's Remi's next-door neighbor."

Jax jerked up his head, his expression hard with disapproval. "Ash . . ."

"I genuinely think he's sketchy," Ash insisted. "He moved in six months ago, he lives alone, and this morning, I caught him peering into her window."

Jax stared at him for another minute, no doubt trying to decide whether Ash was being a crazed ex-boyfriend or a vigilant detective. "Fine," he at last conceded. "I'll check him out."

A portion of Ash's tension eased. He'd already decided he was going to discover everything possible about Doug Gates. Having Jax use the resources of the Chicago Police Department was going to make it a lot easier.

"Is there anything I can do?" he asked his brother.

"Yeah." Jax sent him a grim smile. "Go see Mom."

Ash swallowed a sigh. He'd bet good money his mother had already discovered he was in town and had called Jax to complain he hadn't come by yet. Of all the Marcels, his mother was the best detective.

When Ash was still in high school, the older woman could not only find his pack of cigarettes no matter where he'd hidden them in his room, she had a sixth sense that warned her when he was lying. Plus, she could walk out the door of her house and track down any one of her children, no matter where they were.

It was uncanny.

"Are you coming with me?" he asked.

Jax waved his hand toward his desk, which was hidden beneath piles of folders. "I have a dozen case files I need to look through," he told Ash.

"Unsolved murders?"

"Yep. These are going to take me all weekend."

Ash felt a stab of guilt. Jax already had circles beneath his eyes from working late into the night. Now, he was going to be stuck in the tiny cubicle for the entire weekend.

"Thanks," he said, his voice gruff with emotion.

Jax shrugged. "For doing my job?"

"We both know you're going above and beyond the call of duty on this one."

Jax held Ash's gaze. "You're not the only one who cares about Remi."

Ash gave a slow nod. His family had adored Remi from the moment he'd brought her to dinner. Not only because they knew how happy she made him, but because she was smart and funny and kindhearted. A woman just like his mother.

An emotion that was soft and wistful spread through him. "I know."

Jax rose to his feet, squeezing Ash's shoulder before giving him a small shove out of the cubicle.

"Now go see Mom before you're the next homicide I have to investigate."

Ash lifted his hands in surrender. "I'm going."

Rachel Burke moved across the barren room to stare out the window. Night had settled over the private clinic while she'd been sleeping, revealing the Chicago skyline outlined in lights. She smiled. They shimmered like a thousand diamonds.

It was weird. She'd lived in the city for twenty-four years, but she'd never bothered to admire the view. Probably because Chicago wasn't nearly so pretty up close and personal. At least, not in her neighborhood. Her view had included a grimy street that was lined with crumbling brick apartments and windows covered by wire mesh. Most days, she felt like a rat trapped in a cage.

She grimaced, then released a small grunt of pain. Lifting her hand, she gingerly touched her face. It was nearly healed, but it was still tender.

The price of success . . .

The words whispered through the back of her mind.

That's what the director had told her. If she wanted to achieve her dreams, she had to be prepared to make sacrifices.

The first sacrifice had been leaving her home. Something Rachel had been eager to do. She lived in a pigsty with a drunk for a father and two younger brothers who expected her to be their unpaid maid. She'd wanted out for years, but with no high school diploma or job skills, she'd known she would end up on the streets. Or worse. Her only hope had been her beauty.

She'd been told she was pretty from the day she was born, and while her father had urged her to use her looks to attract a husband who could offer her a stable home in the suburbs, Rachel had refused. She wasn't going to be satisfied with a boring life with a man she had to depend on to provide a roof over her head. She'd seen what it'd done to her mother. The woman had once been as pretty as Rachel, but after years of poverty and enduring beatings from a husband who wasted his paycheck on booze and gambling, she'd looked closer to sixty than forty when she'd died of a sudden heart attack.

Rachel intended to trade in her looks for independence. She'd booked a few local modeling gigs, although none of them paid. And she'd done one commercial for a used auto shop. It wasn't until she'd been contacted by a real director that it seemed her dreams might actually come true.

The second cost of success, however, hadn't been so easy to accept.

Her fingers carefully traced the reconstructed line of her nose. The alterations had been minor, but she'd been reluctant to agree. All she had was her face. What if some quack screwed it up? It was only the thought of being forced to return to her father's apartment that made her go through the surgery.

Thankfully, she'd discovered that once the swelling had gone down and the bruises had faded, the modifications had actually improved her appearance. Her nose was thinner and her lips fuller. Plus, something had been done to make her cheekbones more prominent.

She went from pretty to stunning. And she hadn't had to spend a dime of her own money.

Even better, her isolation at the clinic meant that her father and brothers couldn't be a constant drain on her time or her newly acquired cash. They didn't know where she was, or how to contact her. A win-win situation.

Of course, she couldn't deny that she was starting to get bored . . .

On cue, the disposable phone that was lying next to the bed started to vibrate. Rachel eagerly rushed forward to snatch it off the nightstand and pressed it to her ear. "Hello," she said in breathless tones.

"It's time to take the next step in your career," a voice informed her. "Pack your bag."

The connection was abruptly ended, but Rachel's lips curved into a smile of anticipation.

"Hell yeah."

Chapter Eight

Remi hadn't meant to eat the entire carton of moo shu pork along with all three pancakes. But Ash had remembered her favorite restaurant and her favorite dish. Plus, he'd even brought her favorite bottle of wine.

No woman could resist such temptation.

As they'd perched in front of the breakfast bar chatting about the challenges of teaching, Remi's tension from the day had slowly eased.

That was the Marcel gift. All of the brothers had the ability to make people feel relaxed when they were around. She'd often envied their easy charm, watching as they transformed any gathering, no matter how dull, into an entertaining event filled with laughter.

Swallowing the last bite of her fortune cookie, Remi swiveled the high bar chair and slid off.

"I'm going to have to run an extra mile in the morning," she groaned, wishing she'd changed out of her jeans into her stretchy PJ bottoms.

"We can do that." Ash flipped a leftover egg roll toward the dog, watching him with adoring eyes. "Right, Buddy?"

Buddy swallowed the egg roll in one gulp and answered with a bark. Remi rolled her eyes. Her dog had already given his heart to Ash. And not just because he snuck him table scraps. The two of them had formed an instant connection.

Her heart fluttered. Not figuratively. It really and truly fluttered, like a butterfly zooming from flower to flower. There was something magical about a man who took the time to earn the trust of her dog.

Of course, she already knew that about Ash . . .

Trying to ignore the dangerous thoughts, Remi quickly cleared away the empty cartons, her movements jerky. "Are you ready to start on the files?" she demanded.

He tilted his head to the side, studying her with a curious expression. "You haven't told me about your lunch with your mother."

She grimaced. She didn't want to discuss her mother. She never did. Their relationship was too complicated. Or maybe it wasn't complicated. Maybe it was too superficial.

Whatever the reason, she preferred not to dwell on their awkward relationship. It made her heart twist with a painful sense of regret.

She met his gaze squarely. He'd already told her that he'd spent the afternoon at his parents' house. "Do you want to discuss your lunch with your mother?"

He held up a slender hand. "Touché. My ears are still ringing from the lecture on how a respectful son doesn't wait three months to visit home, regardless of the fact that I had a full teaching schedule for the semester."

She reached for the bottle of wine that was half-full. "You grab the glasses."

He didn't argue, instead taking a glass in each hand and following her into the living room.

"We make a good team," he murmured as they settled side by side on the couch.

She poured out the wine, feeling a heat seep through

her. She told herself it was the alcohol, but she knew it had far more to do with the hard, male body only an inch away.

"Not really." She lifted her glass to take a sip, ridiculously trying to deny the awareness that had sizzled between them from the first moment their eyes met. "We still haven't found anything that could help identify the killer."

He nodded, his expression one of determination. "True, but detective work is a marathon, not a sprint."

"That sounds like something my father would say."

He sent her a wry smile. "It's something every cop says," he told her. "A lot."

Her gaze drifted toward the stacks of manila folders that took up the entire length of her coffee table. Last night, they'd skimmed through the mounds of interviews from the various witnesses, setting aside a handful Ash intended to track down and ask follow-up questions. "I can't believe these are just your private files." She gave a shake of her head, unable to imagine how many boxes must be stored at the police station.

"Interviewing hundreds of potential witnesses is part of the marathon."

She wrinkled her nose, recalling how many times she'd been exasperated with her father when he was late for a school event or missed dinner yet again. In her juvenile mind, she'd leaped to the conclusion that he preferred being with his buddies rather than spending time with her.

"I have a new appreciation for the hours my father spent away from home."

"It's a demanding job."

"But important."

Ash gave a slow nod, his expression grim. "Especially now."

She jerked back her gaze toward the stacks of folders, refusing to dwell on Ash's belief the Butcher was now obsessed with her. She wasn't sticking her head in the sand. Not entirely. It was simply the realization that she couldn't concentrate on finding the killer if she was crippled with fear.

"When did you and my father first realize there was a serial killer?"

He leaned back into the couch, absently drinking his wine. She could sense he was dragging up memories he'd kept buried. She didn't blame him. Being a detective no doubt meant you had to keep all the bad things locked away just to stay sane.

"It was shortly after I became your father's partner," he said. "A woman was found in her home with her throat slit. Our first thought was that her husband was responsible. Or a lover. Statistically, that's the most likely explanation. Then your father noticed the mark on her breast and realized that he'd seen the same mark on an autopsy photo the year before."

Remi was confused. The Butcher's carving on the breast was small, but it was unique. It was hard to believe that the detectives had dismissed it as a random cut. "No one had noticed it before?"

Frustration tightened Ash's features. "The sad truth is that we have too many murders and too few detectives. It wasn't until we began searching through the old case files that we realized there'd been three other women with the exact same mark."

"And you never found any connection between the women?"

"They were all young with dark hair." He deliberately allowed his gaze to skim over her. A silent reminder of the danger that stalked her. "And they were all killed in their homes."

Remi lifted a hand to touch her temple, reminded of the memories that remained trapped in her mind. Would it have made a diffcrence if the cops had realized from the start that they were dealing with a serial killer? Impossible to know for sure.

"Nothing else?" she asked.

A muscle twitched at the base of Ash's jaw, and Remi realized she wasn't the only one recalling her encounter with the Butcher. Hastily, she lowered her hand.

"Not that we could find," he admitted. "None of the victims appeared to know one another, they had various careers, they shopped at different stores. And none of them chose risky lifestyles."

She nodded. She'd watched her father pacing the floor at night, his brow furrowed as he tried to piece together the puzzle. Then she was struck by a sudden thought. "Could any of them have answered an ad to become an actress?"

"That's possible." Ash's lack of astonishment at her cleverness proved he'd already considered the notion the Butcher had used the same tricks to lure his victims in the past. "What young man or woman doesn't dream of becoming a star, no matter what their economic status or career? And for the killer, it would be easy to put an ad in the paper asking for a specific age and physical appearance. A perfect trap." He deliberately paused. "But it doesn't include you, unless you went to an audition you didn't tell me about?"

"No." She set aside the wineglass, using the motion to hide her expression. "I assumed I was chosen because my father was the lead detective investigating the case."

"Or because of me," he breathed, his voice edged with the same awful regret that filled her.

She didn't blame him. Or her father. She blamed herself.

A brittle silence threatened to settle around them, but with an effort, Remi cleared her throat and motioned toward the folders. The past was done. The future was all that mattered.

"We've gone through the witness files," she said, pointing to the two files Ash had separated from the rest. "What are those?"

Ash leaned forward and set aside his own glass, as if he was as anxious as she to put the dark memories behind them.

"Suspect files."

She picked up the folders with a lift of her brows. "There weren't very many suspects."

"Actually, there were dozens, but those files are still at the precinct."

"Why didn't you include these?"

"They were . . ." He hesitated, searching for the right word. "Sensitive."

"Sensitive?"

He tugged the top file from her fingers, flipping it open. "This one was on Steve Davis."

"I don't recognize the name."

"His family owns a chain of discount tobacco shops." He shuffled through the papers in the pile, reading the notes he'd made over five years before. "They have the sort of money that could have quashed any investigation. We had to keep it off the books."

"Why did you suspect him?"

"One of the victims worked as a receptionist at the Davis Tobacco headquarters," he said, offering her an abbreviated version of his thick stack of notes. "After she was fired, she accused Steve of sexual harassment. She'd even hired an attorney. The night before she was murdered, Steve was heard boasting in a bar that he would kill the bitch before he gave her one penny."

She made a small sound of disgust. Steve Davis sounded like a pig. "Did you bring him in for questioning?"

"No. Before we got to that point, we discovered he was left-handed."

"And the killer is right-handed?"

"Yep."

That seemed like a lame excuse to dismiss a potential suspect. "Couldn't he have used his right hand to throw off the cops?" she asked.

"The medical examiner was convinced he would know if the killer had tried that particular trick. Plus, we couldn't find any connection between Davis and the other women." He closed the file and tossed it back onto the coffee table. "He stayed a suspect, but he moved down the list."

She opened the file she held in her hand. "What about this one?" She read the label out loud. "R.H."

"Robert Hutton." His lips twisted with dislike. "He worked in the district attorney's office."

"Bobby?" This time Remi recognized the name. A sound of shock was wrenched from her throat. It had to be a mistake.

Ash's brows drew together at her childhood name for Robert. "Bobby?"

"We went to the same private high school. We all called him Bobby."

A wry amusement twisted his lips. "I suppose I should have guessed."

She ignored his words. The fact that she had a large trust fund had rarely come between them, but Remi had sensed that Ash preferred to forget she'd grown up in a mansion and attended schools that cost more than his parents earned in a year.

"I can't believe he would be a suspect," she said.

"Why not?"

"It might be a cliché, but he doesn't seem the type."

His jaw tightened. As if he was annoyed by her words. "There is no 'type' for a serial killer. It's impossible to predict what might make someone snap."

"You're right. It's just . . ." She allowed her words to trail away with a shake of her head.

She'd known Bobby Hutton her entire life. He was three years older than her, with the sort of boy-next-door good looks that inspired instant trust in people. That was what made him such a good lawyer. Beneath the façade, however, he was a shallow, egotistical man who was consumed with ambition.

A jerk, yes. But she'd never heard any whispers he was violent toward women.

"How well did you know him?" Ash demanded.

She shrugged. "We dated for a short time."

"You dated." His voice was flat. "Why didn't your dad tell me?"

Remi sent him a puzzled glance. Was he aggravated by the thought she'd dated Bobby or because her father hadn't told him?

"We only went out a few times during my freshman year of college," she told him. "It wasn't like we had a meaningful relationship."

His expression remained hard. "Why did you break up?"

She heaved a sigh. "I told you, we were never a couple. We had three or four dates and I quickly realized that his interest wasn't in me."

"I find that hard to believe."

A faint color stained her cheeks at his dry tone. He was right. Bobby had been as eager as any other guy to get her in bed. Still, he'd chosen her for her connections, not her body.

"Bobby has always been ambitious," she insisted. "I

think he calculated that my trust fund, combined with my father's connection to the Chicago Police Department, would benefit his climb up the political ladder."

"Hmm." He didn't look convinced.

Realizing he wasn't in the mood to listen to her arguments, she turned the conversation to more important matters. "Why did you suspect him?"

His eyes narrowed, but he followed her lead. "The last victim, Tiffany Holloway, made several calls to his private cell phone," he said.

Tiffany Holloway was the one victim her father and Ash had discussed in her presence. By then, she'd been spending the majority of her free time either at Ash's apartment or hanging around the precinct. She knew the seventeen-year-old girl had been found in her parents' living room with her throat slit. There'd been no sign of a forced entry and the cops had assumed she'd known her assailant.

The thought that she'd been calling Bobby's private number made her stomach clench with unease. "Did he tell you why?"

"He said she was a waitress at his favorite restaurant and he'd shared his private number with her because she wanted his help to get an internship at the DA's office."

Internship? Remi shook her head. She could accept that any young person would be eager to land an internship in the DA's office. It would look great on a college application. But she couldn't imagine Bobby going out of his way to help anyone, especially a teenager. Not unless there was something in it for himself.

"Did you believe him?"

Ash released a sharp laugh. "No, but he had an airtight alibi the night Tiffany was murdered."

"What do you mean by airtight?"

"He was at your house."

She blinked. "My house?"

"Your parents' estate," he said with a shrug. "Hutton was meeting with your mother to discuss some charity event they were planning together."

Ah. That made sense. Bobby was always eager to promote his supposed dedication to the less fortunate, and her mother had a genuine talent for creating sensational charity events. The two had often worked together.

She'd always been sure to make plans to be away from the house when she knew he was coming over. His ego was big enough to assume she was hoping to spend time with him if she happened to be around . . .

Remi's thoughts were abruptly disrupted as a memory wiggled to the surface. "Wait," she breathed. "I remember that evening."

Ash grimaced. "Like I said, airtight."

Remi's gaze lowered as she skimmed over the notes in the file. Her heart twisted as she easily recognized her dad's handwriting. She would chide him that it looked like chicken scratches and he would tell her that his mind worked too fast for his pencil to keep up.

"November twenty-first," she murmured, lifting her head to meet his curious gaze. "It was a Friday, right?"

He raised his brows in surprise. "Yes."

"My mother didn't meet with Bobby that night."

He stared at her. Was he having trouble processing what she was telling him? Probably. He'd spent years convinced that Bobby had spent the night with her mother.

"Were you there?" he finally demanded.

She shook her head. When her mother had told her that Bobby was coming for dinner, Remi had agreed to join a friend and a few other classmates to cram for a history exam.

"I was supposed to go to a study group, but I felt sick

when I got to the library and turned around and drove back home," she told him.

He tapped his fingers on his knee, silently reorganizing his assumption of what had occurred the night of the murder. He gave a dissatisfied shake of his head. "Did your mother say why Hutton canceled the meeting?"

"She wasn't there when I got home," Remi said. She'd been too relieved when she pulled into the driveway to discover the house dark and silent to consider why the dinner had been canceled. She was feeling like crap and in no mood to deal with Bobby. Or her mother. "I took some cold medicine and crawled into bed."

"Maybe they met somewhere else," he suggested.

"Maybe, but why would he say they met at the house if they were somewhere else?"

He considered the question, at last giving a sharp shake of his head. "You're sure it was the same night?"

She shuffled back through her memories. It'd been over five years ago, and she hadn't had any reason to think about the night since then. Still, she was confident she wasn't mistaken.

"Yeah. I was feeling rotten when Dad got the call the next morning about Tiffany Holloway," she said. "He wanted to take me to the doctor, but I told him to go to work."

Ash continued to tap his fingers against his knee. He was troubled by something. "Surely your dad asked your mother about the meeting?"

She did another scan of the notes. "I don't see any mention of a different location for the meeting or it being canceled." She closed the file and handed it to Ash. "Maybe Dad was like you and just assumed Bobby came to dinner, so he never bothered to ask Mother."

He muttered a low curse, clearly annoyed with himself.

As if he should have known that Bobby had lied. "I think I need to have a chat with Hutton."

"He's the assistant district attorney now," she warned.

A hard smile curled his lips. "All the better."

"Why is that better?"

"He has more to lose."

About to remind him that a career in the DA's office also ensured that he had friends in high places, she was distracted as her dog launched himself across the room, barking loud enough to make her ears ring.

Instinctively, her head turned toward the large window, catching a faint movement before it disappeared. With a sharp gasp, she surged off the couch, her hand pressed against her racing heart. "Ash."

In an instant, he was standing beside her, his arm wrapping around her shoulders. "What is it?"

"Someone was looking in the window," she rasped.

"Stay here."

Before she could protest, Ash was grabbing the coat he'd left on a nearby chair and heading out the front door. Remi cursed and hurried to retrieve her phone from the kitchen. She would give Ash five minutes to return. A second longer and she was dialing 911.

Chapter Nine

Ash darted outside and quickly pressed his back against the house. He didn't want to make himself a target for whoever was lurking outside. Plus, he needed a couple of seconds to let his eyes adjust to the darkness.

Inside, he could hear Buddy still barking, although it wasn't with the same ferocity as earlier. At the same time, he saw a flicker of movement near the corner of the street. Damn. He hurried off the porch, but he knew he was too late. If it was the person who'd been peeking in the window, they'd already disappeared into the darkness.

Of course, he couldn't allow himself to leap to conclusions. It could have been a neighbor heading home.

The thought of neighbors had Ash veering to the right. He stepped around the edge of Remi's house. Next door, the lights were on, and Ash could see a shadow moving behind the closed curtains of the front window. Would Doug Gates have had time to dart back into his home? Probably. But there was no conclusive proof.

With a shake of his head, Ash made a quick circle around Remi's yard to make sure there was no one hiding in the bushes before heading back inside.

Remi rushed to meet him as soon as he stepped through the door, her phone clutched in her hand.

"Did you see anyone?" she demanded.

"No." Without considering what he was doing, Ash wrapped her trembling body in his arms and dropped a light kiss on top of her head. "Whoever it was took off too quickly for me to get a good look at them."

"Who could . . ." Her words trailed away. "Oh, I forgot."

He felt a sharp pang of loss as she pulled out of his arms and headed toward the narrow table next to the front door.

"Remi?"

She grabbed a piece of paper and crossed back toward him, shoving it in his hand.

"I forgot. I found this near the door when we came back from Bailey."

Ash glanced down, reading the brief note.

I need to see you.

What the hell? It didn't sound like a threat. More something a friend would leave. Or a creepy next-door neighbor.

"It wasn't in an envelope?" he demanded.

"No."

"We need to give it to Jax," he abruptly decided. Under normal circumstances, he'd dismiss the note. But these were far from normal circumstances. He wasn't going to risk overlooking any clue. "He can have it checked for fingerprints. Do you have a paper bag?"

"In the kitchen," she said, leading the way.

He was just tucking the paper in a small bag she'd pulled from a cabinet when his phone buzzed. Pulling it out of his pocket, he glanced at the screen.

"Speak of the devil," he murmured, pressing the phone to his ear. "Hey, Jax, what's up?" His brows lifted as his brother revealed he had the background check finished on Doug Gates. "That was quick," he said. Jax was kicking ass on this case. Probably to the point of exhaustion. "Thanks," he said after Jax finished sharing the intel he'd discovered.

Then he rolled his eyes as his brother spent the next few minutes giving him a stern lecture. "Of course I'm not going to do anything stupid," he promised, even as he mentally crossed his fingers. There was a 100 percent chance he was going to do something stupid. "I've got something I think you'll want to see," he said in an effort to distract Jax. "I'll bring it by your office in the morning." He heaved a sigh of resignation as the lecture continued. "I promise, nothing stupid."

Ending the connection, Ash shoved the phone back into his front pocket.

"Why does Jax assume you're going to do something stupid?" Remi asked.

"Older brother syndrome."

"Tell me." Her expression warned she wasn't going to let go of the subject. She called him stubborn, but she was the one who could give lessons to a mule.

"I had Jax run a background check on your neighbor," he grudgingly revealed.

She rolled her eyes. "Of course you did."

"Better safe than sorry."

She paused, clearly torn between her good manners, which said it was rude to spy on her neighbor, and an overwhelming desire to know the secrets Jax might have uncovered.

Curiosity won the battle.

"What did he discover?"

"Doug Gates is a loan officer at a local bank," Ash repeated what Jax had told him. "He was divorced last year and has two daughters."

"That's exactly what he told me."

She looked relieved. Obviously, she didn't want to think her neighbor was a serial killer. Ash, on the other hand, wished he was the Butcher. He could walk next door, arrest the bastard, and bring an end to the threat.

Every day that passed was more opportunity for the killer to strike again.

"Did he also share that his ex-wife has a restraining order against him?"

"Why?"

"She reported that he tried to push her out of the car while they were driving home from the lawyer's office," he told her. "And there was at least one witness who backed up her story."

She flinched, her features tightening with disgust. If Doug had hoped to ever earn Remi's affection, that was effectively dead. Something that pleased Ash more than it should.

"He's obviously a horrible person," she said. "But that doesn't make him a serial killer."

"No, but it reveals he's willing to be violent toward women. And it gives me a reason to check him out."

She looked confused. "Isn't that what Jax just did?"

He shrugged. "I like to get the intel straight from the source."

Her eyes widened as she grasped what he was implying. "You're not going to confront him, are you?"

Ash tucked the paper bag with the note in the pocket of the coat he was still wearing. "We're just going to have a little chat."

She slammed her fists on her hips, glaring at him with a smoldering frustration.

"Ash. Dammit. If you get yourself hurt, I'll . . ." She didn't finish the sentence. Either because she didn't know an appropriately awful threat or because she simply couldn't bear the thought of him being hurt.

Without thought, he leaned forward and brushed his lips over her mouth.

"I love you too," he murmured.

He felt her stiffen in shock and he slowly lifted his head to study her pale face. He wasn't sure if he meant the words teasingly or from the depths of his soul.

Maybe both.

As disturbed as Remi by his impulsive words, Ash turned to leave the kitchen through the back door. Not only was he in a hurry to get away from Remi before she could remind him that they were no longer a couple, but he had an idea of how he could ensure an opportunity to do more than just ask a few questions.

Five minutes later, he was knocking on Doug's door. The porch light flicked on, and he saw the man peeking through the curtain. He disappeared from view and Ash waited for him to pull open the door. And waited. And waited.

The wind swirled and tugged at Ash's coat, the chill slicing through him like a knife. He felt as if his toes had frozen into ice cubes by the time the door swung inward and Doug glowered at him.

"Yeah?"

The man was wearing a wrinkled gray sweat suit that emphasized his paunch. His hair was mussed and the potent scent of whiskey wafted through the air. Gone was the neat and tidy man from that morning. Also gone was his affable smile.

"Ash Marcel," Ash said, holding out his hand. Not because he was overly polite. He just wanted to feel whether Doug's fingers were cold from recently being outside. "We met earlier."

Doug grudgingly clasped his hand for a brief shake. His skin was warm. It was possible he'd been wearing gloves, of course, but Ash was starting to doubt that Doug had been the one peering through the window.

Still, he had every intention of checking out his house while he was there.

"It's late," Doug complained.

"Sorry to bother you." Ash stepped forward, using his larger frame to force the man backward so he could enter the foyer. It was a technique he'd perfected while he was a detective. "But there was someone sneaking around Remi's house."

Doug stiffened, an expression of outrage rippling over his face. "Are you accusing me?"

The man's defensive manner was way too aggressive. Which meant he had something to hide. "You?" Ash offered a faux smile of confusion. "Why would I accuse you?"

Doug's anger faltered and he flushed as he realized that he'd overreacted.

"Why else would you be pounding on my door?"

"I was too late to get a good look at the perp, but I chased him around the house and into your backyard. I think he might have gone into your shed."

"Impossible. I keep it locked."

Ash hid his smile. It wasn't locked. At least not after Ash had given the flimsy door a sharp shove with his shoulder.

"Okay." Ash gave a casual shrug. "I just wanted to make sure the creep didn't manage to steal anything."

Doug's lips flattened. He was no doubt thinking about his new lawn mower stored in the shed, along with whatever tools he might own.

"Damn," he finally muttered in defeat. "I'll check it out."

Ash took another step forward, able to see around the edge of the foyer into a small living room. There was a couch, a low coffee table, and a TV hung on the wall. That was it. Hard to believe anyone would have a home more barren than his own, but there it was.

He turned his attention back to Doug. "I'll go with you, if you want."

"No, you can leave."

"Are you sure?" Ash tried to appear sympathetic. "My whole family is in law enforcement. One call and I can have a patrol car here ASAP."

Doug didn't look reassured. He looked pissed. "I'll take care of it."

"Okay. Have a good night."

Ash turned toward the door and took a couple of steps forward. At the same time, he could hear the sound of Doug hurrying toward the back of the house.

He paused, waiting until he heard the sound of a screen door slamming shut to be sure Doug was outside. Then, knowing he'd only have a couple of minutes, he turned to jog toward a nearby hallway. Pulling his phone out of his pocket, he touched the screen. The light was dim, but it was all he dared to use.

Entering the first room he found, he didn't have to do any searching. It was a spare bedroom with a set of twin beds and nothing else. He peered into the bathroom before entering the last room. It was clearly the one Doug was using. There was a bed that hadn't been made in days. Maybe weeks. A pile of clothes on the floor and a few clean ones hanging in the closet. There was a dresser filled with underwear and T-shirts, except for the bottom drawer that was stuffed with porn magazines.

Ash shook his head as he jogged back up the hallway. Most men used the computer for porn. Doug was either old-fashioned or afraid that his online use was being monitored. Perhaps by an angry ex-wife who was looking for a way to keep his daughters from him.

The kitchen was as barren as the rest of the house, but as Ash entered the dining room, he abruptly realized why Doug had been reluctant to let him in.

Muttering a curse, he moved across the carpet toward the telescope that was set on a tripod and arranged next to the window. He didn't have to look through the eyepiece to know that it wasn't being used to study the stars. It was pointed directly at Remi's bedroom window.

Fury pounded through him as he ripped the expensive telescope off the tripod and slammed it against the ground. There was the sound of glass breaking, but he wasn't satisfied. He stomped on it until the outer casing was shattered and spread across the carpet. Only when he was certain it was busted beyond repair did he turn and storm out of the dining room.

He met Doug, who was entering from the back door. The man jerked to a halt, his eyes widening as he took in the sight of Ash. "What the hell are you still doing in my house?"

Ash folded his arms over his chest. "I wanted to offer you a warning."

"More imaginary thieves sneaking around my house?"

Ash ignored the taunt. "I'm afraid your telescope is broken."

Doug's eyes bugged out before he was trying to cover his ass. "What telescope?"

Ash curled his lips in disgust. "The one you've been using to spy on Remi."

"What? That's a lie." Doug clenched his hands into fists, trying to meet Ash glare for glare. Less than a minute ticked past before he was lowering his head to stare at his feet. "You can't prove anything," he muttered.

Ash snorted. Doug would be a fool if he ever tried to embezzle funds from his bank. He was a terrible liar.

Unless he was pretending to be a terrible liar in the hope of throwing Ash off his trail . . .

He shook his head. Right now, he was focused on the crime he'd caught Doug committing red-handed. "I don't need to prove anything; I know exactly what you've been doing."

"Get out."

"I haven't given you my warning."

Doug lifted his head to glare at Ash. "What is it?"

"You replace that telescope and I'll shove it up your ass," he said, his voice soft and lethal. "Got it?"

Doug's face paled, easily sensing that Ash wasn't exaggerating. He fully intended to follow through on his threat if he caught the man spying on Remi.

"Yeah," he rasped. "I got it."

My windshield wipers slap back and forth, combating the monstrous snowflakes that filled the darkness with a swirl of white.

I cast a quick glance at my latest creation. She is sitting next to me. My fingers twitch. She isn't perfect. Her nose is still wrong, despite the surgery. And she's too short and thick through the hips. I wish I could dump her beside the road and start again. But my sickness is growing too quickly. The last attempt to cut away the evil was . . . sloppy. I had no opportunity to mold the organism into a lasting cure. It had been too unstable, too unpredictable. It had forced me to destroy it before I could fully purge the poison.

It was no wonder I was so swiftly spiraling toward the black hole in the center of my being.

But I can't give in to temptation, I sternly warn myself. Even if my latest creation is flawed, I have no options. I'm infected, not crazy. I can't risk exposure.

My gaze returns to the dark highway even as the vision of sweet, sweet blood dripping over my fingers fills my mind.

Chapter Ten

Jax arrived at the station on Sunday morning just as the sun was peeking over the Chicago skyline. The early start wasn't just because he had an urgent need to hunt down the Butcher. He understood that he couldn't work 24-7 even if Remi was in danger. Nope, he was there at this ungodly hour because of the strange text that had hit his phone at the crack of dawn.

Fortifying himself with a gallon of hot coffee, he drove through the nearly empty streets and pulled into the parking lot. He was still seated in his car, draining the last dregs from his travel mug when there was a sharp knock on his side window.

He jerked his head around to glare at the face outlined in the muted sunlight.

He released an exasperated breath, rolling down the window. Oliver White was a fellow cop who'd worked in the Property and Evidence Unit since Jax graduated from the Academy.

"Shit, Oliver, don't you know better than to startle a man who's carrying? Especially when he hasn't finished his coffee."

The cop shrugged. He was several inches shorter than Jax and several pounds heavier, with a nearly bald head beneath the hat that went with his uniform. "I wanted to catch you before you went inside."

Jax waited for his pulse to settle to a steady pace before unhooking his seat belt and shoving open the door of his car. Then, stepping into the frozen morning air, he studied his companion with blatant curiosity.

"This all seems very cloak-and-dagger, Oliver," he said. "What's going on?"

The man grimaced, his round face ruddy as he reached beneath his heavy coat to pull out a slender file folder. "Yeah, I'm probably being an idiot, but I wanted to give this to you without anyone knowing."

Jax reached out to take the folder. "What is it?"

"A file that was found taped under Gage Walsh's top drawer after he died."

Jax returned his attention to his companion. Had he misunderstood? "Stuck under his drawer?" he demanded. "Or taped?"

"Taped," Oliver insisted, glancing around the nearly empty lot before he continued in a low voice. "The janitor was repairing a bent leg on the desk before he put it in storage. Most of the stuff had been cleared out and any personal belongings had been sent to his widow, so when he found this stuck under the drawer, he didn't know what to do with it. He finally decided to drop it off at the evidence room."

Jax felt a stirring of unease. "What did you do with it?"

"I put it in a box next to the Butcher files. I assumed it had something to do with the case, but . . ." Oliver gave a vague lift of his hands.

"But what?"

Oliver nodded toward the folder in Jax's hand. "When I glanced through it, I couldn't make heads or tails of it. Like it's written in code."

Jax stared down at the file. It sounded like a script from some bad crime show.

A dead detective. A hidden file that could reveal the serial killer, but alas, it's written in code.

He tried to laugh off his ridiculous imaginings, but the unease continued to bubble in the pit of his stomach.

"We all have our own way of jotting down notes," he pointed out. "I'm sure some of mine would look like a foreign language to other people."

Oliver gave a stubborn shake of his head. "I've seen a hundred of Gage's files and they never looked like this. It got me thinking. Why would he write it in such a wacky way? So no one else could read it? Why? And why hide it in a place no one would look?" The words stumbled together, as if he was in a rush to get them out. "Only one answer. Because there was someone he didn't trust. Someone close."

Jax suddenly understood why they were meeting in the frigid parking lot. And why Oliver was acting so weird.

The older cop assumed Gage didn't trust someone in the station. A coworker? A boss? Ash?

No. He instantly squashed the thought. If Gage had any suspicion that Ash was somehow involved, he would have kept Remi far away from her fiancé. Even if that meant locking her in an igloo at the North Pole.

He tucked the file beneath his coat. It was still too dark in the parking lot to read it. Besides, Oliver's odd behavior was making him itchy. He wanted some privacy before he tried to decipher any code.

"Why give it to me now?" he asked Oliver.

"Gage Walsh stood next to me when I was accused of losing evidence during my first year on the job. And he gave me money when he knew my bitch of an ex-wife had taken me for everything I had. I owe him." The male jutted his chin, his expression grim. "If the Butcher is really back, he has to be stopped before he can hurt Remi. That's what Gage would want me to do."

Jax slowly nodded. "You're right," he assured his companion. "And thank you."

"Just catch the bastard," Oliver muttered, turning to head toward his car, parked at the far end of the lot.

Jax watched him walk away, briefly considering the possibility that this had been some elaborate setup. What better way to distract him from the case than to send him on some wild-goose chase with a mysterious file supposedly belonging to Gage?

Then he gave a sharp shake of his head. He couldn't start turning everyone into a suspect. That would only cloud his thoughts and make it impossible to look at the facts with a clear mind.

For now, he would accept what Oliver was telling him was the truth.

Shivering as a blast of air whirled around him, Jax hunched his shoulders and jogged toward the building. Now that he was here, he might as well get some work done.

Once settled at his desk, he tossed aside his coat and opened the mystery file. Usually privacy was as rare as a pygmy three-toed sloth at the station house, but this morning a welcome hush had settled in the air. It wouldn't last, but he was grateful for an hour or so of peace.

The thought had barely formed when he was interrupted by a text hitting his cell phone. It was from Ash. He wanted to see Jax, but he didn't want to leave Remi on her own. Jax sent back a text promising to send a patrol car to keep watch on the neighborhood and telling his brother to meet him at the station.

Once he'd arranged for Remi's protection, he returned his attention to the papers spread in front of him. Oliver had been right. The markings and abbreviations made no sense. At least not to him.

Lost in thought, Jax muttered a curse when he heard approaching footsteps. Swiftly, he was grabbing the pages and shoving them back into the folder.

"Hey, bro." The familiar voice had Jax releasing a sigh of relief as he watched Ash step around the partition.

A wave of warmth crashed through Jax. God, he'd missed his brother. There'd been something incredibly right about entering the squad room to see Ash at his desk. Or hitting the basketball court to shoot hoops after one of them had a bad day. Or spending the weekend at the lake pretending to fish . . .

He swallowed a sigh. Ash had to do what made him happy. Even if it left an aching void in Jax's life.

"You're up early," Jax said, noting the tense lines of his brother's face. Clearly, he hadn't spent a relaxing night in Remi's arms.

A damned shame.

"Not as early as you." Ash did his own bit of inspecting, his gaze lingering on the dark circles beneath Jax's eyes. "Did you get any sleep?"

"Enough." Jax shrugged away his brother's concern. "You said you had something for me to see?"

Ash reached into the pocket of his coat and pulled out a folded paper bag. He tossed it on Jax's desk.

"This was shoved under Remi's front door while we were out yesterday morning."

Curious, Jax opened the bag and glanced at the torn sheet of paper with a scribbled note on it.

I need to see you.

He glanced back up at Ash. "There's not much to go on," he said. "It could have come from anyone."

Ash nodded. "Yeah. I'm probably overreacting, but I hoped you would run the prints."

Jax closed the bag and opened a drawer to drop it inside. He was doubtful that the Butcher would start requesting appointments with his potential victims by sticking notes under their doors, but he was willing to grasp at any straw.

"It will take a while, but I'll get them in the system," he promised, folding his arms on the desk and leaning forward. "How's Remi?"

"Scared, but trying to pretend everything is fine."

"And you?"

"Scared, but trying to pretend everything is fine."

Jax grimaced. He wished he could tell them not to worry, but he couldn't. Not when there was a real possibility that the Butcher was back in town, and that he was focused on Remi.

"We're going to catch the bastard," he said instead. "I promise."

Ash nodded. "I caught sight of the patrol car when I left the house," he said. "Thanks."

Jax gave a lift of his shoulders. "No problem. Everyone on the force wants to make sure Remi is kept safe."

"Let them know I appreciate everything they're doing."

"I will." Jax glanced around, making sure there was no one standing close enough to overhear their conversation. "Tell me what happened last night."

Ash calmly removed his coat, hanging it on the top corner of the partition. "Last night?" He pretended he didn't know what Jax was asking. "Let's see. Remi and I ate some Chinese food. We drank some wine. We went through the old files." He stopped, giving a sudden snap of his fingers. "Oh. I did uncover a new piece of evidence."

Jax grudgingly allowed himself to be distracted. "What evidence?"

This time it was Ash who carefully ensured there was

no one around. "Robert Hutton lied about his alibi the night that Tiffany Holloway was killed."

"Robert Hutton? The one who works in the district attorney's office?"

"Yep."

Jax hissed in shock. Or maybe it was horror. No detective ever wanted to think about a suspect who might create a media frenzy. Politicians. Business leaders. Fellow cops. Members of the clergy. Whether the person was guilty or innocent, it always ended badly for the detective.

"Where did he claim to be?" Jax demanded. He hadn't gone through the old Butcher files. Not yet.

"Meeting with Remi's mother at her estate."

Jax studied his brother's face, waiting to see if this was some sick joke. "Seriously?" he finally demanded.

Ash nodded. "Which was why we didn't go any further with the investigation despite the fact he had phone calls from the victim." He reached for his coat, pulling out a sheet of paper that had been carefully folded and tucked in an inner pocket. He placed it on the desk. "I think he needs a second glance."

Jax unfolded the paper and quickly skimmed through the short interview. Robert had said he'd spent the evening having dinner with Liza Harding-Walsh at her estate to plan a fancy ball for his charity. He then claimed he drove to his town house at ten o'clock and spent two hours going through case notes for an upcoming trial before he went to bed.

Jax glanced back up at his brother. "No one talked to Remi's mother?"

"I didn't." Ash released a frustrated sigh. "I don't know about Gage. He never said anything about Hutton after our initial interview."

Jax made a mental note to go through Gage's files to see

if he had any official interview with his wife. For now, he concentrated on why Ash was convinced the alibi was bogus. "What makes you assume Hutton lied?"

"Remi was sick that night and returned home early from a study group," Ash said. "Neither her mother nor Hutton were there."

Jax didn't ask if Remi was certain it was the same night. It was a question Ash would have asked. "Could they have moved the meeting?"

"Possibly, but I'd like to know why he specifically said he was at the estate the entire evening."

Jax grimaced. Damn. There was no getting around it. He was going to have to get a new statement from Hutton. "So would I," he said.

Ash stepped toward the desk. "I want to go with you when you question him."

Jax snorted. Had his brother lost his mind? "No way."

Predictably, Ash refused to accept Jax's refusal. All the Marcel boys were stubborn, but Ash had an extra dose of pigheadedness.

"Look, if you make it an official visit, you're going to cause a shitstorm," Ash said with a smooth logic. "If the two of us happen to stop by the country club for a casual drink and run into the man . . ." The younger man shrugged. "He can't protest."

"He also won't be forced to answer our questions," Jax reminded his brother. "Plus, if he does become a suspect, he'll have ample opportunity to create a new lie to cover his ass before I can haul him into the station."

"He's going to lawyer up anyway," Ash insisted. "If we approach him casually, we can catch him off guard. He'll be more likely to give something away."

Jax swallowed a frustrated sigh. His brother could be a pain in the ass, but he was also making a good point. The second Hutton sensed his alibi had fallen apart he would have the full power of the district attorney's office behind him. Any investigation would come to a screeching halt.

"I'll think about it," he hedged, not prepared to give Ash any promises. Then, he deliberately changed the conversation. "Now answer my question."

Ash pretended to be puzzled. "What question?"

"What did you do last night?" He stabbed a finger toward his aggravating sibling. "And don't pretend you don't know what I mean."

Ash chuckled, then his smile slowly faded. As if the memories from the previous night were creeping back into his thoughts. "I made a brief visit to speak with Doug," he admitted.

"Shit. I knew it." Jax clenched his hands into tight fists. He'd debated about passing along the information he'd discovered. He'd wanted them to know that Doug Gates had a history of violence, but Ash was always overprotective when it came to Remi. Right now, he was in extreme vigilante mode. Any hint of a threat to his onetime fiancée was bound to send him over the edge. "Is he pressing charges?"

"Not unless he wants to explain the telescope he was using to spy on Remi," Ash growled.

Doug Gates was spying on Remi? Jax carefully planted his palms flat on his desk. It was his way of ensuring he didn't grab for his gun.

"Bastard," he breathed. "Do I need to get an arrest warrant?"

Ash shook his head, his expression grim. "I've taken care of it for now."

Uh-oh. "Is he dead?" Jax demanded.

"No, but he will be if I catch him anywhere around Remi," Ash said without hesitation.

Jax quashed his instinct to have the perv hauled to the station. As much as he wanted to beat the crap out of Doug Gates, Ash could handle the creepy neighbor. It was Jax's duty to find the Butcher. "Do you think he's a suspect?"

"Not really." Ash gave a shake of his head, frustration clearly etched on his face. "But I can't rule him out either."

"Then we keep him on the list of suspects and continue searching for evidence."

"While Remi stays in danger."

"She has a lot of people looking out for her," Jax reminded his brother, knowing the words were empty. Nothing would comfort Ash. Not until the Butcher was behind bars. Or dead.

Ash paused, visibly struggling to regain command of his temper. "Have you found anything in the old files?" he at last asked.

Jax grimaced. "I'm not sure."

"That's less than helpful," Ash said in dry tones.

Jax reached to angle the computer screen on his desk. "Grab a seat. I have something I want to show you."

"Okay." Ash found an extra chair pushed against the nearby wall and placed it next to Jax. "What's going on?"

Jax tapped on the keyboard. "I couldn't find any cases that fit the MO of the Butcher."

Ash muttered a curse under his breath. "But?"

"But I used one of our new search programs." Jax brought up the files he'd found. "They can comb through thousands of files for patterns. First, I looked for anyone who'd been killed by having their throats cut, both male and female. Then I expanded the search to other cities. I couldn't find anything. Finally I put in the physical characteristics of the Butcher's prime targets and searched for any deaths in the past five years. I got a few hits."

Ash leaned forward. "Show me."

"The first victim I found is Carla Tester." Jax enlarged the picture of the pretty, dark-haired woman with a plump face and bright smile. "Twenty-four years old. She worked for the Chicago Transit Authority and died four years ago." Jax brought up the next photo. Once again, the female was dark-haired with pretty features. This one had green eyes and a few freckles sprinkled over her pale skin. "Beth Sampson. Eighteen. She was in her freshman year of college. She died three years ago." Jax pulled up the last picture. The female was older than the others, but she had dark hair and greenish-blue eyes. "Ariel Midland. She was twenty-seven and a hairdresser. She died last year."

Ash sent him a furious glare. "Why didn't anyone tag them with the Butcher killings?"

That had been Jax's first question. The women fit the profile. At least when it came to the physical description of the Butcher's victims.

Then he'd studied the complete records and understood why any connection to the Butcher had been missed.

"Each of the women burned to death in a house fire," he said. "There was no reason to think there was foul play in any of their deaths."

"Three separate house fires?" Ash snorted. "And that didn't raise any questions?"

"They were all at least a year apart," Jax reminded him.

"None of the victims had their throats slit?"

"The bodies were all badly burned and I don't think they did more than a superficial exam. It was assumed they were tragic accidents, not victims of a serial killer."

"Damn." Ash sat back, obviously trying to process the new information. "I don't suppose you can get the bodies exhumed? If we could discover the exact cause of death, and if they had the telltale mark on their breast, we could be certain they were the work of the Butcher."

Jax made a sound of disgust. His brother had obviously been gone from the department too long.

"Are you kidding? I'd need a lot more than a hunch to get the money or a warrant to have the bodies dug up."

"Are you going to investigate them?"

"Yes." Jax held up a hand as Ash's lips parted, no doubt intending to remind him that Remi's life was in danger. "I promise."

Ash sent him a rueful smile. "Thanks. Was there anything else?"

"No." About to send Ash back to Remi, Jax abruptly recalled the reason he was at the office before any reasonable person should be up on a Sunday morning. "Wait." He reached for the folder he'd shoved toward the back of his desk. "This file was found taped under a drawer in Gage's desk after his death."

"Taped?" Ash frowned in confusion, and Jax felt a stab of disappointment. He'd hoped his brother might have some idea why Gage had it hidden, and what the strange markings might mean.

Ash reached to grab the file. "What is it?"

"Hell if I know."

The younger man spread out the papers, his frown deepening as he glanced over the scribbled notes. "It looks like it's written in gibberish."

"None of his other files match this?" Jax pressed.

"No." Ash reached for a map of Chicago that had been photocopied. He pointed toward one of the red circles that had presumably been placed there by Gage. "Those mark where the bodies were found," he said, his fingers moving to the numbers written next to the circle. "And the dates."

Jax had managed to work out that much. He reached for the map and turned it over to reveal the numbers that were penciled on the back. "This is a list of dates as well." He grabbed a second sheet of paper where he'd made his own notes. He touched the first column of numbers. "Some match the nights of the murders." He moved his finger toward the second column. "But not all of them."

Ash studied the list in silence, then he gave a shake of his head. He reached to shuffle through the remaining papers.

"Everything is in initials," Ash muttered, his voice thick with frustration. "There's no way to know what they mean."

"Could be names of suspects," Jax suggested. "Or maybe places?"

Ash shoved the papers back in the folder and rose to his feet. "I'll go back through the notes I pulled out of storage to see if I can find anything that might give us a clue about these."

Jax nodded. If Gage had wanted the folder to be a part of the official investigation, he wouldn't have hidden it in his desk. "You'll let me know?"

"Yeah."

Ash reached for his coat and Jax leaned back in his seat, once again feeling a surge of satisfaction. He hated the reason that his brother was back in town, but he was going to enjoy his company while he was there. "Mom said you stopped by," Jax said.

"I did my duty." Ash slid on his coat, pressing a hand to the center of his chest. "As commanded."

Jax smiled. Ash was like all the Marcel boys. He adored his mother.

"Did she offer you the fatted calf?"

Amusement sparkled in Ash's eyes. "No, but I did get my favorite lasagna and a slice of her homemade chocolate cake with hot caramel dribbled over the top."

Jax rolled his eyes. "Spoiled."

"No way," Ash protested. "Nate was spoiled. You were the favorite, and the rest of us were just the forgotten middle."

Jax snorted. They'd all been loved. Perhaps he was closer to their father than the rest of them, but only because the older man had been eager to get away from a pack of screaming babies and the only way was to take Jax to a ball game or camping for the weekend.

"Speaking of Nate, did Mom tell you he's coming home next week?" Jax said.

"Yes. I've also been ordered to be fitted for my tux before I leave town."

Jax grimaced. No one was happier for Nate than he was. He hadn't met his youngest brother's fiancée, but she sounded perfect for Nate. Still, the thought of being trapped for hours in a formal tux that included a bow tie and one of those stupid cummerbunds was enough to give him a rash.

"Christ. I need to do that too. I keep putting it off in the hopes that Nate will come to his senses and decide to elope," he muttered.

"I don't think it's Nate's decision," Ash said dryly.

"No, I suppose not." Jax heaved a glum sigh.

Ash reached out to pat his shoulder. "I need to get back to Remi."

Jax nodded. "Stay safe."

Chapter Eleven

Ash drove back to Remi's house, slowing as he passed the patrol car to give the cop a small wave. The officer gave a nod and pulled away from the curb as Ash parked in the driveway. He stepped out of the car but, walking toward the front door, he abruptly decided on a detour.

Rounding the edge of the house, he crossed the short distance to peer into Doug Gates's window. He made no effort to hide his approach. He wanted the man to know he was keeping a close watch on him. A quick glance assured him the telescope was gone, and no one was in the dining room or kitchen. Satisfied that the perv had learned his lesson, at least for now, he continued to the backyard.

He did a quick glance around, not expecting to see anything. The sun was shining brightly, and despite the frigid air, there were already people bustling around the neighborhood. But even as he turned toward the house, there was a rustle in one of the bushes next to the small porch.

Ash was moving before he could consider that whoever was lurking in the shadows might have a gun. His only thought was making sure they didn't slip away.

Shoving his arms into the branches, he grasped the quilted material of a coat. Then, gritting his teeth, he pulled the wiggling stranger out of the bushes. There was a blast of foul language from his captive as Ash threw him down and pinned his arms to the hard ground.

"What's your damage, you freak? Let me go," the man yelled.

No, not a man, Ash realized as he gazed into the hood of the coat. The narrow face was dotted with blemishes and a few scraggly whiskers on his chin. He couldn't be more than fifteen or sixteen years old.

"Not a chance," Ash rasped, glaring down at the intruder.

This couldn't be the Butcher. The kid would still have been in grade school when the first woman was murdered. But he might be working for the killer.

Fear flared through the boy's pale eyes, but he remained belligerent. "I haven't done nothing wrong."

"First off, you're trespassing on private property," Ash snapped. "I can probably add stalking and invasion of privacy to the list."

The boy stopped his struggles, his expression suddenly wary. "What are you? A cop?"

"Something like that."

"Why are you staying with Ms. Walsh? I saw a patrol car earlier." He paused to lick his lips. "Is she in trouble?"

There was genuine concern in the kid's voice that made Ash hesitate. Surely if he was the lookout for a crazed serial killer, he would have some convincing cover story? And if he was a common thief, how did he know Remi's name?

"How do you know Ms. Walsh?" he demanded.

"She's my teacher. At the youth center."

The words barely left the boy's mouth when the sliding door opened and Remi stepped onto the back porch.

"Ash?"

"Go back inside," he commanded.

A waste of breath, of course. She stubbornly moved to the edge of the porch to gaze down at the boy who was lying spread-eagle on the ground.

"Drew? What's going on?"

The kid eagerly turned his head toward Remi. "I came here to see you and this lunatic attacked me."

"You can let him go, Ash," Remi said.

He hesitated. He felt like an idiot holding down a boy who was half his weight, but this was no time to make mistakes. "You know him?"

"Yes," she quickly assured him. "He's Drew Tyson. One of my students."

Cautiously, Ash released his hold on the boy's arms. "I caught him hiding in the bushes."

With the awkward movements of a boy who was still adjusting to a recent growth spurt, Drew scrambled to his feet. Next to him, Ash pushed himself upright and grabbed the boy's coat and yanked it open. A quick glance assured him there weren't any weapons hidden beneath the thick material. Drew glared at him but clearly accepted that Ash wasn't going to let him anywhere near Remi unless he was sure he wasn't carrying.

"I was waiting for the cop to leave," Drew said to Remi.

"Cop?" Remi sent the boy a puzzled glance. "What cop?"

Drew pointed toward the corner of the block. "The one who was parked over there."

Remi turned her head, arching her brows in a silent question.

Ash shrugged. "Jax has a few uniforms keeping an eye on the house when they can," he told her.

"Jax asked them to be there?" she pressed.

He shrugged. "You know how overprotective he is." She gave a resigned shake of her head, but before she could chide him, Ash was returning his attention to the boy who was regarding them with a curious expression. "Why are you creeping around here?"

Drew waved his hands in a gesture of impatience. "I told you, I need to talk to Ms. Walsh."

"About what?" Ash demanded.

The boy stuck out his chin. "It's private."

Remi loudly cleared her throat. "Can we have this conversation inside? It's freezing out here."

Ash's gaze remained on the boy. "Do you trust him in your house?"

"Of course I do." She waved a hand toward Drew, who strolled past Ash with a cocky grin before jogging up the steps of the porch.

Remi led the boy inside and Ash quickly glanced through the bushes to make sure there weren't any other lurkers before hurrying behind them. He was stepping into the kitchen as Remi was urging Drew to take a seat at the breakfast bar.

"Have you eaten?" she asked the boy.

"No." He gave a small shake of his head as he pulled off his coat and dropped it on the floor.

Ash leaned against the wall, close enough to keep the kid from causing any problems without making him feel that he was being crowded.

"I'll make you some soup and sandwiches while you tell me why you haven't been in school," Remi said, ignoring the early hour as she pulled out a can of chicken noodle soup from the cabinet and dumped the contents in a bowl.

Drew sent a distrustful glance toward Ash. "I don't want to talk in front of a cop."

"Don't worry." Remi put the bowl in the microwave and moved to pull out four slices of bread. She quickly slathered them with peanut butter. "Whatever you tell me will be confidential."

"Not necessarily," Ash warned.

"Ash." Remi sent him a glare that warned she was close to ordering him to leave the room. Maybe even the house. "He's just a frightened boy."

Drew stiffened his spine, a dark blush staining his cheeks. "I'm a man, not a boy."

Ash battled back his protective instincts. It didn't take a detective to see that the boy was tired and dirty and hungry. Or that he had come to Remi for help, not to hurt her.

"Fine," he muttered. Still, he remained where he was standing.

Remi sighed, clearly deciding he'd conceded as much as he was willing. She finished up the sandwiches and put them on a plate to place them in front of her unexpected guest. "Tell me," she urged.

Drew's sullen demeanor remained, but a hint of fear lurked in the depths of his eyes. He was scared, and like any scared kid, he was trying to cover it with a pretense of indifference.

"Dad got picked up last week," he said.

Remi didn't look surprised. "Drugs?"

Drew hunched a shoulder. "It was a setup. The bas—" He bit off the word as Remi narrowed her eyes. "The cops have been waiting for the chance to throw him back in jail since he got out the last time."

Remi moved to get the soup as the boy devoured the sandwiches in large bites. "Does he have anyone to post bail for him?" she asked, returning to the breakfast bar with the steaming bowl and a spoon.

"No."

Remi continued to move around the kitchen, pouring a large glass of milk and grabbing a napkin before returning to the boy, who'd finished off the sandwiches.

"Where are you staying?" she asked.

"You know." Drew ducked his head to wolf down the soup at the same impressive speed as the sandwiches. "I've been bouncing between friends."

Ash's lips twitched. If the boy thought that was going to satisfy Remi, he was sadly mistaken.

On cue, Remi folded her arms and studied the boy with a stern expression. "Do you have any family I can call?"

"My aunt said she can't take me in." Drew lifted the bowl to drain the last of the soup. "The bitch."

"Drew," Remi chided.

The boy lowered the empty bowl and shrugged. "She says I'm a bad influence on her precious kids, but she's the one who hides her empty bottles of vodka in the garage."

Ash could sense Remi mentally scratching off the aunt from the list of potential caretakers for Drew.

"What about a caseworker?" she asked.

The boy flinched, as if Remi had slapped him in the face. "I won't go back into the system. I'll take my chances on the street."

Remi quickly realized her mistake, reaching for her cell phone sitting on the counter. "We'll work something out," she told Drew. "Let me talk to Mr. Hill."

Drew frowned. "The head dude from the center?"

"Yep." Remi scrolled through her numbers. "He has contacts all over the city."

Drew slid off his stool, his hands curling into tight fists. Ash took a step forward, although he didn't think the boy was angry. More likely he was terrified. Which made him even more dangerous.

"What sort of contacts?"

Remi held the boy's gaze, her expression somber. "Do you trust me, Drew?"

There was a silence before the boy gave a slow nod of his head. "Yeah, I trust you."

"Sit back down and I'll make the call."

There was another pause before Drew was sliding back on the stool. Remi sent him an encouraging smile that any young boy would walk over hot coals to earn.

Or any man, Ash wryly acknowledged.

Remi headed into the living room, dialing Lamar Hill's number. It'd been a shock to glance out her back window to see Ash holding someone on the ground. At first, she'd assumed he'd returned from his meeting with Jax and had caught her creepy neighbor trying to peek in the window. She'd fully intended to call the cops and have him hauled away before Ash could kill him. Then, a closer glance had revealed the intruder was way too skinny to be Doug Gates.

Plus, she was fairly certain she recognized the silver, quilted coat. She'd bought one exactly like it to give to Drew Tyson.

Hurrying onto the porch, she'd felt a flare of relief to see the boy's familiar face. She'd been truly worried that he might take off and they would never see him again.

Of course, she'd had to deal with Ash's overprotective aggression, but once she had Drew settled in her kitchen, she'd been fairly confident she could convince him to accept her help.

Reaching the owner of the youth center, she'd revealed the fact that Drew was at her house and that his dad was back in jail. Lamar was quick to leap into action, putting her on hold as he reached out to his various contacts. In a surprisingly short amount of time, he'd found a perfect place for the teen.

Once assured that Drew's immediate future was going to be taken care of, she returned to the kitchen. She glanced around, finding Ash still keeping an unwavering watch on the boy who sat at the breakfast bar.

At last noticing her presence, both guys turned to glance in her direction. She smiled, moving to grab a cupcake from a tray next to the sink.

Ash had given a lift of his brows when he'd noticed the red velvet cupcakes with piles of cream cheese frosting she'd had delivered from a nearby bakery, but he'd kept his mouth shut. Smart man. She was a stress eater. So sue her.

"Mr. Hill is coming to pick you up," she told Drew as she set the pastry in front of him.

Drew scowled, his face pale and smudged with dirt. She felt a pang of sympathy. He was just a boy being forced to place his life in the hands of strangers.

"Where's he taking me?" Drew demanded.

"He knows a family who does emergency foster care, Wade and Stella Williams. They're going to meet you at the center," she said. "He promised they were decent people and that they are going to take great care of you."

Drew hunched his shoulders, grabbing the cupcake and eating half of it in one bite. "I've heard that a lot," he told her, licking icing off his lips.

"He mentioned that Joe Hearn stayed with them last year and that you can call him and check them out if you want."

A portion of Drew's brittle fear eased at her words. "I remember that," he said in slow, thoughtful tones. As if he was reconsidering whether he was going to take off and disappear before Lamar Hill arrived. "Joe said they were cool. For old folks."

Remi held his pale gaze. "You'll give them a chance?"

Drew finished the cupcake and wiped his hands on his jeans. Typical boy.

"I suppose," he agreed, a stubborn expression tightening his features. "It'll only be for a little while anyway. Dad will get the judge straightened out and we'll be together again."

Not about to encourage the boy's belief that his father was going to be released any time soon, she offered a smile. Right now, all that mattered was keeping him here until Lamar arrived.

"Do you want more milk?" she asked.

"Sure." Waiting until Remi replenished his glass, Drew deliberately glanced toward the silent Ash. "Why do you have cops hanging around?"

Remi hesitated. She didn't want to share what was happening with her. Drew might be street savvy, but he was still just a teen. He shouldn't be troubled with fears of serial killers. Then she squared her shoulders. If she wasn't entirely honest with the boy, he would never trust her again.

"There was a woman murdered a couple of days ago," she said, ignoring Ash's startled glance.

Drew looked uninterested, as if he'd been hoping for something more thrilling than another murder. Then a sudden excitement widened his eyes.

"The one in the park?" he asked. "I seen her picture on the TV last night. She looked like you."

"Yes." Remi suppressed a shiver. "Until they find the killer, I'm going to have some extra protection."

"Do they think he's after you?"

"We just want to be careful."

Drew nodded, the excitement remaining as he tried to act casual. "You're not going to believe it, but I had a friend who was in that park the morning she was found."

It was the last thing Remi had been expecting. She blinked, wondering if he was making up stories to impress her.

"What friend?"

"Roo—" Drew sharply bit off the word, his face flushing with anger at himself. "Nobody."

Ash stepped forward. "Tell me about your friend."

Drew slid off the stool, putting space between himself and the larger man. "I ain't getting him in trouble."

"No trouble, I swear," Remi tried to soothe the boy.

"Bullshit," Drew muttered.

Ash's expression hardened. "Did he see anything?"

"I don't know." Drew held up his hands as Ash scowled with frustration. "I don't. He just told me that he was in the park that morning. Said it freaked him out to think he might have walked past a dead body and not even realized it."

Remi pressed a hand to her stomach. Was it possible there might have been an eyewitness who could ID the Butcher?

"What time did he leave the park?" she asked.

Drew refused to meet her gaze. "He didn't say."

"This is important, Drew," Ash insisted in stern tones. "We need to find the killer before he can harm Ms. Walsh."

The boy stuck out his chin in a mutinous gesture and Remi swallowed a sigh. Ash was no doubt an excellent interrogator when it came to murder suspects, but he didn't seem to know much about scared juveniles.

"I'm sorry. I like you, Ms. Walsh," Drew muttered. "You're the best teacher I've ever had, but if word gets out that I'm a squealer, I'm as good as dead."

"That's fine," she assured the boy, sending Ash a warning glance. "I don't want you to put yourself in danger."

Ash flattened his lips but grudgingly turned his questioning to a less-stressful subject. "How did you know where Ms. Walsh lives?" he demanded.

Drew's tension eased visibly. "Google."

Remi jerked. She hadn't considered how the teen had

known how to track her down. Certainly she'd never given out her address. Not to anyone. Now she studied Drew with a sudden suspicion.

"How long have you been hanging around the house?" she asked.

He gave a vague lift of his shoulder. "Three or four days."

"Did you leave a note for me?"

Color crept beneath Drew's cheeks, emphasizing his youth.

"I didn't have your cell number to call. It wasn't until I shoved the note under the door that I remembered I hadn't put my name on it."

Remi exchanged a silent glance with Ash. They now knew that Drew was the one who shoved the note under her door, and he'd probably been peeking in her window the night before too.

Which meant that it hadn't been the Butcher.

A trickle of relief crept through her. Until this moment, she hadn't realized how horrifying it was to think that the monster was creeping around her property.

Ash folded his arms over his chest, his gaze returning to Drew. "Have you noticed anyone taking an interest in Ms. Walsh while you were hanging around the house?"

"I've seen a few patrol cars parked around the corner."

Remi swallowed her urge to chide Ash for wasting precious police time to keep a watch on her house. Did she honestly want to give up the extra protection? Besides, if the Butcher did have an obsession with her, there was a chance he would decide to seek her out. What better opportunity for the cops to capture him?

Thankfully unaware of her cowardly thoughts, Ash continued to question Drew. "Anyone else?"

Drew glanced toward Remi with a curl to his lips.

"Yeah. I think your neighbor is a perv. I know someone who can take care of him if you want."

Remi gave a shake of her head. She doubted the teen actually knew a hit man, but then again, he probably knew plenty of drug users. One of them might be willing to do anything for their next fix.

"I can handle it," she assured her student, turning her head toward the living room as she heard a knock on the front door. "I think your ride is here."

Drew grimaced but reached for his jacket and pulled it on without protest. A small miracle. As he started toward Remi, however, Ash suddenly reached out his arm.

"Take this," he commanded.

Drew frowned, taking the business card Ash held in his fingers. "What is it?"

"My cell number," Ash said. "Call me if you hear anything that might help keep Ms. Walsh safe."

Drew gave a slow nod. "Okay."

Remi herded the boy out of the kitchen and toward the front porch, where Lamar Hill was waiting for them. She was afraid that the longer she gave Drew to consider the thought of being taken in by foster parents, the more likely he would be to bolt. Thankfully, Lamar was a master at working with troubled boys and quickly had Drew distracted with promises of playing video games once they reached the youth center.

With a small nod toward Remi, the large man efficiently urged Drew toward his waiting car, then pulled away with a squeal of his tires. Remi rolled her eyes. Lamar would always be a kid at heart.

Something she loved about him.

Stepping back into the house, Remi closed the door and headed into the kitchen.

"I hope he doesn't run off," she said, speaking more to herself than the man who was eyeing her with an unreadable expression. "God knows how long his dad is going to be locked up this time."

Ash leaned against the counter as she gathered the dirty dishes and placed them in the sink.

"I appreciate your concern for the boy," he said.

She sent him a questioning glance. "But?"

He hesitated, as if choosing his words with care. "But he had information that might help catch the Butcher. He needs to be interviewed by Jax."

She grabbed a towel, wiping her hands as she allowed a smug smile to curve her lips. "Wouldn't it be easier to go talk with the guy who was actually in the park?"

He looked confused before his eyes suddenly widened. "You know who it is?"

"Drew said 'Roo' before he could stop himself," she reminded him.

"That name means something to you?"

She nodded. "He hangs around the same neighborhood as the youth center," she told him. "Lamar calls the cops when he catches him trying to sell drugs to our kids, but he always comes back. I'm sure that's how Drew met him."

"There could be more than one Roo, but it's not a common nickname." Ash lifted his arm to glance at his watch. "It's early for any drug dealers to be on the streets, but he has to be sleeping somewhere in the area. I'm going to see if I can find him."

"Uh-uh." Remi moved to stand directly in front of her companion. "*We're* going."

His jaw tightened. He intended to be stubborn about this. "Remi."

She shrugged, intending to be even more stubborn. Not

because she felt like Ash wasn't competent to track down Roo, but because she was familiar with the neighborhood. It would be a lot easier for her to get the information they needed. "You don't know what he looks like."

He scowled at her simple logic. "I've been tracking down suspects for a long time," he informed her. "Give me a description and I'll find him."

Remi shook her head. "Roo moves from street to street. No one in that neighborhood will talk to you."

"And they'll talk to you?"

"Most of them," she told him without hesitation. Since volunteering at the youth center, she'd tried to reach out to people living on the streets. It wasn't much, but she knew that every little bit helped to a person in need. "I bring sandwiches and blankets to hand out when it's cold. If Roo is around, we'll find him."

Ash lifted his hands, giving a shake of his head. "Why do I feel like I'm losing control of this investigation?"

Remi smiled. "Either I'm your partner or I'm not."

He released a slow breath between his clenched teeth. As if he was wondering why he bothered to argue with her.

"You're my partner," he conceded.

"I'll drive," Remi said, heading toward her bedroom to grab her coat.

It was almost noon when Remi at last parked her car across the street from the youth center. Despite Ash's sizzling impatience, she'd insisted on stopping at a grocery store to pick up a stack of sandwiches from the deli department.

Now she climbed out of the car and waited for Ash to join her. Holding the grocery bag in one hand, she gave a nod of her head to gesture toward the narrow side street. They walked in silence, Ash on full alert while Remi was more interested in the handful of people who were shuffling along the pavement.

The local streets were home to dozens of people who'd fallen on hard times. Most appeared and disappeared like phantoms, either seeking help and climbing out of the gutters or falling even deeper into the cracks. There were, however, a dozen regulars Remi knew on a first-name basis.

They turned the corner, and Remi caught sight of a familiar form huddled in a doorway. Maggie's thin body was covered by a shabby blanket Remi had brought her last month, and a red knit stocking hat she wore whether it was twenty below zero or eighty degrees was pulled low on her head. She had a few wispy gray hairs that managed to escape and blow around her narrow face that was heavily lined. The woman was probably in her early fifties, but she looked closer to seventy.

Hearing their approach, Maggie quickly shoved something behind her, probably a bottle of cheap vodka. That was her drug of choice. Remi slowed her pace, glancing toward the man at her side.

"Stay behind me," she said in a low voice.

Ash's jaw hardened with a predictable annoyance. "Why?"

"Because you look like a cop," she said without apology. "Maggie won't talk if she thinks you're here to hassle her."

"I don't look like a cop," he protested.

Remi rolled her eyes. "Your entire family was born looking like cops. Just stay behind me."

"What happened to the whole partner thing?" he demanded.

"You're my partner." She deliberately stepped in front of him, glancing over her shoulder. "But back there."

"Christ," he muttered, but he lagged behind her as she approached the older woman.

Either because he trusted her judgment or, more likely, because Maggie hadn't bathed in several days. Maybe weeks.

Remi ignored the stench and moved to squat in front of the woman. She'd met Maggie six months ago, when she'd come into the shelter that was attached to the youth center. Once upon a time, Maggie had been a wife and mother who'd lived in a beautiful town house. Now she struggled to survive.

Remi smiled warmly at the woman. Maggie had told Remi that the worst part of living on the street was that no one ever looked at her anymore. It was as if she was invisible. "Hey, Maggie, how are you?"

Maggie sent a wary glance toward Ash before answering. "Same ol', same ol'."

"Did you get to the clinic to have your feet treated?" Remi asked. The older woman had been complaining about blisters that had become infected on the bottom of her soles.

"Yep. And I got some spiffy new shoes." Maggie pulled back the blanket to reveal the black sneakers.

Remi took a moment to admire the shoes. "Very nice."

Maggie grimaced, an old pain flaring through her dark eyes. No doubt she'd once worn designer shoes. Now she was stuck in sneakers pulled from a charity box. "They at least don't have any holes in them," she said.

Remi held out the grocery bag. "I have some sandwiches."

"Thanks." The older woman hesitantly reached in to grab the food and tucked it under the blanket. As if afraid someone might take it away. Then she sent another glance toward Ash. "Who's that?"

"A friend." Remi glanced over her shoulder, not surprised

to discover that the stubborn man had moved until he was just an inch behind her. "He's here to help keep me safe," she told Maggie.

"About time you figured out how dangerous it is out here." The woman pointed her finger toward Ash. "I hope you're carrying."

Ash shrugged. "I can take care of Ms. Walsh."

Maggie sniffed, clearly disappointed that Ash hadn't pulled out a gun and waved it around. Slowly, she swiveled her head back to study Remi.

"This isn't your usual day to be out here. Unless I've blacked out again."

"No, it's not my usual day," Remi assured her. "I'm looking for Roo."

"Roo?" Maggie looked alarmed. She'd become a mother figure to many of the younger people on the street. At least when she was sober enough to remember them. "Is he in trouble?"

"Nope," Remi assured her. "I just have a couple of questions for him."

Maggie heaved a sigh. "He's not gonna talk. I've tried to help, but he's going down a bad road."

"Have you seen him today?" Remi asked.

Maggie tilted back her head and squinted at the bright sunlight. "No, but it's early for him to be out. This time of day he's usually crashed at that peach house a block east of here."

"Thanks, Maggie." Remi reached out to lightly touch Maggie's shoulder. It felt dangerously frail beneath the blanket. "Go to the shelter tonight. It's too cold to be out here."

The woman nodded. "I'll be in before night falls. You stay safe."

"I will."

Straightening, Remi led Ash away from the woman, who was eagerly pulling out her bottle of vodka to lift it to her lips. A pang of sadness tugged at Remi's heart. Maggie was killing herself, but until she was willing to accept help, there was nothing Remi could do.

She was still lost in her dark thoughts as they reached the corner. About to cross the street, she was halted as Ash reached out to grasp her arm. Turning her head, she met his fierce glare.

"Remi, I've accepted that you're more familiar with this neighborhood than I am, but I draw the line at letting you walk into a crack house."

Chapter Twelve

Ash squared his shoulders and braced himself for an argument. One that he was fully prepared to win.

But even as Remi's lips parted to inform him that she was perfectly capable of taking care of herself, her eyes widened.

"There he is," she breathed, jerking away from his grip to hurry down the sidewalk. "Come on."

They headed north rather than east as Remi jogged toward the lone figure strolling at a leisurely pace.

"Hey, Roo," she called out.

The person quickly turned to reveal a lean face that was older than Ash had expected. He guessed Roo was in his early twenties, with pale features that looked chapped from the cold. His dirty blond hair was kept in long dreads and he had a dozen piercings in various places on his ears and face. Most surprising, however, was the clear intelligence in his brown eyes.

This Roo might be a dealer, but he didn't abuse his product.

Catching sight of Remi and Ash walking in his direction, Roo muttered a nasty curse. Obviously, he'd been hoping for a customer. "I haven't been selling to your pathetic delinquents," the young man growled. "So if some crybaby told you I—" Roo bit off his words as Ash halted directly in front of him. His dark eyes narrowed with suspicion. "What the hell is going on?"

Ash heard Remi heave a sigh before she was stepping to stand at Ash's side.

"He's a friend."

"Yeah, right," Roo muttered. "Do I have 'stupid' tattooed on my forehead?"

Ash pretended he didn't notice Remi's wry glance. Okay, maybe he did look like a cop. It wasn't like he could do anything about it.

Reaching into his pocket, he pulled out his money clip. Without a badge to force the dealer to talk, he was going to need another incentive. "I need information and I'm willing to pay for it," he told the younger man.

Roo continued to eye Ash as if he'd just crawled from beneath a rock, but he didn't take off. "I've told you guys I ain't no snitch," he snapped. "Find some other sucker."

"This isn't about your drug suppliers or your clients," Ash assured the dealer.

"Right." Roo shivered as a sharp wind whipped around the corner, easily cutting through his thin coat. "That's how it always starts. Just tell me this. Or tell me that. And the next I know, you have your hand up my ass and I don't have any choice but to be your damned narc."

Ash pulled out a twenty-dollar bill, holding it up in a silent temptation. "This is a one-time deal," he promised. "You never have to speak with me again." Ash was careful not to claim that Roo might not have to talk to the cops. One step at a time.

The dealer's gaze lingered on the money, his fingers tapping against the side of his legs as he considered the danger of answering Ash's question against the benefit of a quick twenty bucks.

At last, the money trumped his caution. "What do you want?"

"Tell me about Friday morning."

Roo sent a quick glance toward Remi, as if baffled by the question. "Friday morning?" He gave a shrug of his shoulders, returning his gaze to Ash. "Got up late. Hooked up with my girl around noon. Same as any other day."

"You left out your trip to Jameson Park."

Roo jerked, alarm rippling over his face before he could disguise his reaction by jutting his chin to an aggressive angle. "I don't know what the hell you're talking about."

"You were there," Ash said, his words a statement.

Roo shook his head. "Whoever told you that is a liar. A dead liar."

"Video surveillance doesn't lie," Ash drawled. He wasn't claiming he had video of Roo, just that it didn't lie.

Roo flushed with a sudden burst of anger. "That dick promised me there were no cameras."

Ash hid his smile of satisfaction as he gave another wave of the twenty. "What dick?"

Roo reached for the money. "Just a local dude."

Ash jerked back his arm, keeping the twenty just out of reach. "I need a name."

Roo sent him an angry glare. "It doesn't matter."

"No name, no money."

"We called him Weed," Roo snapped, lunging with surprising speed to grab the crisp bill from Ash's fingers. "He was killed in a drive-by last week."

Ash watched Roo stuff the twenty into his pocket, his gaze flicking down to Ash's money clip with an unmistakable eagerness. He might not be a user, but he was clearly in desperate need of cash. Ash peeled off another twenty and shoved the clip into his pocket. No need tempting the man into doing something rash.

"So why were you in the park?" he asked, once again holding up the money.

Roo narrowed his gaze, as if considering the possibility of tackling Ash and taking the money. Then, without warning, his guise of a badass drug dealer was shattered to reveal a young man who was tired of struggling from day to day.

"Look, I'm getting squeezed out here. Most suppliers want a dealer who's still young enough to peddle their shit at the schools. Or tweakers who are willing to work for a taste of the product. I need cold, hard cash to eat and pay the rent," he confessed in a harsh voice. "A few months ago, Weed expanded his business to the north. He said the rich kiddies had deep pockets and a taste for oxy. He was selling as many pills as he could get his hands on."

Ash nodded. He'd spent a year in Vice before passing his test to make detective. The drug epidemic had been overwhelming then, now . . . it was mind-boggling. "In the park?" he demanded.

Roo nodded. "He'd get there before dawn and wait for them to stroll in with their uniforms and designer backpacks and a big wad of cash. He'd hand them a baggie and they'd scurry off to their fancy schools."

Ash heard Remi muttering something beneath her breath. Probably something about jerks who peddled poison to children. He felt the same disgust. "So you decided to take over his territory after he was murdered?" he demanded.

Roo stuck out his lower lip, which was pierced with a gold hoop. "If I don't, someone else will."

Ash sent Remi a mocking glance. "Capitalism is alive and well."

"Screw this," Roo muttered. "I need to bounce."

"Wait." Ash moved to block the dealer's path, still holding the twenty in his fingers. "What did you see in the park that morning?"

Roo kept his gaze on the money. Was he reminding himself why he didn't just kick Ash in the nuts? Probably.

"Nothing," he finally ground out. "It was completely empty."

Ash studied him in disbelief. "Empty?"

The younger man gave a jerky wave of his hand. "There were a few joggers and a man standing next to the lake. I guess he was fishing."

Ash made a mental note to search along the beach. Pretending to fish would be a great way to fade into the background. "No students?" he pressed.

A look of disgust tightened Roo's narrow face. "Not that I could find. Either they already found a new supplier or they got scared off when they heard their candy-man was shot in the head."

Or Weed had lied, Ash silently added. The dealer would be a fool to give away the location of his sweet spot to a competitor. Not that Ash cared one way or another. All that mattered was finding out if Roo had seen anything that could help them. "You didn't notice a woman who might have looked like Ms. Walsh?"

The dealer glanced toward Remi before giving a shake of his head. "Nope."

Ash studied the younger man's expression. "You're sure?"

"Yeah, I'm sure," Roo insisted. "Ms. Walsh is a pain in the ass, but if I'd seen someone who looked like her, I would have remembered."

The younger man's expression was sardonic, but he couldn't entirely hide the hint of respect for Remi. The same respect he'd noticed when Maggie and Drew were talking about Remi.

She might not have the exact teaching career she'd dreamed about, but she was making a difference in the lives she touched. And he couldn't be prouder of her.

His heart swelled, but he resisted the urge to turn and gather Remi in his arms. At some point he would have to deal with the emotions that weren't buried as deeply as he thought they had been five years ago. But not now.

"You can't remember anything that might help?" He gave a wave of the cash.

Roo was silent, as if searching his mind for some information that might get him the money. "There was one thing," he at last said.

"What?"

"I was nearly run over when I was leaving."

Ash didn't know what he was expecting, but it wasn't that. "Run over?" he repeated. "By a car?"

"No, by a herd of rabbits." Roo smirked at Ash's confusion. "Of course it was a car."

Ash ignored the dealer's sarcasm. "Tell me what happened."

Roo held out his hand. "No money, no talk."

Ash handed over the twenty. "Now tell me."

The bill disappeared into the pocket with the first one. "I was leaving the park—" Roo started.

"Which exit?" Ash interrupted.

"The one with the weird-ass lions."

Ash lifted his brows. "Griffins?"

"Whatever." Roo shrugged, unperturbed that he didn't recognize the mythical creature. "When I reached the exit, a car was gunning its engine behind me, and the next thing I knew it was jumping the curb. I had to leap into the bushes to keep from getting hit."

Ash started to dismiss the incident. There were a thousand crazy drivers in the city. He'd almost been run over a dozen times. Then he paused, forcing himself to try to imagine what had happened that morning. The park would have been quiet. Just a few joggers and a man fishing, Roo had said. The killer had followed Angel into the wooded area. Or lured her there to meet him. Then he'd struck, slicing her throat and leaving the telltale mark on her breast.

What would he be feeling? Elation? Panic? Cold-blooded satisfaction? One thing was certain: He would want to be far from the area before the body was discovered.

"Do you think it was intentionally trying to hurt you?"

"Naw. There was a patch of ice on the road. I think they lost control." Roo suddenly squinted his eyes, as if struck by a thought. "'Course, they did cause me a lot of pain, and my clothes were ripped to hell. If you find out who it was driving the car, I want some money for the damage they caused."

"I'll keep that in mind," Ash said with a wry smile. Roo was a born hustler. "Do you remember anything about the vehicle?"

"Yeah. It was impossible to forget."

"Why do you say that?" Ash demanded.

"It was a yellow Mustang with flames painted on the side." Roo described the car without hesitation. "You don't see many of those around."

There was a shocked sound from Remi as she abruptly took a step forward. "Are you sure?"

Roo sent her a puzzled glance. "The thing nearly rammed up my ass. I'm sure."

Ash reached out to wrap an arm around Remi's shoulders even as he firmly diverted Roo's attention back in his direction.

"Did you see which way it headed?"

"North."

"Anything else?"

"I went home."

Ash studied the thin face framed by the dreads for a long, silent moment. The younger man's words had rung true, but Ash wasn't an idiot. Roo was a skilled liar and manipulator. "If you were involved or know who killed that woman, you're going to have an easier time if you go to the cops now," he warned in tones that had made grown men tremble.

Roo, however, had faced down gangbangers, rival dealers, and God knew how many cops. He wasn't going to be intimidated.

"I wasn't involved and if you have the surveillance you claim, you know I wasn't," he drawled, throwing Ash's words back in his face. "I'm outta here."

This time Roo turned and jogged across the street, his back stiff with unspoken warning. He was done with the interview.

Keeping his arm wrapped around Remi's shoulders, Ash steered her back to the car. Her face was pale in the afternoon sunlight, and several strands of her dark hair had been pulled loose from their braid by the stiff breeze.

He knew exactly what was wrong with her as he urged her into the passenger seat before hurrying to take his place behind the steering wheel. Remi was too distracted to drive.

She waited until he'd pulled away from the curb and headed out of the shabby neighborhood before she at last asked the question that was trembling on her lips. "The car that nearly hit Roo . . ." She twisted her fingers in her lap. "It sounded like my dad's."

Ash forced himself to give a casual shrug. She had

enough to worry about without adding ghosts to her fears. He intended to have the answer of whether the car had any connection to her father by the end of tomorrow.

"Gage wasn't the only one with a Mustang in Chicago," he said.

"No, but as Roo said, the yellow with flames on the side can't be that common," she insisted. "I remember Dad telling me that he had his custom painted."

"I'm sure it's a coincidence," he said, sending her a quick smile.

Remi settled back in her seat, her expression troubled. She wasn't satisfied, but she accepted that Ash didn't have the answer she wanted. At least not yet.

"Did you believe Roo?" she instead asked.

Ash snorted, turning onto the main thoroughfare, heading toward the west side of Chicago. "Not as far as I can throw him," he said.

He could feel her gaze lingering on his profile. "Do you think he was at the park?"

Ash grimaced. "Yeah, I think he was there. I'm just not sure everything he told us was the truth."

"Why would he lie?"

That was easy enough to figure out. Ash had interviewed hundreds of witnesses and all of them had a reason to tell him something that wasn't the full truth.

"Habit. Covering for a friend. Covering for himself," he said. "A desire to 'stick it to the man.'"

She heaved a frustrated sigh, her gaze drifting toward the windshield. Her brows tugged together as she leaned forward, belatedly realizing they weren't headed toward her house.

"Where are we going?"

"I thought we'd have an early dinner at Tiramisu," he told her.

When they'd first started dating, the small Italian restaurant had been their favorite place to eat. It'd been quiet and romantic, and the food was the best in the city. He told himself that he wanted to allow her to relax and enjoy a good meal. It had nothing to do with trying to remind her of the days when they were happy together.

His lips twisted as he returned his concentration to the traffic darting around him.

"Shouldn't we go tell Jax what we found out?" she asked with a distinct lack of enthusiasm.

Was she as eager as he was to forget the world for an hour or two?

Ash tightened his hands on the steering wheel and silently reminded himself not to press for more than Remi was ready to offer. If he spooked her, she'd once again turn away from him. He couldn't risk that.

"I'm hoping my brother finally went home to get some rest," he told her. "I'll go see him in the morning. Right now, we have nothing to do but enjoy a few hours of peace."

She released a slow breath. "Okay."

Chapter Thirteen

Rachel tried to suppress her burst of frustration. What had she been expecting? A penthouse suite at the Four Seasons? The director had been very clear that this role was going to be demanding. Not only by insisting on the alterations to her face but by spending a few weeks rehearsing her role. She had to practice how to style her hair and put on her makeup. She had to wear different clothes. And most importantly, she had to learn how to walk and talk so she could be believable as Remi Walsh.

She'd already started by studying the newspaper clippings while she was at the clinic. First, she concentrated on the ones of Remi Walsh when she was a young socialite. The papers had loved to photograph her. She was lovely, rich, and engaged to a handsome detective. Plus, she was often attending charity events that encouraged reporters to attend.

Then she studied the news after the poor woman had been attacked by the Butcher. She'd been hounded by the press as she'd left the hospital and then when she'd gone to the police station to offer her official statement.

Remi had changed from a vivacious woman with a quick smile to a pale imitation who had ended her engagement and faded into the shadows. Rachel understood that it was imperative she capture that change. Something she found harder than she'd expected. What did it feel like to know your father sacrificed his life to save you? Rachel didn't have a clue. Her own father would have bailed at the first hint of danger, leaving her to deal with the crazed killer. He was all about self-preservation.

With a sigh, she glanced around the room that was supposedly an exact replica of Remi's bedroom the night she was attacked by the Butcher. It was elegant rather than pretty, with an ivory satin and gold décor. Just the sort of princess bedroom Rachel always dreamed of having. But there was no window, or it had been boarded over behind the heavy curtains that had been pulled tightly together, giving the sensation she'd traded one prison for another.

Unease crawled through her, feeling as if she had bugs scurrying across her skin. She wished she'd stop thinking about prisons. This was a new beginning for her. A way to hit the Restart button on her life. She wasn't going to screw it up because of her sudden bout of anxiety. It was just nerves trying to get the best of her.

She'd escaped from her ugly fate. From now on, there was nothing but opportunity in her future. Right?

"Why have you stopped?"

The words from the director crackled through the speaker in the ceiling, reminding Rachel that she was being constantly watched.

Dammit.

She squared her shoulders and concentrated as she walked across the room and perched on the edge of the bed.

There was an edge in the director's voice that warned Rachel she wasn't performing up to the level that was expected of her.

Time to up her game.

* * *

Ash rolled out of bed at the crack of dawn, ready to join Remi in her morning run. Once they returned, however, he waited for her to hit the shower before he was grabbing his car keys and heading out of the house. He wasn't trying to be sneaky. Okay, maybe a little sneaky. But he wanted to have the opportunity to check out Gage's Mustang without Remi.

Calling Jax to make sure that he would send a patrol car to keep a watch on the house, Ash cut through the side streets to reach the elegant mansion north of town. Parking around the corner, he used a narrow opening in the hedges to enter the grounds. Remi had shown him the nearly hidden pathway after they started dating. Her mother had never fully approved of Ash. He didn't know if it was because he was a cop or because his family didn't own a big house and a membership at the country club. Whatever the case, it was easier to avoid her disapproving glare when he wanted to spend a few minutes with Remi before heading to work, or to his apartment at the end of his shift.

Now he strolled along the edge of the neatly trimmed bushes, circling the pool house to head toward the detached brick garage that was three times the size of most homes. According to local gossip, Liza Harding-Walsh's grandfather had used the building as a speakeasy during Prohibition, while her father had run an illegal gambling parlor there in the sixties and seventies. Ash was fairly certain, however, that Gage had never used the building for anything but a place to park his cars.

Cutting through the empty garden, Ash did his best not to be seen from the mansion without actually getting on his hands and knees to creep over the flower beds that were covered in straw. If he got caught, he wanted to be able to claim he was there for a friendly visit, not to illegally search for evidence.

The sky was leaden overhead with the looming threat of snow. Thankfully, the wind had turned from turbo to merely breezy. The temperature was still frigid enough to turn his breath into puffs of icy mist, but he could feel his nose. A minor miracle during a Chicago winter.

Hurrying toward the back door of the garage, Ash was brought to an abrupt halt by the sound of a male voice calling out.

"Stop! What are you doing?"

Muttering a curse beneath his breath, Ash forced himself to turn and meet the accusing glare of Albert Martin.

"Easy, Albert," he said, lifting his hands. "It's me."

The longtime gardener, chauffeur, and all-around handyman widened his hazel eyes in surprise.

He was a short man with a solid frame and dark hair that was balding in a pattern that looked like someone had shaved a stripe down the center of his head. His skin was darker than Ash's and his features a combination of his multiracial background.

Albert had worked at the estate for years, and Ash knew he was one of Gage's most trusted employees.

"Detective Marcel?"

Ash lowered his hands, smiling in what he hoped was a casual manner. "It's just Ash now."

"That's right. You became a teacher, right?" the older man asked.

"Not according to some of my students," Ash assured him in dry tones. "How are you?"

Albert patted his stomach, which was still flat beneath his heavy coveralls. During his time of dating Remi, Ash had watched the older man bustle around the estate. He worked as hard as three men put together.

"Getting old."

Ash snorted. "You'll outlive us all, Albert," he said

with absolute confidence. "What about your family? Are they well?"

Albert nodded. "My wife is still working at the hospital and the boys have started their own landscaping business."

Ash quickly dredged through his memories to recall that Albert was married to a nurse and that they had two sons who must be in their midtwenties.

"Good for them. You must be proud."

"Yes, sir." A smile of pure satisfaction curled Albert's lips before he was casting a quick glance toward the nearby house. No doubt he was reminding himself that he was on duty. He cleared his throat, returning his gaze to Ash. "Can I ask what you're doing here?"

Ash rapidly searched his mind for a response that wouldn't get him run off the property. Then, with a flash of inspiration, he realized he had the perfect excuse standing right in front of him. "I actually wanted to chat with you," he told his companion, waving his hand toward the nearby garage. "Can we get out of the cold?"

Albert didn't hesitate. "Sure."

Pulling out a large ring with dozens of keys, he unlocked the door and pushed it open. Ash quickly followed behind him, wanting to get a good look before the man had a chance to change his mind.

Albert switched on the overhead lights, revealing the long, open space. Ash glanced around, suddenly recalling his amazement the first time Remi had brought him into the garage. It was completely paneled in a dark, glossy wood, even the ceiling. The floor was a polished cement with flecks of color that glittered like jewels. There were five bays for the cars in front of him, and on the far end were built-in cabinets that went from floor to ceiling. And across the room, set in the wall, was a massive safe painted a bright red with an old-fashioned gold lock on the front.

It was easy to see why people might assume this place was more than just a garage.

"It looks just the same," he murmured softly.

"Mrs. Liza wanted everything to be kept just as it was before—"

Albert always referred to the Walsh family like a servant from the Old South. Probably at Liza Harding-Walsh's insistence. She liked to remind people that she was a person of importance.

"Yeah, I get it," Ash said, reaching out to lightly pat Albert's shoulder.

Ash knew Albert had been devoted to Gage. The two of them enjoyed working on cars together, as well as both being avid Chicago Bulls fans. The servant was still clearly grieving for his old friend.

"It's hard to let go," Albert said.

Ash nodded, feeling the old ache in the center of his being. Gage Walsh had been his mentor, his partner, and the man who was going to be his father-in-law. And he missed him every damned day.

"Is the rest of the staff still around?" he asked, casually strolling down the center of the room.

"No, it's only me and Ms. Hodges now," Albert told him.

Ms. Hodges was the housekeeper. A middle-aged woman who Remi swore had the patience of a saint to deal with her mother.

"That must keep you busy."

Albert shrugged. "It's not too bad. Mrs. Liza rarely entertains at home anymore, and she drives herself unless she's attending a formal event."

Ash continued forward, wondering if there was a reason Liza no longer wanted a dozen servants flittering around the place. Had her finances tightened? Or had she decided that it was ridiculous to have such a large staff to take care of one woman?

Dismissing the question from his mind, Ash studied the cars parked in the bays. One was a glossy black Bentley that was worth a fortune. In the middle was a silver sedan. And at the far end was the Mustang.

"Which car does Liza drive?" he asked.

Albert nodded toward the sedan. "The BMW."

"Never the Mustang?"

Albert moved to stand beside Ash, his expression suddenly tight with suspicion. "What's going on, Detective?"

Ash didn't bother to remind the man that he was no longer with the force. For those who knew him in Chicago, he'd always be a cop. "I'm not sure if you heard the news that a young woman was found with her throat slit in a nearby park?"

Albert nodded slowly, his expression still wary. "My wife was telling me about it."

"Did she say that the victim looked exactly like Remi?"

He heard Albert suck in a sharp breath. "You think that monster is killing again?"

"I do. That's why I'm back in Chicago."

A genuine horror tightened Albert's features. "Have you told Miss Remi?"

Ash nodded. "I'm staying at her house."

"Good. She needs you." Albert held Ash's gaze, almost as if he was silently chiding him. "She's *always* needed you."

Ash snorted. Did the man think he was the one who pushed her away? "She wouldn't agree with you," he said.

Albert waved away his explanation. "Her head was all messed up. Can you blame her?"

Did he blame her? Ash gave a mental shrug. Maybe a little. He'd tried to be the man she could turn to in times of trouble, but it hadn't been enough. The knowledge had destroyed a small piece of his heart.

Still, he would give his life to make sure she was safe.

"I know, Albert," he said with a small sigh. "Which is why I'm going to make damned sure she doesn't have to go through anything like that again."

Albert squared his shoulders, his face hardening with determination. "What can I do?"

Ash's lips parted to offer a glib lie, only to have the words dry on his lips. There was no mistaking Albert's fierce desire to help. He'd known Remi since she was a baby.

"I've been doing some investigating separate from the police," Ash forced himself to confess.

Albert tilted his head to the side. "Why would it be separate?"

"I'm no longer with the force," he reminded his companion. "Which actually is a good thing. I don't have to worry about all the tedious rules and regulations."

"Is that legal?"

"I don't care," Ash said without apology. "Gage sacrificed everything to try to protect Remi. I plan to do the same."

A deep sadness touched Albert's face before he was giving a firm nod. "That's true." The man stepped closer to Ash and lowered his voice, as if worried they might be overheard. "What are you investigating?"

"I've been trying to locate anyone who might have been in the park the morning the woman was murdered."

"Did you find someone?"

"I did."

Albert looked impressed. "They saw the Butcher?"

Ash grimaced, silently reminding himself to ask Jax to check the surveillance tape for joggers and fishermen. It was a long shot that one of them could be the killer, but it would be a perfect way to fade into the background.

"Impossible to know for certain," he admitted. "But he did give me one clue."

"What was it?"

Ash took a second to consider his response. If the Mustang had no connection to the park, he was going to upset Albert for no reason. And if it did have a connection . . . He shuddered. In truth, he hadn't fully considered the possibility or the potential fallout.

Giving a small shake of his head, Ash shoved aside his sudden doubt. Instead, he glanced toward Gage's car. "The man who was in the park was nearly run over by a yellow Mustang with flames painted on the side," he told his companion.

Albert made a choked sound as he moved to stand in front of the Mustang. As if he intended to protect it from Ash.

"You can't think it was this car?"

"I have to check." Ash offered an apologetic smile even as he moved to the side of the car, his gaze running over the glossy automobile. In the shadowed bay, it was hard to determine if there was any indication it'd recently been driving through the park. "Does anyone use the Mustang?"

"No one but me." Albert's tone was oddly tight. Like he was being strangled by some unseen source. "I take all the cars out at least a couple of times a month to make sure the engines are running smooth."

Ash gave an absent nod, rounding the back of the car. "When was the last time you had the Mustang out?"

"Not the morning the woman was killed, if that's what you're asking."

Ash jerked up his head, studying Albert's flushed face with a pang of regret. Clearly, the man had assumed he was there to accuse him of the crime.

"I'm not trying to imply you were involved, Albert," Ash assured him.

"Right," Albert growled. "Everyone always blames the ex-con." He pointed a finger at Ash. "But I'll tell you this, I love Miss Remi as if she was my own daughter."

Ash held up his hands in apology. The older man wasn't just angry, he was deeply hurt. "I know. I'm not here to accuse you, I swear."

Albert jutted out his chin. "Then why look at the car?"

Ash chose his words with care. "It's possible that someone besides you drove it."

"Who else would drive it?" Albert demanded. "Mrs. Liza? Ms. Hodges?"

Ash shrugged. He had to agree it seemed unlikely the two women were involved. "I was thinking more about the employees who've worked here over the years," he clarified. "I remember Gage complaining that his home had a revolving door for the staff."

The stiffness in Albert's shoulders slowly eased. Still, his expression remained guarded.

"Mrs. Liza can be demanding," he admitted slowly.

Ash pressed his lips together to prevent them from curling into a mocking smile. Liza Harding-Walsh was a tyrant when it came to her employees. Gage had told him more than once that he never bothered to learn the names of the maids and gardeners. They were certain to be gone by the end of the week.

Only Ms. Hodges and Albert had remained longer than three months.

"Very diplomatic," he murmured.

Albert's brows snapped together, as if he was offended by Ash's response. "Do you know how I got a job here?" he asked.

Ash was caught off guard by the question. Gage had

talked about Albert during their time as partners, although he hadn't ever abused the older man's privacy. "All Gage said was that you needed a job as a condition of your parole."

Albert folded his arms over his chest. "I'd just finished serving a six-year stint for car theft," Albert admitted. "Before that, I'd been in and out of trouble since I was in grade school. No one wanted to hire me and I don't blame them. I was a bad risk."

Albert's tone was flat, but Ash sensed the older man carried deep scars. Had he endured a violent childhood? Or was it just regret for his bad choices? Hard to say.

"Gage clearly had faith in you," Ash told his companion. And it was true. Gage had trusted this man as much as he trusted anyone. "He understood that you'd paid for your crimes and were ready for a new start."

Albert lifted his brows, as if surprised by Ash's words. "Mr. Gage wasn't the one who hired me," he said. "It was Mrs. Liza."

Ash took a full second to absorb what the handyman was telling him. "Liza hired you?" he demanded, wondering if he'd heard wrong.

Albert nodded. "Yep."

Ash shook his head, trying to picture Liza Harding-Walsh choosing an ex-con to work at her elegant mansion. "How did she know about you?" he demanded in confusion.

"My uncle worked for her family."

"Ah." A derisive smile curved Ash's lips. Remi's mom was so rigidly proper and such an important member of Chicago society, it was easy to forget she came from a family of gangsters.

"Uncle Jake called Mrs. Liza, and she agreed to give me a chance as a handyman around the estate." Albert eyed him, clearly sensing Ash's lack of appreciation for what the older woman had offered. "I'll always be grateful. If it hadn't been for her, I would have been back in jail."

Ash dismissed the tiny voice in the back of his mind that questioned whether Albert's uncle had a way to force Liza to give his nephew a chance. He was prejudiced against the older woman after she'd made it painfully clear he wasn't good enough for her daughter.

Something a trained detective understood was dangerous. It blurred his ability to see clearly.

"But the other employees weren't as loyal to the Walshes?" he asked.

"They weren't loyal to anyone," Albert said in disgust. "They spent more time trying to avoid work than just doing it. I wasn't sorry to see most of them go."

"How many of them had keys to the garage?"

Albert studied him, as if waiting for him to finish the sentence. "How many since when?"

Ash considered the question. They'd never precisely pinpointed the start of the Butcher's killing spree. It was assumed it had been going on at least three years before they discovered the connection of the murders, but it could have been longer.

"Let's make it in the past ten years."

"Ten years?" Albert stared at him in confusion. "Are you serious?"

"Unless you've had the locks changed since then?"

Albert shook his head. "I doubt the locks have ever been changed."

"I just want an estimate," Ash assured him.

The handyman thought for a second before offering his guess. "At least six or seven stayed long enough to be given keys to the garage."

"And any of them could make a copy."

"Along with anyone else who worked here."

Ash braced himself. He didn't need Albert's grim expression to know he wasn't going to like what he had to say. "What are you talking about?"

"Mr. Gage always tossed his keys in a bowl on the kitchen counter when he came home."

"Damn." Frustration bubbled through him. He understood Gage's lack of concern for security. Who would steal from a cop? But it doubled the number of people who could have keys in their possession. If he decided they needed to be investigated, it was going to take forever. He swallowed a sigh as he turned back toward the car. "Do you remember the last time you had the Mustang out?"

This time Albert answered the question. "It was the first of the month."

"And it hasn't been moved since then?"

"Nope."

Ash circled the back of the Mustang. He really wasn't much of a car guy. Most mornings, he got into his vehicle, turned the key, and hoped it started. Now he wished he'd paid more attention to his father's lectures on the care and maintenance of his vehicles. Maybe he would be able to detect some small clue that would prove it hadn't been out of the garage for the past two weeks.

"Are you here every day?" he finally asked.

"I have the weekends off unless Mrs. Liza needs me to drive her to an event."

Ash strolled to the side of the car, peering into the interior at the yellow leather seats and sleek dashboard. Gage had once taken Ash on a ride through the back roads outside the city in his beloved Mustang. The older man had scared the shit out of Ash as he'd raced over the gravel roads at a speed that would make anyone see their life flashing before their eyes.

That was the last time he'd been in the car.

"When do you usually arrive for work?" he asked Albert.

"I try to be here around eight." The older man smiled with wry amusement. "It used to be earlier, but my wife put her foot down and insisted that we have breakfast together."

"I don't blame her," Ash said, silently acknowledging that it was possible for someone to have taken out the Mustang on Friday and have it back before Albert arrived at the estate.

He bent down to study the tires.

"What are you doing?" Albert asked.

"The witness told me that he'd had to jump into a ditch to avoid the car, which nearly ran him down," Ash said. "If this is the car, there might be some damage."

Albert moved to stand at his side. "Is there anything?"

Ash reached under the wheel well, searching for a stray branch that might have got stuck up there.

"Nothing," Ash said, glancing up at the man standing beside him. "Do you check the odometer?"

"Only to see if it's time for an oil change. I don't keep a weekly log or anything."

Accepting that there was no way to prove or disprove this was the car Roo claimed was in the park, Ash started to rise to his feet. At the same time, his gaze caught sight of a small lump behind the tire.

Ash reached out to grab the object, pulling it from beneath the car.

"What's this?" He rose to his feet, allowing the overhead lights to reveal a black leather glove. He held it toward Albert. "Yours?"

Albert reached toward it, a weird expression on his face. "No." His eyes became distant, as if he was overwhelmed with memories. "It belonged to Mr. Gage."

Ash jerked with shock. Gage's glove? The man had been dead for five years. It couldn't have been lying on the garage floor since then, could it?

"Are you sure?"

"Positive. They were a gift from Mrs. Liza." Albert turned over the glove to reveal the gold G.W. that was stitched on the cuff. "She had them monogrammed."

Ash reached out to take back the glove, running his fingers over the butter-soft material. He should have guessed it belonged to Gage. It was too expensive for one of his staff to own.

So where the hell had it come from?

"Could the gloves have been in the Mustang?" he demanded. It was possible someone had accidentally kicked the glove when they were climbing in or out of the car.

Albert gave an emphatic shake of his head. "No. He only wore them when he was forced by Mrs. Liza to go with her to a fancy event."

Ash believed the man. Gage was a cop who came from humble beginnings and liked the simple things in life. Ash had always been amazed that he'd ended up marrying Liza Harding. Of course, he'd never doubted that Gage adored his wife. It truly was a case of opposites being attracted to each other.

"Where did he usually keep them?"

The handyman waved a hand in the direction of the nearby mansion. "I guess he probably had them with the rest of his clothes in his closet."

Ash conjured up his memory of the tour of the house Remi had given him after they'd first started dating. He knew that her mother and father each had their own suites with large bedrooms, walk-in closets, and a connecting bathroom. He hadn't found it odd. Rich people seemed to need a lot more space. Plus, a detective had crazy hours. It was hard to share a bed when a person was being called out in the middle of the night.

"What did Liza do with Gage's clothes?"

The sadness returned to Albert's face. "Nothing. She locked the door to his private rooms and no one has been allowed in there. Not even Ms. Hodges." There was a faint buzzing sound, and Albert pulled his phone from the pocket of his coveralls. He glanced at the screen. "I have to go," he said.

Ash nodded, allowing the man to escort him out of the garage, although he kept the glove. He'd discovered all he could for now.

"Thanks, Albert," he said as they stepped into the brisk morning breeze.

Albert sent him a worried glance. "Just keep Miss Remi safe."

"You have my word," Ash promised in soft tones.

Chapter Fourteen

Remi reeled off several fine curses when she stepped out of the bathroom to realize that Ash had disappeared while she was showering. Grabbing her phone, she'd had every intention of calling him and demanding he return so she could go with him. They were supposed to be partners, weren't they?

Then, with a grimace, she tossed her phone on the kitchen counter. She was no longer Ash's fiancée. Which meant she didn't have the right to call and demand that he do anything. Even if he had promised they would work together to stop the Butcher.

Pretending she didn't care where Ash might have gone, Remi returned to her bedroom. Pulling on a casual pair of jeans and a cable-knit sweater, she braided her hair and headed into the third bedroom, which she'd converted into an office. She intended to spend a few hours at the youth center this afternoon and she wanted to create several worksheets that would help with her tutoring.

It was nearly nine a.m. when a knock on the door interrupted her concentration. Remi left her office, feeling more curious than alarmed. She didn't have any doubt that Ash had made sure there was a cop watching her house. He was nothing if not predictable.

Still, she glanced through the spyhole in the door before pulling it open with a flare of surprise.

"Mrs. Marcel?" she breathed, staring at the woman she hadn't seen in years.

June Marcel was a small woman with a halo of dark curls and a dimpled face. She looked far too young to have grown sons, but it was her frenetic energy that most people first noticed. It buzzed around her like a force field. Remi didn't know if it was the result of being the mother of four epically active boys, or just a natural part of her.

This morning, she was wearing the same plaid coat Remi remembered and holding a well-used Tupperware container.

"No one calls me Mrs. Marcel," the older woman chided. "I'm June. Or Mom."

A dull pain throbbed through Remi. Once, she'd shyly called this woman Mom. It wasn't in an effort to latch on to a mother figure. She already had that. It was a symbol that she'd become a member of the Marcel family.

"Come in," she murmured, stepping back so the older woman could enter the house. "I'm afraid Ash isn't here right now. I could call him if you want."

June waited until Remi had closed the door and turned to face her. "I'm not here to see my son," she said with a smile that could warm even a frigid Chicago morning. "I'm here to see you."

"Me?" Remi felt a sudden jolt of anxiety. When she'd seen June standing on her porch, she'd just assumed she was here to see her son. "Why?"

"We haven't had a nice chat in years."

Remi wasn't fooled by the sweet smile and innocent expression. By chat, the woman meant a quizzing that would rival the Spanish Inquisition.

"I . . ." Remi licked her dry lips, searching for a reasonable excuse to escape. "Actually . . ."

June held up the Tupperware container. "I brought coffee cake."

Remi's mouth instantly watered. Like Pavlov's dog. There was no one who could cook like June Marcel. "Cinnamon pecan?" she asked.

June's eyes sparkled with an evil amusement. "That's the one."

Remi's lips twitched. "You should have been the detective," she told the older woman. "You could make the most hardened criminal talk."

"I'll take that as a compliment."

Conceding defeat, Remi turned to lead June through the living room. "Let's go into the kitchen and I'll make some coffee."

June walked behind Remi at a leisurely pace, giving the older woman plenty of opportunity to glance around the living room with obvious curiosity. "What a charming house," she said.

"It suits me," Remi said, crossing the kitchen to start the coffee maker.

Eventually, June appeared and set the container on the breakfast bar before she was shrugging out of her coat. "Ash mentioned it belonged to your grandparents?"

"It did." Remi collected two mugs and spooned two teaspoons of sugar into June's. She assumed the woman still had her sweet tooth. "I have a lot of great memories here."

"And that's what makes a house a home."

"Yes," Remi agreed.

This house wasn't a showstopper, but it had a warmth that came from the love her grandparents had shared. She gathered two plates and a knife before returning to pour out the coffee. By the time she'd climbed onto the high stool, the older woman had the cake cut and a large slice was shoved in front of her.

Remi didn't protest. She would take another jog in the gym at the youth center. There were some calories more worthy of sweat than others.

She took a big bite, the cinnamon and sugar and butter hitting her tongue with glorious perfection.

"Yum," she breathed. "Just as delicious as I remember."

June settled on a stool next to her, sipping her coffee as she studied Remi demolishing the cake with a smile of pleasure.

"It's been too long," the older woman finally said. "I thought about calling, but I didn't know if you would want to talk to me."

Remi sent her a startled frown. "Why wouldn't I?"

June cleared her throat, obviously choosing her words with care. "I was never sure of the reason you broke off your engagement to my son. I was afraid you might be angry with the entire Marcel clan."

Remi glanced down at her nearly empty plate, feeling a pang of guilt. She'd been so caught up in her own emotional trauma that she'd never considered how her retreat from Ash might have affected others.

"I was never angry with anyone." She forced herself to lift her head and meet June's searching gaze. She owed the older woman that much. "Certainly not you."

June reached out, lightly touching Remi's hand. "It's not my business, but if you weren't angry, why did you push Ash away?"

Remi resisted the urge to shake off the woman's touch. She didn't want to talk about the past. Especially not now. The return of the Butcher had stripped away the thin layer of protection that had allowed her to pretend her life was getting back to normal. It left her feeling raw and vulnerable.

"It was too painful," she forced herself to admit.

June squeezed her fingers. "Did you blame him for your father's death?"

"No," she sharply denied. "Never."

A sad expression settled on the older woman's face. "That's what he believed."

Remi flinched. She wanted to tell June that she hadn't realized what she was doing to Ash, but the words stuck in her throat. For five years, she'd told herself that she wanted to protect the man she loved. She'd already lost her father; she couldn't bear to put Ash in danger.

And that was a big part of her need to build a barrier between them. But it wasn't the full reason.

"I didn't blame him, I blamed myself," she confessed, her voice oddly harsh. "It was all my fault."

June stiffened her spine, a sudden anger flashing through her eyes. "Nonsense. How could you even think such a ridiculous thing?"

"It's not ridiculous." A queasy sensation rolled through her stomach. She'd had endless nightmares about the horror her father must have endured when he walked into the house to try to find her. No one knew exactly what had happened. She'd been unconscious in the kitchen, and while there'd been a gruesome amount of blood on the living-room floor to indicate her father had received a killing blow, his body had never been found. Somehow, the fact they'd never had a proper burial for him had only made it more difficult to put the past behind her. "My dad was trying to save me when he was murdered."

"Exactly," June said in a stern voice. "He was killed by the Butcher, not you."

Remi swallowed a frustrated sigh. June didn't understand. How could she?

"But he wouldn't have been there that night if I hadn't called to say I thought I was being followed," Remi reminded her companion.

June leaned toward her, her features soft with sympathy. "You think your father would have preferred that you hadn't called, that you'd become another victim?"

"No, but—"

"The only one at fault is the Butcher," the older woman insisted.

They were the same words Remi had heard over and over again. Until they'd become a yammering chorus that gave her a headache.

"Logically, I understand that." She gave a sharp shake of her head. "But my heart still says that my father would be alive if it wasn't for me."

"So you're punishing yourself by pushing everyone away?"

Remi's brows snapped together. "That's not what I'm doing," she protested.

"It's not?"

"I just . . ." Remi closed her mind to the accusation. She had too much to process. She was adding to the mess in her mind. Instead, she fell back to her most convenient excuse. "I can't put anyone else in danger."

June's hand moved to rub over Remi's shoulder in a soothing motion. "What danger?"

Remi pushed aside her empty plate, hating the feeling that her stomach was being twisted into knots. She'd struggled for years to get rid of the awful sensation. Now it was back with a vengeance.

"I've always known the Butcher would return." She glanced toward the kitchen window, as if expecting to see the monster standing in the middle of her yard. Sometimes it felt like he was there even if she couldn't see him. "And that he would strike again." She drew in a shaky breath. "I'd already lost my father. I wasn't going to lose Ash."

"But you did."

Remi hissed at the soft words, as if she'd been struck by an unseen weapon. Or maybe she'd just been hit by the truth.

Either way, it was painful.

"Stop trying to make sense of what was going on in my mind," she pleaded. "It's a disaster in there."

A deep sorrow darkened June's eyes before she was briskly grabbing Remi's empty plate and filling it with another slice of coffee cake.

"There's one way to clear the clutter," she said, returning the plate directly in front of Remi.

"Don't say a therapist," Remi groused, reaching for her fork. She'd take two jogs tonight. Right now, she needed the sweet, ooey goodness. "I know they're fabulous for some people, but I'm not interested."

June shrugged, grabbing her mug of coffee. "Then talk to me."

Remi swallowed the large chunk of coffee cake she'd shoved into her mouth. "You?"

"I'm a pretty good listener."

Remi believed her. "You'd have to be, with four boys."

June studied her with a somber expression. "Remi, I consider you a part of my family, whether you are engaged to Ash or not," she assured her. "You can trust me. Whatever you tell me will never leave this room. Let's start with the night you were attacked."

Remi shoved another bite of cake into her mouth. "There's really nothing to talk about. I don't remember anything from that night," she mumbled.

"Nothing at all?"

With a sigh, Remi set down her fork. June wasn't going to be satisfied until she'd heard every detail of the few scraps of memory Remi possessed.

"I remember that I went to my classes and that I stayed late on campus to attend an open house at the art gallery," she said, barely able to recall the young coed who'd been filled with a belief that nothing could steal her glorious future.

"Alone?" June asked.

"Yep. It was worth extra credit in my art appreciation class. And Ash was working." Remi wrinkled her nose. At the time, she'd been more resigned than annoyed when Ash had called her to say he wouldn't be able to join her for the event. Being a detective meant his schedule was always crazy, but with a serial killer on the loose, he'd practically disappeared from her life. "As usual."

June heaved a small sigh. "A Marcel trait, I'm afraid. Only Nate has learned there's more to life than his job."

Remi shook herself out of her dark memories, offering her companion a small smile. "I haven't told you how happy I am to hear Nate is getting married," she said. She hadn't known Nate as well as the other brothers. His job with the FBI had kept him away from home most of the time. But she'd always enjoyed his lighthearted teasing when they'd been together. "I hope his fiancée appreciates what a great guy she's going to have as a husband."

"Ellie is wonderful," June said with genuine satisfaction, holding Remi's gaze. "My boys have shown excellent taste in women."

Color rushed to Remi's cheeks. There was no mistaking the older woman was referring to her. "I wouldn't say that."

"I would," June insisted. Then, with a grimace, she

returned the conversation to the past. "What happened after you left the art gallery?"

Remi swallowed a sigh. The sooner she was done with the story, the sooner she could try to tuck it into the back of her mind.

"I was supposed to meet Ash after he was done with his shift," she continued with a pang of wry amusement. She'd been eager to show off a new outfit she'd bought the day before. A rare display of vanity. "So I decided to go home and have a quick shower and change my clothes before I went to his apartment."

"Is that when you noticed you were being followed?"

"Yes." Remi's amusement abruptly vanished. Her skin prickled with unease, as if she was back in her car on that fateful night. "I'd been edgy ever since Ash admitted they were looking for a serial killer. That's the reason I looked in my rearview mirror when I pulled out of the parking lot."

"What did you see?"

"Headlights behind me," Remi said.

"You couldn't see the vehicle?"

"No." She'd tried, but the darkness of the night and the blinding brightness of the headlights reflecting from the rearview mirror had made it impossible. "At first, I told myself it was meaningless that a car was pulling out of the parking lot at the same time as me. There were lots of people coming and going from the campus no matter what time it was."

"When did you get worried?"

It'd been a slow, steady process from unease to downright terror.

"I usually drove home through the side streets. It could take longer, but I avoided the traffic." She didn't have to add that the streets in the wealthier neighborhoods were wide and impeccably maintained. They were also clear of traffic jams. "After the third or fourth turn, I knew it couldn't be a coincidence that the headlights were still right behind me."

"Is that when you called your father?"

Regret sliced through Remi. It'd been sheer impulse that had her digging in her purse for her phone and calling her father. At the time, she'd simply wanted the reassurance of his voice. No one could offer a sense of security like Gage Walsh.

"Yes. I didn't know what else to do," she said, her voice thick with pain.

June wrapped her arm around Remi's shoulders, giving her a tight squeeze. "That's exactly what you should have done."

"If I could go back in time . . ." Remi whispered.

"What happened next?" June demanded, clearly eager to distract Remi from her raw sense of guilt.

Remi lifted her hand, pressing her fingers to her temple. Recalling that night always gave her a headache. The doctors said it was psychosomatic. She didn't care. It hurt like hell.

"It's all fuzzy. The doctors think the drugs affected my memories." Remi shrugged. "All I know is that they found my car parked in the garage. And when I woke up, I was lying on the kitchen floor."

"My poor dear," June breathed. "You must have been so afraid."

Yes, she'd been afraid. And confused. And desperate to get help. But at the time, she hadn't realized just how horrifying the night was about to become.

"I managed to clear the fog enough to call 911, but then I blacked out again. When I regained consciousness, I was in the hospital." She was forced to halt and clear her throat. "That's when I was told that the cops had found my father's blood in the living room."

"Oh, Remi." June gave her another squeeze before she was pulling away to study Remi with a stern expression. "It was a horrible thing. But there was nothing you could have done to change what happened."

Remi shuddered. "I think that's what terrifies me the most."

"Why?"

"We like to believe we have control over our lives." Remi shook her head. "It's scary to know how little we really do."

Expecting the older woman to try to convince her that the world wasn't totally random, Remi was caught off guard when June released a sharp laugh.

"No crap," she agreed. "With four boys, I've accepted that life is crazy and messy and sometimes so scary I can barely breathe."

Remi blinked at her blunt honesty. "I don't know how you stand it."

June sipped her coffee before answering. "A lot of sleepless nights. An occasional bottle of wine. And faith that I have the strength to endure what fate has in store for me."

The words made perfect sense. Deep inside, Remi knew she had the power to overcome the past. Her parents had raised her with the belief that she could achieve anything, no matter what the hurdles. But the grief and continuing fear that her torment wasn't over had stolen her confidence.

"I've lost my faith," she breathed.

June reached out to place her fingers beneath Remi's chin, tilting it up as if she was encouraging her to go into battle. And maybe she was. A battle not only against the Butcher but her own sense of worth.

"I believe in you, Remi. I know my son believes in

you," June told her in fierce tones. "Accept our strength until you find your own again."

Remi wrinkled her nose. She wanted to reassure the older woman, but it was easier said than done. "I don't know if I can."

With brisk motions, June was climbing off the stool and grabbing her coat. "Promise that you'll at least think about what I said."

Remi gave a nod. "I promise."

"Good." June grabbed the plates and carried them to the sink. "I have to go, but I'm having a dinner for Nate and Ellie on Sunday." She turned back to send Remi a stern glance. "I expect you to be there."

Remi felt a warmth spread through her, suddenly realizing just how much she'd missed this woman. She wasn't just Ash's mother, she was a friend.

"Yes, ma'am," she promised.

"Good girl." June turned to head out of the kitchen, thankfully leaving the coffee cake behind. "Call if you need anything."

Wrong. It was all wrong.

I'd been so certain that the effort to create a perfect replica of my obsession would cure the sickness that was spreading with alarming speed. Or at least offer a few months of respite. Instead, it seemed to be making everything worse.

Clenching my hands, I watch my creation walk from one end of the room to another. I have her perch on the edge of the bed. I have her braid her hair. She has been practicing hard and her natural ability to mimic others has given her a talent the last one lacked. I try to convince myself this will be my salvation.

It doesn't work.

Against my will, I remember my fingers warm and sticky with blood. The feeling had banished the darkness, easing the gnawing pain in the center of my soul.

The malignancy doesn't care that it has been fed only days ago. Or that its hunger threatens to expose my secrets.

No. The disease is crawling through my veins and invading my mind. It has to be cut away before the madness consumes me.

Chapter Fifteen

The front door was pulled open as Ash stepped onto the porch. He conjured up his most charming smile as he studied Remi's face in the light that spilled from the house.

"I'm home."

"Hmm."

She turned to walk back into the living room, and Ash took a selfish second to appreciate the fine shape of her backside, which was shown to advantage in her soft jeans. Then, giving a shake of his head, he was hurriedly stepping inside and closing the door. It was freezing outside. Plus, he knew Remi well enough to sense she was pissed.

"I recognize that 'hmm,'" he said. "You're mad."

Coming to a halt in the center of the living room, she turned to face him. "You don't have to sneak away while I'm in the shower. If you have to go somewhere without me, you can just walk out the door."

He winced at her frosty tone. "Ouch."

She shrugged. "I just mean that you're free to come and go as you want."

"Stop." Ash stepped forward, cupping her face in his hands. He felt a genuine remorse for his childish flight that morning. "I'm sorry. I left without telling you where I was going because I didn't want to worry you. I won't do it again." Lowering his head, he brushed an impulsive kiss over her lips. "I promise."

Remi blushed, but she thankfully didn't pull away from his touch. "Why would I be worried?"

"Because I went to your mother's estate to check out the Mustang," he confessed.

He felt her stiffen. "You said it was a coincidence."

"I had to know for sure."

"And?"

Ash grimaced. "I have more questions than answers."

Her expression tightened with frustration. And something else. Was it fear?

"I don't understand," she rasped. "Was it my father's car that nearly ran over Roo or not?"

"It's really impossible to say yes or no," he told her. "There was nothing to show that it had been out of the garage since Albert had last driven it."

She blinked in confusion. "Albert was driving it?"

"He takes out all the cars to keep the batteries charged and check for any problems."

"Oh." She wrinkled her nose, her tone rueful. "Sometimes I forget how spoiled I was when I lived with my parents. I just got in my car and assumed it would be ready to go. I never even filled up the gas tank until I moved out."

His fingers brushed over her cheeks, fascinated by the soft satin of her skin. He didn't want to talk. Especially not about the Butcher. He just wanted to savor the feel of her beneath his hands.

"I didn't realize food didn't magically appear on my plate at dinnertime until I got my own place," he assured her. "Kids are supposed to be spoiled."

She trembled at the heat that sparked between them. "Speaking of food," she hastily tried to distract him, "your mother stopped by this morning."

"Ah. That explains why you taste like cinnamon." His gaze lowered to the lush temptation of her lips. He desperately wanted to kiss her again, but he sensed she was too edgy. One wrong move and she'd be pushing him away. "What did she want?"

Remi shook her head. "Not until you tell me what you found out."

Ash wanted to assure her that he'd found nothing. Why worry her? Then he had a memory of her face when she'd opened the door tonight. If he kept shutting her out, how could he expect her to lower the barriers that kept him at a distance?

"Like I said, it was impossible to know if it'd been driven or not," he said.

"But?" she pressed.

"But I discovered there could be a dozen former employees who had keys made to the car."

She furrowed her brow at his accusation. "Why would anyone want to use my father's Mustang?"

It was a question that had plagued him for the entire day. He'd shuffled through dozens of various explanations. None of them had truly satisfied him. But one did stand out as the most likely.

"It's distinctive," he reminded Remi.

"Exactly," she said.

"What better way to draw attention from yourself than to drive a vehicle that could easily be traced to your father?"

A hint of frustration rippled over her face. "Why draw attention to himself at all? He could have slipped in and out of the park unnoticed."

Ash twisted his lips in a humorless smile. "I have a wacky theory."

"Tell me."

Ash had to force out the words. "The Butcher isn't satisfied with killing anymore," he said. "He needs to punish you."

Her eyes widened. "Me?" she breathed in shock. "For what?"

Ash swallowed as he watched her face pale. This was precisely what he'd wanted to avoid. Unfortunately, he had no choice but to continue. "Surviving."

She took a second, as if she was struggling to clear a lump from her throat.

"So why hasn't he tried to kill me?"

Ash didn't have an easy answer to her legitimate question.

"It's possible that right now he's enjoying the hunt, and it has the added pleasure of tormenting you," he suggested.

"By killing other women?"

"By ensuring the women look exactly like you. And then using your father's Mustang and deliberately trying to run down a pedestrian so it would be sure to be noticed," he said. He couldn't come up with any reason to use that particular vehicle and then commit a hit-and-run except to draw attention to themselves. "The killer didn't realize Roo wasn't about to call the cops and report the car that nearly hit him."

Horror darkened her eyes. "If you're right, that would mean the Butcher is someone who worked for my parents."

Ash gave a slow nod of his head. "Or someone who visited the house and happened to wander into the kitchen. Albert said that your father would leave his keys in a bowl on the counter."

"God." She stepped away from his clinging touch, biting her lower lip. "Have you told Jax?"

"Not yet." In an effort to keep himself from reaching out to pull her close, Ash slid off his coat and tossed it on a nearby chair. "It's still just a theory, and he has enough real leads to concentrate on. I did my own investigating."

"Did you find anything?"

Ash rubbed his hands over his chilled face. It'd been a long day, and without the assistance of the police department database, he'd been forced to track down the past employees with his feet, not a computer.

"I discovered that three of the former employees have left town and two have been in the Cook County jail for the past year."

She arched her brows. "Jail?"

"Drugs."

"Oh." She didn't look particularly surprised. Obviously, the old saying was true: It *was* hard to find good help. "Did you track down anyone you could talk to?"

"Roy Parker."

"The name is vaguely familiar," she murmured.

"He worked cleaning the pool and mowing the grass around six years ago."

She heaved a small sigh. "There were so many."

"No crap."

She ignored his muttered words. She was used to having a full staff that remained mere shadows in the background. In his house, they never hired out duties. It was his father's opinion that God gave you children to take care of chores.

"What did he say?" she demanded.

Ash hid his urge to shudder. Roy Parker had reminded him of the perps he used to arrest when he still carried a badge. Whiny. Cunning. And always trying to turn a situation to his own advantage.

"He remembered that the keys to the garage and the cars were always available."

She hunched her shoulders, a wistful expression on her

face. Was she recalling the innocent days when they'd never worried about evil touching their lives?

"We never thought about it. I tossed my own keys in the bowl."

Ash pressed on, hating the knowledge he was causing Remi pain. "He also recalled that there were at least three other part-time workers who came and left in the six months he worked for your parents."

"Did my mother fire them?" she demanded.

He shrugged. "I don't know about the part-time workers, but Roy admitted it was your father who told him to leave and not come back."

She jerked, clearly caught off guard. "Dad?"

"Roy claimed he was caught sneaking an extra cigarette break in the pool house, but I can't imagine that's the full story," he said.

Surprisingly, Remi gave a firm shake of her head. "That could have been enough to get him fired."

"A smoke break?" Ash studied her in confusion. "That seems a little harsh."

"Not the smoke break, being in the pool house," she clarified. "There's an old story that my grandfather used to take anyone who double-crossed him there to be punished."

"Punished?" Ash lifted his brows. He'd heard lots of stories about the Harding family. He'd assumed most of them were exaggerations. "A stern chiding?"

She looked almost embarrassed. "A little more old school, I'm afraid," she admitted, obviously not wanting to admit that the pool house had been the site of extreme violence. "Once my grandfather died and my mother inherited the estate, my father had the doors locked to keep out trespassers who thought they would see a ghost, or worse, take a picture of the place and sell it on eBay. As far as I know, it hasn't been used for thirty years."

"The dangers of a colorful past," he teased lightly.

She offered a rueful smile. "'Colorful' is one word for it."

Sensing her unease at discussing the family business they'd hoped to bury in the past, Ash was quick to change the subject. "That's all the man could tell me," he said. "I'll try to track down the other employees tomorrow."

She gave a small nod, a visible shiver racing through her. "It gives me the creeps to think the Butcher might have been strolling around my house."

"It's more likely I'm chasing shadows," he reminded her, reaching into his pocket to pull out the soft object he'd stuffed in there earlier. Now that Remi was already upset, he might as well finish with the last of what he'd discovered. "I did find this," he said, holding it out.

Gingerly, she reached out to grab the object, smoothing the soft leather with her fingers. Then she gave a tiny gasp, her gaze lifting to reveal her pained recognition. "That's my father's glove."

"I found it under the Mustang," he said. "Albert swore it shouldn't have been in the garage."

"So how did it get there?" She glanced down at the glove in her hand. "And where's the other one?"

"Your guess is as good as mine."

She slowly lifted the glove to her face, rubbing the soft leather against her cheek as a heartbreaking tear slid down her face.

"Can't the bastard let my father rest in peace?"

Unable to bear the sight of her raw grief, Ash gently tugged the glove from her hand and placed it on the low coffee table. Then he turned back to gather her in his arms.

"Tell me why my mother was here," he urged, hoping to give her the opportunity to regain control over her emotions. She'd always hated people seeing her cry.

"She asked about the night I was attacked," she said in

a hoarse voice. "And she wanted to know why I broke off our engagement."

"Christ," Ash breathed. Talk about leaping from the frying pan into the fire. "I'm sorry, Remi. I love my mother, but she can't help sticking her nose where it doesn't belong."

A shaky smile curved her lips, her face still tragically pale. "I think she's worried I might hurt you again."

He mentally cursed his meddlesome mother. He adored her, but she was way too fond of interfering in matters that were his own business.

"I'll say something to her," he promised.

"No. She's your mother," Remi protested. "It's her job to be worried about you."

"I've been taking care of myself for a long time," he reminded her.

There was a short silence before Remi asked a question that sounded as if it'd been on her mind.

"Does your family blame me for your decision to leave the force and move away from Chicago?"

Ash lowered one arm and wrapped the other around Remi's shoulders. This sounded like a conversation that might take a while. They might as well be comfortable. "Let's go into the kitchen," he said, urging her forward. "I want a piece of that coffee cake before it disappears."

She managed a wry smile. "You know me too well."

He bent his head to brush his lips over the top of her head. "I intend to know you better."

He heard her breath catch at his low words, but she firmly pulled away as they entered the kitchen. "Did you eat dinner?" she asked, clearly hoping for some task to keep herself busy.

Ash swallowed a sigh. *Patience.*

"Unfortunately," he admitted. "The price of getting information out of Roy was taking him out for a burger and a beer. I think he ate half a cow and slurped down a pony keg before I could leave."

"A hefty price," she agreed, hovering near the doorway.

Sensing she might decide to bolt to the seclusion of her bedroom, or even take off to spend the evening with one of her friends, Ash took drastic action.

He knew one certain way to keep her in the kitchen. Grabbing two plates and a knife, he moved to the counter to cut a couple of large slices of his mother's coffee cake.

Placing one on each plate, he settled on the high barstool and pointed toward the second plate. "Here."

She placed her hand on her stomach, but she couldn't disguise her desire for the gooey sweetness. "No. I already ate three slices."

"Come on," he urged. "You know you want it."

She blew out a heavy sigh, moving to settle on the stool next to him.

"Fine, but if I can't fit into my jeans tomorrow, it's entirely your fault," she warned, taking a large bite.

"I'll take full responsibility," he assured her, pressing a lingering kiss on her lips. "Mmm. Cinnamon," he whispered.

Chapter Sixteen

The sweet, buttery richness seemed to melt on her lips as Ash brushed his mouth over hers. It was glorious. Remi sighed as a decadent pleasure jolted through her. She wanted to crawl into his lap and spend the rest of the night indulging in his sensual kisses.

Dangerous, a voice whispered in the back of her mind.

Especially when she felt battered and bruised by the thought that someone who'd worked for her family might be responsible for her father's death. Now wasn't the time to give in to her vulnerable emotions.

Reluctantly pulling back, she cleared her throat. "I asked you a question earlier," she reminded him, not surprised when the words came out as a harsh rasp.

Ash's eyes smoldered with suppressed desire, but he readily straightened and grabbed his fork to concentrate on his coffee cake. He was a man who had enough confidence in his skills as a lover to wait until she was completely comfortable in a more intimate relationship.

"The answer is, no, my family didn't blame you for my leaving Chicago," he assured her, taking a large bite. "They would be the first to tell you that I always make my own decisions."

She placed her elbow on the counter, resting her chin in the palm of her hand as she studied his finely chiseled profile.

"You were happy as a detective."

"I was. I loved my job," he assured her. "But after your father died, I needed to get away to clear my head."

She got that. Ash and her father had been closer than just partners. They'd been like father and son. She didn't doubt for a second that he'd been as devastated as she'd been by his death.

"Why not take a two-week vacation in Oklahoma with Nate?" she asked. "Quitting your job and moving away from Chicago was extreme."

He gave a small shrug, continuing to eat his cake. "I needed to remember why I'd decided to go into law enforcement. When a friend asked if I'd be interested in a position at the university, I agreed. Going back to school seemed like the perfect solution."

Remi tried to imagine him standing in front of a group of eager college students. She couldn't do it. He would always be a detective in her mind. "Was it a perfect solution?"

"At the time," he assured her. "There's nothing quite like the energy and enthusiasm of students just beginning the journey into their careers."

"Yes."

He smiled at her fervent agreement. "I guess I'm preaching to the choir."

He was. She loved being a part of young students' lives, hoping to mold them into the best people they could be. Especially those who society quite often assumed weren't worth the effort of saving.

"You said 'at the time.'" She continued to study him, tracing each hard line and curve of his face. "Have you changed your mind?"

"Being back in Chicago has made me realize I'm homesick." He turned to meet her searching gaze. "Not only for my job as a detective but for the people I love."

Excitement sizzled down her spine. "You're coming back?"

His gaze swept over her. "I'm considering my options."

There was more sizzling, making her pulse go wild. "That will delight your mother."

Without warning, he swiveled the barstool, reaching to grasp her shoulders. "Just my mother?"

The kitchen suddenly seemed smothering. Was she having a hot flash? Surely she was too young for that?

"I'm sure your whole family will be happy."

His fingers slid over her shoulders and down her arms. "And you? Will you be happy?"

"I . . ." The words died on her lips.

He leaned forward, his breath brushing over her cheek. "Tell me, Remi. Have you missed me?"

Any thought of denying the long years of misery without him was banished by the sight of the yearning in his eyes. This man had given her his heart without hesitation. How could she continue to batter it?

"Yes," she breathed.

"Say it."

She clicked her tongue. "Bossy."

His hands moved to span her waist, his expression beseeching.

"Please."

She paused, then, with a hesitant movement, she lifted her arm to brush the tips of her fingers down his jaw. His five-o'clock whiskers pressed against her skin, sending a shiver of anticipation through her.

"I've missed you."

He released a husky groan, his lips pressing against her

forehead. "I've ached for you, Remi." His voice was low, harsh with a remembered pain. "I wake in the morning and my arms are empty. I sit at the breakfast table and I'm all alone. I see something funny and I turn to share it with you, but you aren't there."

"I'm sorry."

"No." He lifted his head to gaze down at her. "This isn't about blame. I just want the barriers to be gone."

"I'm afraid." The words left her lips before she could halt them.

He blinked, obviously startled. "Of me?"

"Of us," she said, not sure how to explain the emotions that continued to haunt her. "The future."

His fleeting concern eased. "Ah. Then let's take this minute by minute."

Her lips twitched. "Live in the now?"

"Exactly."

She took a second to consider his offer. At last she gave a slow nod. "I can do that."

"Me too." With a wicked smile, he slid off the barstool. Then, grabbing her knees, he parted her legs so he could step between them. Remi instinctively tilted back her head, giving him the perfect opportunity to cover her mouth in a deep, searching kiss. Not that she was about to protest. Instead, she lifted her arms to wrap them around his neck. "Cinnamon. Sugar," he murmured against her lips. "And everything nice."

She shivered as the heat that had been smoldering inside her flamed into an inferno. "I don't feel nice right now," she informed him.

He chuckled. "How do you feel?"

"Naughty."

He pressed his hips between her legs, allowing her to

feel the hard thrust of his erection. "I'm feeling pretty naughty myself."

She licked her lips, tasting the clinging cinnamon. "I'm going to have to learn how to make your mother's coffee cake."

"It's not the coffee cake," he whispered. "It's you."

"Probably a good thing," she admitted. "I hate to cook."

His hands slid up her waist, gently cupping her breasts. "You have other talents."

She leaned back to send him a chiding glance. "Ash."

He released a sudden laugh. "I meant your ability to touch the hearts of students who most people would consider lost causes." He held her gaze. "I admire you for that."

Remi felt a blush stain her cheeks. "Thank you."

The wicked smile returned as he used his thumbs to tease at the tips of her nipples. "Although this talent isn't too shabby."

Remi shivered, arching against his hard body. "You're not too shabby yourself."

He used the tip of his tongue to trace her lips. "I'm just getting warmed up."

Remi tangled her fingers in his hair. She wasn't prepared to sleep with Ash. Not tonight. But she was fully onboard with the pleasure of sharing a few sugar-and-cinnamon kisses.

Rachel shivered. The wind felt like a knife slicing through her. It didn't matter that she had on a puffy parka and a stocking hat and matching gloves. Nothing was capable of combating a Chicago winter. Especially not when she was standing in an abandoned lot in the middle of the night.

"How much longer?" she muttered, stomping her feet in an effort to keep the circulation going to her toes.

Had she actually wished she could get out and breathe some fresh air? Now she just wanted to be back in her cozy rooms. They might make her feel claustrophobic, but at least they were warm.

There was no answer and she turned, trying to peer through the thick shadows. She'd been in this neighborhood once or twice, and each time it felt like she was taking her life in her hands. Which, of course, was the point of her being there.

The director was insistent that Rachel couldn't be convincing in her role unless she truly felt terror. As if Rachel hadn't been raised in a neighborhood where her creepy landlord loitered in the hallway so he could cop a feel when she passed by him or dodging bullets while she was walking down the street.

Still, she had to admit there was something unnerving about standing alone in the darkness. It was one thing to confront her familiar dangers. She'd learned how to cope with the grabby landlord by giving him a faceful of pepper spray. And she rarely walked the streets after dinner. It gave her a sense of security.

Now she was surrounded by the unknown. Anything could be lurking in the dark. And worse, she suspected there was going to be some nasty surprise that was intended to teach her how to react to the scene in which her character was being followed by the killer.

The thought made her as twitchy as the time her dad had tried to detox.

"Shit," she groused. "I'm freezing my ass off."

There was a crunch of footsteps against the broken pavement.

"At last," she muttered.

"Don't move," the director barked.

Rachel froze, battling the urge to turn. She wanted to see what was coming. She knew, however, that this was a test. If she failed, she might very well be sent home, her dreams shattered.

She would endure anything before she allowed that to happen.

With a grim effort, she conjured the image of her father. At this time of night, he would be passed out on the sofa. Her brothers would be stumbling home from their own evening of partying, making a mess in the kitchen that she would be expected to clean up.

The thought helped to steady her nerves as she felt an arm circle her shoulder and grasp the collar of her coat. She held herself still even when she felt the hand tugging down the puffy material. She was confused. Was she being filmed? Did they want a better view of her face?

She remained oblivious to the threat even when something was pressed against her throat.

It wasn't until the gush of warm blood flowed down her neck and drenched her sweater beneath her parka that she finally understood.

This wasn't a rehearsal.

It was the finale.

Jax was sound asleep when his phone rang. It wasn't unusual to have his night interrupted, but he wasn't on call, so he knew as soon as he opened his eyes that it had to do with the Butcher.

Crawling out of bed, he stretched his muscles, which felt stiffer than usual, and pounded down a large mug of coffee as he pulled on his clothes. He tried not to think how much harder it was every year to get himself moving as he headed to his car and drove across town. Or how he was shivering despite the fact that he had the heater blowing at full force.

He was getting old. No doubt about it.

Thankfully, he'd shaken off most of his aches and pains by the time he reached the abandoned lot. Climbing out of the car, he weaved his way through the cluster of gawkers, cops, and paramedics to take charge of the crime scene.

He crossed to the center of the lot, not surprised to discover the young, dark-haired woman with her throat cut. Still, he felt as if he'd been punched in the gut as the lights the patrol had set around the area revealed the female's features. She looked like Remi. Not an exact replica. But closer than mere coincidence.

Gritting his teeth, he forced himself to concentrate on gathering the evidence and sending the uniforms to canvas the area. The bastard was bound to make a mistake at some point. No one was perfect. He just had to be diligent enough to catch it when it happened.

It was still dark when he at last returned to his car, although there was a hint of a predawn glow at the edge of the horizon. He hesitated. He could go home and try to get a couple of hours sleep. Or head to the office. Or . . .

He put his car in gear and headed for the distant suburb.

Another innocent girl with her throat slit and the telltale mark on her breast. He was done with this shit. It was time to start rattling some cages to see what fell out. And he knew exactly who would be willing to help.

Pulling out his phone, he called Ash. He didn't want to bang on the door and scare poor Remi.

Twenty-five minutes later, he pulled next to the curb in front of the bi-level house and climbed out of the car. The door to the house was opened as he stepped onto the porch and Ash was outlined by a dim table lamp. He was wearing a pair of jogging pants and his hair was mussed. Clearly, he'd just crawled out of bed.

"Come in," he invited Jax, closing the door behind his brother and resting a hand on a large dog that was eyeing Jax with steady suspicion. "This is Buddy."

"Hey, big boy." Jax held out his hand, waiting for the dog to give a cautious sniff before he scratched the animal behind his ear. Buddy remained watchful, but he settled down next to Ash. Jax lifted his head to meet his brother's gaze. "I hope I'm not interrupting anything?"

Ash folded his arms over his bare chest. "Stop being nosy."

Jax deliberately glanced around the open foyer that offered a view of the living room and into the kitchen. The house was small but comfortable. Like his parents' home.

"I'm a detective," he reminded his brother. "It's my job."

Ash didn't look impressed. "What's happening in my bedroom is not your job."

Jax's lips twitched. "Meaning I didn't interrupt anything."

"I assume you didn't wake me up just to be a pain in the ass?"

Jax's brief amusement faded. "There's another body."

Ash's jaw clenched, but it was obvious he'd been expecting the news. "You think it was the Butcher?" he demanded.

"Her throat was slit."

"And the mark?"

"Yep."

"Damn." Ash lowered his voice, as if afraid they might be overheard. "Did she look like Remi?"

"Long dark hair, slender, pretty."

Ash held his gaze. "Was it natural?"

Jax hesitated. He wasn't worried about sharing information about the case. He was already risking his job by involving his brother. But he was reluctant to admit just how much the woman had looked like Remi.

"I'll have to wait for the medical examiner's report, but I suspect she'd recently had some work done," he said.

Ash grimaced, but he didn't press for more details. "Was she found in the same park?"

"No. It was an empty lot."

"Another change from his usual pattern."

Jax shrugged. "There's more."

"What?"

"The killer intended to burn her body."

"'Intended'?"

Jax shuddered. The scent of charred flesh had smacked him in the face the second he'd arrived at the crime scene. There was nothing quite so sickening. Thankfully, it'd been limited to her feet and legs.

"She was drenched in gasoline and lit on fire. It was sheer chance that a patrol car was driving past and the officer had the good sense to put out the flames before the woman was burned completely."

Ash reached out to give his brother's shoulder a squeeze. He was one of the few people who understood the stress of working a serial killer case. It was one thing to deal with a drive-by shooting. Or a pissed-off boyfriend. Someone died, and you investigated until you could put the guilty party in jail.

With a serial killer, the clock was always ticking. Either you found them or they murdered again. And again. And again.

It was like having a noose around your neck that was constantly tightening.

"I don't suppose he happened to notice anyone in the area?" Ash asked.

"No." Jax had interviewed the cop. He'd been so rattled,

he'd barely been able to give an account of what had happened. "He was too busy trying to put out the fire and call for an ambulance. It wasn't until I arrived that I had a sweep of the neighborhood made. So far, no one admits to seeing anything."

"Of course not." Ash muttered a low string of curses. "This destroys my theory."

"What theory?"

In brisk, concise words, Ash shared the events of the past twenty-four hours.

"You've been busy," Jax said in dry tones.

Ash shrugged. "I knew you wouldn't have time to investigate everything."

Jax suspected Ash was more worried about upsetting his potential mother-in-law.

He needn't have worried. Jax was happy to allow Ash to deal with Liza Harding-Walsh. Unless they had more than the dubious testimony of a drug dealer, he wasn't going to try to get a search warrant for the Mustang. A judge would laugh him out of his office.

"What was your theory?" he asked instead.

"I thought the Butcher was deliberately attempting to terrify Remi," Ash said, glancing toward an opening that led to a hallway. Jax assumed it led to the bedroom where Remi was still sleeping. "First by ensuring his victims look *exactly* like her and then by using her father's prized Mustang to make a flashy escape from the park."

Jax gave a slow nod. It made sense. He'd assumed the cosmetic operations were to satisfy the killer's need for a specific look in his prey, but it was quite possible it was meant to send a message. The bastard was clever enough to know that the victim's images would be spread all over the media. And that Remi would realize he was creating clones of her.

"It's a good theory," he admitted.

Ash made a sound of disgust, running his fingers through his mussed hair. "Not if the killer tried to burn the body tonight," he pointed out. "What would be the point of having a victim who looks like Remi if you're going to destroy the body?"

Jax grimaced. Maybe the killer panicked and feared he could be connected to the victim. Or perhaps he was simply overcome by an urge to watch the body burn. Or it could be a thousand other possibilities.

"Trying to peer into the mind of a serial killer is always a waste of time," he reminded his brother.

Ash gave a firm shake of his head. "There should be a pattern."

"Yes, but the pattern only has to make sense to the killer, not to us."

Ash flattened his lips, frustration smoldering around him like an invisible cloak. Jax sympathized. This case was giving him an ulcer. He could only imagine what it was doing to his brother.

"Do you know anything about the victim?" Ash demanded.

"Not yet." Jax lifted his hand to rub the back of his aching neck. The coffee was wearing off and the weariness was creeping into his bones. "I'm headed to the medical examiner's office to light a fire under Feldman's ass. Hopefully, I can get the Jane Doe moved to the top of his list."

There was the sound of approaching footsteps, and the brothers turned toward the hallway to watch as Remi strolled into the room. Buddy yelped in pleasure, racing to dance around her feet and tug on the hem of her knee-length robe.

Jax smiled. When Ash had first started dating the

daughter of his partner, he'd seen nothing but trouble ahead. Not only because Gage was hyperprotective of Remi, but she had been raised in a way that was utterly foreign to the Marcel clan. They didn't do private schools, or formal debutante parties, or summers in Europe.

They were more backyard BBQs and Friday-night football games.

It'd only taken a few months, however, for Jax to realize Remi was much more like her father than her snooty mother. Plus, there was no mistaking just how devoted Ash was to the young woman. Jax had gone from skeptical to fiercely hopeful the two would make a match of it.

And even after the two of them had ended the engagement, Jax remained hopeful they would get back together. Whatever their problems, they'd loved each other with an intensity that didn't just die.

"Ash?" She moved to stand beside her onetime fiancé before turning toward him. "Hey, Jax."

"Morning, Remi." Jax watched as Ash wrapped an arm around her shoulders. It wasn't possessive. Just the instincts of a man who craved the closeness of a certain woman. "Sorry. Did we wake you?"

She shook her head. "No, I usually get up early."

Jax leaned forward, planting a quick kiss on her sleep-flushed cheek. "It's good to see you, Princess," he said, using the affectionate nickname he'd given her years before.

She snorted, but something in her expression eased at his teasing. Had she been afraid things had changed between them?

"Same old Jax," she murmured, her smile filled with a fondness that warmed Jax's heart.

"Hmm." He tilted his head to the side. "Is that an insult?"

"You know it isn't," she murmured.

He held her gaze. "You've been missed."

Her eyes darkened with something that might have been regret before she was squaring her shoulders and visibly bracing herself for bad news. "I don't suppose I have to ask why you would be here at such an early hour," she said. "There's been another murder."

"I'm afraid so."

Chapter Seventeen

Ash tightened his arm around Remi's shoulders as she swayed in horror.

He'd wanted to signal to Jax to keep his mouth shut. Remi was stressed enough. The last thing she needed was another death weighing on her mind.

But there'd been no point. Remi wasn't stupid. She would know that Jax wouldn't show up before dawn unless he had news about the Butcher. And besides, it would soon be plastered all over the TV.

"Do you want to sit down?" he asked in a low voice, his gaze skimming over her face that had paled despite her attempt to try to prepare herself for Jax's words.

"No, I'm okay." She stiffened her spine, her gaze focused on Jax. "Are you sure it was the Butcher?"

"I'm waiting on the report from the medical examiner," Jax hedged, his expression revealing he wasn't going to go into any gory details of the crime.

"But you suspect it's another victim?" Remi pressed.

"Yeah."

She pressed a hand to the center of her chest, as if to contain the pain in her heart. "We have to stop this," she rasped.

Ash brushed a kiss over the top of her head, but before he could speak, Jax was answering her plea.

"That's actually why I'm here."

Ash lifted his head to study his brother's grim face. He'd assumed he'd just wanted to share the news about the most recent murder. "What do you need?"

"I thought you might join me for brunch."

For a second, Ash was certain he's misheard his brother. "Brunch?"

"The mayor's office is hosting a media day to salute the brave men and women in blue," Jax said.

Ash remained confused. Jax had never been one to enjoy the political side of his job. In fact, if an event involved a suit and a tie, he did everything in his power to avoid it.

"And?"

"And I called a friend on the way over and she—"

"She?" Ash interrupted with a lift of his brows.

Jax narrowed his gaze. "Can I finish?"

Ash sent him an innocent smile. "I'm not stopping you."

"He hasn't changed either," Remi said in dry tones.

"No shit," Jax muttered, although Ash didn't miss the hint of pleasure in Jax's eyes. Once the brothers had been practically inseparable. Not only because they both worked in the same office but because they shared the same interests. Ash knew that his self-imposed exile had been tough on Jax. "She informed me that Robert Hutton sent his RSVP."

Ash was jerked out of his rueful contemplations. Hutton. Just the man he wanted to see. "Do you have an invitation?"

Jax shrugged. "No, but that's not going to stop me from showing up."

"What time?"

"I'll pick you up at nine."

"I'll be ready," Ash assured him.

Jax glanced toward Remi. "We need to have dinner and catch up."

"You can come over tonight." Remi smiled with anticipation. "I'll make spaghetti."

"Oh." Jax cleared his throat. "You know . . ." A deer-in-the-headlights expression spread across his face. No doubt he was recalling the night Remi made them a pot of chicken and dumplings and it turned into one soggy lump of dough. Or maybe the meat loaf that had something that tasted suspiciously like coffee grounds in it. "I'll have to take a rain check. I'll be eating something at my desk for the foreseeable future."

Remi wasn't fooled for a second. "My cooking isn't that bad," she groused.

Jax sent Ash a taunting smile. "I'll let you field that one." He reached out to tug a lock of Remi's hair. "See ya later, Princess."

With a wave, Jax turned and left the house. He was swift to close the door, but a brutal blast of cold air still managed to swirl inside. Ash hurriedly steered Remi away from the entryway and into the warmth of the kitchen.

Almost as if she was operating on autopilot, Remi immediately moved to switch on the coffee maker.

"Are you going to confront Bobby about where he was the night Tiffany Holloway was killed?" she demanded.

Ash hesitated. He didn't want Remi anywhere near Hutton. But he wasn't sure if it was because he suspected the slimy bastard was hiding something or because she used to date the man. "That's the plan."

Remi opened the cabinet to pull out a couple of worn mugs. "Do you want me to go with you?"

Ash studied her profile in surprise. She sounded like she had no interest in joining them.

"I was bracing myself for your insistence on being included," he admitted.

She poured the coffee, spooning in sugar before moving to hand him his mug.

Ash felt a small flare of warmth. Ridiculous, but he loved the fact that she could make his coffee without having to think about how he liked it. It assured him that their former intimacy wasn't entirely destroyed.

"Actually, I think I'll visit my mother," she said, catching him off guard.

Ash set aside his mug, frowning at his companion. "If you wait—"

"No," Remi interrupted sharply. "She won't talk if you're around."

Well, that was true enough. Liza Harding-Walsh would have her tongue cut out before she uttered more than icy, barely polite chatter in his presence. Ash assumed the older woman was terrified that if she tried to be nice, Ash might assume he was welcome in their pedigreed family.

A horrifying thought.

"I don't like you going there alone," he growled.

She looked predictably confused. "It's my home."

"That's what scares me," he muttered.

Remi shook her head, clearly refusing to allow his heebie-jeebies to affect her. "The Butcher would have had hundreds of occasions to attack me at the house if he wanted."

Ash couldn't argue. He didn't even know what was bothering him. He had no proof the car that'd tried to run down Roo belonged to Gage. Or that the killer had any connection to Remi's family estate.

Besides, as Remi had just pointed out, she'd been in and

out of the house on a weekly basis. If the killer had wanted to hurt her, he'd had plenty of opportunity.

Still, he found he couldn't completely shake his unease.

"The one thing we know is that he's unpredictable," he muttered.

She made a sound of impatience. "I can't stay locked in this house."

"Why not?"

She glared at him. "Be serious."

"Okay." He heaved a resigned sigh. "But I want you to call me before you go and as soon as you leave."

Her lips flattened, and it was obvious she wanted to tell him to back off. But, perhaps recalling that he was only trying to protect her, she placed her mug in the sink and turned to head out of the kitchen.

"I'm going to change and then go for a run," she said.

"Buddy and I will join you," he called out as she headed for her bedroom.

"Of course you will," she called back in sarcastic tones.

Ash glanced down at Buddy, who was regarding him with a gaze that warned he was treading close to getting thrown in the doghouse.

The adrenaline is pumping through me. A glorious antidote to the poison that fills my veins. It excites and soothes me at the same time. An intoxicating sensation I clutch like a lifeline.

But it wouldn't last.

I could already sense the euphoria slipping away.

I sit in the dark, staring at the house down the street. I try to conjure the memories, needing to savor them to keep my sanity.

Closing my eyes, I visualize the sight of my creation

standing in the empty lot. Her fear had been a tangible force that seeped deep inside me. It was better than any hit of Xanax. I'd wanted to spend hours just watching her shiver in terror. I don't know why the sight eases the gnawing hole in the center of my soul. I only know I can momentarily breathe.

Then, all too quickly, the woman is gathering her courage and turning around. The sight reminds me that I am exposed. As much as I might desire to prolong the glorious culmination of my efforts, I can't risk someone noticing our presence in the neighborhood.

Commanding the creature to hold still, I move out of the shadows. One step. Then two. I come close enough to catch the scent of the familiar soap. My stomach unclenches at the sweet scent even as my hunger sharpens.

I need more.

The curse of my illness.

More. More. More.

I wrap my arms around her, tugging down the coat to offer me unimpeded access to the tender flesh of her throat.

Only blood would truly ease my suffering.

I force open my eyes.

After purging my cancer, I cover my tracks and return home. I shower and intend to go to bed. My symptoms should be sated for at least a few weeks.

But rather than crawling beneath the sheets, I find myself driving to the unassuming house in the quiet neighborhood.

It's dangerous. Even though I've eased my demons, I know I'm not impervious to temptation. I proved that once.

Still, I linger.

And the sickness begins to spread.

* * *

Ash sat in the passenger seat of his brother's car and blindly stared out the window as they headed to the fancy hotel just north of the Loop.

After his jog with Remi, Ash had taken a quick shower and changed into fresh slacks and a chunky silver sweater. Not quite up to the mayor's standards, but he didn't plan to attend the brunch as a guest.

Now he tried to concentrate on the upcoming encounter with Robert Hutton even as he stewed on the thought that Remi would soon be heading to her mother's estate. Logic told him that she would be perfectly safe. His heart, however, hated every second she was out of his sight.

He had it bad.

"You're quiet." Jax at last broke the silence, sending Ash a questioning glance. "Is anything wrong? Beyond the obvious?"

"I feel . . ." Ash searched for the word that captured the prickling unease that plagued him. "Itchy."

"A premonition?" Jax demanded, perfectly serious. The older Marcel was a big believer in gut instinct.

Ash shook his head. "More a knowledge that serial killers eventually spiral out of control," he said. "Every minute that passes puts Remi in more danger."

Jax muttered a curse as he swerved his way through the thick traffic. In the morning sunlight, Ash could make out the shadows beneath his brother's eyes and the tension in his unshaven jaw.

"The only way to protect her is to find the Butcher," Jax said.

Ash sent his brother a sour glare. He didn't need to be told what had to be done. What he needed were clues to lead him to the killer.

Keeping his frustrated words to himself, Ash returned

his gaze to the side window, watching as his brother pulled into the parking lot next to the hotel.

"It doesn't look like a very big crowd," Ash murmured, taking in the nearly empty lot.

"The event doesn't start for another hour," Jax explained.

Ash felt a stab of impatience. He had a dozen things he could be doing. "Then why are we here?" he demanded.

Jax drove toward the side entrance. "I want to catch Hutton before he goes inside."

Ash's gaze skimmed over the handful of cars already parked at the back of the lot. He assumed they were employees at the hotel. Then he noticed the glossy black Mercedes pulled into a distant corner. That didn't belong to a waiter. Or a maid.

It was more instinct than true curiosity that drew his attention to the vanity plate of the Mercedes. RHUTTONIV.

Robert Hutton the Fourth.

He reached out to grasp his brother's upper arm. "Pull behind the dumpster," he commanded in sharp tones.

Jax swerved toward the large trash receptacle, bringing the car to a halt before glancing toward Ash in confusion. "What's going on?"

Ash pointed toward the Mercedes they could see around the edge of the dumpster.

"It looks like Hutton decided to get here even earlier."

Jax frowned, his lips parting as if to demand how Ash knew that was Robert Hutton's car only to snap shut when he noticed the plates. "Why would he arrive an hour before the event starts?" he demanded instead.

A good question. Ash ran through a mental list of possibilities, only to come up blank.

"Either he's moonlighting as a member of the waitstaff

or he's hoping to impress the mayor by showing up before anyone else," he finally concluded.

Jax dismissed his theory with a shake of his head. "The mayor won't even be here, so there's no one to impress with his punctuality. It's one of those PR events they set up to get the district attorney's staff and the chief of police on the front page of the papers."

Ash didn't miss the edge of disdain in his brother's voice. "You don't sound very impressed."

"I understand the politics of it," Jax said, glancing toward the hotel that no doubt was charging a fortune to host the fancy brunch. "We need the publicity the mayor can offer us to get the funding, but I wish we made more of an effort to reach out to the people we're supposed to be serving." He gave a frustrated shake of his head. "They need to be reassured that we're listening to their concerns, and that's not happening when we're having fancy brunches where only the most elite of Chicago are invited."

Ash shrugged. "You can make the change when you become chief."

Jax sent him a horrified glance. "Christ, don't even suggest that."

"Why?" Ash had been only half-teasing. He couldn't imagine anyone better than Jax Marcel to be chief of the CPD. He would be hard but fair, and he would demand the very best of his employees. "The only way to have the future you want is to take charge," he pointed out.

"I could say the same to you," Jax said in dry tones.

The vision of Remi filled Ash's mind. That was the future he wanted. The woman he loved, and a return to the job that had once filled him with a sense of purpose.

The Butcher had stripped that away from him. Perhaps capturing the killer could give it back.

"I'm trying," he said with a sigh.

Jax turned off the engine and unhooked his safety belt before turning in his seat. "Remi looks at you like she did five years ago," he abruptly told Ash.

"How's that?"

"Like she found her treasure at the end of the rainbow."

Ash's breath caught in his throat, aching to believe his brother's claim before he told himself that he was being ridiculous. "Right," he said with a snort.

"It's true," Jax insisted. "I envy you for that."

Not entirely convinced that his brother hadn't mistaken Remi's gratitude for his presence with something more intimate, Ash distracted himself with his brother's love life.

It wasn't nearly so complicated.

"You've had your opportunities," Ash reminded Jax.

Although all the Marcel men had been raised to treat females with the respect they would offer their own mother, Jax had spent his early years dating any number of beautiful, talented, and intelligent women. Including an FBI agent Ash had thought might be "the one."

"I . . ." Jax allowed his words to trail away as a car drove past the dumpster and headed toward the back of the lot. "Looks like the security team has arrived," he muttered.

Ash made a sound of shock. He recognized the man behind the wheel of the sedan.

"Isn't that O'Reilly?" he demanded.

Jax leaned forward, his attention focused on the car as it parked next to the Mercedes. "Yes."

"Why would he work security?" Ash demanded in confusion. He assumed there would be some uniforms on duty, but why would you have a detective?

"He wouldn't," Jax muttered, his hands curling into fists on his lap as O'Reilly crawled out of his car and glanced around the parking lot before hurrying to enter the passenger seat of the Mercedes. "I guess we know why Hutton was here so early. He had a meeting set up."

Ash shook his head in confusion. "Why would he meet with O'Reilly?"

"And why here?" Jax added. "Hutton has a fancy office just a few blocks away."

"Both good questions."

"Yeah. So how do we get them answered?"

"First, we wait," Ash told his brother, knowing Jax must be feeling the same urgent need to rush across the parking lot and confront the two men that was searing through him. Only the knowledge that they were more likely to get information by dividing and conquering kept his ass in the car.

Ten minutes later, O'Reilly was back in his sedan and driving out of the lot.

"I'm done waiting," Jax announced.

Ash unbuckled his seat belt and pushed open the passenger door. "Fine. You take care of O'Reilly. I'll deal with Hutton."

His brother scowled. "Ash."

"You can't risk confronting Hutton," Ash told him. "Not when he could get you fired with one phone call."

Jax muttered a curse as he glared toward the Mercedes. "He's involved. I don't know how, but he's involved."

"I'll take care of it. You go after O'Reilly." Ash slipped out of the car. "I'll call you when I'm done."

Jax leaned across the console, his expression worried. "Ash, Hutton might be a spoiled rich boy, but he's cunning and ambitious. I don't doubt he would go to any lengths to protect his pampered ass."

Ash nodded. He knew his brother was right. Any man could be dangerous if he was backed into a corner.

"I'll be careful."

Jax heaved a sigh. "I wish I believed that."

"You worry about yourself." Ash turned the tables on his brother. "O'Reilly will be carrying. Probably more than one gun."

Jax offered a wry smile. "Let's just both agree not to get shot today."

"Deal."

"Call me," Jax demanded as Ash slammed shut the door and turned to head across the parking lot.

Chapter Eighteen

Ash ignored the icy wind that cut through his coat as he took a wide route toward the Mercedes. He preferred that his prey didn't realize he was being hunted. Especially when Hutton was in a car and Ash was now on foot.

For once, however, his timing was perfect. He was just approaching the car when the driver's door was shoved open and Robert Hutton stepped out.

The man was two inches shorter than Ash, around five ten, and slender, with black hair he kept brushed from his lean face. His eyes were dark, and his skin had a faint olive tint even in winter, as if he had some Italian heritage in his background. Currently, he was wearing an expensive trench coat and silk gloves that covered a suit that was no doubt hand-tailored.

Ash smirked as he stepped directly behind Robert. All he was missing was a cane and a monocle to be the image of a cartoon rich dude.

"Hello, Hutton," he said.

The assistant district attorney gave a small jump as he whirled around to discover who'd managed to sneak up on him. His brows drew together, confusion clouding his expression before he managed to recognize who was standing in front of him. "Ash Marcel?"

Ash offered a twisted smile. "The one and only."

The man's gaze moved over Ash, taking in his clothing, which wasn't designer but cost more than most cops were able to spend.

"I thought you moved away from Chicago?" he finally said, clearly deciding that Ash hadn't reached a position that meant he had to be more than vaguely polite.

Ash's smile remained firmly pinned in place. "I'm visiting for the holidays."

"Ah." Hutton took a step back, no doubt intending to turn away. "Enjoy your time with your family."

"Actually, I was hoping we could have a chat," Ash said, subtly shifting to block the man's path.

Hutton looked predictably confused. "A chat about what?"

Another blast of wind swirled through the parking lot, feeling like a solid wall of ice.

"Let's get in your car," Ash suggested. "It's too cold to stand out here."

Clearly impatient, Hutton reached into the pocket of his coat and pulled out a gilt-edged business card. "Call my secretary and make an appointment," he commanded. "I'm having brunch with the mayor. So if you'll excuse me . . ."

Ash ignored the card, allowing his smile to fade.

"We can chat in your car or we can chat inside, but I don't think you want anyone to overhear what I have to say," he said, his words a blatant threat.

Hutton frowned, glancing around as if ensuring that Ash was there alone. "What the hell is going on?"

"I'll tell you as soon as we're in your car."

Hutton narrowed his dark eyes. "You've always been an annoying ass."

"True." Ash shrugged. It was hard to argue with the truth. Then he moved to pull open the door of the Mercedes. "Shall we?"

There was a tense silence as Hutton glanced toward the nearby hotel. Was he debating the notion of walking away and daring Ash to follow? Probably. At least until the news van pulled in and parked smack in front of the door.

The media had arrived.

"Fine."

With a petulant expression, the man crawled back into his car and slammed the door. Ash hurried to the passenger side and slid inside before Hutton could lock him out. He sank into the supple seat, his knees barely fitting beneath the glove compartment.

It was a great car, but not made for a man his size.

Hutton turned to send him a sour glare. "What do you want?"

Ash leaned his back against the door, pretending to make himself comfortable. He had years of experience interviewing the toughest criminals in the city. This pretty boy wasn't going to know what hit him.

"Have you heard the rumors that the Butcher has returned to Chicago?"

Surprisingly, the man flinched. Had Ash hit a nerve?

Before he could pinpoint the source of the man's unease, Hutton had smoothed his expression into a bland mask. No doubt it was a trick he'd learned in law school.

"I don't have time to listen to gossip," he scoffed. "My office deals with provable facts. Until there is an arrest and I have the proof I need on my desk, I don't have time to worry about a mythical serial killer who might or might not have returned to Chicago."

Ash studied his companion with open suspicion. Most district attorneys would be salivating to be handed a high-profile serial killer to take to trial. It was a straight shot up the career ladder.

So why was Hutton pretending he couldn't be bothered with the animal who was stalking the streets of his city?

"Mythical?" Ash snorted. "You make him sound like a unicorn, not an evil, cold-blooded killer."

"I have actual criminals waiting to be prosecuted," Hutton said in smooth tones. Too smooth. "That's what I focus on. Investigating is your job. Wait—" The aggravating idiot paused, then, lifting his hand, gave a snap of his fingers. "You're not a cop anymore, are you? You're some sort of teacher."

"Some sort," Ash agreed in a dry tone.

"If you want to discuss the Butcher, I suggest you go talk to your brother," Hutton continued. "It's his job to track him down."

Ash hid his flare of satisfaction. Hutton had known that Jax had caught the case. Which meant he was paying closer attention than he wanted to admit.

But why not just confess his interest?

Unless there was something he had to hide.

"I'm talking to a lot of people," Ash said, keeping a close watch on Hutton's face. "Including Remi Walsh."

Hutton looked more bemused than worried at Ash's explanation. "Sweet Remi. I really should give her a call. We're old friends, you know."

"So she told me." Ash was proud he didn't drive his fist into Hutton's face. It was very mature of him. "Along with another interesting fact."

"The reason she dumped you?" Hutton mocked.

Ash just smiled. He'd grown up with brothers who'd specialized in tormenting him. He wasn't going to be provoked by an amateur.

"We happened to be discussing old times and she mentioned an evening when she was supposed to go to a study group, but she felt ill and had to return home," he said.

Hutton looked genuinely puzzled. "Seriously? This is why you're wasting my time?"

Ash held up his hand. "I'm not done."

Hutton peered down at the watch strapped around his wrist. Rolex, of course. The man was nothing if not predictable.

"You have one minute to finish."

Ash ignored the warning. "The night she returned home coincidentally happened to be the same night that you told me you were at her house having dinner with her mother."

Something flickered in the dark eyes, even as Hutton kept his expression carefully bland. "I don't know what you're talking about."

"Of course you do." Ash leaned forward, using his height advantage to gaze down at his companion. "I interviewed you along with Detective Walsh after Tiffany Holloway was discovered murdered in her home."

Hutton leaned back, nearly smacking his head on the window. "That was a long time ago."

"Five years."

"I don't really remember," Hutton stubbornly insisted.

Ash made a sound of disgust. "You don't remember? How many times have you been interviewed by the cops about your relationship to a murder victim?"

"There was no relationship," Hutton snapped, far more easily goaded than Ash. "The girl approached me about an internship and I agreed to assist her."

"So you do remember?"

Hutton's jaw clenched. "I remember being harassed by

you and your partner. Lucky for you, I didn't take my complaint to your captain."

Ash arched a brow.. "Your number was in her phone. Did you expect us to ignore your possible connection?"

"I expected you to have the brains to know I couldn't possibly be a serial killer."

Ash didn't miss the fierce sincerity in the man's voice. He sounded truly offended that he could possibly be a suspect. Then again, he was a professional liar.

He probably practiced in front of a mirror.

"Then why did you lie?" Ash demanded.

"About what?"

Ash once again managed to avoid the urge to plant his fist in the man's face.

"Your supposed alibi on the night Tiffany died."

Firmly cornered, Hutton glanced around, as if hoping for inspiration to strike. When nothing happened, he pointed toward the passenger door. "This is a ridiculous waste of my time. Get out."

"I'm not finished," Ash told him.

Hutton stuck out his lower lip, as if he was a twelve-year-old boy, not a polished attorney. "I am."

Ash rolled his eyes. It was a good thing Hutton was born rich. He never would have survived without a trust fund.

"I'm having this conversation, either here or in front of the press," he warned.

The lip stuck out another half inch. "I'll have you locked up for harassment."

Ash shrugged. "You don't scare me."

"You think I don't have influence?"

"Not with me. I'm no longer with the Chicago Police Department," Ash bluntly reminded the man. "Are you done with your threats?"

Hutton slashed his hand through the air. "I'm done. Period. As you just pointed out, you no longer carry a badge. Which means I don't have to answer your questions."

Ash wasn't fooled by the man's bluff. There was no way in hell Hutton was letting Ash anywhere near the media, who continued to arrive in the parking lot.

"Let's go, then," Ash murmured, reaching for the door handle.

Hutton muttered a curse. "Why are you pushing me?" he hissed.

"I want the truth."

"Why?"

Was the man serious? Maybe he'd lived in a world of deceit for so long, he'd forgotten that there were people who actually preferred not to wade through the muck.

"Because Remi is in danger," he snapped.

Hutton looked confused. "She's no longer your fiancée. What do you care?"

Ash gave a slow shake of his head. He'd met some weasels in his day, but this man . . .

He was as weaselly as they came.

"She will always be my concern." Ash allowed a warning silence to fill the car. He didn't want Hutton to mistake just how serious he was. "And I'll do anything necessary to protect her. Including destroying your career."

Hutton licked his lips. He might be a weasel, but he wasn't stupid. "Now who's making threats?"

"Mine aren't empty," Ash assured him.

Hutton turned his head to glance at the lot, which was rapidly filling with cars. Ash sensed the man desperately wanted to shove open his door and simply walk away. Perhaps he was even scouring his mind with something to blackmail Ash into leaving him alone.

At last he turned back to Ash. "I had nothing to do with the Butcher."

"Then tell me where you were that night."

"With Liza, as I told you."

"A lie," Ash growled. He was at the end of his patience.

"You can't prove that."

Ash held his wary gaze. "Are you certain?"

Hutton studied him, perhaps looking for some hint that Ash was fishing for information. But catching sight of Ash's clenched jaw, he heaved a harsh sigh.

"Fine. I didn't meet with Liza that night. She called and canceled."

Ash felt a stab of surprise. He'd assumed Hutton was the one to bail on the evening.

"Why?" he demanded.

"She didn't say and I didn't ask."

That seemed unlikely, but Ash wasn't interested in Liza Harding-Walsh. At least, not right now.

"So where did you go?"

"Nowhere." He gave a vague lift of his shoulder. "I stayed home."

"By yourself?"

"Yes, by myself." A flush touched the man's face, as if he was embarrassed to admit that he'd been without a ready date. "It was too late to make other plans."

He had no alibi. How many other nights had the weasel supposedly been home alone when women were getting their throats slit? Had he been so infuriated by Remi's refusal to consider him as a potential boyfriend that he'd gone over the edge? It didn't take much to provoke men with fragile egos.

"How did you know Tiffany Holloway?"

"I told you," Hutton muttered.

"Yeah, and we know how much that's worth," Ash said in dry tones.

Hutton tried to stiffen his spine. "I've answered your questions, now get out of my car."

Ash didn't budge. "Were you with Tiffany that night?"

"No," Hutton rasped, pointing a finger in Ash's face. "You're not pinning her murder on me."

Ash knocked away the finger. Hutton was quick to assume Ash thought he was involved with the girl's death. A guilty conscience?

"There's no way in hell you gave out your private cell number to a waitress who supposedly wanted to be an intern." He flicked a taunting glance over the man's expensive coat. Men like Hutton never helped anyone unless there was something in it for themselves. "We let it go in the past because you had an airtight alibi. That alibi is gone, and I'm not going to stop digging until I find what you were doing with her."

"I didn't kill her," Hutton insisted. "Leave it alone."

"Never." Ash held the man's gaze. He wanted him to see the truth staring back at him. "Not ever."

Hutton's hands curled into frustrated balls. "If I was the Butcher, I would just slice your throat and dump you in the trash."

Ash wasn't worried. Strange. He probably should be, considering he wasn't carrying.

"Jax drove me here."

It'd been an offhand threat, but suddenly Hutton looked more worried than he had since Ash had insisted they have this chat. Why? It took a full minute for Ash to work out the fact that the assistant district attorney was wondering if Jax had managed to see O'Reilly climbing out of the Mercedes.

There was a tense silence before Hutton made an explosive sound of anger.

"If you tell anyone what I'm about to say, I swear I will destroy everyone in your family," he snarled.

Ash allowed the threat to stand, even as he inwardly scoffed. His brothers would twist this idiot into a pretzel and dump him in the river if he tried to hurt any of them.

"I'm listening," he said.

Hutton took a second to gather his thoughts, his hand smoothing back his hair before he was tracing the knot of his silk tie with the tip of his finger. Was he ensuring it was perfectly square?

"I met Tiffany at one of the endless charity events I'm forced to attend. She was working for the catering service," he finally admitted. "I was bored and started chatting with her. She chatted back and made it clear she was interested in a little off-duty fun. At the end of the night I asked her if she wanted to go for a drink."

Ash's brows snapped together. "She was seventeen."

Hutton flattened his lips, his expression defensive. "I didn't know that. Not until it was too late."

Ash grimaced. Hutton might not have known Tiffany was still in high school, but he most certainly had to know she was too young to legally drink alcohol.

"Too late?" he demanded.

"You know what I mean."

"Before you had sex with her."

Hutton sent him an aggravated frown. "When I realized how young she was, I told her we couldn't see each other anymore. She wasn't happy."

"That's when she called you?"

"Yes."

"And she ended up dead."

"I couldn't believe it." Hutton curled his lips in disgust. He clearly didn't have any sympathy for the poor girl who'd been brutally murdered. His only concern was for himself. "I'd assumed I'd managed to escape unscathed from the potential scandal, only to land in the middle of a murder investigation."

"So you lied about your alibi."

Hutton looked unrepentant. As if lying to a law official investigating a serial killer was nothing more than a trivial oversight.

"After I realized my number was going to show up on Tiffany's phone, I called Liza and asked her to say we were together the night she died."

"And she agreed?" Ash demanded, not bothering to disguise his shock. He clearly was going to have to have a conversation with Remi's mother.

Not something he was looking forward to.

Maybe Jax . . .

Hutton interrupted his dark thoughts. "She was as eager as I was to have a reasonable alibi."

Ash tucked any questions about Liza and her willingness to offer Robert Hutton an alibi in the back of his mind. That was a problem for later. "Did Tiffany ever mention that she was being harassed by anyone?" he asked.

Hutton shook his head. "We didn't do a lot of talking."

"Christ." Ash felt a stab of disgust. "You're a piece of work."

Hutton flushed, but with a determination that warned Ash the man was done with the interview, he shoved open the car door and climbed out.

"You have your truth, now go back to whatever rock you crawled from beneath and leave me alone."

Ash slid out the opposite side of the car and pulled his

phone from his pocket as Hutton stormed across the parking lot. He wanted to pass on what he'd learned before Jax confronted O'Reilly. Then he needed to head toward the line of taxis parked in front of the hotel.

It was too damned cold to wait for his brother to return.

Chapter Nineteen

Jax strolled through the police station, stopping to chat with a friend before heading to his office. After his conversation with Ash, he wanted to give O'Reilly plenty of opportunity to start whatever sneaky task Hutton had sent him to do.

If he could catch him in the act, he'd have the leverage he needed to force the traitor to talk.

Ten minutes later, he stepped around the partition to discover O'Reilly shuffling through the files on his desk.

"Somehow I knew I would find you here, O'Reilly," he drawled.

The man squawked in surprise, jerking up his head to regard Jax in horror. "Marcel." The detective straightened, his eyes darting around as if seeking inspiration. "I was hoping to talk to you."

Jax's lips twisted into a humorless smile. "No, you weren't. You were hoping I wasn't coming in to the office so you could look through my files."

The man snorted, folding his arms over his chest. "You're becoming paranoid in your old age, Marcel. Have you thought about retirement?"

"Every day," Jax assured him.

"Yeah, well . . ." O'Reilly took a step backward, clearly eager to flee.

Jax moved, ensuring the man would have to push him aside to get out of the cubicle. "Where are you going?"

"I have things to do."

"I thought you wanted to chat?"

The man stepped to the side. "It can wait."

Jax moved to block him, like an awkward dance that might very well lead to violence. "Actually, it can't," he said.

O'Reilly's square face flushed with anger. "What's wrong with you?"

Jax allowed his gaze to roam over the man's coat, which was stained and wrinkled, and down to the leather shoes that were in dire need of a polish. He wasn't a snob. Far from it. But he did have a firm belief that a detective had to take pride in their appearance.

How could anyone take you seriously if you looked like a slob?

"I don't like liars," he drawled. "Or spineless snakes who have no morals or loyalty."

The flush darkened to an ugly purple. "You'd better not be talking about me," he blustered.

"Or what?" Jax demanded. "You'll call your favorite lawyer in the district attorney's office?"

O'Reilly sucked in a sharp breath, his head turning to make sure that no one was close enough to overhear their conversation. "I don't know what you're babbling about."

Jax rolled his eyes. He hoped O'Reilly never played cards. His poker face sucked. "Why were you meeting Hutton this morning?"

"I wasn't."

Jax held up his hand. "Don't bother. You're an awful liar. Plus, I saw you in the parking lot less than half an hour ago."

The flush drained from the man's face, leaving it pale with fury. "Are you following me?"

Jax deliberately paused. "Not you."

"Oh." O'Reilly was quick to pick up the implication that it'd been the assistant district attorney under surveillance. "What's your interest in Hutton?"

"I'm asking the questions."

O'Reilly hunched his shoulders. "I don't have to tell you anything."

"Then I'll take it to the chief." Jax smiled, the warning spilling off his lips before he fully thought through the threat.

Did he really want to admit to the chief that he was putting the screws to a fellow detective, and that his brother, who was no longer on the force, was harassing one of the young, hotshot lawyers from the district attorney's office?

Thankfully, O'Reilly didn't challenge him. "Take what to the chief?" he demanded.

Emboldened, Jax allowed his smile to widen. "That you're working with Hutton to cover up a crime."

"Crime?" The man's bloodshot eyes flared with unmistakable fear. "Bullshit. There's no crime."

Jax tilted his head to the side. There was a harsh sincerity in the man's voice that suggested he was convinced he wasn't doing anything illegal.

Still, there was no way O'Reilly could believe it was normal to be sneaking through another detective's case files.

"What about a cover-up?" he demanded.

O'Reilly glanced away, his jaw clenched as he considered his limited options. Either he confessed the truth to Jax and dumped all the blame on Hutton, or he risked continuing to lie and hoped Hutton's payoff would be enough to cover the potential loss of his job.

Jax made the decision easier for him.

"I already know Hutton was sleeping with Tiffany Holloway right before she was murdered," he told his companion. "And that he lied about his alibi the night she was killed."

"How—" O'Reilly bit off his question, belatedly realizing he was revealing more than he wanted to. "Sounds like you should be talking to Hutton, not me."

Jax conjured a suitably mysterious expression. "It's being handled."

"By who?" he demanded.

"It's being handled outside the department."

The detective shifted from foot to foot, his mind no doubt filling with images of Internal Affairs. Or worse. The feds.

"Shit." O'Reilly looked sick, any loyalty to Hutton forgotten as he hurried to save his own skin. "I didn't do anything."

"You're working for Hutton," Jax pressed.

O'Reilly shook his head. "I did him a couple of favors, nothing else."

Jax stepped closer. It was possible Hutton was the secret serial killer. He'd certainly been acting in a suspicious manner. Plus, he'd admitted that he was involved with one of the victims and had gone to extreme methods to keep his relationship with Tiffany Holloway a secret.

But after confronting the assistant district attorney, Ash had been doubtful that he was more than a sexist jerk. And now Jax was beginning to agree.

If O'Reilly was covering a series of murders, he'd either have been a lot more careful not to be caught or he'd be demanding a lawyer before he talked to anyone.

Right now, he seemed worried about his job, not death row.

"Tell me about the favors," Jax commanded.

"Five or six years ago, Hutton stopped by my house and said he needed my help," the man revealed.

Jax grimaced. He hadn't been to O'Reilly's place, but he'd heard it was a pigsty south of town that was in constant danger of being condemned.

"That must have been a surprise," Jax said, unable to imagine the fussy Robert Hutton risking his designer shoes in such a neighborhood.

O'Reilly snorted. "I don't think he'd ever been in my part of town before. He kept looking around like he was afraid he might get shot in the back."

That didn't sound unreasonable to Jax. He'd probably do the same.

"Why was he there?"

"He admitted he'd been banging the waitress and wanted me to keep my ears open," the man said.

"For what?"

"Any connection to him. He was worried about word getting out he was with an underage girl."

That matched with what Ash had told him. "And that's all he was worried about?"

A sneer touched O'Reilly's bluntly carved features. "It didn't help that the girl was chilling in the morgue. He thought his career would be over."

Jax dismissed the man's stunning lack of empathy for a dead seventeen-year-old girl. Really, that was the least of his offensive personality traits.

"And now?" Jax studied O'Reilly's face, noticing the broken blood vessels and sagging skin along the jaw. He looked like a man who'd been hitting the bottle pretty heavily over the past months.

Maybe years.

"The same thing." The detective gave a restless lift of his shoulder. "He called when he heard the chatter that the

Butcher was back and wanted to make sure his name wouldn't get involved."

"How were you supposed to do that?"

Resentment sparked in the man's eyes, revealing that his partnership with the assistant district attorney wasn't a happy one.

"He didn't give specific directions," he muttered. "He just said to do it. Like I'm some sort of miracle worker."

Jax shook his head. Had Hutton assumed the detective would steal evidence if it threatened to implicate him? Probably.

"Why were you meeting with him this morning?"

O'Reilly glanced toward Jax's desk, where the top file was lying open. "He said he'd heard there was another murder. He wanted me to look through your notes."

Jax frowned in confusion. "He thought he might be implicated?"

O'Reilly scowled at the question. "Of course not."

"Then why does he want you nosing through my private files?"

"He believes that whoever is out there is a copycat killer," O'Reilly explained. "He demanded that I search through the evidence and come up with some proof."

Jax was confused. Why would Hutton believe the killer was a copycat unless he had some evidence . . . ?

Belatedly, he realized this was actually a clever ploy by Robert Hutton. "If you found a way to claim the latest killings are by a copycat, all the old case files would be put back in storage," he said.

The detective nodded. "Yeah, and he can stop worrying that someone is going to ask the wrong questions and his name is going to get splashed across the front page of the paper."

Jax folded his arms over his chest, ready to be done

with this conversation. He had a thousand things waiting for his attention. Starting with a double-check of the old files to ensure that there was no other connection to Robert Hutton or Detective O'Reilly. Their story that this was nothing more than panic over sex with an underage girl was plausible, but they remained on his suspect list.

"Call Hutton and assure him that it's not a copycat," he told O'Reilly. "And that if I catch him interfering in my investigation again, I will have him publicly hauled down to the station and grilled in front of the entire department."

The older man sent him a jaundiced glare. "Fine."

Jax moved aside, but even as the detective stepped forward, Jax was struck by a sudden curiosity. "Hey, O'Reilly."

"Now what?" the man groused.

"What does Hutton have on you?"

His gaze skittered away. "Nothing."

"You didn't help him out of the goodness of your heart," Jax pointed out. "So how did he blackmail you?"

O'Reilly let his features harden into a peevish expression, clearly resenting Jax's question. Surprisingly, however, he answered. "He made a call to the chief."

"And?"

"And it got Internal Affairs off my back," O'Reilly snapped.

Jax abruptly recalled Ash's explanation of why Gage Walsh had dumped this detective as a partner. "Gage was right," he said in disgust. "You were stealing from the evidence room."

"I took a few pills and a bag of weed no one would ever miss," the older man groused, his tone defensive. "I needed the money. My mother was sick."

Jax didn't think his opinion of the man could actually plummet, but the fact that he'd try to blame his lack of morals on his sick mother . . . Christ. He was a spineless slug.

Jax pointed a finger in O'Reilly's square face. "Come near my desk again and I'll shoot you."

"No need to be such a dick," the detective muttered, stomping away.

"I haven't started being a dick," Jax called out, a sudden heat touching his cheeks as a uniformed officer appeared around the corner, his expression worried.

"Everything okay, Marcel?" he demanded.

"Just peachy," Jax assured him, dropping into his seat behind the desk.

He'd wasted enough time on O'Reilly. He needed to concentrate on the actual killer. And how the hell he was going to track him down.

Remi stood near the pool house, hoping to block the wind that swirled through the gardens of her mother's estate. It also gave her an opportunity to peek through the shutters that covered the window of the decaying building.

Once, when she'd been a young teenager, she'd snuck inside. She hadn't known what she wanted to see, but a few of her classmates had recently shared the crazy stories that revolved around her grandfather and his habit of shooting his enemies inside the small building.

The whole experiment had been a disappointment. There'd been nothing to see beyond the open bar area that still had a few Mason jars filled with moonshine and dusty tables that were shoved against the wall. And, in the back, a couple of bathrooms with showers for people who actually used the pool house to change out of wet bathing suits.

There were no skeletons hidden in the cabinets or blood on the tiled floor.

And worse, her father had caught her while she was looking around and grounded her for a week. He said he was worried about the ceiling falling on her head, but she thought it had more to do with the gruesome past of the place.

He never discussed the fact that he'd married into a family of gangsters. It was as if he was determined to erase the past by simply ignoring it.

Now she stood there, trying to imagine her father firing a gardener for sneaking in for a cigarette. It seemed extreme, but not more extreme than the dozens of other servants who'd been fired by her mother.

Almost as if the thought of Liza Harding-Walsh had conjured her from thin air, the older woman stepped around the edge of the pool house.

As always, Liza was elegant, dressed in one of her designer pantsuits that clung to her curvaceous body and a matching tailored coat. And despite the breeze that was sending puffs of snow spraying through the air, her dark hair was pulled into a sleek, perfect knot at her nape.

It was amazing.

"Remi, what on earth are you doing?" she asked, genuine surprise touching her beautiful face.

"Mother." Remi grimaced as she stepped away from the window. This was the house where she grew up, but she suddenly felt like an intruder. "You startled me."

Liza arched her brows. "Not as much as you startled me. I glanced out the window to see a shadowy figure skulking around my yard."

"And you came out here alone?" Remi sent her a chiding glance. "You should have called the cops."

Liza waved a slender hand toward the mansion on the other side of the covered pool.

"I knew Albert was working nearby," the older woman told her. "There was a frozen pipe in the kitchen this morning and he's making sure it doesn't burst."

Belatedly, Remi heard the sound of a shovel hitting hard dirt. Poor Albert. It was too cold for the older man to be outside working, but he would no doubt be offended if she tried to make him call for a plumber to weatherize the pipes.

"You still shouldn't have come out here alone," Remi said.

A strange expression rippled over the woman's face as she glanced toward the pool house.

"I thought . . ."

Remi felt a strange sensation scuttle down her spine. Like spiders scurrying over a web. She shivered, instinctively wrapping her arms around her waist. "What?"

"Nothing." Her mother smoothed her expression to the familiar polite mask. "Are you going to tell me what you're doing here?"

Remi glanced over the vast backyard. She'd spent a lot of her childhood lying next to the pool or playing tennis on the court next to the back fence. She'd been happy here, even though she didn't have a lot in common with her parents. She'd known she was loved and protected and had the opportunity to do whatever she wanted with her future. A rare gift.

Of course, when she'd lived here, she'd concentrated far too much on her resentment that she was a neglected daughter who didn't get nearly enough appreciation. Like every other teenage girl.

Her lips twitched, a small measure of her unease fading. She always overreacted when she was with her mother. Today, however, she needed to make sure she didn't act like an emotional child.

If she wanted her mother to answer questions, she was going to have to lure her into a sense of comfort.

"Just having a look around," she said. "It's been a while since I spent any time here."

Her mother looked skeptical. "It's freezing."

Remi moved to wrap her arm through her mother's, steering her around the edge of the pool. "I was just getting ready to come inside."

Her mother allowed herself to be led toward the mansion, her gaze lowering to the glove that was still clutched in Remi's hand.

"What are you holding?" she demanded.

Remi had a brief regret that she'd brought the glove. It'd been an impulsive desire in case she ran into Albert. She wanted a chance to ask him about the Mustang and why her father's glove would be on the ground.

Now she tried to think quickly. The last thing she wanted was to upset her mother. Especially today.

"I found it on the ground," she lied smoothly.

Liza jerked it out of her hand, her face tightening with an expression that was impossible to read.

"That belongs to your father," she rasped, her fingers stroking over the embroidered initials on the cuff.

"Yes," Remi agreed in gentle tones.

"I don't understand." She frowned, glancing around the frozen ground. "How did it get here?"

"I don't know."

"This should be locked upstairs." Her voice was sharp with an anger she rarely revealed. "No one is allowed in your father's rooms. No one. I need to talk to my housekeeper."

Remi grimaced; this wasn't starting out as well as she'd hoped. "The glove could have been lost years ago, Mother," she tried to soothe. "Beneath a bush or in the hedge. The wind probably untangled it and it landed here. Please don't blame your staff."

"Perhaps." Liza carefully folded the glove as they entered the back door of the house.

In silence, they slid off their coats and hung them on the hooks next to the door. Then they headed into the kitchen.

"We should have coffee," Liza announced, firmly heading across the tiled floor.

Remi wandered behind the older woman. "Do you want me to make it?"

"I'm capable of switching on the coffee machine," Liza assured her, flicking buttons on the space-age, stainless-steel monstrosity.

Remi was frankly impressed. It looked like you needed a master's degree to figure out the thing. Leaning against the counter, she heaved a small sigh and allowed her gaze to roam over the large room.

The cabinets were painted a bright white, with silver countertops and a white marble floor. The ceiling was high and there was a bank of windows that overlooked the pool. It all combined to create an atmosphere of bright cheerfulness that lifted Remi's mood.

"This has always been one of my favorite rooms," she murmured.

"The kitchen?" Her mother looked surprised. "You hate to cook."

Remi's lips twisted. She wondered if that would be put on her gravestone. It certainly was the one thing everyone knew about her.

"I love the view, and it always smells like fresh-baked bread." She nodded toward the small white table set beneath the windows. "Dad and I used to sit over there and eat our morning cereal."

Her mother filled the mugs and crossed to join Remi. "I remember."

Remi sipped her coffee, turning her head to study her mother's profile. "Have you ever thought about selling the estate?"

Liza jerked, as if she'd been struck by an unseen blow. "Selling?"

"It's a lot of house for you," Remi said, genuinely curious. She understood her mother's loyalty to the family estate, but it had to be lonely in the huge house. "You might be more comfortable in a smaller place."

Liza looked confused. "This has always been my home."

"Not always. Didn't you and Dad live downtown when you were first married?"

Liza waved away her early days of living in an apartment, the diamonds on her fingers sparkling with a blinding brilliance. "Yes, but it was less than a year before my father died and we moved into this house."

Remi had secretly wondered how her father felt about moving into the home of his in-laws. Especially because the reputation of this place was hardly suitable for a cop. As far as she knew, he'd never revealed anything but satisfaction to call this home, but she didn't doubt he would have preferred someplace less . . . ostentatious.

Liza Harding-Walsh, on the other hand, obviously didn't find the house grandiose. Not even for a woman on her own.

"What about your mother?" Remi asked. Liza never talked about Remi's grandmother. And on the few occasions on which Remi had spent time with the old woman, there'd been a hushed formality about the event, it had made her feel like she was at a funeral.

"She went to Florida after Dad's funeral. She said she

couldn't bear another Chicago winter." Liza shrugged. "Lawrence and his family moved into the house she built after she died."

"I wish I had the chance to get to know my grandparents," Remi said. "I've heard all the colorful stories, of course, but I really have no idea what they were like as people."

Liza sipped her coffee, her eyes growing distant, as if she was traveling back in time. Perhaps to when she was a young girl in this kitchen. "My father was a difficult man." Her lips twisted into a wry smile. "Most people say I take after him."

Remi would agree with that, but she kept her thoughts to herself. Today was about peace and harmony and getting the information she needed.

"Was he a good father?" she asked.

Liza took another sip of coffee. "He was distant and short-tempered, but there was nothing I loved more than spending time with him."

Remi didn't miss the genuine affection in her mother's voice. It was odd. This was the first time they'd ever had a conversation about her mother's side of the family. Probably because her father had usually looked uncomfortable as soon as Patrick Harding was mentioned. It had never been overt. Nothing she'd really noticed as a child. But looking back, she realized he had subtly avoided any conversation about the Harding clan.

"Do you have any special memories of your dad?" Remi asked.

Liza gave a slow nod. "He would take me on his Friday morning rounds."

Remi frowned in confusion. "Rounds?"

"We would travel around Chicago in a big limo and visit the local restaurants and nightclubs," her mother said, her voice filled with a childish pleasure. "I would be given a special table with a plate of treats while Dad would discuss business with the owners. I felt like a princess."

Remi hid her grimace. She'd known her grandfather was in the protection racket. But to think about the man driving around in a limo with his daughter in tow, no doubt threatening the business owners with some hideous fate if they didn't pay up . . .

She cleared her throat, trying not to look shocked. "Did Uncle Lawrence ever go with you?"

Liza flattened her lips. "He was a momma's boy."

"You weren't close with your mother?" Remi asked, although the answer was obvious.

Liza abruptly set aside her mug, her hand not quite steady. Could she still be that troubled about the past? After all these years?

"I think she was jealous of the time I spent with my father," Liza said. "She wasn't a strong woman. She depended on Dad to take care of everything. I think that's why I had a difficult time being a good mother to you. I didn't have much of a role model."

Remi felt a stab of guilt. She'd been so self-absorbed, she'd never considered the fact that Liza might feel inadequate as a mother. Or that their distant relationship might have pained the older woman. "We've managed to muddle through," she insisted.

A fleeting smile touched Liza's face. "I was always thankful that your father was so devoted to you."

So was Remi. Deeply grateful. She once again held her tongue. "How did Grandpa feel about you marrying a cop?"

Liza blinked, as if caught off guard by the question. "He wasn't happy. In fact, he threatened to disown me."

Remi wasn't surprised by Patrick Harding's horror at having a cop marry into the family. She was, however, deeply surprised that her mother would have risked her inheritance to be with her father.

"But you married him anyway?"

"I fell in love with him the first day we met. Nothing ever changed that." Liza clutched her hands together, her expression suddenly fierce. "I would have done anything for him."

Chapter Twenty

Remi gave a slow nod. "That's the one thing I never doubted in my life," she said.

Liza's sent her a curious glance. "Your father?"

"The fact that the two of you loved each other."

The older woman's eyes remained distant, as if her thoughts lingered in the past.

"No one ever understood me like your father," she said in low, soft tones. "That's the key to a happy marriage. Knowing all your partner's faults but still loving each other."

Remi set down her mug, her mouth dry and her heart twisting with a sharp pain. "I had that," she breathed.

"Excuse me?"

"That's the way I felt when I was with Ash," Remi clarified. "Complete."

Not surprisingly, Liza's features hardened at the mention of Remi's ex-fiancé. "I heard he was back in town."

Remi was annoyed by her mother's stiff tone. "I never understood why you didn't like him."

Liza widened her eyes and Remi prepared herself for the pretense that she didn't understand what Remi meant: It was the usual game. Liza would display a fleeting disdain for Ash, then retreat behind her barriers of indifference the moment she was challenged.

Surprisingly, this time Liza actually answered the question. "It wasn't personal."

"It felt personal," Remi informed the older woman. "Especially to Ash."

"I didn't want you to marry a cop," Liza said, the words sounding as if they were being dragged out of her.

Remi was baffled by the explanation. Was her mother just making some excuse to avoid admitting she thought the Marcel family was beneath them?

"Why not?" she demanded. "You married a cop."

"Yes." Liza turned, wandering toward the center of the kitchen, her hands smoothing the jacket of her ivory pantsuit. "I loved your father very much, but his career was a constant strain on our relationship."

"It's a demanding job," Remi agreed.

Liza made a sound of impatience, as if Remi couldn't possibly comprehend. "It wasn't demanding, it was all-consuming," she corrected. "Do you know how many dinners and special events I was forced to attend alone?"

It would have been impossible for Remi to forget. Her mother might have found it difficult to reveal her emotions to her daughter, but that had never been a problem with her husband. She'd griped, she'd complained, she'd sulked whenever Gage announced he had to go in to work. If it'd been up to Liza Harding-Walsh, her husband would have remained at her side night and day.

Remi rushed to the defense of her father. "He was a good cop."

"He was," Liza agreed. "And I had to accept that his family would always come second."

Remi studied her mother with mounting confusion. "I thought you said you were happy?"

"We were," Liza insisted. "Very happy. But that didn't

mean there wasn't a cost to his career. One I had to pay along with Gage."

Remi got it. She truly did. When she'd been dating Ash, there'd been times when she'd wanted to storm down to the station and demand that he leave. He'd missed her birthday party, the spring formal at college, and the Christmas dinner she'd prepared, although that one might have been on purpose. She'd tried to cook duck and it had ended up as dry as sawdust.

But she'd been so very proud of him and what he was accomplishing. Plus, he was doing what he loved. How could she ever take that away from him?

"I suppose every job has its pros and cons," she murmured, a wistful sadness tugging at her heart.

"This was more," Liza insisted, her hands pressed against her stomach and her face oddly pale. "It was like being with my father all over again. The secrecy. The refusal to discuss what was troubling him, no matter how many times I pleaded with him to be honest. And his darkness. The terrible darkness."

The spiders returned to skitter down Remi's spine. "What darkness?"

Liza made a small sound, as if belatedly realizing she was revealing stuff she'd never wanted revealed.

"Nothing." She turned back to Remi, a meaningless smile on her lips. "I'm being silly."

"Mother, did Dad . . ."

"I allowed my emotions to overcome me at times." Liza overrode Remi's demand to know more about the darkness in her father. Clearly, she had no intention of discussing what she'd meant. "I wanted things to be easier for you."

Easy. Remi sighed. Ash hadn't been easy. Unlike her other boyfriends, he'd never cared about her wealth or social position. He hadn't even cared about her looks, although he told her that she was beautiful. He'd demanded her heart, her soul, and a permanent place in her life.

Nothing less would do.

Looking back, she wondered if his desire to claim her so completely had unconsciously freaked her out. "Should love be easy?" she murmured, speaking more to herself than her mother.

"Probably not." Liza heaved a small sigh. "I'm sorry I tried to interfere. I know you've been unhappy since the engagement was broken."

"That had nothing to do with you," Remi said. And she meant it. She'd become resigned to her mother's lack of welcome for Ash into the family. That hadn't influenced her decision to break off the engagement. "I was going through a lot."

There was an awkward pause. The death of Remi's father was yet another subject they never discussed.

"Yes." Her mother cleared her throat. "Is Ash planning on staying in Chicago?"

Remi's heart skidded, as if it was a car that hit black ice. Was it excitement at the thought of Ash being back in Chicago? Or terror that he might leave again?

She really wasn't sure.

"I think his plans are still up in the air," she told her mother.

"Is he here for work?"

"He's helping his brother with the Butcher case."

Liza made a sound of distress, her hand lifting to touch her throat. Almost in an unconsciously protective manner. Remi didn't blame her. The Butcher had destroyed both their lives.

"Then it's true," her mother rasped.

Remi nodded. She'd assumed her mother must have

seen the endless news covering the latest murders. "I'm afraid so."

She sent Remi a worried frown. "You should move back here until he's caught. It's not safe."

Remi didn't remind her mother that nowhere was safe. Not even this estate. Neither of them needed a reminder of that horrible night.

"Ash is staying with me," she told her mother instead.

"Ah." Liza glanced away before forcing herself to meet Remi's steady gaze. "Why didn't he come with you today?"

"He's with Jax."

Her mother abruptly narrowed her eyes. "Tell me why you're here, Remi."

Remi hesitated before squaring her shoulders. It was time to do what she'd come here to do. "I do have a question for you," she admitted.

Liza stiffened, her expression wary. "Yes?"

Remi had considered a dozen different ways to get the information she wanted from her mother. In the end, she accepted that she would simply have to be honest.

"We were going through the old interviews Ash and Dad conducted five years ago."

"Why?"

"To see if he'd overlooked anything."

"And had he?" Liza asked.

"Not so much overlooked as was lied to," Remi told her mother.

Liza tried to hide her impatience. "By a witness?"

"Robert Hutton."

"Bobby?" Liza stared at Remi in surprise. No one expected a man in Robert Hutton's position to be involved in a crime. "Why would he lie?"

"He told Dad that he was with you the night Tiffany Holloway was murdered."

Her mother looked blank, as if all emotion had been wiped from her face. "Then I'm sure we were together."

Remi gave a firm shake of her head. "I came home early that night. He wasn't here. And neither were you."

Liza waved her hand in a dismissive motion. "How could you possibly remember?"

"Because I was still sick the next morning when Dad was called and told that there'd been another murder," Remi said. "Dad was trying to convince me to call a doctor while you were complaining that he was supposed to accompany you to some luncheon."

Liza clicked her tongue. "Fine. Then we must have moved the meeting."

"Bobby has already admitted he lied and you called to cancel the meeting." She shared the information that Ash had texted her just as she'd arrived at the mansion.

A sudden silence filled the kitchen. Was her mother trying to recall that particular night? After all, she hadn't had any reason to think about it for years. Or was she crafting some lie?

At last, she gave a restless lift of her shoulders. "What are you asking me?"

"Where did you go that night?" Remi demanded bluntly.

Liza tilted her chin, her lips pursed. "I don't want to discuss it."

It wasn't the reaction Remi had been expecting. She'd assumed Liza would either deny knowing what she was talking about or smoothly explain that she'd been called to a different charity meeting that had some sort of emergency.

It was amazing how dramatic some of those people could be over a luncheon to save an old theater or support some local politician.

"Please, Mother, it might be important," she murmured, her voice pleading. "Why did you cancel that night?"

Liza paced across the floor, staring into the back mudroom as if seeking some source of inspiration. "I told you that I allowed my emotions to overcome me," she at last said, her voice so soft it was hard for Remi to catch the words.

"Mother?"

Liza's narrow shoulders tensed. "Your father told me that he had a difficult case. I even knew it had something to do with a serial killer called the Butcher. But I didn't truly comprehend the amount of time it would force your father to spend away from home."

Remi nodded. She'd been equally unhappy at the endless hours her father and Ash had been forced to work, although she'd tried to be supportive. She understood they were under a lot of pressure.

"What does that have to do with canceling your dinner with Bobby?" she asked.

Liza kept her back turned. "Your father had told me that he was spending the evening with Ash, interviewing some businessman, and he couldn't join Bobby and me for dinner."

Remi shuffled through her memories. "That's true. Ash called me to say he was going to be busy. That's why I decided to go to the study group that night."

"I impulsively asked the housekeeper to make a plate of dinner for him," Liza continued, almost as if she hadn't heard Remi. Perhaps she was too lost in her thoughts. "You know how I hated it when he would eat at one of those greasy diners."

Remi swallowed a choked laugh. Her mother might have loved her father, but she'd never fussed over his health.

"Actually, I remember you saying that you hoped he got

heartburn when he admitted to going to the diner," she reminded her mother.

Again, Remi's words were ignored. "I called the station to ask him to meet me in the parking lot," Liza continued.

"And?"

"And I was told he wasn't there."

Remi waited for more. When her mother remained silent, she gave a shrug. "That's not unusual," she pointed out. "It's not like he had a desk job. He spent as much time driving around Chicago as he ever did at the station."

"I asked when he was expected back," Liza abruptly continued. "They told me he'd gone home hours ago and wasn't expected back that night."

"So?" Remi remained puzzled. "It was probably just a mix-up."

Liza slowly turned, her face still pale and her expression strained. "Yes, but I was already feeling fragile. I was suddenly convinced he must be lying to me."

"Dad?"

"He was a handsome, charming man. Women were always throwing themselves at him. And—"

"You can't be serious," Remi interrupted despite her best effort. She wanted her mother to explain why she'd offered an alibi for Bobby Hutton, but she couldn't ignore the implication that her father would ever cheat. He had his faults. She knew that. He could be selfish, and obsessed with his job, and he forgot important events, but there was no one more loyal.

Liza looked oddly defensive. "It was a natural concern. My father always had a mistress. Sometimes more than one. It was expected of a man in his position."

Remi scowled. "Dad would never have cheated on you."

"My heart believed that, but my head was . . ." Liza

faltered, a blush suddenly staining her cheeks. "Confused. He'd been so distracted. So distant. I had to make sure."

Remi studied her mother in amazement. Liza Harding-Walsh had always seemed so invincible. As if nothing could touch her. Certainly nothing so mundane as jealousy. The realization that she'd been vulnerable enough to fear her husband was interested in another woman made her more human.

"What did you do?" Remi asked, truly interested.

"I canceled my dinner with Bobby and drove down to the station," Liza admitted in stiff tones.

"Was Dad there?"

"No. I could see right away that his car wasn't in the lot."

Remi studied her mother's face. There was an expression she couldn't fully decipher. Almost a desperation.

"I waited in my car," Liza said. "I felt like a fool, but I couldn't leave."

"How long did you stay there?"

"Two hours." Liza shrugged. "Maybe three."

"What happened?"

"Eventually, your dad drove into the lot, along with Ash, and pulled a man from the back seat of his car." Her lips twisted, the strange expression lingering on her face. "It was obvious he'd been out searching for a criminal. Or maybe it was a witness they intended to question. Either way, he'd been working while I'd sat there like a silly old woman."

Remi felt a tiny pang of regret she'd forced her mother to reveal her weakness. She knew it would scrape against Liza's considerable pride to admit what she'd done that night. "You were upset," she murmured, her tone soothing. "Did you talk to Dad?"

Liza shook her head. "Not until later. He asked about Bobby's alibi."

So . . . her father had known that Bobby hadn't been at the house that night. Did he talk to the younger man? Did Bobby confess his connection to the victim?

"I wonder why he never told Ash?" Remi spoke her thoughts out loud.

"I'm sure he didn't want to embarrass me." Her mother sucked in a slow, deep breath, her features hardening. "Is there anything else?"

Remi tried to think of what she should ask. There was no doubt information that could help Ash, but right now she didn't want to dwell on the past. Or the glimpses her mother had given her into her vulnerable heart.

It made her feel as if her entire world was being turned upside down.

"I thought we could have lunch together," she offered, without realizing the words were going to come out of her mouth.

Liza widened her eyes, clearly startled by Remi's offer. "Today?"

Remi had a second of remorse. Did she really want to spend another hour or more making small talk with her mother? Then she squashed the familiar unease.

Perhaps she and her mother could forge a new relationship.

Not necessarily the traditional mother-daughter bond, but a mutual love for her father and the suffering they'd endured.

"Unless you have other plans," Remi said.

"No." Liza hesitated, then the polite smile curved her lips. "That would be nice."

Chapter Twenty-One

Remi settled back into the sofa, sipping her wine as she watched Ash polish off a piece of deep-dish-style pizza she'd picked up before she'd come home.

After she'd had lunch with her mother, she'd gone to the youth center for a few hours. Not only had she needed a distraction from the unsettling memories her meeting with her mother had dug up, but she'd hoped she might see Drew.

She wanted to make sure he was settling into his foster home.

The teen never made an appearance, but she did talk to Lamar, who reassured her that he'd been by the house the evening before and Drew was happy for now.

The knowledge Drew was in good hands had lifted the shadows from Remi's heart, and, determined to celebrate, she'd stopped for pizza and wine.

A good thing, because Ash was in dire need of comfort food after his encounter with Robert Hutton. Unlike Ash, Remi hadn't been particularly surprised to discover that Bobby had been sleeping with Tiffany Holloway. He'd always liked his women young and eager to please. Or that he'd lied to her father and Ash when he'd been interviewed. He was charming, intelligent, and spineless.

On the other hand, Ash had been shocked by Remi's

revelation that her mother had canceled the dinner with Bobby because she'd been worried and jealous that her husband might be sneaking around.

He'd known Remi's father was an upright, honest man who would never, ever, have cheated on his wife.

"So we're back where we started." Remi broke the comfortable silence with a small sigh. "No suspects. No clues. Just another dead body."

Ash grimaced, turning on the sofa to face her. "Unfortunately, that's the nature of detective work. A hundred promising leads that fizzle out before you find the one that doesn't fizzle."

She sipped her wine, relieved to hear the reassuring edge in his voice. She depended on Ash to be her rock. If he was beginning to doubt his ability to find the Butcher, her anxiety was going to come crashing back.

"Fizzle?" She studied him with a small smile. "Is that cop talk?"

"Yes indeed," he assured her, his expression serious. "Fizzle. Poof. Sputter out. All very technical."

She pursed her lips, pretending to consider his words. "Do you teach that to your students?"

He polished off his wine and set his glass on the low coffee table. "It's more of an on-the-job training vocabulary."

Remi shook her head, poking his chest with the tip of her finger. After Ash had come home, he'd showered and changed into a crisp white dress shirt and dark slacks. She'd slipped on a pair of jeans and her favorite fuzzy sweater. The one that clung to her slender curves.

It'd been a deliberate choice, although she didn't let herself consider the reason behind the decision.

"I've heard the vocabulary at the station and the words didn't include fizzle or poof," she informed him.

He chuckled. They both knew the language at the station was crude and usually filled with obscenities.

"We had a wide and varied method of communicating," he told her.

She nodded toward the nearly empty box on the table. "More pizza?"

"Good Lord, no." He patted his flat stomach. "I already ate twice as much as I should have. I've missed Chicago-style pizza. No other place makes it right."

Her lips parted to demand whether he'd made the decision to stay in town. It wasn't her business. Not anymore.

Plus, she wasn't sure she wanted to hear the answer.

"Do you want to go through more files?" she demanded instead.

He didn't even glance toward the boxes she'd stacked near the window to clear the coffee table for dinner. "Not tonight."

She felt excitement curl through the pit of her stomach. He was looking at her in a way she remembered. One that had always made her tremble with anticipation.

"Do you have plans with Jax?"

"Nope." He placed his arm along the back of the sofa, his fingers lightly brushing her shoulder.

She cleared a strange lump from her throat. "Your mother?"

"Nope." He leaned forward, surrounding her with the warm scent of male skin and soap. "Tonight I'm all yours."

There were more curls of excitement. "What am I supposed to do with you?"

His fingers slipped beneath her braid, teasing the sensitive skin of her nape. "What do you want to do with me?"

Suddenly, Remi understood the meaning of a "loaded question."

She could think of a lot of things she wanted to do with

Ash Marcel. Most of them involved his clothes off, a can of Cool Whip, and a cherry. It was an image that had been implanted in her brain the first time she'd ever caught sight of him.

"Honestly?" she asked.

"Yeah."

"I'm not sure."

An expression of satisfaction settled on his face. Clearly, he was pleased by her fluttering bemusement. "Then we'll start with an easier question."

She found herself swaying forward. As if she was being sucked in by the sheer force of his personality. Or maybe it was the potent beauty of his male features.

"That sounds dangerous," she breathed.

"Only a little dangerous." His fingers moved to stroke over the pulse hammering at the base of her throat. "Do you still want me?"

Heat rushed to her cheeks. She hadn't expected him to be so blunt. "I'm not dead," she muttered.

"Thank God." His hand cupped her cheek. "But that doesn't answer my question."

Remi lowered her lashes, trying to hide her expressive eyes. "Ash, there's not a woman with a pulse who wouldn't want you."

His fingers tightened on her cheek. "There's only one woman I care about." His thumb brushed the stubborn line of her jaw. "Tell me. Do you want me?"

She didn't know why he needed her to say the words, but it was obviously important to him.

"Yes." She forced herself to speak the truth. "I want you."

"Good," he rasped, his fingers tugging at the band around the end of her braid to release her hair. He smiled as the heavy curtain spilled over her shoulders, threading his fingers through the dark strands. "I love the feel of your hair. Ebony silk."

"I keep thinking I should cut it off," Remi said, not sure why she was babbling but unable to stop herself. "It's constantly in the way."

"Sacrilege," Ash growled, tugging a curl. "Do you know how many nights I've spent fantasizing about the feel of your hair, brushing against my bare chest?"

Her breath tangled in her throat. "Why would your chest be bare in your fantasy?"

A slow, wicked smile curved his lips. "Because you stripped off my clothes, of course."

She trembled, barely remembering to breathe as his head lowered until their faces were just inches apart.

In the past, their lovemaking had been more than mere sex. It had been a glorious mixture of affection and pleasure and sheer fun. Some evenings, they barely got through the front door before they were yanking off their clothes with eager haste. And other nights, she would spend an hour peeling off each article of his clothing, exploring his body with her lips and tongue.

Unable to resist temptation, she slowly reached up to undo the top button of his shirt. "Like this?"

She heard him suck in a sharp breath, a hint of color staining his cheeks.

"Exactly like that."

She fumbled, her fingers trembling. It had been a long time. Too long.

"Ash," she breathed. The five years melted away, leaving Remi raw and vulnerable.

They'd been so happy together. Everything was perfect. They'd savored being in each other's company, whether it was making love or just watching an old movie and eating popcorn. They'd made plans for the future. They'd discussed where they would live and how many children they would have. They'd even talked about traveling around the world after they retired.

Then the future had been smashed by the Butcher and she'd done exactly what her mother did.

She'd retreated.

It'd been the easiest thing to do to avoid the pain. Now she wasn't sure she knew how to bring down the barriers that protected her.

As if sensing her trepidation, Ash covered her hands with his own, helping her finish her task. Then he shrugged out of his shirt, tossing it aside before pressing her palms flat against his chest.

"That's better," he murmured.

The feel of his warm skin against her palms sent sizzles of anticipation searing through her. Like someone had just poured lava directly into her veins. She tilted back her head, meeting his smoldering gaze. "What do you want from me?"

"Isn't it obvious?" he asked, his hands skimming down her body to grasp the hem of her sweater. Then, with one smooth motion, he had it yanked over her head.

His smile widened as he cupped the soft swell of her breasts, barely hidden beneath the sheer lace of her bra.

She shivered, her mouth suddenly dry. "Beyond the obvious."

"I don't think you actually want me to tell you what I want," he warned in soft tones. "Let's just pretend this is about sex. At least for tonight."

"I . . ." His thumb rubbed the tip of her nipple, and Remi's brain went blank. "I can't think when you're touching me."

"What's to think about?" His lips brushed over her forehead before moving to nuzzle her temple. "We can keep this simple if you want."

Pleasure darted through her, making her toes curl and her back arch in silent invitation. Maybe he was right. This didn't have to be complicated.

Ash was still trying to figure out what he wanted to do with his future. Not to mention the fact that he was fully preoccupied with his hunt for the Butcher. She, on the other hand, was still working through her fear, and guilt, and her need to punish herself.

Why not forget everything for a few hours and enjoy being together?

"Simple is good," she agreed, her hands exploring the hard muscles of his chest.

"Mmm." His lips skimmed over her cheek, finding the tender curve of her ear. "Just good? I'm trying for great."

She forced air in and out of her lungs. Ash didn't have to *try*. He was naturally great. One touch—one kiss—and she was melting into a puddle of panting need.

"You were always an overachiever," she said in a soft whisper.

He used the tip of his tongue to trace the shell of her ear. "It's all a matter of dedication."

"Really?" She struggled to concentrate on his words. Her heart was thundering, her body zinging with electric jolts of anticipation.

"Oh yeah." His fingers moved to her back, easily un-hooking her bra. "You have to be willing to practice. And practice. And . . ." He lifted his head, his words drying on his lips as he watched the scrap of lace fall away.

"Practice?" she offered, a sense of joy spreading through

her heart as he cupped her breasts with a gentle reverence. As if she was a rare, precious treasure.

Remi melted a little more. Who wouldn't love a man who made her feel so cherished?

"Exactly," he agreed, his voice husky.

She trembled. "Do you practice a lot?" The words left her lips before she could halt them, and she grimaced with instant regret. Lifting her hand, she placed it across his mouth. "Sorry; don't answer that."

He reached to wrap his fingers around her wrist, gently pulling her hand away from his face. "Remi, you know me," he said.

She nodded. She did know him. Even if he'd taken a lover during the time they were apart, he would have treated her with the same loyalty and respect he had always given her. Which meant that if he was willing to be with her, he wasn't currently dating any other woman.

He wouldn't cheat. Or lie. Or pretend. Period.

"I do, Ash," she assured him, wrapping her arms around his neck.

He groaned, burying his face in the curve of her throat. "It's you. Only you."

She tilted her head to the side, allowing him greater access to her neck. "You left because I pushed you away."

He trailed a path of kisses to the hollow beneath her ear, his fingers busy undoing the zipper of her jeans. "I think we both needed time to process what happened."

"I'm not sure I did much processing," she admitted, leaning back against the sofa cushions as Ash efficiently stripped off her remaining clothing. A cool breeze brushed over her bare skin, and instinctively, she glanced to the side to make sure the curtains were closed. She was still freaked out by the thought of her neighbor skulking around, peering in her windows. Once assured no one could see inside, she returned her attention to the man leaning over her. "I think it was more hiding and hoping I could convince myself it was all a bad dream," she admitted.

He shrugged, his gaze slowly moving over her naked form, as if reacquainting himself with every curve and angle. It was a little unnerving.

"Whatever works," he assured her.

She smoothed her hands up and down his arms, gazing up at his gorgeous face. She'd pretended it was working. That she'd put the past behind her and was getting on with her life.

But she'd been lying to herself and everyone else. She hadn't been getting on with her life. She'd been sticking her head in the sand while the world passed her by.

"I think it's time now for the processing," she told Ash.

Something that might have been satisfaction flared through his eyes as he slowly lowered his head. "I can help with that," he promised, brushing his lips lightly over her mouth.

Back and forth. Back and forth. The touch was as gentle as the brush of a butterfly, but it ignited sparks that heated her blood to a fever pitch.

Her toes did more curling. "More of your over-achievement?" she teased, her fingers smoothing over his shoulders and down his back.

She loved the erotic combination of his warm, silky skin and the hard muscles beneath. She loved his rich, male scent. And the weight of him pressing her into the cushions.

"I'll let you be the judge," he assured her, his tongue touching the pulse that raced at the base of her neck.

"Me?" She deliberately angled her hips to press against

the thickening length of his erection. "You mean I get to give the teacher a grade?"

Ash's breath hissed between his teeth, a dark color staining his cheeks. "Remember my fragile ego," he growled, kicking off his shoes before he was wrestling off his slacks and silk boxers.

Remi's lips curved into a smug smile as he muttered a curse. She liked his fumbling haste. It reassured her that she wasn't the only one overcome with lust.

"Fragile?" she mocked, allowing her gaze to take a slow, thorough survey of his body. He wasn't quite as muscular as he'd been before. No doubt he spent more time sitting behind a desk. And there was more hair on his chest, while his shoulders looked wider. But he still had the sort of long, lean form that a man half his age would be proud to show off. "The Marcel men have steel-plated egos," she reassured him.

He grabbed her legs, stretching them across the sofa so she was lying flat against the cushions. Then, reaching down, he grabbed a condom from the back pocket of his slacks before he was settling on top of her.

"There're other parts of me that feel steel-plated at the moment."

Remi shifted beneath him, allowing him to settle between her parted thighs. She groaned at the feel of his hard arousal pressing in precisely the perfect spot.

"So I noticed," she said with a groan.

His lips moved to trace a line of kisses down her nose and over her cheeks. At the same time, his hands moved over her body. He cupped her breasts, teasing her nipples into tight, aching beads. Then they moved down, following the curve of her waist before grasping her hips.

"You, on the other hand, are soft and smooth and just as beautiful as I remember," he said in a husky voice.

Remi shivered, wondering if he could also feel the extra pounds she'd put on, and the lack of perkiness in her breasts. She wasn't overly vain, but she had a mirror. She knew she was beginning to age. "It's been five years."

He nuzzled his lips down the side of her throat. "I know."

"Things change," she told him.

"What things?" His voice was distracted, as if he was having a hard time following the conversation.

Perhaps because he was distracted by the sight of her tightly budded nipples. He stared at them as if he was starving.

"I'm not twenty-three anymore," she warned.

"If you're worried you look any different to me, you can stop. I love every inch of you," he rasped, bending his head to run a rough tongue over the tip of her breast. "And even when time actually does start to change things, I will still love every inch of you," he assured her. "Including this." He sucked her nipple between his lips, teasing the tender nub with his teeth and tongue until her fingernails were biting into the flesh of his lower back. "And this," he told her, licking the lower curve of her breast before he kissed down the center of her midsection. He dipped his tongue into her belly button, making her squirm. "And this." He headed downward.

"Ash." She reached down, her fingers threading through his hair as he tugged her legs wider, giving him full access.

"I will always want you, Remi Walsh," he swore, licking his tongue through her damp heat.

Remi forgot her fears. Her vulnerabilities. And anything beyond the feel of the sweet, sweet pressure that was building with every sweep of his tongue.

Her back arched, her fingers tugging at his hair as a violent blast of excitement exploded through her. This was exactly what she needed.

She studied Ash's flushed face, shivering at the raw tenderness that lurked in the depths of his eyes. There was no mistaking this was more than a one-night stand for him. But she refused to consider the future. Tonight was about pleasure, not emotions.

Bliss cascaded through her as he continued to stroke over her clit. She felt like she was being seared from the inside. She needed more.

She needed him buried deep inside her.

"Please, Ash."

He chuckled. "That's what I'm trying to do, Remi. Please you."

Her mouth went dry, that delicious force continuing to swell. "You please me anymore and it's all going to be over."

"Then we'll do it again," he assured her, pushing his tongue inside her.

Remi made a sound of stunned need, her gaze riveted to the sight of him lying between her legs.

"Come for me, Remi," he commanded, pressing his tongue deeper and deeper. As if his words were some sort of magical cue, a brutal orgasm burst through her, making her body shake from the sheer pleasure.

She cried out, trembling from head to toe at the glorious release.

Still, Ash wasn't done. His tongue pushed in and out of her body, swiftly teasing her back toward another climax.

She groaned as he turned his attention to her swollen nub and gently sucked it, at the same time sinking a finger deep into her body.

Remi groaned. It was too much. He was bewitching

her in a haze of sensual pleasure. How would she ever be the same?

Seemingly satisfied that he'd completely decimated her, Ash began to slide up her body. "Are you ready for me?"

"I need you inside me."

He took time to kiss the tip of each tightly furled nipple as he slid on the condom. Remi grasped his shoulders and parted her legs so he could settle between them.

She gazed up at the man who'd lingered in her fantasies even after she'd turned her back on him. His lean, male features were flushed with passion, the satin of his hair mussed from her fingers, his eyes smoldered with passion.

He was her man. It was as primitive and simple as that.

There would never be anyone who could replace him.

The thought had barely formed when he plunged into her wet channel with one hard surge of his hips.

She made a sound of raw pleasure at the sheer intimacy of their connection. It felt as if they were one.

He stared down at her, his gaze lingering on her flushed cheeks. "Okay?"

She nodded, unable to speak.

Holding her gaze, he thrust his hips forward, rocking into her at a fierce, ruthless pace.

Her nails sank into the soft flesh of his backside, her hips lifting off the sofa to meet his hard thrusts. Unbelievably, she felt another surge of hunger race through her. Clearly, she'd been needing this. More than she realized.

He dipped his head down to claim her mouth with a kiss that demanded her complete surrender.

She didn't mind. In fact, she loved it. Remi wrapped her legs around his hips, bracing herself as another massive orgasm began to clench her lower muscles.

"I've missed you, Remi," he muttered against her lips,

their bodies moving together with a primitive intensity. "I've missed us."

Her fingers tangled in his hair as his hands slipped beneath her hips to tilt her to an angle that allowed him to thrust even deeper.

His cock hit a glorious spot deep inside her, sending her hurtling over the edge, the orgasm ripping through her as she cried out his name in dazed pleasure.

Chapter Twenty-Two

Jax arrived in front of the run-down apartment building, not surprised to discover it was shrouded in a grim silence. Just a couple of blocks away, the early rush hour had already started as people dashed to catch the bus or train to get to work on time. Here, however, very few had actual jobs. This was a place for those who were barely keeping a roof over their heads.

Crawling out of his car, Jax made sure it was locked tight and then touched the gun that was holstered beneath his coat. He didn't intend to use it, but he wanted to be prepared.

After the medical examiner's office had called with an ID on the murdered woman, Jax had done his research. He'd discovered that Rachel Burke lived with her father and brothers in the cramped apartment. There hadn't been much more on her. She'd never been arrested, she didn't have a driver's license, and her work record was spotty at best.

Her father, Allen Burke, on the other hand, had been arrested on half a dozen occasions. Mostly public intoxication or fighting at the local bar. There'd also been one petty theft charge that had landed him in the Cook County jail for a week. The brothers were following in their father's footsteps, although they were young enough that their crimes were in the hands of the juvenile system.

Jax climbed the stairs to the front door of the apartment building, not surprised to discover it was unlocked. He couldn't imagine the owner particularly cared about the safety of his tenants. He crossed the dark lobby and climbed the stairs to the third floor. He wasn't going to take the elevator. His luck hadn't been that great lately.

He pulled out his phone to double-check the apartment number before halting in front of the door at the end of a dark, narrow hallway. Then, unzipping his coat so he had ready access to his gun, he pounded on the door.

Nothing. He pounded again. And again. Five minutes later, the door cracked open to reveal Allen Burke. Jax pressed his lips together, hiding his wry smile.

The tall, thin man looked just like his mug shot. At one time he might have been handsome, but now his dark hair was sticking up like it hadn't seen a comb in years. His face was jaundiced, with dark circles beneath his bloodshot eyes. And there were spidery veins on his prominent nose from years of hard drinking. Jax's gaze lowered to take in the clothes that were wrinkled and stained. They hung off his gaunt body as if he'd found them in a dumpster.

"Shit," Allen rasped, peering at Jax as if he was having trouble focusing his eyes. "What time is it?"

"Almost eight," Jax said.

Allen muttered a curse. "What sort of jackoff goes around banging on doors at eight in the morning?"

Jax pulled aside his coat to reveal the official ID card he had clipped to his belt.

"The sort that carries a badge," he told the man. "I'm Detective Marcel."

Allen's face pinched into a sour expression. "If you're

here to tell me my daughter's dead, I already know. I had to spend an hour at the morgue last night."

Jax frowned. The man sounded put out, like the death of his daughter had been a huge inconvenience. "I'm sorry for your loss," he forced himself to say.

"Yeah. Don't know what the hell we're going to do without her." Allen glanced over his shoulder. "The place is a mess."

Jax grimaced, even as he tried to remind himself that everyone grieved in their own way. He'd seen parents who were stunned, some who were angry, some disbelieving, and others pretended it was all some huge mistake. "Can we go inside?" he asked instead.

Allen scowled with a sudden suspicion. "Why?"

"I have a few questions."

"About what?"

Jax narrowed his gaze as he heard a door open down the hall. He didn't like having his back exposed. Especially not in this neighborhood.

"Inside," he commanded.

"Christ, I hate cops," Allen muttered as he stepped back.

Jax quickly stepped through the opening and closed the door behind him. Then, he made a quick survey of his surroundings to ensure there was no one lurking in a dark corner.

They were standing in a small living room that had a sofa nearly hidden beneath blankets and dirty clothes. It looked like that was where Allen had been sleeping before Jax woke him up. There were also a couple of recliners that were equally covered by dirty clothes. Empty pizza boxes were tossed around the room.

Jax shuddered. Not so much at the obvious filth that coated the apartment. It was more the stench that clung to the air that was making his skin crawl. As if there was something toxic hidden beneath the layers of dirt.

On the plus side, it appeared they were alone, although he assumed the two Burke brothers were asleep somewhere in the apartment.

Reaching the middle of the room, Allen turned to glare at Jax. "What do you want?"

Jax reached into the inner pocket of his coat and pulled out an old-fashioned notebook and pencil. He hadn't mastered the ability to jot down his thoughts on an electronic pad.

"When was the last time you saw your daughter?" he asked.

Allen shrugged. "A few weeks ago."

"Can you be more specific?"

"Not really." Allen rubbed his jaw, which was dark from his unshaved whiskers. "The days all run together."

Jax studied the man. His words weren't slurred, but Jax could catch the scent of alcohol on his breath. Just how much drinking had he done last night?

"But she lived here?" he pressed.

Allen shrugged. "Yeah. She lived here."

"Tell me about her."

Allen looked confused. "Whadda ya want to know?"

"Her job, her hobbies, her friends." Jax shrugged. "Any boyfriends."

The man glanced around the apartment, as if searching for inspiration. "There's nothing to tell."

"Nothing?"

"Rachel went and dropped out of school her sophomore year and then started taking odd jobs she hated. None of them lasted more than a couple of weeks." He shook his head in disgust. "That's why she was still living here. I let her stay as long as she helped take care of the boys."

Jax grimaced. He sensed that Rachel was the only one

who was expected to earn her keep in the apartment. Beneath the piles of clothes and pizza boxes, the carpet was worn, but it had a few rugs spread over the worst spots, and there were curtains and pretty, framed pictures on the wall. That wasn't the work of Allen or his boys.

"Generous," he said in dry tones.

Allen stuck out his lower lip, like a petulant child. "She had a place to live and food on the table."

Jax shook his head. He wasn't going to argue with the idiot. "Did she have a job when she disappeared?"

"She told me that she was doing some modeling, but you know what that means."

"No. I don't."

Allen hunched his shoulders. "Probably taking her clothes off for men," he muttered. "Girls always have a way to get easy money."

Jax clenched the pencil tightly in his hand. Allen Burke made his skin crawl, but right now, he couldn't risk punching the bastard in the face. He needed answers about Rachel and how she might have come in contact with the Butcher.

"Do you have the address of the modeling agency?" he asked between clenched teeth.

"It wasn't official or nothing. She would get an email or a message on that page thingy of hers."

Page thingy? Jax frowned before he realized what the man meant. "Facebook?"

"Whatever." Allen waved a hand toward the door. "Next thing, she would be plastering her face with makeup and taking off."

Jax flipped back through his notebook, studying what Ash had discovered about Angel Conway when he'd traveled to her hometown. He felt a flare of satisfaction. Yes. Angel had been a wannabe actress and model. Ash had also suspected she was discovered by the killer through her Facebook page.

"Rachel had a computer?" he asked. Was it possible they could find an email for the Butcher?

The possibility sent a sizzle of anticipation through Jax. They'd been chasing shadows for so many years, it seemed hard to accept they might have an electronic trail to lead them to the killer.

Allen licked his lips, an odd expression on his sallow face. "Yeah, she bought a laptop a couple of years ago."

Jax stepped forward. "Where is it?"

"I . . . uh . . ."

Jax scowled. What was wrong with the man? Then, Jax was hit by a sudden realization. Was the man using the computer for some illegal activity? Porn? Dealing drugs? Downloading pirated movies?

Right now, he didn't give a shit.

"Allen, all I'm looking for is Rachel's communication with anyone offering her a job," he said in stern tones. "I'm not interested in anything you might have been doing on there."

He'd expected the man to be reassured. After all, he'd given him a free pass.

Instead, Allen cleared his throat, as if he was being choked. "The thing is . . ."

Jax rammed the paper and pencil back into his pocket. He was tired of being jerked around by this loser. The Butcher was no doubt stalking his next victim even as Jax was wasting his time in this apartment. Every second the bastard remained out there put another woman at risk.

"I can get a warrant for it," he warned.

Allen folded his arms over his chest, his expression defensive. "It's not here."

Disappointment poured through him like acid. "Did she take it with her?"

Allen's eyes darted around. He was about to lie. Jax knew all the signs. Then, as if realizing that trying to deceive a cop wasn't the best idea, the man heaved a rasping sigh.

"One of the boys sold it," he admitted in clipped tones.

Jax paused, allowing the words to sink into his brain. "You sold your daughter's computer?"

Allen shifted from foot to foot, his face flushing. "She wasn't here."

Was he lying? Maybe he was still afraid there might be something on the computer that might get him in trouble? Or had he really been sleazy enough to sell his missing daughter's computer?

"Who did you sell it to?" he demanded.

"It wasn't me," Allen insisted, no doubt sensing Jax's gut-deep disgust. "It was my boy."

"Then who did your boy sell it to?" he demanded through clenched teeth.

Allen shrugged. "Someone on the street."

Without warning, Jax reached out to grab Allen's dirty sweatshirt, twisting it until the neckline tightened around the man's throat.

"Do you think I won't arrest you?" he snapped.

The bloodshot eyes widened in a sudden burst of fear. "For what?"

"Interfering in a murder investigation."

"How am I interfering?"

"You're withholding information," Jax accused.

"Bullshit."

Jax gave the man a shake. He didn't believe in police brutality, even when he was dealing with a scumbag. But the fear that the Butcher was slipping through his fingers was making him a little crazy. "Then where is the computer?"

"I woke up and the boys were partying," Allen stammered. "I asked them where they got the—"

Jax made a sound of impatience as the man cut off his words. "Drugs?"

Allen gave a small nod, as if unwilling to say the word out loud. Did he think Jax was wired? Idiot.

"They told me they'd given Rachel's computer to their dealer," he continued in a whiny voice. "It was too late for me to do anything about it."

Jax tried to imagine his father's response if one of them had been missing and a brother had stolen their personal computer and sold it for drugs. It would have been epic.

And not in a good way.

"What's the dealer's name?" he demanded.

"I don't know his name." Allen squawked as Jax twisted his hand so the material of the sweatshirt bit into the man's throat. "All I know is that he hangs out on the corner a block south of here."

Jax shoved the man back, releasing his grip on the shirt. He was afraid he might accidentally break the fool's neck.

"Where are your sons?"

Allen glanced around, as if wondering if they might be hidden beneath the piles of clothes.

"Probably crashing at a friend's house," he finally muttered. "I haven't seen them since last night."

Jax wasn't surprised the man didn't have any idea where his sons might be, despite the fact that they were both underage. He was, however, baffled by his complete lack of concern that his only daughter had been lured from her home and brutally attacked.

"Don't you care at all that your daughter was murdered?" he ground out.

Allen jerked, his flush turning an ugly shade of red. "Of course I care."

"Really?" Jax scoffed. "She goes missing, but instead of calling the cops, you pawn her computer for a few drugs?"

"I told you, it wasn't me . . ." Allen started to protest, only to snap his lips together as he met Jax's fierce glare. "All right, I'm a shitty father," he admitted in grudging tones. "What do you want from me?"

"I want to know if Rachel was contacted by her killer, and why she didn't fight back when she was being attacked." He held the older man's gaze. "Did she say anything before she left?"

Allen started to shake his head, but he stopped, his brow furrowed, as if he was struck by a sudden thought.

"Not to me," he said. "But I heard her talking to herself in the bathroom."

"What was she saying?"

Allen snorted. "She was pretending she was accepting an Academy Award. She was always doing stuff like that."

"She wanted to be an actress," Jax murmured. Just like Angel. And perhaps all the other victims.

As Ash had pointed out, it would be easy to use the promise of a modeling or movie contract to lure a young, vulnerable woman into a trap.

"Yeah." Allen glanced across the room at an open door Jax assumed led to the bathroom. "I told her to get the hell out so I could take a shower. She yelled back that she was going to become a famous actress and she was going to leave me to rot in the gutter."

Jax tried to visualize the scene. It was probable that Rachel had been playacting. How else could she make her life in this apartment bearable? But then again, she might have been promised the ability to make her dreams come true.

"Anything else?" Jax asked.

Allen scratched under his arm, leaning down to grab a

half-empty bottle of vodka from the floor. "There might be something in her room."

"Do you mind if I search?"

Allen screwed off the lid of the cheap liquor, taking a deep drink. Then he burped as he waved his hand toward the short hallway at the back of the room. "Knock yourself out."

Jax rolled his eyes. "You're a real winner."

"Hey." Allen pointed a finger at Jax. "Not all of us were given a good job in this world. Some of us have to scrape just to get by."

Jax gave a humorless laugh. "Do you think they came to my house and handed me a badge?"

Allen shrugged, clearly in no mood to accept he had no one to blame but himself for his crappy life. "There are people who have luck, and those who don't."

Jax shook his head, stepping over the pizza boxes as he headed for the hallway. "There are people willing to put down the bottle and work for a better future."

"I'm going back to bed," Allen muttered.

Jax ignored him as he entered the first door on the right of the hallway, thankful to discover it was scrupulously clean, with a frilly bedspread and dresser with a large mirror.

This had to be Rachel's bedroom.

He reached into the back pocket of his slacks to pull out a pair of rubber gloves, snapping them on before he stepped over the threshold.

Crossing the floor, he pulled open the closet door. There were several empty hangers, which he assumed meant she'd packed a bag to take with her. But there were still enough clothes inside to suggest she intended to return to the apartment. He turned to search through the dresser. There was nothing there that might offer a clue where she'd gone.

He shoved his hands under the mattress and then pulled aside the bedcover to look under the pillows. He was hoping for a diary. Did women still keep them? Or at least a letter from a boyfriend who might know where Rachel was going.

Nothing.

He straightened. Obviously, he'd have to wait until he could get a warrant to get Rachel's phone and email records. More time wasted while the Butcher continued to hunt the streets of Chicago.

He was walking toward the door when his attention was captured by a scrap of paper next to a small trash can. Jax bent down to grab the note, glancing at the scribbled writing.

There was one word.

Paradiso.

What the hell?

I watch the waitress as she scurries to keep up with the morning crowd. This is one of those upscale pastry shops, so there's not much on the menu beyond muffins and croissants and a dozen different types of coffee.

The waitress is only vaguely satisfying. Her body is sleek and slender beneath the sweater and jeans. And her black hair is long enough to be kept pulled into a ponytail. But her skin is too dark, as if she spent time in a tanning booth. And her eyes are the wrong shape. They're too round and a strange gray color. Plus her nose is way too wide.

Not that it mattered. I'd already tried creating the perfect specimen and what had it accomplished? Nothing. I'd wasted time and energy and money without the cure I so desperately desired. In some ways, the prototypes had only made my sickness worse.

Spiraling out of control . . .

The words whispered through my mind.

I'd spiraled before. Five years ago. Back then, I'd been halted before I could hit bottom. I'd even managed to come back to my senses.

Or at least I'd diverted my hungers. Nothing could truly appease the suffocating urges. It was a disease. One that was refusing to be cured. No matter how much blood flowed.

Blood, blood, blood.

I sip my coffee, my gaze following the waitress. She smiles, but it doesn't reach her eyes. Is she sad? Bored? Ready for her tedious life to be over?

No. I try to remind myself she is young. It's possible she is still filled with hope that her future will be better. That was doubtful, of course. She had a crappy job. She wasn't particularly beautiful. She smoked; I could smell it clinging to her clothes. And she didn't have enough personality to be considered charming.

Just a dull, average woman. Who would miss her? Who would care?

I eat my muffin and sip my coffee. The chatter washes over me. It had always been like that for me. When I was in this mood, I was alone no matter how many people were around.

I understand that sounds clichéd. Everyone felt they stood apart from the world, but my loneliness is more.

Mine is cold. An emptiness that echoes through my soul.

I have told myself it wasn't my fault. It was a darkness implanted while I was too young to fight against it. There was nothing I could have done to change my destiny.

We all have a destiny. Don't we?

Even the waitress. I set aside my empty coffee cup and wrap my fingers around the knife set next to my muffin plate. The young woman was reaching the end of her shift. In a few hours, she would be walking home.

I'd followed her before.

I knew her apartment was several blocks away from the pastry shop.

On such a cold day, she would no doubt be eager to accept a lift. Even from a stranger.

Silently, I rehearse the exact words that will convince the woman I can be trusted.

Chapter Twenty-Three

Ash was surprised to open his eyes and discover the pale winter sunlight was streaming into the bedroom. What time was it? About to reach for his phone, Ash was halted as a low, tortured whimper echoed through the air.

With a frown, he turned his attention to the woman tightly wrapped in his arms. Instantly, his heart melted. He hadn't actually made a conscious decision to sleep with Remi last night. But sitting next to her on the couch as they ate pizza had been a potent reminder of all the wonderful evenings they'd spent together.

Suddenly, he couldn't wait any longer.

He still loved her. He would *always* love her. And eventually, he would convince the stubborn woman that they belonged together.

And he didn't regret their night of heated passion. Their lovemaking had been just as glorious as it had been five years before. And while he wished they could openly discuss the future, he was prepared to be patient.

They had enough to worry about right now.

On cue, Remi resumed her whimpering. Gently, Ash pushed her dark hair from her cheek, studying her sleep-flushed face.

After making love on the couch, Ash had carried Remi to her bed. Then he'd devoted the next few hours to exploring her from head to toe and back again. Which would explain why he'd slept so late.

"Remi, wake up," he urged in a husky voice. Her body twitched, her breath rasping between her parted lips. Ash's heart clenched with concern. His hand reached out to cup her cheek as he leaned down to speak directly in her ear. "Remi."

The whimpering stopped as she lifted her lashes to study him with a fierce intensity.

"Ash?" she breathed.

He skimmed his lips down the line of her jaw before planting a soft kiss on her lips. "I've got you."

She wiggled against him, her hands grasping his upper arms. "Hold me."

He gave her lower lip a gentle nip. "You never have to ask." He slowly lifted his head, searching the shadows that darkened her eyes. "Was it a bad dream?"

"I . . ." Her words dried on her lips.

"Remi." Ash stroked his fingers down her cheek. "Talk to me."

"I think it must have been a dream, but it seemed so real." She shivered, her gaze skittering away. "Too real."

"Tell me," he urged in low tones.

She hesitated, clearly reluctant. But as he continued to gaze down at her in silence, she heaved a resigned sigh.

"It was that night," she muttered.

"The night you were attacked?"

"Yeah."

Ash grimaced, his fingers tucking her hair behind her ear. "I'm sorry."

She looked confused. "Why are you apologizing?"

"Because the two of us being together has obviously stirred up old memories," he explained.

"No." Her fingers moved lightly over his bare chest. "I've had nightmares before. Just not like this one. It was . . ." She shook her head. "Weirdly vivid."

Ash battled to keep his muscles from tensing. He didn't want Remi to know that he'd been desperately hoping her memories would return. The last thing he wanted was to put any pressure on her. Especially not when she might be right.

It was quite possible she'd had a nightmare.

"Maybe if you talk about it, you'll feel better," he told her, his fingers continuing to stroke over her pale features. "What happened?"

Remi sucked in a deep breath, as if gathering her courage. "It started out like the others. I was being followed as I drove home."

Regret tugged at Ash's heart. He hated causing Remi pain, but this was too important. He had to know what was in her dream. "You're safe," he whispered. "You're right here in my arms."

Her body arched closer, perhaps seeking his warmth, but her expression remained distant. As if she was lost in her dream.

"After that, things usually go blank in my dreams. Just like they did that night."

"What happened this time?"

Her fingers curled, her nails biting into his chest. Ash didn't protest. He could endure a little pain. Anything to make it easier for her.

"I was in the car, and then everything was dark," she said, her voice a mere whisper. "I don't remember driving into the garage or getting out. But this time, I was suddenly in a tunnel."

Ash felt a stab of surprise. "A tunnel? Underground?"

She paused, considering the question. "I'm not sure. There weren't any windows."

He allowed his fingers to thread through her hair, savoring the sensation of the silky strands. "Tell me what you see," he prodded in gentle tones.

She tilted back her head, her brow furrowed. "Ash, it was a dream."

He gave a light tug on her hair. "Humor me."

"Fine." She closed her eyes, as if trying to recall the specific details. "There are a line of bare light bulbs running down the middle of the ceiling," she said at last.

"What about the floor?"

"It was dirt. So were the walls." Her voice held an edge of puzzlement. Obviously, she didn't recognize her surroundings. "It must have been underground, but I don't know where it is or how I got there."

"Are you alone?"

He felt her sudden shiver. "No. There's someone behind me."

His fingers cupped her nape, gently massaging the tense muscles. "Can you see their face?"

"No." Her voice was unsteady. "I'm afraid to turn around."

"Shh. It's okay, Remi." Ash squashed the impulse to press her for more details about the person behind her. He wasn't interrogating a witness. He had to be careful not to spook her into refusing to discuss her dream. Instead, he leaned down to brush his lips over her forehead. "Do you remember anything else about the tunnel?"

She took a moment before she answered. "There was a smell."

"Do you know what it is?"

"Bread."

"Bread?" Ash studied her in confusion, wondering if he'd heard her correctly. "Are you sure?"

She nodded slowly. "Freshly baked bread."

He tried to think of why there would be bread in a tunnel. "Could you be beneath a restaurant or a bakery?"

"No. It smells like home."

Ash stared down at her in confusion. Maybe it had been nothing more than a strange dream. "Here?"

"No, my childhood home," she clarified.

"Oh." That made more sense. "Are there tunnels beneath your mother's estate?"

She glanced at him as if he was out of his mind. "Of course there aren't any tunnels."

Once again he didn't press her. He wanted her to concentrate on the dream.

"What else do you remember?"

She shivered. "It's cold. Really cold."

He considered his next question. "Are you wearing the clothes you had on when you attended the art gallery opening?"

Her lips parted, no doubt intending to tell him that she hadn't noticed what clothes she had on in her dream. Then her eyes widened.

"Yes," she breathed. "I had on the same jeans and sweater. And my boots. They were crunching against the dirt floor."

Ash's certainty that this was more than a dream was increasing by the minute. "Do you have on your coat?"

"Yes. And my gloves." She wrinkled her brow, trying to concentrate on her fading memories. "But I don't have my purse."

That made sense. When Ash had gotten to the estate that night, he'd found her purse and backpack in her car.

The discovery had told him that Remi had been attacked while she was still in the garage. She would never have left her purse and phone in the car. The question had always been whether she'd been the one to unlock the door to the house and switch off the security system. Or if she'd already been unconscious and the Butcher had the ability to break into the house without setting off the alarm.

Now he had a new theory.

The Butcher had followed her home, then attacked her in the garage. From there, he'd used the hidden tunnels to force her into the house.

Which meant he was familiar with the estate.

"How long were you in the tunnel?" he asked.

"I don't think it was long. A few minutes maybe."

Long enough to get from the detached garage to the house, Ash silently acknowledged. "Did anyone speak?"

"No. It was quiet." She trembled against him, her nails digging deep into his skin. "Scary quiet."

He ran a soothing hand up and down her back. "Do you realize you're in danger?"

She shook her head. "I'm more confused than anything. As if I've been drugged. My knees are so weak, I can barely walk."

That fit in with the results of her medical report after she'd been taken to the hospital. The doctors had found a puncture wound from a needle on the side of her neck, and traces of Midazolam in her system.

"Do you know where you're going?" he asked.

"I don't know." She halted, seemingly struck by a sudden thought. "Wait. There are stairs ahead of me."

"Describe them," Ash commanded.

"They're just stairs."

"What are they made of?"

She frowned, as if wondering why he was interested in something so mundane.

"They're wooden," she said at last.

Ash nodded. He was assuming the tunnel had been built

for secrecy, not beauty. Which would explain the dirt floor and wooden stairs.

"How many steps?" he asked.

"Five." Remi shrugged. "Maybe six."

Not many. That would mean the tunnel wasn't deep. "Do you climb them?"

"Yes." She grimaced, as if enduring physical pain at the memory. "I'm barely able to stay upright, my knees are so weak. I'm crawling up each one."

Ash kissed the top of her curls, hating the need to force her to relive the horror of that night. He could only hope that her sacrifice would lead to the unmasking of the Butcher.

"Why don't you stop if your knees are so weak?" he asks, his hands continuing to trace up and down her spine.

"There's something pressing into my back."

"A gun?"

"No. It's sharp."

His hands halted, his breath wrenched from his lungs. *Shit.* He should have guessed what it would be.

"A knife," he breathed in a harsh voice.

"Yes."

Silence filled the room at the mention of the knife. Both of them were tortured by the knowledge of just how many women had been brutally killed by having their throats sliced open.

At last, Ash cleared his throat. "Do you remember anything else?"

Her brow furrowed as she lifted a hand to touch her temple. As if she had a sudden headache.

"Everything is going dark," she told him.

The drugs must have been about to knock her unconscious, Ash realized. "Did you reach the top of the stairs?"

"I don't think so." She paused, the denial forgotten as she sucked in a sharp breath. "Yes. I did reach the top. I was on my hands and knees, then a door opened and there was a blinding light. And the scent of fresh bread was much stronger. As if I was standing in the kitchen. I thought I must have died and was on my way to heaven."

Ash was confused. "Did the person behind you open the door?"

"I don't know." She continued to rub her temple. "It just opened, and the light was all around me."

Ash tried to imagine what had happened. Remi had been on her hands and knees, presumably on some sort of landing. Was the door opened from inside? Or had the killer reached around her to open it?

Or maybe there was a hidden switch in the wall that would activate it.

"Did you go into the house?"

She stiffened abruptly, her head tilting back to reveal her stricken expression.

"No," she breathed. "It had to have been heaven."

Unease curled through his gut. "Remi?"

"I heard my father's voice," she rasped.

Ash made a choked sound. Gage? Had his onetime partner caught the Butcher when they were in the tunnel? But if he had, why had his blood been found in the living room?

"You're sure?" he demanded.

Remi's hands flattened against his chest as she arched away. "Ash, it was just a nightmare," she insisted, her voice edged with something that sounded like panic.

It was obvious she'd endured enough. Perhaps it was the memory of her father. Or maybe it was some deeply buried memory that was still struggling to come to the surface.

Whatever the case, her nerves were close to snapping.

"Maybe," he murmured, his hands resuming their exploration of her back.

It was time for a distraction. And he knew the perfect way to take her mind off her bad dreams.

"It was." Her tone was harsh. "I promise you, there are no mystery tunnels beneath my mother's home."

He lowered his head, allowing his lips to nuzzle the corner of her mouth. "Hmm."

Her hands slid up his chest, her fingers grasping his shoulders. "What?"

He traced her lower lip with the tip of his tongue. She tasted so sweet. Warm and feminine. Deliciously familiar.

"You know, I'm suddenly finding it hard to concentrate," he informed her in husky tones.

"Really?" Her fingers tiptoed up his shoulders until she tangled them in his hair. "Why is that?"

"Because I woke with a beautiful, naked woman in my arms," he admitted, stealing a slow, lazy kiss.

"That does sound distracting," she murmured against his lingering lips.

Ash lifted his head, staring down at the woman who'd remained in his heart no matter how many miles were between them.

It was a relief to watch her relax beneath his teasing. And to catch a glimpse of the passion darkening her eyes. But even as he cupped the softness of her breast, he knew that neither of them had forgotten the darkness that haunted them.

Right now, however, he intended to concentrate on the sheer bliss of having Remi wrapped in his arms.

"I missed having you in my bed," he whispered, his head dipping down so he could run his tongue over the tip of her nipple. He smiled as he felt her quiver in pleasure. "I even missed your snoring."

She gave a sharp tug on his hair in protest even as her back arched in invitation for his touch. "I don't snore."

"It's cute," he assured her, teasing the tender nipple with the edge of his teeth.

She turned so she could wrap her leg over his hip. Ash's breath rushed out on a low hiss as she nestled against his hardening cock.

"At least I don't kick," she said, her lips curling into a smug smile as he took several seconds to process her words.

Hell. A man wasn't supposed to think when he had a soft, willing woman pressed against him. Was he?

"I kick?" he finally managed to rasp.

"Like a mule," she assured him.

"Should I kiss you and make it all better?"

He didn't wait for her to answer as he brushed his lips down her body. She trembled, her arms wrapping around his neck.

"That's not where you kicked me," she murmured.

"No?" He chuckled, his hands grasping her hips as he kept her from squirming beneath his searching caresses. "Don't tell me. I want to find the spot myself."

She released a low groan, her lashes lowering as she gave in to the waiting bliss.

"Overachiever."

Chapter Twenty-Four

Jax was climbing into his car and about to pull away from the decrepit apartment building when he received a text from his mother.

I have to see you. Now.

Jax told himself not to overreact. His mother tended to use whatever methods were necessary when she wanted something. Still, he couldn't prevent the urge to speed through the backstreets as he drove straight to the 1950s ranch house in the suburbs.

Like most houses in the neighborhood, it was built on a small lot with a fenced-in backyard. The vinyl siding was white, although Jax had a vague memory of it being a weird shade of avocado in the past. There was also an attached garage his father had recently expanded.

The driveway was packed with the cars of holiday guests that had already descended, forcing Jax to park in the street. Locking the car, he jogged across the frozen yard and pulled open the door. It didn't matter how many times he tried to convince his mother to keep the house secure, she refused to listen. She claimed she would move before she would keep herself locked away like a prisoner.

Entering the cozy living room that was currently being used as a spare bedroom for Jax's aunt and uncle, he tiptoed his way into the L-shaped kitchen.

As expected, he found his mother standing next to the kitchen sink, washing dishes.

A portion of his tension eased as she turned at the sound of his footsteps. She smiled with a sunny welcome that assured him no one in the family was injured.

"Jax." She grabbed a dish towel to dry her hands as she headed across the floor and pressed a kiss to his cheek. "I'm so happy to see you."

He glanced down at her with a frown. "I got your text. Is everything okay?"

"That's exactly what I intended to ask you," she said, abruptly moving to close the kitchen door. She turned back with a shake of her head. "I swear, I'm going to start spending the holidays in the Bahamas. I haven't had any peace for a week."

"Mom, what's going on?" Jax pressed.

She didn't answer. Instead, she pointed toward the kitchen table in the center of the floor.

"I want you to sit down," she told him. "Then I want you to tell me what you would like for breakfast."

"Breakfast." He studied his mother, wondering if the stress of her houseguests had tumbled her over the edge. "I'm working this morning. Do you need something or not?"

She pursed her lips, continuing to point at the table. "I'm not talking until you sit down and tell me what you want for breakfast. Is that clear?"

Jax paused. He was way too busy to be playing games. Then again, he knew that tone. When his mother was in this mood, a smart man simply did what she wanted.

"A western omelet and toast," Jax muttered as he grudgingly walked forward and flopped into one of the wooden seats.

Bustling around the kitchen with the intensity of a general going into battle, his mother pulled out the ingredients from the fridge. Then, grabbing a banana, she placed it on the table.

"Eat this while I'm cooking," she commanded. "You need your vitamins."

Jax heaved a sigh, obediently slipping off his coat before he peeled the fruit and stuffed it into his mouth.

"You're a very frustrating woman, June Marcel."

She turned back to the counter, chopping vegetables and whisking eggs that she tossed into a skillet. Never halting her fluid movements, she grabbed the coffeepot and filled a mug with the steaming black nirvana.

"It's part of my charm," she assured Jax, setting the coffee in front of him.

Jax grabbed the mug, taking a deep sip. He sighed in pleasure. His mother knew exactly how he liked his coffee.

"Is Nate here?" he asked.

"No, he should be home tomorrow," his mother said. As far as the older woman was concerned, this house would always be home for the Marcel boys. "You'll join us for dinner at seven."

It wasn't a request, but Jax gave a vague shrug. "I'll have to see. This case—"

His mother interrupted. "Is consuming your life and making you crazy."

Jax snorted. "Is that an official diagnosis?"

"It's a mother's diagnosis," June informed him, grabbing a plate and sliding the omelet out of the skillet before gathering the toast and slathering it with her homemade jelly. "Here." She placed the plate and utensils in front of Jax. "I want you to eat every bite."

"I'm not a child," Jax protested, even as he grabbed a fork and dug into the food with unmistakable gusto.

He hadn't realized how hungry he was until he started eating.

"Then stop acting like one," his mother chided, taking a seat next to him as she sipped her own coffee.

He ate a slice of toast before he demanded an explanation. No one could cook like his mom. "What are you talking about?"

She offered a mysterious smile. "I have my connections at the station."

Jax narrowed his eyes. "Monica?" he asked, knowing the dispatcher played bridge with his mother.

"Among others," she murmured.

Jax grimaced, polishing off the last of his omelet. "And what did your spies tell you?"

"Not spies," June corrected him. "Concerned friends who keep me informed on the welfare of my son."

"That sounds a lot like spies."

His mother pretended she didn't hear his accusation.

"They tell me that you're working day and night. And that you drink gallons of coffee without eating a decent meal. They also say you are starting to look like a zombie." She reached out to touch the shadows beneath his eyes. "They were right."

Jax couldn't lie. The evidence of his lack of sleep was etched on his face.

"I can rest and eat later," he said. "Right now, nothing matters but finding the Butcher."

"Your health matters."

Jax ate his second slice of toast before pushing away his empty plate and swiveling in his chair to confront the woman who was regarding him with open concern. "Remi is in danger, Mom," he said in a low voice.

"I know." Her expression was somber. "And I understand that you and Ash have to do everything possible to find the killer."

"So why am I here?"

"Because you're . . ." The older woman heaved a sigh.

"I'm what?"

"You are my Jax." His mother gazed down at her coffee cup, as if trying to find the words. "You've always been the protector of the family."

Jax frowned. "Dad is the protector."

June lifted her head, her expression wry. "Yes, but he was married to his job. Just like you are now," she pointed out. "And when one of your brothers was in trouble or needed help, you were the one to rush to their rescue."

Jax felt a blush heating his face. His mother made him sound like he was some sort of superman. "I think you're exaggerating."

She held his gaze. "Who drove five hours in the middle of a snowstorm to pick up Ty when he got stuck in a ditch?" she demanded.

Jax reached for his coffee. It was true that his brothers had a habit of turning to him when they didn't want their parents to know they'd gotten in trouble. But it wasn't that he had any special talents. He just happened to be the oldest.

"Ty had to be back for football practice or he would have lost his scholarship," he said, his lips twitching as he recalled the frantic call that had woken him from a deep sleep.

He thought his middle brother was going to cry when he realized he might not be back in time for early morning check-in.

"And he didn't want to tell us he'd snuck out of his dorm room to attend the concert despite his curfew."

"He was an idiot, but he didn't deserve to lose a chance at a good education," Jax said. Playing college sports could be grueling, and Jax understood his brother's need to blow off steam.

He'd ignored his coach's curfew once or twice himself. Thankfully, he'd never gotten caught.

"You were also the one who found the boy who stole Nate's bike and forced him to give it back," his mother reminded him.

Jax chuckled. He'd nearly forgotten Sam Perry, the neighborhood bully. He'd been three inches taller and fifty pounds heavier than Jax, but he'd gone down with one good punch to the face.

"I took great pleasure in hitting that jerk," he admitted. "I think I broke his nose."

His mother sent him a rueful smile. "I have a hundred other stories that are the same."

"Let's give them a pass," Jax insisted.

"My point is that you'll drive yourself into a hospital bed if someone doesn't take care of you," his mother said, reaching to cover his hand with hers. "And until you find that special woman, that task belongs to me."

Jax snorted at the subtle jab. "You're hitting all the buttons today. My job. My lack of a wife."

"Because I love you."

He turned his hand so he could give her fingers a tight squeeze. "I know that, Mom."

"Good." She settled back in her chair, studying him with a stubborn expression. "Now tell me what's bothering you."

"Wouldn't you rather discuss the wedding?" He tried to distract her.

She held his gaze. "Tell me."

Jax accepted defeat. His mother wasn't going to give up until she'd gotten the information she wanted.

"Unfortunately, there's nothing to tell," he told her. "Every clue that might lead me to the Butcher has turned out to be a dead end."

"Those poor women." The older woman grimaced. "It's creepy that they all look like Remi."

"All serial killers have a preference in their prey."

"I suppose that's true."

Jax hesitated, not sure what Ash had revealed to their mother. "Of course, in the case of the Butcher, he's taken it a step farther," he said.

June looked confused. "Why do you say that?"

"It hasn't been shared with the media, but the last two victims had plastic surgery shortly before they were killed."

"Does it matter? Lots of women have work done," she said, clearly unaware there'd been more to Ash's return to Chicago than the simple fact the victims resembled his ex-fiancée. "I don't know why. Beauty comes from the heart," she continued.

"The surgeries weren't just to make them pretty. They were done to make them look more like Remi."

Her mother's eyes widened, her hand lifting to press to the center of her chest.

"Oh sweet Jesus," she breathed. "Why would they do that?"

"My assumption was that they were either convinced to have the work done by the Butcher," he drummed his fingers on the table, the familiar frustration bubbling through him, "or it was done by force."

"Do you think the Butcher is a surgeon?" his mother demanded.

It was a thought that had gone through his mind.

"It's possible. Certainly, none of the clinics I've contacted are willing to admit the victims were patients," he told her. "If their work was done in Illinois, it was done off the books."

June took a second to gather her composure, her face pale with concern for Remi. "The surgery could have been done out of state," she said.

"I'm checking, but it's a slow process." Too slow, Jax silently acknowledged. It could take weeks, even months, to get the information he needed.

"What about the women?" his mother abruptly demanded.

Jax shook off his aggravation at his inability to track down where the women had their surgeries.

"What do you mean?" he asked his mother.

"Surely their families knew they were going to have the operation?"

Jax shook his head, not willing to tell his mother that their families hadn't paid enough attention to the victims to know what was happening in their lives. It only upset the older woman when she had to accept that not all children were given the same love and devotion she lavished on her boys.

"Not that I could discover. But they both wanted to be actresses," he said, changing the direction of the conversation. "I'm guessing it would have been easy to convince the women to leave home, and even have plastic surgery, if they thought they were going to get a part in a movie."

His mother arched her brows. "That would be a clever trap." She considered the possibility for a moment. "Have you checked with the talent agencies?" she finally asked.

Jax wrinkled his nose. "Yet another thing I'm in the process of doing."

"I could help."

"Absolutely not."

His mother stiffened, and Jax instantly regretted his harsh tone. In his defense, the last thing he'd expected was for her to offer her assistance.

He didn't want his mother anywhere near this god-awful case.

"Jackson Robert Marcel," June snapped, making him flinch at the use of his full name, "I've lived in this city my entire life. Just as my parents did. And their parents."

"I know."

"I have dozens of friends who have dozens of friends who have dozens of friends. At least one of them is bound to work in the entertainment industry," she continued. "They would be able to tell me if any of the agents were asking to find women who look like Remi."

"I appreciate . . ."

His mother frowned as his words trailed away. "Yes?"

Jax reached for his coat, pulling the scrap of paper from his pocket. He had the perfect solution. Not only could he soothe his mother's temper by allowing her to assist him, there was a chance she might have the information he needed. As she said, her family had been in Chicago forever.

"Actually, I do need your help," he said.

June's expression eased, her ruffled feathers smoothed by his agreement. "It's about time you appreciated my wealth of knowledge," she informed him in tart tones.

"I've always appreciated you," he assured her, reaching out to lightly touch her hand.

This woman was nothing less than a miracle.

She'd been a devoted wife who never complained when her husband was working 24-7 and a mother who'd showered love on her four sons, all while making sure they never felt smothered.

Of course she was bossy, he silently admitted as she leaned toward him.

"Tell me what I can do."

He held out the piece of paper. "I found this in the bedroom of the most recent victim."

Smoothing the wrinkled note, June read the word out loud. *"Paradiso."* She lifted her head, looking confused. "What does it mean?"

Jax swallowed a sigh. "I was hoping you could tell me."

She glanced back down, her brow furrowed. "I think it translates to paradise," she said at last.

"Could it be a talent agency?"

She silently considered his question. Then she shook her head. "I don't think so."

"A hotel?" he suggested. "An apartment building?"

"No." She stroked her fingers over the paper, as if hoping it would give her inspiration. "But there's something familiar about it."

Jax remained silent. He hated when people bombarded him with questions when he was trying to pinpoint a memory. Then, with a sudden surge, June was out of her chair, a satisfied smile curving her lips.

"There's a picture," she said.

Jax lifted himself to his feet. "A picture?"

"Come with me," his mother commanded, leading him across the linoleum floor and pushing open the kitchen door. She glanced over her shoulder with a grimace. "I hope your Uncle Clark is still asleep. He starts demanding his breakfast the second he crawls out of bed."

Jax chuckled as they quietly moved through the living room to his parents' bedroom. Uncle Clark was his father's brother who traveled from one relative to another, mooching food and money until he was politely urged to move on.

Once in the bedroom, his mother closed the door and

headed for the large dresser that was pushed in a corner. Jax watched her pull open the bottom drawer with a frown.

"What are you doing?"

"I'm looking for my mother's old photo album," she muttered, bending down to begin pulling out old boxes and stacks of papers.

"Why?"

The older woman made a sound of impatience, waving a hand toward the double bed in the middle of the room. "You sit there and be quiet."

Jax rolled his eyes, obediently perching on the edge of the mattress. "Yes, Mother."

"Good boy."

She returned to her task, leaving Jax with nothing to do but glance around the room that hadn't changed in the past thirty-odd years. The bed had been hand-carved by his grandfather, along with the dresser and matching armoire. The flower quilt had been stitched by his mother. She'd also sewn the curtains that covered the windows.

It was old-fashioned, but it had a shabby comfort that Jax realized made the place feel like home.

"Here it is," his mother announced at last. Straightening, she carried over a photo album that had a worn cloth cover and plastic sleeves inside that had yellowed with age. She settled next to him on the bed and flipped through the pages until she found the photo she wanted. She pointed a finger at the top picture. "There."

Jax bent his head to study the blurry image. He could make out a young, slender woman dressed in a tight, sleeveless dress with her dark hair pulled into a mass of curls on top of her head. She was standing in front of a marble fountain, glancing at the camera with a flirtatious smile.

"That's Grandma?" he muttered in surprise. He remembered his Grandma Ruth as a frail, faded woman who had a stash of chocolates hidden in her bedside table to hand out when Jax visited her at the nursing home.

"She wasn't born old," his mother chided. Her finger moved to point at the long, Mediterranean-style building behind her. "Look at the sign."

"Paradiso." Jax stiffened in shock. When he'd asked his mom for her input, it'd been nothing more than an act of desperation. Plus, the bonus of getting out of trouble. Now he could only shake his head in amazement. Luck had finally decided to smile on him. "When was this taken?"

"Around fifty, maybe fifty-five years ago."

"Do you know where it is?"

"At the time, it was a few miles north of the city," his mother answered. "By now, I'm sure it's surrounded by suburbs."

Jax tilted the photo album, trying to peer through the yellowed plastic. He would have taken it out of the sleeve if he hadn't been worried it would disintegrate at his touch.

"Is it a hotel?" he asked, studying the building. It was two stories, with a red-tiled roof, and in the picture, it looked like it spanned several hundred feet across the manicured grounds.

Too big for a private residence.

"A spa," June corrected.

"Spa." Jax glanced toward his mother. "Like a health spa?"

"Yes. It was opened by a . . ." She paused, digging through her memory for the name. "A Dr. Bode," she finally announced. "My mother spent a week there after a nasty bout with the flu."

A health spa.

Jax shook his head, thoroughly baffled.

"What did they do there?" he demanded.

June shrugged. "Mom said she swam in an indoor pool in the morning, then rested in the afternoon. She also had to drink some nasty tonic that was supposed to clean out the toxins from her body. She was convinced she was drinking a bunch of mushed-up weeds they'd found in the yard." The older woman chuckled. "In fact, she said the whole place was a scam, but she stayed because she was so happy to have a few days away from a house filled with screaming kids." She sent Jax a teasing smile. "It wasn't until I had you boys that I understood what she was talking about."

Jax's lips twisted. They were probably lucky his mom hadn't walked out one day and never come back.

"Is this spa still open?" he demanded.

"I'm not sure." His mother gently closed the photo album, placing it on the mattress. "I remember hearing that it'd been taken over by Dr. Bode's son, but I don't know anyone who's ever been there."

Jax glanced toward the ugly oil painting of their house that hung on the wall opposite him. It'd no doubt been created by one of his brothers, and it would have looked a lot better on top of a bonfire, but his mother had hung it with obvious pride.

"Why would the name of an old health spa be in my victim's bedroom?" he muttered.

"Well," the older woman leaned toward him, speaking in a conspiratorial whisper, "my mother told me a rumor she heard when she was staying there."

"What rumor?"

"That Dr. Bode started his spa with money that was given to him by the mob," she told him.

Jax resisted the urge to roll his eyes. This was Chicago. Every rumor had something to do with the mob. Usually it ended with Al Capone being involved.

"Why would the mob give money for a spa?" he obediently asked.

"Because he had a clinic there that he used to give new faces to people who wanted to disappear," she continued. "You know, if they had to get away from the feds."

Jax's resigned amusement was forgotten as he realized exactly what his mother was telling him.

"Dr. Bode was a plastic surgeon?"

She nodded, a smug smile curving her lips. "He was."

"I have to go." Jax jumped to his feet, pulling his phone out of his pocket.

He needed the address for the *Paradiso*.

"Don't forget dinner tomorrow night," his mother called out.

Jax lifted his hand in agreement, although he barely heard her words.

He had a real lead.

The hunt was on.

Chapter Twenty-Five

Ash watched as Remi sipped her coffee and nibbled on a blueberry muffin. They'd just crawled out of bed, although it was closer to lunch than breakfast. Now he was struggling to shake off his delicious sense of lethargy.

There was nothing he wanted more than to spend the rest of the day with Remi, making love and curling up on the couch to binge-watch their favorite movies.

Unfortunately, he was going to have to postpone his fantasy. At least until he'd discovered whether there was anything to his suspicions.

Pushing aside his empty coffee mug, he cleared his throat. Remi wasn't going to be happy. But he had to do this.

"Do you have any plans for today?" he asked.

She reached for her phone, scrolling through her calendar. "No, but I might go to the youth center later."

"What time?"

"When school gets out. Around three." She set down her phone, studying him with a curious expression. "Why? Is there something you'd like to do?"

His gaze narrowed, taking a slow, thorough inspection of Remi from the top of her dark hair, rumpled from sleep, down to the tips of her bare toes. She'd wrapped a silk robe around her body, but the material was thin enough for him to see through. The sight wrenched a low groan from his throat.

"A dangerous question," he warned in a husky voice.

A flush stained her face. "Ash."

He gave a wistful shake of his head. Soon the damned Butcher was going to be in prison. Or better yet . . . dead. But until then, he had to make sure his first priority was keeping Remi safe.

He reached across the breakfast bar to stroke his finger down her reddened cheek. "As much as I want to stay here, I have something I need to check out."

She dropped her half-eaten muffin, regarding him with a sudden wariness. "I don't like the sound of that."

He shrugged. "It's just a theory."

"What do you need from me?"

"I want you to invite your mother out for lunch."

"My mother?" She jerked her brows together, staring at him as if she was certain she'd misheard him. "I just had lunch with her."

He grimaced. He knew he was asking a lot. Mothers— even his own—were best enjoyed in small doses. That way you could truly appreciate them.

"I know you did," he said in apologetic tones. "But I need to get her away from the estate for an hour or so."

She slid off her stool, her face pale. "You don't believe it was a nightmare."

Her words were a statement, not a question.

"I'm not sure," he said. And he wasn't. Right now, he was grasping at any straw he could find. "That's why I have to check it out."

She wasn't satisfied with his words. "Why not go there and ask my mother?" she demanded. "If anyone would know about secret tunnels, it would be her. She's lived there most of her life."

He shook his head. He wasn't prepared to admit that he was afraid Liza Harding-Walsh would refuse to let him step foot on the estate. He'd deal with his future mother-in-law later.

Right now, he wanted to get in and out of the estate unnoticed.

"I'm not ready to involve anyone else," he told her. "Not until I have some actual evidence."

"Evidence of what?"

"That someone who worked for your family is the Butcher," he said.

She snapped her lips together. Ash knew it had to be hard for her to accept that someone she'd known, and perhaps liked, was responsible for the grisly murders. But what other explanation could there be? If her dream had been real, the killer had to have ready access to the estate. That was the only way they could have stumbled across the tunnels.

"At least call Jax," she requested at last.

His fingers slid down her cheek, his expression apologetic. "As you just said, right now, we don't know if this is anything more than a bad dream. If I find anything, I'll let him know." He stroked a soft caress down the side of her neck. "I promise."

She wrinkled her nose. "I don't like the thought of you going there alone."

"I'll have a quick look around and leave," he assured her. "You'll know exactly where I'll be, and I'll keep my phone on in case I need to call for backup." His fingers threaded into her hair. "Everything will be fine."

She glared at him, her jaw jutting to a stubborn angle. "I still don't like it."

Ash heaved a sigh. "Just an hour. Please?"

She continued to glare at him before snatching the phone from the counter.

"Fine," she reluctantly conceded. "I'll ask my mother, but don't be disappointed if she won't go. Since Dad died, she doesn't like to leave home unless it's for one of her charity events."

He watched as she turned away from him, pressing the phone to her ear. A pang of regret sliced through him. She was worried about him. He understood. The return of the Butcher not only reminded her that she was in constant danger, it had ripped open the wounds of her father's death.

With an effort, he squashed the urge to reach out and take the phone from her. The sooner he could search the estate, the sooner he could get back home and hold her in his arms.

After a brief conversation, Remi lowered the phone and turned back to face him.

"Well?" he prompted.

"She agreed," Remi said, her expression tight. "We're meeting at her favorite French restaurant. It's only a couple of blocks from her house."

Ash grimaced. "Snails and foie gras? Better you than me."

She shrugged. "It's an acquired taste. And the wine is superb."

He rounded the end of the breakfast bar, wrapping his arms around her waist.

"You could order an extra bottle," he suggested. "We'll share it tonight."

She lay her hands flat against his chest, pushing him away. "If I have to spend another day with my mother, I'm drinking the extra bottle myself."

"Then get two," he teased. "I like when you're tipsy."

She sniffed, refusing to be charmed. "I'm going to take a shower."

Ash instantly felt his body hardening at the thought of Remi naked and wet. "Would you like me to wash your back?"

She gave another sniff. "Buddy needs a walk and his breakfast."

With that, she pivoted on her heel and left the kitchen. Ash gave a sad shake of his head, glancing down at the dog, who was regarding him with an accusing expression.

"I knew it was only a matter of time before I ended up in the doghouse," he assured the canine. The sound of the bathroom door slamming echoed through the house. Buddy barked. "Yep. Doghouse," Ash muttered.

Hoping to avoid any arguments about his plans for the day, Ash took the dog on a quick walk, returning to the house to pull on a pair of jeans and heavy sweater. Then, grabbing his coat, he headed out to his car.

The morning sunlight had disappeared behind a layer of sullen clouds, but on the plus side, the wind had died down. A blessing as he parked his car a block away from the elegant estate and walked back to hide in the high hedge. It was cold but not unbearable.

Or at least it wasn't for the first fifteen minutes. Eventually, his toes began to go numb and his teeth were chattering.

At last, he caught sight of the BMW pulling out of the front gates. Eagerly, he pushed his way through the hedge and skirted the back of the mansion. If his theory was right, the night Remi was followed, she must have managed to park her car before the killer attacked her. That indicated that the opening to the tunnel was somewhere in the garage.

He paused in front of the door of the garage, using the

key he'd borrowed from Remi. Then, slipping inside, he quickly closed the door behind him.

It was shadowed inside, but Ash didn't turn on the lights. He couldn't risk attracting unwanted attention. Instead, he pulled a small flashlight from his pocket and swept it around the cavernous space.

Walking forward, he ignored the cement floor. If there was a large hole cut in the pavement, Remi would have noticed. The opening had to be a lot more discreet.

Instead, he moved to tap on the walls. He wasn't sure if he was going to be able to detect a hidden door, but he'd seen this method used in the movies.

Feeling like a fool, he moved along the paneling, knocking every few inches. He'd managed to reach the far corner when he heard the sound of the door opening.

Cursing at his crappy luck, Ash slowly glanced over his shoulder to watch Albert step into the garage. He had a brief moment of madness when he considered darting behind the Mustang. Thankfully, it quickly passed.

He was a grown man who'd once carried a badge, not a teenager who was terrified of getting in trouble.

Flicking on the overhead lights, Albert had reached the middle of the floor before he realized he wasn't alone. The older man instinctively lifted the heavy wrench he was carrying, clearly intending to bash the intruder on the head.

Then, with a frown, he slowly lowered his hand. "You again?"

Ash smiled, cautiously moving forward. "I'm like a bad penny," he said. "I just keep turning up."

Albert glanced around the garage, as if making sure nothing had been stolen. Once reassured everything was where it was supposed to be, he returned his attention to Ash. "Mrs. Liza isn't here."

"I know," Ash admitted.

Albert frowned. "I don't think you should be poking around without her approval."

Ash held up his hands, considering the best way he could convince the man to let him search the property.

"I understand your loyalty to your employer, Albert, but this is extremely important."

Albert remained wary. "I've kept an eye on the Mustang. I swear it hasn't been moved."

Ash paused, not sure how much he wanted to share. Then he gave a mental shrug. Right now, honesty seemed like the best policy.

At least a small amount of honesty.

"Have you noticed anything strange?" he asked.

"Like what?"

"Any old employees hanging around?"

"No. It's only me and the housekeeper now."

"None of the previous staff have stopped by for a visit?" Ash pressed.

"No." Albert studied Ash in confusion. "Are you interested in any particular employee?"

"Perhaps one who revealed an interest in Remi when they worked here?"

Albert's lips pinched in disapproval. He had enough fatherly affection for Remi to have been disturbed by an employee stepping over the line.

"There's more than one name I could give you," he admitted. "Ms. Remi was a pretty girl and she was always friendlier than she should have been with the staff. She didn't realize her kind heart could lead to trouble."

"Amen," Ash muttered. He'd chided her more than once about being so friendly with her fellow college students. He told himself that he was concerned one of them might take advantage of her. Looking back, he suspected a portion of his fear had included the knowledge that the college was filled with young, handsome men who had plenty of time to spend with a beautiful coed.

"But none of them have been back at the estate. Not since . . ."

Albert didn't have to finish his sentence. He meant that no one had been there since the night Gage was murdered.

Stymied, Ash shifted the conversation to the reason he'd come to the estate. "What do you know about the history of this place?"

Albert was clearly baffled by the question. "Chicago?"

"No, this estate."

"Oh." He glanced around. "I think it was built by Mrs. Liza's great-grandfather. Or maybe it was a great-great-grandfather." He shrugged. "All I know for sure is that it's been in the Harding family ever since then."

"I've heard it was used as a speakeasy during Prohibition. Is that true?"

The older man's spine stiffened, as if he was offended by Ash's question. "I'm old, but I wasn't working here during the twenties."

"There must be a few mementos from that time," Ash insisted. "I remember the house being filled with antiques."

Albert abruptly walked around Ash, heading toward the cabinet to place the wrench inside. Was he trying to hide his expression?

"The family doesn't like anyone discussing what happened in the past," he said.

"Well, I'm soon going to be part of the family, I'm sure no one will mind," Ash assured the older man.

Albert whirled back to regard Ash with raised brows. "The engagement is back on?"

Ash wrinkled his nose. He couldn't lie. Not about his relationship with Remi. It was too important.

"I'm working on it," he said.

Albert smiled, seeming to assume his words meant the engagement was all but official. "Congratulations."

Ash held up his hand. "Thanks. But before we can celebrate, we have to stop the Butcher."

Albert moved back to stand in front of Ash. "You haven't had any luck?"

"Perhaps." Ash tried to act casual, even as he closely monitored the older man's reaction. "Remi is beginning to recall the events of the night she was attacked."

Albert jerked, as if he'd been struck by lightning. "Truly?" He cleared his throat. "That would be a miracle."

Ash frowned. Albert looked more concerned than delighted that Remi was starting to remember. Of course, if Ash wasn't so desperate to track down the serial killer, he would be worried himself.

The memories could only bring her pain.

"It is a miracle," he agreed. "But it's still fuzzy. Last night, she remembered being in a dark tunnel."

"In a cave?" Albert asked in confusion.

"No, she thinks she was beneath this estate."

Albert's eyes widened, his hands clenching at his side. "Here?"

Ash covertly moved so he was between the older man and the door. Albert had a weird look on his face. He couldn't be sure the man might not suddenly decide to bolt. "It occurred to me that one of Remi's ancestors might have found it useful to have a way to allow their guests to enter and leave the place without attracting unwanted attention," he smoothly suggested.

Albert's lips parted, then he gave a slow shake of his head. "It's been years. I'd almost forgotten about them."

The air was jerked from Ash's lungs. It hadn't been a bad dream. He could see the truth etched on the older man's face.

"You know about the tunnels?"

Albert twisted his callused hands together, his gaze darting toward the door before he leaned toward Ash. Was the man afraid there might be someone lurking outside who might overhear them?

"Shortly after I started working here, Mr. Gage told me he was worried about some old passages," he confessed.

Gage? Ash was caught off guard. He hadn't expected his old partner to know about the tunnels. Why had he kept them secret from Remi and himself?

The question reminded Ash of the hidden file that had been given to Jax. Yet another secret his partner had kept from him. He was beginning to suspect he hadn't known Gage as well as he thought.

He gave a shake of his head, concentrating on the man standing in front of him.

"Why was he worried?" he demanded.

Albert hunched his shoulders. "He said he was afraid that they were aging and might collapse."

That made sense. If they'd been built a hundred years ago, it was likely they'd become unstable. "Did he want them filled in?"

"No, he didn't want to risk causing any damage to the buildings," Albert said.

Ash frowned. He didn't understand how filling the tunnels could cause damage, but he was a detective, not a structural engineer. "What did you do?"

"We took some lumber down there and braced the tunnels," Albert explained. "Gage wanted to make sure they wouldn't collapse."

"Anything else?"

"We sealed all the entrances to make sure no thieves could sneak inside," Albert told him. "Plus, Mr. Gage wanted to keep out any nosy employees. They would sometimes snoop around." The older man's expression twisted into disgust. "One even dug up the gardens, looking for old skeletons."

Ash could sympathize with Gage's reluctance to discuss the illegal activities of his wife's family. As well as his eagerness to hide the physical proof.

Still, it seemed odd that he'd never mentioned the passages to his own daughter. After all, Remi would inherit the estate someday.

"Is there an entrance to the tunnels in the garage?" he asked, silently chiding himself for becoming distracted.

What did it matter why Gage hadn't mentioned the tunnels? Right now, he wanted to see them for himself.

The older man looked wary. "I don't know if I should be telling you."

"Albert, this is for Remi," he said in pleading tones. "If the killer had her in the passageways, he might have left a clue to his identity."

There was a long silence as Albert mulled over his loyalty to his employer against his love for Remi. Finally, he heaved a resigned sigh.

"Okay." He nodded across the garage. "Over here."

Ash followed the man as he headed directly for the old-fashioned safe that was set in the paneled wall.

He'd noticed it before. It was hard to overlook a heavy steel door that stood seven feet tall and five feet wide, with a spoked handle in the center. But he'd assumed it was decorative. Only a bank needed a safe that large. And even if Remi's relatives had wanted a place to store secret stuff, why would they put it in the garage?

Now he watched in silence as Albert bent in front of the door and started to turn the combination from left to right to left to right. At last, he reached for the handle and gave it a turn.

There was a faint creak, then the door slid open.

Curious, Ash stepped forward, peering into the dark. He could see shelves on the side walls, but they were empty.

"Where's the entrance?" he demanded.

Albert pointed toward the back wall of the safe. "There's a hidden door."

"Clever," he murmured. He was impressed. If someone broke into the safe, they would be searching for gold or valuables, not entrances to secret passageways. "Who has the combination?"

Albert shrugged. "Just me now that Mr. Gage is gone. He changed the lock after we finished our work."

"What about Liza?"

"She never had any interest in the tunnels."

Ash frowned. He found it hard to believe that the older woman didn't have access to every inch of this estate. She was obsessed with her family home.

Then he dismissed the older woman from his mind. She might consider the tunnels a part of the estate that was better left forgotten.

Moving forward, he entered the safe and glanced around. The overhead lights battled against the murky darkness, allowing Ash to make out footprints visible in the dust on the floor. He leaned down, but it was impossible to tell the size.

He glanced over his shoulder at Albert, who hovered near the entrance. "Have you been in here recently?"

Albert shook his head. "Not for years."

So who'd been in the safe? Ash straightened, moving toward the back of the container.

"How does the hidden door open?" he asked.

"There's a switch on the floor that looks like a rock," Albert said. "Just step on it."

It took a minute for Ash to locate the small chunk of stone that looked as if it had been randomly dropped. Reaching out his foot, he gingerly pressed it down. There was another creak, then the back wall of the safe slid aside to reveal an empty darkness.

His nose wrinkled as he caught the scent of rich earth and stale air. "Are there lights?"

"Yeah." He heard Albert move into the safe behind him, running his hand under one of the shelves until he found the switch. Ash heard a click, then a dim glow allowed him to see the stairs leading downward.

"Wooden steps," he breathed, his mouth feeling oddly dry as he recalled Remi's description of her dream.

"What?" Albert questioned.

"Nothing." Ash shook his head as he considered his options.

They were limited. He could call Jax and hope his brother could get a warrant to search the tunnels. Unfortunately, it seemed unlikely that a judge would allow the cops to invade Liza Harding-Walsh's estate unless there was compelling evidence. And so far, all he had was the entrance to a passageway that Remi had seen in a dream.

He could walk away and have Remi return to talk to her mother about any employee who might have discovered the tunnels.

Or . . .

"I'm going down," he announced abruptly.

He heard Albert mutter a curse. "Detective, that isn't a good idea."

Ash released a sharp laugh. "I've been hearing that a lot lately." He glanced over his shoulder, his expression somber. "Call 911 if I'm not back in half an hour."

Albert pursed his lips. "I don't like this."

"I can't say I'm crazy about it," Ash said. "But I have to see what's down there." He held the older man's gaze. "Watch my back."

Albert gave a slow nod. "I'll be here."

Chapter Twenty-Six

Jax pulled to a halt in front of the pale pink building with the tiled roof. The *Paradiso*. It took up an entire block, with long wings that had tall windows and arched openings that led to an inner courtyard. Jax climbed out of his car. The spa had the feeling of old Hollywood. A place where Mary Pickford and Douglas Fairbanks might have spent a quiet weekend away from their hordes of fans.

But as he walked forward, it was easy to see it was faded. And a little tarnished. The flagstone walkway was crumbling beneath his feet. And as he neared the sprawling structure, he could see the windows were dingy, with layers of dirt.

He paused as he caught sight of the sign across the middle of the double doors.

FOR SALE BY OWNER

Well, well, well.

Angling away from the front entrance, which was heavily padlocked, he walked through an arched entry and stepped into the courtyard.

A smile touched his lips as he caught sight of the marble fountain in the center of the tiled floor. It was empty now, with a layer of mold, but there was no mistaking it was the same fountain he'd seen in the photo. He was standing in the same spot as his grandmother. The knowledge tugged at his heart and he took a second to imagine her strolling through the elegant spa, perhaps laughing and chatting with another guest.

It was nice to think of her when she was young and happy, and feisty enough to slip away from the demands of her family for a little peace and quiet. He now understood where his mother had gotten her backbone.

With a shake of his head, Jax walked toward the glass door that led toward the east wing of the building.

He grabbed the handle and pulled. Locked. He swallowed a curse, pivoting to cross the tiled floor to try the door to the west wing.

He was reaching toward the handle when he caught sight of a shadowed form moving across the wide foyer inside the building. With a quick movement, he unzipped his heavy coat to give himself ready access to his gun.

As the form neared the glass door, Jax could start to make out details. He pressed his lips together, suppressing his smile. The person looked exactly like the clichéd owner of a fancy spa.

He was slender, with a delicate build, and he was wearing a gray cashmere sweater and a pair of dark slacks that no doubt cost a fortune. His silver hair was carefully brushed to hide a growing bald spot, and as he pushed open the door, Jax caught sight of dark, bronzed skin that looked like it came from a tanning bed. The leathery color contrasted sharply with the unnaturally white teeth.

Jax guessed his age to be close to sixty, but with his lean face frozen by Botox injections, it was hard to be certain.

"We're closed," the man stated in a clipped voice.

Jax forced a smile to his lips. "I noticed the for-sale sign on the front door."

The man ran a suspicious glance over Jax's worn leather coat and down to his shoes, which came from a department store.

"You're interested in purchasing a spa?"

"Not personally," Jax said, trying to avoid a direct lie.

"Are you a real estate broker?"

Jax lowered his voice, speaking in a confidential tone. "I'd like to keep everything off the record until I've had a chance to look around," he said. It was perfectly true. "Are you the owner?"

The man remained suspicious, but he gave a nod of his head. "I'm the owner. What do you want to see?"

Ah. This was Dr. Bode. Just the man he wanted. Jax felt a stab of satisfaction as he brushed past Bode to enter the foyer. "Let's just wander around while you tell me about the history of this place," he suggested.

The doctor hesitated, looking annoyed at having his day interrupted. But then again, he was clearly anxious to sell the place.

"My father bought the property in the late fifties," he said, leading Jax across the tiled foyer, which had a high ceiling, a marble floor flecked with gold, and frescoes of palm trees and flamingos on the walls. "This lobby and the outer courtyard are part of the original mansion."

Jax hid his grimace. It was not his style, but it might have been the fashion back then. "Do you know who he bought it from?"

There was the faintest hesitation. "Frank Pruitt."

Jax recognized the name. It was well before his time, but there were stacks of boxes at the station that included Pruitt's arrests for extortion, illegal gambling, and even murder. Not one had led to a conviction. He had powerful friends in high places.

Then he had suddenly disappeared. Had the elder Dr. Bode given him a new face in exchange for the property?

"The name is familiar," he murmured.

"He was a prominent businessman," Bode said, heading across the floor to the hallway.

Jax followed, obediently standing next to the older man as he pulled open the first door to reveal an empty room that had a faded carpet on the floor and a tall window that needed to be washed.

"This is one of the private rooms for the guests. As you can see, everything is built from the highest-quality material." Bode pointed toward the crown molding near the ceiling and then toward the built-in cabinets. "You don't get that sort of workmanship nowadays. Perfect if you wanted to convert the spa into a hotel." He sent Jax a too-white smile. "And on the upper floors there are larger suites you could keep for premium guests or convert into smaller rooms to double the occupancy potential. Would you like to see them?"

"Not now." Jax stepped back. "Are there rooms in the other wing as well?"

"No, but there's an indoor pool with a hot tub and a steam room, as well as a small gym and a full kitchen," Bode quickly assured him.

Jax began strolling down the hallway, entering the foyer so he could peer out the glass door.

"What about the upper floor?" he demanded.

"It was a clinic until I closed it a few years ago."

Jax glanced toward the man, not having to fake his curiosity. "What sort of clinic?"

"The spa used to offer beauty treatments, and I performed cosmetic surgery on guests who wanted more than a facial."

"You're a doctor?" Jax feigned surprise.

"Yes."

There was an edge in the man's voice that told Jax he didn't want to discuss his career as a physician. Why not? Jax was guessing he had something to hide.

"Do you still do surgery in another clinic?"

"No, I gave up my license when I decided to retire." A muscle twitched at the base of Bode's jaw, assuring Jax that the doctor hadn't given up his license willingly. "The clinic could be renovated if you wanted to create more rooms."

"Can I see?" Jax demanded, wanting to inspect the clinic for himself.

It should be easy to determine if it'd been used recently.

Bode seemed to come to the same conclusion. Licking his lips, he reached into his pocket to pull out an ivory business card.

"I'm busy today. If you want a full tour, I suggest you ask your client to call me to make an appointment for next week," he said, pressing the card into Jax's hand.

Jax dropped the card on the floor, his smile fading. No more games. He needed answers. And he was going to get them one way or another.

"Actually, I'm going to insist we do it now," he said, pulling aside his coat to reveal his badge, attached to his belt.

Bode frowned, leaning down to study the ID. "'Detective Marcel,'" he read out loud, slowly straightening with a confused expression. "What's this about?"

"I have a few questions."

"About the spa? I assure you, all my zoning permits are in order."

"I'm a homicide detective," Jax told the man. "I'm not interested in permits."

"Then what do you want?"

"I told you." Jax narrowed his eyes. "I would like to see your clinic."

Bode shifted from foot to foot. "Why? It hasn't been used in years."

"I don't believe you." Jax's voice was hard.

"Check with the medical board," the man tried to bluff. "They'll tell you I haven't worked as a doctor."

"I assume they took your license?"

Anger flared in Bode's eyes. "Yes. It was all a mistake, but they stole my ability to work as a surgeon."

Jax couldn't care less why the doctor had lost his license. "You couldn't perform surgery legally, but that didn't mean you couldn't do it in secret."

It was a direct hit. Bode clenched his hands, his face paling despite the leathered bronze of his skin. "I think I should call my lawyer."

Jax shrugged, pretending to be indifferent to the threat. Inside, he was reminding himself to be careful. He could get a warrant to search the place, as well as force the man to talk even with a lawyer, but it would take ten times as long.

He couldn't risk the delay. Not with a serial killer stalking Remi.

"Right now, I'm just looking for information," he said, giving a casual shrug. "But if you want to make this official, we can finish our conversation downtown."

There was a brittle pause as Bode silently weighed his options. No doubt his logic was warning him to keep his mouth shut, but his pride was balking at the horror of being hauled into a police station.

Oh, how the mighty have fallen.

"Information about what?" he demanded at last.

Jax released a silent breath of relief, reaching beneath his coat to retrieve the photos he'd tucked into the pocket of his suit jacket.

"These two women," he said, holding them out.

The doctor took the photos, sucking in an audible breath as he obviously recognized Angel Conway and Rachel Burke.

Bode coughed, reluctantly lifting his head to meet Jax's steady gaze. "What about them?"

"They recently had plastic surgery."

"And?" Bode tried to look bored. Instead, he looked like he'd swallowed something nasty. "There're a thousand plastic surgeons in Chicago."

"And all of them have denied having these women as patients," Jax said.

Bode abruptly shoved the pictures back into Jax's hand. "I don't know what that has to do with me."

Jax carefully tucked the photos into his pocket, considering his words. Obviously, the doctor was determined to deny any knowledge of the victims. Time for a different approach.

"There's a rumor your father used to make extra money offering mobsters new faces."

The man blinked, confused by the sudden accusation. "My father died twenty-five years ago."

"I know." Jax folded his arms over his chest. "I thought you might have followed in his footsteps."

Bode forced out a harsh laugh. "Are you claiming those girls are mobsters?"

"I'm saying you might have been in need of cash." Jax deliberately glanced toward the wall where the palm trees were peeling and the flamingos had faded from pink to a nasty shade of salmon. "Why not do a little nip and tuck off the books?"

Bode grimaced, seeming to at last realize that Jax wasn't here on a whim. "Even if I did a few small procedures, and I'm not admitting anything—"

"Of course not," Jax interjected in dry tones.

Bode ignored his interruption. "Why would a homicide detective be involved?"

"Because those two women are now dead."

"What?" Bode jerked at Jax's blunt explanation. "That's impossible."

"Don't you watch the news?" Jax demanded.

Bode gave an absent shake of his head. "I have better things to do with my time. Besides, I've been preoccupied." With a sharp movement, the doctor turned to pace across the foyer before spinning back to glare at Jax. "Dead. Are you sure?"

Jax squashed his pang of disappointment as he studied the man's horrified expression. He hadn't known. No one was that good an actor. *Dammit.* Jax had realized it would be a long shot for Bode to be the Butcher, but he'd still clung to the hope. It would have solved all his problems.

Of course, even if he wasn't the killer, he had to know who was, he told himself.

"It's my job to be sure," he told the older man.

"What happened?" Bode demanded. "An accident?"

"Both of them had their throats cut open."

Bode gasped, lifting his hand to his neck. "They were murdered?"

"Yep."

"At the same time?"

Jax shook his head. "No, it was a few days apart."

"This is . . ." Bode paced back toward Jax, his heels clicking on the tiled floor. The sound echoed eerily, reminding Jax that they were all alone in the building.

Cautiously, Jax shifted his hand so it was near his holstered gun. "What?" he asked.

"Unbelievable," the doctor breathed.

Jax had intended to conduct the interview in the clinic, but now that they'd started, he didn't want to give the man time to reconsider his need for a lawyer. "Tell me about the women," he commanded.

Bode nervously smoothed his hands down his cashmere sweater, a film of sweat on his face despite the chill in the air.

"Angel came to me first," he abruptly confessed.

Jax didn't pull out his notebook and pencil. He'd take the good doctor down to the station to make an official statement later. For now, he wanted his hands free in case he needed his gun.

Even if Bode wasn't a danger, this was a big building. Anyone could be hiding in one of the rooms.

"How did she find you?"

Bode shrugged, he eyes darting from side to side. He was trying to come up with a feasible lie.

"I've been doing Botox parties for the past three years," he finally said.

Jax was confused. "Botox parties?"

Bode gave a wave of his hand. "A group of friends get together at my clinic. We have wine and cheese and I give them Botox injections."

Jax snorted. What happened to Tupperware parties? "Angel wasn't old enough for Botox," he pointed out.

"Are you kidding?" Bode looked amazed by Jax's stupidity. "Any woman who cares about maintaining her beauty begins preventive care in her twenties."

Jax wrinkled his nose. He supposed it was fine for a

woman to do whatever she wanted with her own face, especially if it made her happy. But his mother was one of the most beautiful women he'd ever seen, and it was completely natural.

"Fine." He held the man's gaze. "Angel couldn't afford your party."

"She heard about me from one of the ladies." The words were said in a rush. A certain sign the man was lying. "She came to me and asked if I could do more extensive work."

"What sort of work?"

"The usual."

Jax stepped forward, poking his finger in the center of the man's chest. "Don't screw around with me, Bode," he snapped. "What work did you do on her?"

The doctor took a stumbled step backward, a drop of sweat hanging from the tip of his nose.

"She wanted me to make her look more like Remi Walsh," he ground out, reaching up to brush away the sweat. "She was the girl who was attacked by the Chicago Butcher a few years ago."

Jax's gut twisted, even as he felt a blast of satisfaction. He and Ash had been right. There was someone out there deliberately creating victims who looked like Remi.

"I know who she is," he said in cold tones. "Why would Angel want to look more like her?"

"She told me they were making a movie about the Butcher. She had the role of Remi, but she wanted to look more believable." The doctor sounded defensive, as if he could make excuses for operating without a license on a young girl who had been lured to her death by her dreams of fame. "She paid in cash, so I didn't really care why she wanted the surgery."

Jax bit back his urge to tell the doctor he thought he was a total scumbag. He'd save that treat for later.

"And Rachel?" he asked.

"She came to me a week or two later," Bode admitted. "She told me the same story."

Jax frowned. He'd already surmised the doctor wasn't the sharpest tool in the shed. He'd managed to lose his license and the spa he'd inherited was crumbling to dust. But he wasn't stupid.

"You didn't think it was odd that they would need more than one actress to fill the role of Remi Walsh?"

"I assumed the first one didn't work out," Bode muttered, his lips twisting with disgust. "To be honest, I wasn't surprised."

"Why?"

"She was kind of flaky." Bode glanced toward the glass door at the opposite wing. "Plus, I caught her searching the clinic for painkillers. It was obvious she was an addict. It was only a matter of time before she did something to get fired."

His words echoed what he'd learned from Angel's autopsy. She had traces of drugs in her system, and enough physical damage to reveal she'd been abusing opioids for years.

"You're telling me that two women just wandered in off the street, plopped down a stack of cash, and asked you to make them look like Remi Walsh?" he demanded, his tone mocking.

"More or less."

Jax struggled to leash his anger. The doctor was seriously pissing on his last nerve. Time to turn up the heat.

"They stayed here after the surgery, didn't they?" he demanded, already guessing this would be the perfect location for the killer to keep them isolated from their friends and family.

Bode hunched his shoulders. "They remained here for

a few days. Just so I could keep an eye on their incisions. After that—"

"They were murdered," Jax interrupted, his tone blatantly accusing.

"I told you, I didn't know."

"Two women." Jax stepped until he was towering over the man, his expression hard with warning. "Both made to look like the Butcher's preferred victim. And now both dead."

Bode pulled a handkerchief from his pocket, wiping his forehead. The motion allowed the dim light to sparkle off the large diamond on his pinkie. "What are you implying?"

"The killer has a fascination with Remi," Jax continued. "And a sharp knife that might very well have been a scalpel. Does that remind you of anyone?"

Bode was shaking his head before Jax finished speaking. "No way in hell are you pinning this on me."

Jax abruptly reached out to grab the front of the man's sweater, twisting it until he forced him onto his tiptoes.

"Then tell me the truth," he growled.

"I did." The words came out in a sputter as Bode stared at Jax with a nervous gaze. "The women came to me, they asked for the surgery to look like Remi Walsh, and that's what I did. Once they left the clinic, I never saw them again."

Jax glared down at him. "They didn't come here alone, did they?"

"I'm not sure what you mean."

Jax gave him a violent shake. He was done. The man was going to give him the answers he needed or he was driving him downtown and throwing him in jail. Maybe a day or two locked in a cell with a bunch of hardened criminals would loosen his tongue.

"Someone brought the girls to you. The same someone who had the stacks of cash," he insisted.

"I . . ." Clearly realizing he was about to be introduced to the delights of the Illinois penal system, Bode released a harsh sigh. His shoulders slumped and his eyes dimmed with defeat. "Yes."

Jax felt a blast of elation. Finally. He was about to put an end to the Butcher. Once and for all.

"Tell me."

Chapter Twenty-Seven

Ash had never considered himself a coward. During his years in law enforcement, he'd proved he was capable of facing down armed suspects and even running into a burning building to save a child.

But he couldn't deny that it took a considerable effort to force his feet to carry him down the stairs. He wasn't crazy about tight, dark spaces, and there was a sense of malevolence that choked the air.

Or at least it felt that way to Ash.

No doubt it was his imagination working overtime, but that didn't keep a prickly unease from crawling over his skin.

He shivered, moving down the cramped tunnel with slow, cautious steps. It was freezing down here, but the light at least allowed him to search for any clues that might have been left behind.

Exactly what sort of clue that might be was something he hadn't fully contemplated. A wallet with an ID? A monogrammed handkerchief?

He grimaced, walking down the center of the tunnel. He was forced to duck beneath the light bulbs that hung from bare wire. The low ceiling emphasized the cramped size of the tunnel. On the other hand, he was reassured by the sight of the wooden posts that were driven into the walls. At least he could be hopeful that the passageway wasn't going to collapse on him.

He wasn't sure how much time passed—it felt like an eternity, although it was probably no more than five minutes—when he caught sight of the stairs in front of him.

Satisfaction raced through him. *Yes.* Remi hadn't been dreaming. There was a passage from the garage to the house. And whoever attacked her was familiar enough with the estate to have stumbled across the opening.

On the point of climbing the stairs to see if he could figure out how to open the door, he came to an abrupt halt as he caught sight of something on the ground. Bending down, he grabbed the object, smoothing it out to discover it was a glove. And not just any glove. It matched the one he'd found in the garage.

Ash frowned in confusion.

Why would Gage's glove be in the tunnel? Had he lost it when he was putting in the braces?

He was trying to imagine why Gage would wear his expensive leather glove to do manual labor when the heavy silence was shattered by the explosive echo of a gunshot.

Ash dropped the glove, his mind going blank with shock.

Then instinct kicked in, and he pivoted to spring back down the passageway. At the same time, he pulled out the gun he'd holstered beneath his coat. He'd decided before leaving Remi's house that there was no way he was going to search the estate without a weapon.

Now, he silently thanked whatever impulse had urged him to come armed.

Skidding to a halt as he neared the stairs, he pressed his back against the wall of the tunnel. He strained to hear what was happening in the garage.

Had Albert been shot? Maybe even killed? It seemed likely. Otherwise, the man would have called down to warn Ash that they were no longer alone.

Ash clenched his teeth, waiting for the mystery shooter to come down the stairs. Whoever it was couldn't leave him alive now that he'd found the tunnels. But even as he braced himself to kill the intruder, there was a familiar creak.

He cursed. The door was closing.

Unwilling to risk dashing into view and being shot, Ash forced himself to inch his way along the tunnel, then cautiously up the steps toward the garage.

His mouth was dry and his muscles tense as he headed upward, but his mind was crystal clear. Years of training had ensured that danger intensified his ability to focus. As if adrenaline was a turbo-booster.

At last reaching the top step, he placed his hand against the door and pushed. It refused to budge.

Ash didn't waste his time trying to force open the door. There had to be a hidden switch. Tucking his gun into his holster, he used both hands to search the walls, then bent down to search the stairs.

There was nothing.

Refusing to contemplate the thought that he was effectively buried alive in the tunnel, he grimly turned around and headed toward the other end. There had to be a way out. In her dream, Remi had seen a bright light and smelled bread. He was betting the entrance opened into the kitchen.

Ash was halfway down the passage when he abruptly

sneezed. He came to a halt as he realized that a cloud of dust was filling the air. What the hell? He squinted up at the ceiling, horrified by the fear that it was preparing to collapse.

It was only when he heard the footsteps that he realized there might be worse things than a cave-in.

Glancing over his shoulder, he peered through the dust, expecting to see a figure walking toward him. Instead, there was a strange grinding noise as a portion of the wall directly across from him slid inward.

Another secret door.

Caught off guard, Ash watched as a form appeared in the opening. He froze, trying to process who was stepping into the passageway.

Liza Harding-Walsh.

He shook his head as his brain scrambled to accept what he was seeing.

Why was she there? She was supposed to be at lunch. And how had she entered the tunnels? More importantly, *why* had she entered the tunnels?

Slowly, his stunned gaze lowered to where she was holding a handgun. Christ. This was no accidental encounter. The weapon was pointed directly at his heart.

"I knew you couldn't keep your nose out of my business," she said in tones sharp enough to slice through the thick air.

Business. What business? Ash struggled to clear his mind. He'd just prided himself on his clear focus in the face of danger. Now it felt like his brain was coated with molasses.

"Do you mean the tunnels?" he asked.

An oddly delighted expression touched the pale, perfect face. "They're wonderful, aren't they?"

"Wonderful?"

"Yes." She waved a gloved hand toward the passage that led back to the garage. "My great-grandfather built them during Prohibition."

Ash's mouth was dry and his heart was skittering around his chest. He wasn't sure what was happening, but he sensed the woman wasn't stable.

It wasn't just the gun she had pointed at him; it was the fevered glitter in her eyes. He suddenly feared it was going to take a miracle for him to survive the next few minutes.

And he had to survive. He had to find Remi and make sure she hadn't been harmed.

"To hide alcohol?" he asked, cursing himself for not having pulled his own gun as soon as he'd caught sight of the older woman. He'd just been so damned shocked. Now he had to hope he could get close enough to knock the gun from her hand.

"Among other things. He built the finest speakeasy in the county beneath this estate." She heaved a small sigh, as if she was wishing she was back in the past. "It was glorious. Politicians and movie stars and the most powerful men in the world came here to drink and gamble. I have the pictures."

"You must be very proud."

She sniffed, as if sensing he wasn't as impressed as he should have been. "You wouldn't understand. You're—"

"What?"

Her lips curled with contempt. "Common."

"Yeah, my relatives were boring, law-abiding citizens," Ash mocked before he could halt the words.

This woman had treated him like he carried the plague when he was engaged to Remi. Now he wondered if it was because she possessed some weird obsession with her daughter.

She sneered at his claim. "As I said. You wouldn't understand."

Ash forced himself to take a deep breath. Right now, he was supposed to be keeping Liza distracted, not conducting a childish argument about who had the better relatives.

"I thought you were having lunch with Remi." He glanced over the woman's shoulder. There was a soft light glowing behind her. "Where is she?"

"I'll take you to her," Liza promised, holding out her hand. "As soon as you give me your gun."

Shit. He'd accepted that he couldn't grab his weapon, pull it out, and shoot before Liza put a bullet through his heart. But as long as he had it on him, there was a chance he would have an opportunity to use it.

"I'm a professor, not a detective," he reminded the older woman. "I don't carry a weapon."

Her contempt remained firmly etched onto the older woman's face. "You lie about as well as Gage did. I suppose it must have something to do with being a cop." She pointed a finger toward her feet. "Place your gun on the ground and kick it toward me."

Ash studied Liza with a sense of unreality. It was as if he was looking at a stranger. Not only because she was wearing clothes that probably were stolen from her housekeeper, but because she was holding the gun with an expertise that warned she was comfortable with firearms.

Had Gage insisted she learn? Or was it something she'd picked up from her father?

He was betting on her father. Reluctantly, he pulled out his gun and placed it on the ground. Then, with the tip of his toe, he shoved it across the ground. For now, she had the upper hand. Until he knew if Remi was safe, and that Liza didn't have a partner hidden in the tunnels, he had to play the game by her rules.

Straightening, he watched her grab the gun and tuck it in her purse. Never once did she take her gaze off him.

"Take me to Remi," he commanded.

"She's this way." She backed down the tunnel, keeping the gun pointed at him.

Ash shuddered, forcing himself to move forward. It was like the woman's gaze was causing his skin to crawl. Had he noticed it before? he absently wondered. Had he sensed there was something off about the woman?

Hard to say. He'd always assumed their strained relationship was because he hadn't come from a fancy family with a huge trust fund.

Now . . .

He shook his head. He didn't know. Just as he didn't know where Remi was. Or if Liza had shot poor Albert. Or what she intended to do with him. He suspected the older woman was involved in the murders, but he had no idea if she was a delusional pawn or the mastermind.

The new tunnel angled away from the house, he was guessing toward the center of the backyard. Then he stepped through a framed doorway, and his eyes widened. He'd been expecting a cave. Or another staircase.

Instead, he was standing in a room that was as big as a house, with the same glossy paneling that had been used in the garage. At one end of the space was a long bar with a polished mirror that was set in a fancy bronze frame. The floor was carpeted, and several small tables and comfortable chairs were arranged around the room.

His gaze shifted toward Liza. "Where are we?" he demanded.

"Below the pool house."

"This was the club?" he guessed.

"Yes."

He turned in a slow circle, taking in the stuffed animal heads on the walls and the crystal chandeliers that hung from the ceiling.

"Impressive," he said, unable to imagine how much time and effort it'd taken to build the place.

"Yes, it is," Liza agreed, strolling forward, a wistful smile on her lips. "I wish I could have seen it when my great-grandfather was entertaining."

Ash hid his grimace. Some other time he might have found the club interesting, but now there was only one thing he cared about.

"Where's Remi?" he demanded again, moving quickly toward an open doorway.

Liza called out something, but he didn't hear. He was busy finding the switch to turn on the light. Then he made a strangled sound as he gazed around the smaller room. He assumed he'd become numb after all the shocks he'd endured, but he discovered he was still capable of feeling as if he'd been kicked in the head.

The room was an exact duplicate of Remi's bedroom. Not similar. Not faintly akin. It was a perfect match. Hell, it even smelled like her room. Not perfume, but a fresh, clean soap.

The only thing missing was Remi.

"Christ," he breathed.

"Money can accomplish whatever you desire," Liza drawled.

He swiveled around to regard the woman with a bizarre sense of disbelief. Had he fallen asleep and was he having some weird dream? That's what it felt like.

"Why would you have Remi's room put down here?" he demanded.

The older woman scowled at him. "You know why."

"No, I truly don't."

She made a sound of impatience. "Because of the disease, of course."

"Disease?" Ash frowned. Had he misheard? "What disease?"

She gave a sharp motion with her hand, leading him across the room toward a mahogany door set in the paneling. She reached out to pull it open, revealing a small closet.

"It started here," she said.

Ash's confusion only deepened. Had Liza gone completely crazy? It seemed more than a little likely. "What started?"

Her gaze skimmed over the club, her expression becoming distant as she conjured up old memories. The gun, however, remained squarely aimed at Ash.

"My father refused to let me play down here," she told him, her voice fond as she spoke of her parent. "So of course I snuck down whenever I could escape from my nanny."

Ash clenched his teeth, fiercely trying to pretend he gave a crap about the words coming out of her mouth. Inside, his heart was screaming with the need to escape from the suffocating tunnels and find Remi.

"Was it still a club?" he forced himself to ask.

She shrugged. "My father occasionally had parties down here. Mostly, he used it to conduct his business."

"And the closet?" He tried to steer her to the point of her reminiscing.

"One morning I was playing down here, and I heard my father approaching." Her hand smoothed over the wood of the door. "I didn't want to get in trouble, so I hid in here."

"Did he find you?"

"No." A flush crawled beneath her skin. "He was preoccupied with his visitor. They were arguing about an overdue debt. I was only nine or ten at the time, but I knew it was a mistake. My father didn't like when people refused to pay the money they owed him."

Ash grimaced. "I can imagine."

She ignored his dry words, lost in her memory. "They continued to argue, and it was hot and stuffy in the closet, so I decided to crack open the door." She paused, a visible shudder shaking her body. "That's when I saw."

Ash's preoccupied attention was captured by the strange quiver in Liza's voice. It was a mixture of fear and acute excitement. He'd heard it once before. Just before the perp he was chasing threw himself in front of a speeding bus.

"Saw what?"

"My father." Her eyes reflected the light from the chandeliers. "He grabbed a knife from the bar and stabbed it in the man's heart."

Ash's breath hissed between his teeth. He'd known Remi's grandfather wasn't a saint, but he hadn't been prepared to hear he was a cold-blooded killer.

"Christ."

"I closed the door and waited until my dad's men had taken away the body," Liza continued. "Then I crept back to my room."

Ash felt an unexpected flare of pity. No young child should witness their father committing such a heinous act of violence. It had to screw with their mind.

Was that the reason Liza was unbalanced? It was as good an answer as any.

He took a furtive step forward. It wasn't that he wanted to be closer to the woman. In truth, he felt as if he was being shrouded in evil as he neared her. But if worse came to worst, he intended to shove her into the closet and escape before she could shoot him in any vital organ.

Not his best plan, but the only one he had at the moment.

"You didn't tell anyone?"

She sent him a confused glance. "Of course not. I wanted to see it happen again."

He couldn't disguise his horror. "A murder?"

"Punishment. Death. Blood." A dreamy pleasure softened her features. "It became a game to try to sneak down here so I could see my dad deal with his enemies."

Ash's stomach heaved, and for a second he was afraid he might vomit. He'd spent years dealing with hardened killers, many of them completely unrepentant after they'd taken the life of another.

But none of them had savored the murders.

"How many people did he kill?"

Liza shrugged. "Only a few. He usually allowed his bodyguards to convince his guests to pay their debts."

Ash gave a slow shake of his head, trying to imagine a young Liza hiding in the closet as her father's goons beat the shit out of someone. Or worse, her father sticking a knife in their heart.

"I'm sorry you had to see that."

Her pleasure drained away, leaving her face pale. "It . . . damaged me. At least that's what my mother claimed when she caught me down here," Liza admitted. "She insisted my father take me to a hospital in New York. They gave me medication to make me better."

Ash was caught off guard. He'd somehow expected Liza's parents to be indifferent to her sick fascination with death. But at least her mother obviously realized they needed to do something extreme to help her daughter.

"Did you get better?" he asked.

"For a while," she said, a wistful smile touching her lips. "I came back to Chicago and eventually fell in love with Gage. He . . ." She took a second to consider her words. "He centered me," she finally said. "When we were together, I felt safe. The darkness couldn't find me."

A horrified fear suddenly flared through Ash. "Did Gage know?"

"There was nothing to know," Liza snapped, as if she was offended by his question. "I was fine. At least until the baby."

"Remi?"

Anger rippled over the woman's face. "I didn't want children," she rasped. "I think I knew deep inside that I was too fragile for motherhood."

His brief sense of sympathy for this woman was erased by her petulant words. "So why did you get pregnant?"

"To please Gage." Her voice dripped with a bitterness that would poison any soul. "He wouldn't admit how desperately he wanted a child, but I could sense his yearning. I wasn't enough for him. I'd lost my father. I couldn't lose my husband. So I gave him a daughter."

Ash shuddered. He was getting a glimpse of Liza's twisted brain. It wasn't pretty. First had been the trauma of witnessing her father's brutality. Then God only knew what cocktail of drugs the doctors had shoved down her throat in the institution. And then the jealousy of her own daughter.

It had all combined into a toxic brew.

Ash's mouth went dry, a slow certainty growing in the center of his being.

"Gage loved Remi very much," he managed to mutter.

Liza's face twisted, the fevered glitter in her eyes intensifying as she allowed the thought of her daughter to work her into a rage. "He called her a precious gift."

"She *was* a gift," Ash insisted, taking another small step forward. He was going to have to do something quickly. The woman was about to snap. "For all of us."

"Not all of us." Liza lifted the gun until it was pointed directly at Ash's face. "She brought back the cravings."

Ash tensed his muscles, preparing to attack. "The cravings for what?"

The woman released a laugh that sounded like something straight out of a horror flick. "Blood. Death."

"You're the Butcher," he breathed.

She smiled with a sick pride. "I am."

Chapter Twenty-Eight

Remi hadn't intended to drive past her mother's estate on her way to the restaurant. Not only was it out of her way, but she didn't want Ash to know just how worried she was about him.

He was a big boy who could take care of himself, she'd whispered over and over. But somehow, her car kept making turns toward the street that ran along the side of the estate. As if it had a mind of its own.

As she slowed, however, her attention was distracted by the sight of her mother scurrying along the sidewalk with her head down and a large purse clutched in her hands.

Remi frowned. Had her mother's car broken down? No. If there was something wrong with the BMW, she would have called Albert and waited for him to come to pick her up. It wouldn't matter if she was ten miles away or a block.

What was going on?

She pulled to a halt next to the curb and put the car in Park. Then, swiveling in her seat, she managed to catch sight of her mother disappearing through the hedge.

A strange sensation crawled over her skin. Was it a reaction to the knowledge her mother was going to be pissed if she caught Ash sneaking around the house while she was gone? Or a premonition?

Without giving herself time to consider the wisdom of her urge to follow her mother, Remi switched off the motor and climbed out of her car. She barely noticed the snowflakes that were drifting from the low-hanging clouds. She was too intent on listening to the fading sound of Liza's footsteps.

Picking up her pace, Remi wiggled through the opening in the hedge. Once in the backyard, her gaze tracked her mother as she hurried across the frozen ground. For once, the older woman wasn't wearing the designer heels she adored. In fact, she had on a pair of rubber boots that Remi had never seen before. Odd. Really odd.

Expecting Liza to head for the mansion, Remi halted when her mother instead crossed directly toward the garage. Maybe there was something wrong with her car.

Remi hurried to the back of the garage as her mother entered through the front door. Then she pulled out her cell phone and pressed Ash's number.

"Pick up, pick up," she muttered.

Of course it went directly to voice mail. Did he have it turned off? She cursed, dropping the phone back into the pocket of her coat. She had to distract her mother.

Taking a step toward the corner of the garage, Remi fell to her knees as the silence was abruptly shattered by the blast of a gun.

She crouched low, her sluggish brain trying to process what was happening. Had the shot come from inside the garage? Yes. It'd been too loud to have come from the house.

Oh, God. Her mother. Scrambling on all fours over the frozen ground, Remi cautiously lifted herself upright. Then, barely daring to breathe, she leaned to the side to peer through the window. It took a couple of seconds for her eyes to focus. And even after she could see, she struggled to figure out what was going on.

There was a man lying on the ground. But he was too

short and bulky to be Ash. Then his head flopped to the side and she jerked with shock. Albert. And next to him, her mother was standing over him, staring down with a strange expression.

Remi frowned in confusion. Had Albert accidentally shot himself?

The thought had barely managed to form before the older woman took a step back, and the purse she had slung over one shoulder swung aside to reveal that she was holding something in her hand. Something that looked like a . . .

Gun.

Remi pressed a hand to her mouth, watching as her mother entered the large safe that was open. Then, before she could wrap her mind around the fact that Albert was injured and her mother was seemingly doing nothing to help him, the older woman reappeared.

Deep inside, Remi knew she should be dumbfounded by the sight of her mother calmly walking past the possibly dying Albert with a gun in her hand. It was unthinkable. As if she was peering into a bizarro world.

Instead, a strange certainty settled in the center of her soul.

Her mother had pulled the trigger.

Remi's stomach twisted into a tight knot, autopilot taking over as Liza headed for the door of the garage. Crouching down, Remi listened to the crunch of her mother's footsteps. Where was she going? It wasn't toward the mansion. She could hear the boots squeaking against the tiles around the pool.

The pool house?

Not bothering to try to figure out what the woman was up to, Remi hurried in the opposite direction. Darting around the corner of the garage, she pushed open the door.

She paused, forcing herself to glance around before stepping inside. She still wasn't sure exactly what was happening. Or if there was someone else running around the estate. She couldn't help Ash if she stumbled into a trap.

Once convinced there was no one hiding in the shadows, she entered and rushed toward the body on the floor. At the same time, she pulled the phone from her pocket and dialed 911, demanding an ambulance and as many cops as they could send. Then she crouched next to Albert and reached out her hand to place it against his throat.

"Please be alive, Albert," she whispered.

Her fingers pressed against his skin, relieved to discover it was warm. That was a good sign, wasn't it? She was concentrating fiercely, trying to feel for a pulse, when his head turned and, without warning, his eyes opened.

Remi barely managed to swallow her startled scream. "Oh thank God," she rasped. "Hang on, Albert, the ambulance is on its way."

His lips parted, blood dribbling down his chin as he tried to speak.

She'd known Albert most of her life. He'd treated her like she was his daughter. Now his face was a terrible shade of gray and blood was leaking from a gaping wound in the center of his chest.

It didn't seem possible he could survive, but she grimly held on to hope.

"No, save your strength," Remi pleaded, her hand moving to smooth back his hair.

He held her gaze, finally managing to force out one word. "Marcel."

"Do you mean Ash?" She leaned in. "He's not here. It's just me."

"Tunnels," the man managed to choke out. "Warn him."

As quickly as they'd opened, his eyes slid shut and his

body went limp. Remi surged upright, realizing what Albert was telling her. Ash was in the tunnels. She had to find him.

Glancing down at the unconscious Albert, Remi sent up a quick prayer that the ambulance would arrive in time. Then, unable to battle against her overwhelming need to make sure Ash hadn't been hurt, she headed toward the safe.

It couldn't be a coincidence that the door was open. Not when her father had always sworn the combination to the lock had been lost.

Remi warily entered the safe, ignoring the voice in the back of her mind that was warning her to wait for the cops to arrive. She didn't know where her mother was or what she was doing, but Remi had an unmistakable sense that Ash was in danger.

Inspecting the small space, she frowned. Where was the entrance to the tunnel? Her gaze lowered to the floor, studying the footprints visible in the layer of dust. They led to the back wall of the safe. She took another step forward, her toe landing on a rock. There was the sound of a soft click, then a creak, as a hidden door slid open to reveal a set of stairs leading to an underground passage.

A blast of musty air swirled around Remi, filling the safe with the scent of rich dirt. At the same time, she heard the sound of her mother's voice drifting from below.

Remi swayed, nearly falling down the stairs as she was hit with a dizzying wave of memories. It was as if triggering the hidden door had opened a matching door in her mind.

Suddenly, she was reliving the night when she'd been attacked. And now she had pulled into this very garage and jumped out of her car. She was at the point of running to the house when the vehicle that had been following her pulled in next to her.

She could remember vividly the acute relief when she realized it was her mother. She'd even laughed at her ridiculous overreaction. At least until her mother had moved with surprising speed to stand directly in front of her, lifting her arm and slashing it toward her neck.

Remi had been too surprised to move, and even when she felt the stab of pain from the hypodermic needle, she'd simply stared at the older woman in confusion. But then her mother had pulled the knife from beneath her coat, and Remi had known that the danger was horrifyingly real.

Numb with shock and whatever drug had been pumped into her system, Remi allowed her mother to force her into the safe and down the steps into the tunnel.

Christ. It was no wonder she'd blocked out the memories.

Her dark thoughts were interrupted at the sound of Ash's voice.

He was in the tunnel. With her mother.

Without considering the fact that she'd just had flashbacks of her mother drugging her and threatening her with a knife, she headed down the stairs. She'd reached the bottom step when she caught sight of Ash and her mother disappearing down a side tunnel. Remi forced her feet to carry her forward, following behind them. But when she reached the doorway, she found herself hesitating as she listened to her mother tell Ash about her twisted childhood, and her revelation that she should never have given birth to Remi.

Her words just confirmed what Remi had already suspected. Liza Harding-Walsh had never loved her. She'd been incapable of seeing her daughter as anything but an unwelcome intrusion into her life.

A disease.

A distant part of her brain acknowledged this was a pain she would have to deal with at some point. But not now. Any childhood issues became inconsequential when she heard Ash name her mother as the Butcher and her mother agree.

A part of her had known, of course, but she hadn't been able to process the truth. So she'd simply blanked it out. And now the older woman was going to kill Ash unless Remi could stop her.

Stiffening her spine, she forced herself to step through the doorway, her gaze darting around the surprisingly large space that looked like it'd been used as a nightclub. How could she have lived on the estate for the majority of her life and never realized there was all this just below her feet?

With an effort, she shook off her sense of unreality and turned her attention toward the two people who were standing near an open closet. Her heart squeezed with fear as she caught sight of her mother pointing a gun at Ash.

She didn't know how she was going to convince her mother not to shoot. The older woman was obviously bat-shit crazy. But she had to try.

"I thought we were supposed to meet for lunch?" she said, strolling forward.

Ash whipped his head around, sending her a horrified glare. "Remi," he snapped. "Get the hell out of here."

She ignored the command, her attention focused on her mother, who was smiling at her with smug satisfaction.

"I knew there must be a reason you wanted me away from the house," the older woman told her. "You never invite me to lunch. I snuck back to find your . . ." She sent a sour glance toward Ash. "Boyfriend trespassing on my private property."

Remi came to a halt in the center of the room. It wasn't

just fear of her mother, although there was plenty of that bubbling through her gut; it was more a sense that there was an evil surrounding the older woman. Remi had an irrational horror that she might become contaminated.

Tilting her chin, she tried to act as if her heart wasn't slamming around her chest with an erratic refusal to find a rhythm and stick with it.

"You shot Albert." She didn't know why, but they were the first words that burst from her mouth.

Her mother arched her brows, as if baffled that Remi couldn't comprehend her need to kill the man who'd devoted his life to her. "A pity, I'll admit," she said. "He's been a loyal servant, but he's not stupid. After today, he would know about my little secret. I couldn't let him tell anyone."

Remi slowly shook her head. "So many people hurt and all because you wanted me dead."

"Yes," Liza swiftly agreed. "It's your fault."

"Bullshit," Ash growled, moving to stand at Remi's side. He pointed a finger at the older woman. "It was you. No one else."

Remi sucked in a sharp breath. Was the man trying to get himself killed? Reaching out, she gave his arm a warning squeeze, trying to silently tell him that the cops were on the way.

They just had to stay alive until they arrived.

"When did this all start?" she demanded, trying to distract her mother from Ash.

Liza glowered at Ash, clearly trying to decide whether to pull the trigger. Then she gave a small shrug. "Ten years ago."

"Ten years?" Remi didn't bother to hide her shock.

"The first woman I killed was an accident. I saw her, and she reminded me of you. The next thing I knew, I was following her to her house." Her mother shrugged, as if she was discussing an impulsive decision to get a tattoo. "I didn't know why. Not until she was lying on the ground with her throat slit."

Nausea rolled through Remi. "Oh my God."

"It was awful, of course, but the sight purged the poison that had been escalating inside me." There wasn't a trace of guilt on the older woman's face. In fact, there was a glitter in her eyes that suggested she was relishing the memory. "It was over a year before I felt the darkness return."

Remi swallowed the lump in her throat. "Is that how you found all your victims? Just seeing them on the street?"

"No." Liza shook her head. "Some I encountered during my charity work. There were always the catering and cleaning staff I hired for my events, as well as the occasional models if I included a fashion show. Sometimes I would see their picture in the paper. In the past few years, I began to use social media."

"That's how you found Angel and Rachel," Ash accused.

Liza sent him a frown, as if annoyed he would intrude in their conversation. "Yes," she snapped.

"Why did you carve a C into their flesh?" Ash demanded.

"They were my cancer. Their death was meant to end the disease."

Ash continued to press her. "Did you mark the women you killed and burned?"

Liza paused, her lips parting in surprise. "Very good, Detective," she murmured, clearly assuming no one had connected the deaths of those women to the Butcher.

Remi grimaced. When Ash had told her Jax had discovered more victims, she'd been horrified. Now that she knew they'd been brutally murdered and set on fire by her own mother . . .

She didn't have words to describe her revulsion.

"Why not just kill me?" she burst out.

Liza looked oddly offended by the question. "I may be sick, Remi, but I am your mother," she chastised. "I tried to battle the urges."

Remi shuddered. Since her earliest memories, she'd blamed herself for her mother's lack of affection. Her childish mind had been convinced it had to be her fault, that she wasn't lovable.

Now she knew it had nothing to do with her. Liza Harding-Walsh was completely insane.

"Until the night you followed me home from the art show," Remi reminded her mother. She needed to keep the older woman talking. The cops had to be close.

Liza kept the gun pointed at Ash even as her attention was focused on Remi. "There was a voice in my head that was telling me the only way to destroy the malignancy was to cut it out of me," she said, as if that was all the excuse she needed to kill her own daughter.

Remi paused, battling against the urge to try to make sense of her mother's madness. "You took me through the tunnels," she instead said.

"Yes." She offered a condescending smile. "I wanted you to be in your room, surrounded by the things you loved."

"Nice," Remi muttered. "What happened?"

"You passed out before I could get you in the house." Her mother's face tightened with something that might have been pain. "Then the door opened and your father appeared."

Remi released a startled gasp, unable to imagine her father's reaction. "That must have been a shock to him," she rasped.

"No. He confessed that he'd begun to suspect I was the killer weeks before," Liza admitted.

"The file," Ash muttered.

Remi glanced at him in confusion. "What file?"

"Your father had a file hidden in his desk, with a map of the murder locations along with notes that were written in code," he explained, glancing toward Liza. "I'm guessing he was trying to determine if his wife could have crossed paths with the victims before they died."

"Oh." Remi gave a shake of her head, disgusted with her gullibility. Of course, in her defense, Liza possessed an extraordinary talent for lying. "You never believed Dad was having an affair. You canceled dinner with Bobby because you were planning to kill Tiffany Holloway."

Her mother sniffed at the note of repugnance in Remi's voice. "I could sense Gage was watching me," she said. "Sometimes I would even catch him tailing me when I drove around the city."

"What happened that night?" Remi demanded.

"He found us on the stairs. You'd already collapsed, so he carried you into the kitchen," Liza told her. "Then we went into the living room, so we could talk. He insisted that I tell him everything."

Remi could easily visualize her father. He would have been distraught, perhaps even in a panic, but he loved his wife. He would be desperate to help her, no matter what she'd done.

"Did you confess?"

"Yes." Liza clicked her tongue. "A mistake, but I hoped he would understand."

Remi shivered. "Of course he didn't understand. No one would."

Liza pretended she didn't hear Remi. Or maybe she truly hadn't. She looked lost in her memories.

"He pleaded for me to go to a hospital. I knew what he meant. He was going to lock me in some horrible institution with crazy people for the rest of my life." The older woman made a choked sound. "I couldn't let that happen."

A terrible fear curdled in the pit of Remi's stomach. "What did you do?"

Liza's features hardened. "I pretended to agree. Then, when Gage came toward me to give me a hug, I slashed his throat."

"You . . ." Remi swayed, momentarily afraid she might pass out. Then a strong arm encircled her waist, keeping her upright. She'd known her father was dead. It didn't matter that they hadn't found his body. Deep in her heart, she'd known he was gone. But the realization that her mother had slaughtered him just to protect her terrible secret threatened to overwhelm her. "I thought you loved him?"

Fury darkened her mother's eyes, offering a rare glimpse of the emotions that stewed just beneath the surface.

"I loved him with all my heart." She jerked her hand to the side, pointing the gun at Remi. "It was because of you. If you'd never come into our lives, everything would have been fine."

The accusation didn't hurt Remi. Her mother was incapable of taking responsibility for the evil she'd committed. Besides, Remi was still reeling from the image of her father lying in the middle of the living-room floor with his throat cut.

"What did you do with him?" she rasped.

The emotion was wiped from Liza's face. Almost as if she could turn it on and off like a switch.

"There's a special trapdoor behind the bar. It took me a half hour to wrap his body in the plastic my father kept in the garage and drag him down here." Her gaze flicked toward the bar before returning to Remi. "By the time I got back, I heard you calling the police. There was no time to clean up, so I grabbed some clothes and headed to the garage. I didn't want to be found at the estate."

Remi swayed again, her gaze lowering to the ground. "He's down there?" There was a shrill edge to her voice, revealing the swelling hysteria that made it hard for her to breathe.

Sensing her horror, Ash pressed his lips to the top of her head, his arm tightening around her waist. "Shh."

"I had no choice," Liza insisted.

Remi was forced to pause and gather her shattered thoughts. Later, she could grieve a second time for her father, she grimly reminded herself. And try to process the damage her mother had wreaked on dozens of families.

For now, she was supposed to be keeping the woman talking. Something Liza was oddly happy to do.

"After he was dead, why not kill me?" Remi asked.

"Before Gage died, he made me swear I wouldn't hurt you. I tried to keep my promise. I truly did." Liza restlessly shifted, as if she was growing bored with the conversation. "But my illness became overwhelming."

Remi barely heard her mother's pathetic excuses. Instead, she clung to the fact that her father had used the last of his strength to try to protect her.

Proof of just how much he'd loved her.

It was Ash who continued the conversation, perhaps knowing it was imperative that they play for time. "You had the women surgically altered to look like Remi?"

Liza sent him a dismissive frown. "Dr. Bode is a personal friend and always in need of cash. It was easy to convince him to help me."

Remi grimaced. Those poor girls. "Why would you go to such an effort?"

"I thought they would help to prevent the darkness from returning so swiftly. I sensed that I was spiraling out of control," she finally admitted, a nerve twitching next to her eye. Where the hell were the cops? "But they only made it worse."

Ash gave Remi's waist a warning squeeze, as if he was sensing the same brittle tension in the air.

"You killed Angel in the park," he said, the words an accusation, not a question.

"Yes. She was such a disappointment." Liza's tone was sharp, clearly blaming Angel for getting her throat slit. "She was prostituting herself for drugs."

"Why did you drive the Mustang?" Ash demanded.

Liza looked confused. As if she barely recalled the murder. "What?"

"You drove Gage's car to the park."

"Oh." The older woman shrugged. "I knew Angel would recognize mine. I didn't want her to know I was following her. I'd forgotten just how awful it was to drive when there was snow on the road." She shook her head. "I nearly killed myself."

Remi didn't miss her mother's concern for herself and not for the young man she'd nearly run over. Of course, it was becoming clear that Liza Harding-Walsh was incapable of looking at the world beyond her own needs and desires.

Before Ash could speak again, the sound of sirens echoed through the tunnels.

Remi's mouth went dry as she watched the older woman stiffen in fear.

"This has to end, Mother," she pleaded softly.

"It does." A hectic flush stained Liza's face, her hand lifting the gun to aim it at Remi's forehead. "And there's only one cure."

Without warning, Ash was rushing forward, plowing into Liza in an attempt to knock away the weapon. He was quick, but Liza's finger managed to squeeze the trigger. The gunshot was deafening in the underground space, and Remi screamed as the two hit the floor with a heavy thud. She stumbled toward Ash as he rolled onto his back, the front of his shirt coated in blood.

Was it his or her mother's?

The question was answered when Liza scrambled to her feet. She was disheveled but clearly unharmed.

"Ash," Remi cried, falling to her knees next to him.

No, no, no. She'd lost her father. She couldn't lose Ash. It would break her.

"Remi." Ash reached up his arm before she could determine the extent of his injuries, trying to tug her behind him. "She has another gun in her purse."

Remi glanced up. She hadn't realized her mother had dropped the weapon, but now she was struggling to yank open her handbag. A voice in the back of her mind told Remi to make a dash for the door. There was a chance she could escape before her mother could get out the gun and shoot her. But she didn't budge. She wasn't going to leave Ash. It didn't matter what happened to her.

But before her mother could find the gun, Remi caught the sound of footsteps stomping through the tunnels.

The cavalry had arrived.

A miracle.

"It's over," she rasped.

Her mother glanced toward the door, her face going blank as the footsteps sounded just outside the door. There was no way out this time.

"Yes." Liza dropped her purse, something that might have been relief rippling over her face. "Thank God. It's over."

Moving like she was on autopilot, the older woman walked toward the bar. Remi watched in confusion. Was her mother going to have a last drink before being hauled off to jail?

Feeling as if she was frozen in place, Remi remained kneeling next to Ash even as she saw her mother reach beneath the bar to pull out a long knife. She couldn't believe the woman was delusional enough to think she could overpower Remi.

But while Remi prepared to fight off the older woman, Liza merely smiled as she lifted the knife and pressed it against her throat.

Remi made a strangled sound as she quickly ducked her head. She was going to have enough nightmares. She didn't need to add the sight of her mother dying.

Ash tightened his grasp, pulling her tightly against his side as the police—led by Jax—rushed into the room.

Chapter Twenty-Nine

Nate and Ellie's wedding had been a small, simple church ceremony with only family in attendance. It had been beautiful, emphasizing the glowing happiness between the bride and groom. The reception, on the other hand, was a loud, noisy affair with at least a hundred people crammed into the rented VFW hall.

Remi was sitting at a back table with Ash. He'd insisted he didn't feel up to joining the mass of people who were dancing near the DJ and flashing lights, but she suspected he'd been worried she would be feeling battered by the chaos.

And, in truth, she couldn't deny that she was nearing her limit. She loved the Marcel family, but they could be overwhelming. And she was still feeling raw from recent events.

Snuggled close beside Ash, who was holding her hand, she smiled politely at one of the numerous great-aunts who had appeared from the crowd. Ash hadn't scoped out the layout of the hall properly, which meant he hadn't realized the path to the bathroom passed next to their table. Over the course of the past two hours, they'd had every guest at the reception stop by to chat.

"Such a beautiful ceremony, wasn't it?" the older woman

breathed, her red hat, which matched her silk dress, tilted at an odd angle. That and the flush on her plump cheeks revealed she had been enjoying the heavily spiked punch.

"Yes, Aunt Harriet," Ash readily agreed.

The woman sent Ash an arch glance. "I assume we'll soon be hearing the church bells ringing for you two?"

Remi kicked his heel beneath the table. Ash grunted but kept his answer vague.

"Who can say?"

The woman heaved a disappointed sigh before heading toward the bathroom.

Ash sent Remi a chiding frown. "I don't know why you insist on keeping everything such a secret," he said.

In this moment, Remi had to admit it seemed like a stupid decision. Ash was always a potently attractive man. But today, he was downright gorgeous.

Allowing her gaze to run over his hard body, encased in a gray tuxedo, she felt her mouth go dry. Then, with an effort, she sternly reminded herself of exactly why she'd insisted they remain silent.

In the past month, Ash had been rushed to the hospital with a gunshot wound to his shoulder. Thankfully, the bullet had gone through without causing any major damage and it was healing quickly. Then, the word that Liza Harding-Walsh was the Chicago Butcher had spread through the city like wildfire. Remi was barely able to leave her house without being hounded by reporters. Eventually, the horde had grown tired of her refusal to speak, but not before Liza had been plastered across every major news outlet in the country.

It'd all combined to turn their lives into a circus that had sucked the time and attention of Ash's family. Remi had been grimly determined to make sure that today, she and Ash remained firmly in the background.

"Because today is for Nate and Ellie," she said. "I'm not going to distract from their wedding by announcing our engagement."

Ash scowled, lifting her hand to press it against his lips. "I want to see my ring on your finger."

Her heart fluttered. Just like it was supposed to when the man she loved gazed at her as if there was no other woman in the world.

"In a few days, I promise," she said in husky tones.

The past weeks had been a nightmare. The interview with the police to answer their endless questions. The quiet burial of her mother in the family crypt. The legal paperwork to have the Harding estate destroyed.

The one silver lining had been Ash's steadfast support. Without him, she was fairly sure she would have locked herself in her bedroom and never come out.

"I'll try to hold on to my patience," he assured her. "But just as a heads-up, it's not my finest virtue."

Her lips twitched. "Shocker."

"Hmm." He tilted down his head to gaze at her with a teasing expression. "I'm not the only one with a lack of patience."

"I don't know what you're talking about."

"I heard you this morning, yelling at that poor lawyer."

She arched her brows at his accusation. "I wasn't yelling."

"No?"

"I was emphatically reminding him that I want every penny of my inheritance to go into the fund for the Gage Walsh Center," Remi insisted. She'd barely had time to arrange for her mother to be cremated in a private ceremony before the family lawyer was contacting Remi to inform her that she was now the owner of the estate, along with an obscene amount of money. Remi had resisted the urge to refuse the inheritance. Instead, she'd spent a few days considering how she could use the money to do something good. At last, she'd hit on the idea of creating a group home for youth who needed emergency care. Like Drew, when his dad was thrown in jail. They would have a safe place to stay until they could be returned home, or to a more permanent foster care location. "If I wanted a portion of the money in stocks, or bonds, or my personal bank account, I would have asked for it."

He pressed another kiss on her fingers. "You made your point."

Heat touched her cheeks. Okay. Maybe she had been yelling. "I just want to get things going."

He smiled down at her. "I like seeing the sparkle back in your eyes."

She knew what he meant. For days, she'd struggled to put one foot in front of the other. She'd felt smothered by a shroud of guilt, as if it was somehow her fault she hadn't recognized that her mother was a serial killer. But slowly, she'd come out of the darkness, accepting that she'd been a victim, like all those other women.

She could either wallow in misery or make the most of the life she had been given.

"I can't change the past, or the horror my mother spread through this city," she said. "But at least I can make sure my father's name is remembered for something fine and decent."

Ash bent down to lightly kiss her lips. "I'm proud of you, Remi Walsh."

"I couldn't have done it without you, Dr. Marcel," she assured him.

"Oh." He lifted his head, suddenly smiling. "I heard from the dean."

"Did they find a replacement?" she asked.

Ash had spoken with the college to request that they release him from his contract.

"Yes. I'm officially unemployed."

"Are you sure about this?" Remi demanded. As much as she wanted Ash to return to Chicago, she couldn't bear for him to someday regret giving up his career in teaching. "I don't want you leaving the opportunity to be the hottest professor on campus for me."

"It's time," he assured her. "I'll have to settle for being the hottest detective in Chicago."

"Hold on," a male voice drawled from behind them. "That title is already taken."

Remi glanced over her shoulder, flashing a smile at Ash's brother, who looked equally handsome in his tux.

"Jax. Have a seat." She waved an inviting hand to the chair across the table.

Jax had been the first cop through the door to find Ash and Remi lying on the ground, with her mother bleeding to death near the bar. He'd been the one to hustle the paramedics to load Ash into the ambulance and carry him out of the tunnels. And to make sure Remi didn't have to deal with anything but going to the hospital to be with Ash.

Since then, he'd stopped by her house every morning, keeping Ash occupied so he didn't go stir-crazy before his wound was healed. And to keep Remi updated on the ongoing investigation. He didn't want her caught off guard if they found more bodies.

She would never forget all he'd done for them.

Jax, however, gave a shake of his head, his gaze moving toward a red-haired woman who was sipping a glass of champagne near the dance floor.

"Naw," he drawled. "I'm making the rounds."

"Hmm. Be careful," Ash warned. "Weddings are always

filled with our gene pool. You should probably make sure you're not hitting on a cousin."

Jax rolled his eyes. "Why did I ever want you to return to Chicago?"

Ash flashed a smug smile. "Because you love me."

"I can't imagine why," Jax said in a dry tone, giving a shake of his head. Then he placed a hand on Ash's shoulder, careful not to press against his wound. "Hey, Mom wanted me to swing by to tell you it's time for you to leave."

"Leave?" Ash arched his brows. "It's been a long time since I had a curfew."

"She's worried you're overdoing it," Jax told him.

"I'm fine," Ash protested. "And Nate is only going to get married once. At least, that's the plan."

They all glanced toward the dance floor, where Nate and Ellie were leading the conga line.

"Nate's married, the cake has been cut, and all that's left is the drinking," Jax pointed out.

"And the fighting," Ash protested. "It wouldn't be a Marcel wedding without someone getting a black eye."

Jax snorted. "Yeah, that's why Mom wants you out of here."

"She's right," Remi broke into the brewing argument. "Time to go home."

"I'm all healed up," Ash said, heaving an impatient sigh. "I swear."

"Then prove it." Remi rose to her feet, flashing an inviting smile.

Ash blinked, his gaze slowly roaming down the floaty silver dress that swirled around her body. It was perfectly cut to look modest—then she moved, and it slithered over her curves with remarkable results.

With a jerky surge, Ash was on his feet. "You know what, I think it is time to head home." He glanced toward Jax, his expression distracted. "Tell Nate I'll come see him before they head back to Oklahoma."

"Will do," Jax agreed. "Now go."

Ash wrapped an arm around her shoulders, gazing down at her with an expression that made her heart melt. "Ready?"

She reached up to lightly touch his face. It had taken years, and more pain than she'd ever imagined she'd have to endure, but at last she could offer her heart to this man without hesitation.

"I really and truly am."